"*Bump and Run* is outrageous, opinionated, and most important, funny as hell." —Phil Simms, CBS Sports, Super Bowl–winning quarterback, New York Giants

"This is a rowdy, raunchy take on pro football in the style of Dan Jenkins's *Semi-Tough*." —*San Antonio Express-News*

"The novel goes deep into the fast-paced, dirty world of football, with the unique, inside perspective of the author, a *Daily News* sports columnist." —*New York Daily News*

"Sportswriter Mike Lupica tosses a bomb to the end zone with this spirited and funny fictional look at the money monster that the game has become . . . It's certainly a lot of fun to read." —*The Detroit News*

"Fans of contemporary, irreverent—and decidedly adult—humor will enjoy this novel . . . Everyone is fair game for Lupica's sardonic skewering—players, owners, media, rap stars, organized crime, strippers, politicians, etc." —*The Cleveland Plain Dealer*

ALSO BY MIKE LUPICA

NONFICTION

Reggie (with Reggie Jackson)

Parcells: The Biggest Giant of Them All (with Bill Parcells)

Wait Till Next Year (with William Goldman)

Shooting from the Hip

*Mad as Hell: How Sports Got Away from
the Fans—and How We Get It Back*

The Fred Book (with Fred Imus)

Summer of '98

FICTION

Dead Air

Extra Credits

Limited Partner

Jump

Bump and Run

MIKE LUPICA is

"DROP-DEAD HILARIOUS."
—*New York Daily News*

"THE FUNNIEST THING GOING IN SPORTS."
—*The Orlando Sentinel*

"GET READY TO RUMBLE!
Sportswriter Mike Lupica takes you on a wild, witty, funny,
colorful, quirky and sometimes touching ride...daring to
touch on a subject where no man has gone before."
—*Lexington Herald-Leader*

Praise for *FULL COURT PRESS*

"Lupica talks the talk, a pro at picking up the rhythms of locker-room voices. In other words, it's a howl."

—Elmore Leonard

"Lupica skillfully controls a multilayered plot that ridicules the greed and vanity dominating too much of professional sports territory." —*The Washington Post*

"Brutally accurate, unsparingly funny satire—a naughty delight for true basketball fans." —Carl Hiaasen

"A story with plenty of laughs, but even more heart. This novel must have been as much fun for Lupica to write as it is to read." —*Book Magazine*

"As always, Lupica entertains with his lively pacing, screwball characters and insider's knowledge of professional basketball." —*Publishers Weekly*

"You needn't be a hoops fan to enjoy this tale of life in the fast-break lane . . . The story's full of twists and turns and tension, athletic, romantic and otherwise . . . irreverent, sometimes sidesplitting, dialogue and a page-turning narrative."

—*The Sunday Oregonian*

"A convincing inside look at what motivates those in professional basketball, and what it's like to be an athlete, coach or owner." —*Rocky Mountain News*

"An excursion into the world of basketball that women and men will enjoy." —*The Lexington Herald Leader*

"A fast-breaking sports novel . . . a slam-dunk tale."

—*BookBrowser*

continued . . .

Praise for *BUMP AND RUN*

"A big-time touchdown of a book—a hilarious tale of life behind the scenes in the raunchy, rowdy world of pro football."

—Dave Barry

"Truly hip, uproariously funny, and my God, it might even be true. *Bump and Run* places Lupica high up among the funniest guys writing fiction."

—Elmore Leonard

"High-profile sportswriter Lupica goes for the gold with this quip-fueled romp . . . Reminiscent of Peter Gent's *North Dallas Forty* and Dan Jenkins's *Semi-Tough*, this is a deliciously wicked tale of contemporary professional sports and the people who, for better or worse, run the game."

—*Publishers Weekly*

"Captures the beer-and-blood flavor of the NFL."

—*Entertainment Weekly*

"Irreverent, funny . . . and all fiction aside, dead on point."

— Al Michaels, *ABC Monday Night Football*

"Even if you don't give a rat's *ss for professional football, you should read this savagely hilarious novel."

—Pete Hamill

Full Court Press

MIKE LUPICA

JOVE BOOKS, NEW YORK

FULL COURT PRESS

A Jove Book / published by arrangement with
G. P. Putnam's Sons

PRINTING HISTORY
G. P. Putnam's Sons hardcover edition / October 2001
Jove edition / November 2002

ISBN: 0-515-13364-7

A JOVE BOOK®
Jove Books are published by The Berkley Publishing Group,
a division of Penguin Putnam Inc.,
375 Hudson Street, New York, New York 10014.
JOVE and the "J" design
are trademarks belonging to Penguin Putnam Inc.

PRINTED IN THE UNITED STATES OF AMERICA

10 9 8 7 6 5 4 3 2 1

For Pete Hamill, William Goldman, Esther Newberg.
And, of course, Taylor McKelvy Lupica.
In the writing of these books, they are the home team.

This book would not have been possible without the expertise of three people in particular:

Nancy Lieberman, who not only believes a woman will play in the NBA someday but believes it should have happened already.

Paul Westphal, whose vision of the game has always been as pure as Eddie Holtz's.

Susan Burden, MSW.

⚾ **one**

All Eddie Holtz really knew about Monaco was that Grace Kelly got old and fat there after she married the guy Eddie's mother had always called Prince Reindeer.

It was different with his mother, who could talk about Monte Carlo and Monaco as if she were talking about Long Island City. But then she'd been fixed on the princess for as long as Eddie could remember. "I've always felt a bond," she'd say, "maybe because we're both the daughters of brick-layers." Then she'd sigh and say, "One of us grew up to marry a Grimaldi and one of us married your father, may the sonof-abitch rest in peace." Eddie never knew whether that was true or not, the bricklayer part, he always had trouble separating fact from fiction with his mother, who didn't stop keeping scrapbooks on Princess Grace until she died in that car crash on the same road Eddie'd driven down from Cannes — the Grand Corniche — which was scarier than the Cyclone ride at Coney Island. When he finally pulled up in front of his hotel, the Loew's–Monte Carlo, actually finding 12 Avenue Spel-ugues on his own, he wondered how come more people didn't end up dead on the side of that Corniche. You thought you were going fast enough on the twisty roller-coaster turns, but even when you pushed it up to seventy or eighty there'd be some lunatic right behind you flashing his lights and blowing his horn, waving at you to get the hell out of the way.

Eddie couldn't remember whether it was the crash or a stroke that had killed Princess Grace, but after making the drive himself he saw where it could just have been the road that finally blew all her circuits.

It made the Grand Central Parkway look slower than a funeral procession, Eddie decided. He'd promised his mother he'd go to Monaco Cathedral to visit Princess Grace's tomb—"For someone who had all the advantages, she really had a very difficult life," Catherine Holtz had told him sadly—but now he was just going to say a couple of fast Hail Marys that he and the Renault had made it here in one piece.

The whole eastern part of the Riviera that Eddie'd seen was pretty much what he'd expected from the movies, especially his mother's all-time favorite, the one he'd seen on Turner Classic Movies right before he came over, with the young Grace Kelly giving it up to Cary Grant during the fireworks. Except that even in Monte Carlo, with the drop-dead view of the Mediterranean from his balcony, he noticed they were doing the same dumb-ass thing he'd seen everywhere he'd been the last two weeks, Barcelona, Lisbon, France, even Rome: trying to make it more American than judge shows on TV.

It hadn't taken long for Eddie to figure out that Europeans loved pretty much everything American except Americans.

The whole continent was mean people with accents.

The night before he'd passed up the Italian restaurant at the hotel—Le Pistou, Eddie loved the idea of one of these restaurants finally admitting it was pissed off—and ended up eating the worst Tex-Mex food of his life at a place called Le Texan, which served him right. And tonight, on the way to Stade Louis II for the game, he'd stopped at a bar Larry Bird had told him about from when Bird was with that Olympic Dream Team back in 1992. The Summer Olympics had been in Barcelona that year, but Bird and Jordan and Magic and the rest of them had played a couple of tune-up games in Monte Carlo.

Bird said you had to go into the place on the name alone: Le Freaky Pub.

Eddie thought it looked like about nine thousand joints on Second Avenue, just without cable or beer that was cold enough. Jesus, you only had to get thirsty one time over here to find out this was the anti-ice capital of the world.

He nursed a couple of almost-cold ones anyway, killing an hour or so, eyeballing the tall girl barmaid. The rest of the time he tried to translate some of the conversations at the bar without having to run to the men's room every few minutes and check out *Langenscheidt's Universal Phrasebook*. He didn't usually drink before he scouted a game, but tonight was a little different; there was as much chance of his being interested in somebody besides Earthwind Morton as there was of old Prince Reindeer, who was supposed to be in the crowd, running out and dunking the ball during the pregame warmups.

Out loud in Le Freaky Pub, Eddie Holtz said, "What the hell am I doing here?"

The girl bartender smiled and said, *"Pardonez-moi?"*

Eddie made a motion with his hands, like he was waving off a shot. "No problemo," he said.

This close to the end of his scouting trip, Eddie figured it was all right to start going with his own universal phrases, screw *Langenscheidt's*.

It was weird, though, having to come halfway across the goddamn world to see Earthwind. When they'd both still been in the NBA ten years ago, before Eddie blew out his knee, all he'd had to do to watch Earthwind play was put on Sports-Center on ESPN. If the Knicks had a game that night, the highlights were always about him, the way they were always about Jordan when he was still playing, at least before Earthwind tried to put the gross national product of Bogotá up his nose. Now Eddie had to come to Monte Carlo to see if Lavernius (Earthwind) Morton, playing for Olympique Antibes in France's First Division Men's League, had enough left for the New York Knights to bring him back for one more shot.

"You still any good?" Eddie had asked over the phone when he'd called from Paris.

"Only thing sweeter than myself over here is *le poo-say*," Earthwind said. "Myself has done exactly what all those jive counselors told me: replace one jones with another."

"So you replaced dope with what?" Eddie said.

Earthwind whooped and said, "Some of dem mada-*mo-selles*, baby."

The basketball arena was part of the big soccer stadium that Eddie thought could have been called Meadowlands on the Med. The night before, he could actually hear the cheers from the soccer game as he sat on his balcony with the big boy martini he'd fixed himself from his minibar. He knew there used to be a First Division team in Monte Carlo but didn't remember if it was still there. Eddie did know that Earthwind had missed the last couple of games for Antibes, which bothered the shit out of him, considering the guy's rap sheet with the coke and crack and even heroin, which Eddie'd always thought of as the main event. So this was Eddie's last chance to get a look at him in person before he flew back to New York to give his report to Michael De la Cruz, the Knights' owner.

And if Earthwind was washed up, Eddie was going to have to tell the boss the truth: After having been to Spain and Italy and up and down France, he wasn't even coming home with a decent roll of film.

Oh, there'd been a couple of guys in Spain who might be able to give the Knights ten minutes a game. And there was a Russian kid playing for Bologna named Arvy Daskylmilosevic, who in addition to having the world's longest last name could occasionally shoot threes as if they were layups. But as little as De la Cruz knew about basketball—even though he'd managed to convince himself it was he and Dr. Naismith back at the beginning, cutting the hole in the peach basket—Eddie knew he couldn't bullshit him with those guys.

Eddie couldn't even do that with himself, not when it came to basketball.

"I'd like you to come back with somebody who can win us

some games," he'd told Eddie. "But not as much as someone who could sell us some goddamn tickets."

So Earthwind Morton, who was supposed to be clean finally, was pretty much the whole ballgame. He was the one De la Cruz wanted. People love comeback stories, he'd told Eddie. The sportswriters can write the same stories they've already done about the other junkies, and the fans will eat it up.

He'd gone through the same rap on the phone the other night, getting all revved up like he could, like he was still pitching tech stocks. Eddie'd finally said, "I'm not as worried about what the fans are going to eat as I am with my man Earth."

Michael De la Cruz wanted to know what that meant, and Eddie said, "I saw a picture of him in *L'Equipe* the other day? The French sports paper? The guy looks like he swallowed Notre Dame."

Eddie pronounced it right, "Not-rah Dahm," so his boss, still pretty new to sports, wouldn't confuse the cathedral with the Fighting Irish football team.

The p.r. guy from Olympique Antibes, Jean-Claude something, another guy with an attitude when Eddie'd talked to him on the phone, had forgotten to leave him a ticket. Eddie'd found that out when he'd called over to Stade Louis II in the afternoon, but the concierge at Loew's, Lebortvaillet, had said he'd take care of it, and did.

Eddie overtipped Lebortvaillet when he came downstairs. The guy just took the fistful of those Monegasque coins that were the same as francs, and shrugged. France, Monte Carlo, it didn't matter where you were, it's like they all took some kind of course in not giving a shit. Most of these bastards, even the well-meaning ones, were like the old joke about New York City.

"Could you tell me how to find the Hotel du Paris, or should I just go fuck myself, *s'il vous plaît?*"

The cab to the arena took him through the kind of tunnel where Princess Di had got it, and dropped him on the arena side of the Stade Louis sports complex. The sign outside said it was Antibes vs. Lyon Villeuranne, eight o'clock. Lebortvaillet had said the game was an exhibition to benefit one of

Princess Stephanie's charities. Or maybe it was Princess Caroline, he wasn't sure. Eddie remembered that one of them had had her hair fall out one time and the other was in the car when Princess Grace bought it, he just couldn't keep them straight anymore. Lebortvaillet said that out of respect for the royal family, each team had sent at least five of its best players, and that the rest of the rosters would be filled out with some of the better college kids from Monte Carlo and as far up as Cannes and Nice.

Eddie had watched some tape on Earthwind back in New York, but now he needed to see if the guy, even in a charity game, could still do things on a basketball court only one other point guard his size—Magic—had ever been able to do.

Inside, Stade Louis II looked as if it might belong to some small Division I college team back home. Iona, someplace like that, or the gym where Rutgers played its home games. It was about the size of Alumni Hall at St. John's, Eddie's alma mater, with the same kind of theater balcony, except this was a lot newer and not nearly as much of a dump. There were maybe twenty rows of seats on either side of the court, nothing behind the baskets and then maybe twenty more rows in the balcony. The blue seats down by the court looked as if they'd just gotten a new paint job and were supposed to be the color of the sea. Eddie's seat in the balcony was bright red. He sat up there sipping the local version of Perrier, waiting for the game to start.

He'd walked around trying to find a Coke, but the snippy girl at the concession stand acted offended that he'd even asked for one.

It was the variation of the look you got when you asked for directions in Paris or someplace, as if you'd broken a law not knowing if you were on the right *rue* or not.

"We 'ave no Coke for you," the girl said. "We 'ave water, wiz or wizzout gas."

Eddie knew that one; it meant carbonated or not.

"Wiz," Eddie said.

Earthwind, he saw when both teams came out for warm-ups, had definitely put on a few since the NBA had kicked him out after he'd failed his fourth drug test in two years. They'd called it a life sentence at the time, but you could apply for reinstatement after three years if you could show you'd been a good boy. Earth, which is what the playground boys used to call him back in the city, had also added a few tats, one on his neck that resembled a knife scar. Or maybe it *was* a knife scar; Eddie remembered reading something in the gossip page in *Sports Illustrated* about how a bunch of guys from Antibes, Earth included, had gotten into it outside some club on the Left Bank after the Division I All-Star Game a couple of months earlier and ended up in jail for the night.

It took only the first few minutes of the game for Eddie to see that the crazy sonofabitch still had some ball in him, underneath all the tat graffiti and rolls of jiggle and the tits he seemed to have grown while he'd been over here.

Eddie knew that most of the playground shuck and jive was for his benefit. When Eddie had still thought he could come all the way back from the reconstructive surgery on his knee and Earthwind Morton had been an All-Star with the Knicks, they'd go down to the playground on West Fourth Street in the summer, just wait on the side until it was their turn to get into a game. Once they did, they'd play all night. Earthwind wasn't doing anything harder than grass; it'd be a couple more years before he'd upgrade into the heavier stuff. So he was still the fastest big guy anybody'd ever seen in those days, every bit as big and strong as Magic at six-nine, but faster, even better with the ball, especially on the run, built like a football tight end, not an ounce of fat on him in those days. Shit, he really could run like a good wind in those days. Sometimes in the summer, they'd get bored with West Fourth, or the jive-ass summer league games uptown, and go over to Penn Station, jump on the Metroliner, go down to the Baker League in Philadelphia, and kick some ass down there, on a whim, just for the fun of it.

Now just about everybody was faster, even the white guys in Stade Louis II, and it didn't matter, because Earthwind was better than all of them, even sweating gravy, making his shots from the outside, doing it up like a Globetrotter for the royals when he'd play with his back to the basket, even giving a high five to Princess Stephanie—the lady next to Eddie pointed her out—as he went past her one time.

Another time in the first half, after he made a three from so far outside Eddie thought it was a thirty-footer, Earthwind ran by the small press table, grabbed the p.a. guy's microphone, and said, "Yo, all you *madames et monsieurs*: Where's the damn love here?"

A few minutes into the second half, Olympique Antibes was ahead twenty points and Eddie was starting to think about heading back to Le Freaky Bar, or this other place he'd heard about, called DC, when the Antibes coach put in what looked like one of the local kids, a guy about five-ten or five-eleven and so skinny Eddie thought he might be a high school kid, wearing an old green Celtics cap pulled down tight over his eyes, his jersey looking to be about three sizes too big. Eddie looked at the single-sheet program the wiz-or-wizzout girl had handed him when she sold him his Perrier, looking to see who No. 14 was, the one who thought he was so cool he didn't have to take off his fucking hat.

D. Gerard, it said. Eddie saw that they let him go in for Black Messiah Lewis, an old Syracuse teammate of Earthwind's, at the point. Earthwind stayed in the game but went to center now, where he wouldn't have to run too much more the rest of the night, which Eddie thought was good, he didn't want to have to call Michael De la Cruz when the game was over and tell him the good news was that Earthwind could still play and the bad news was that he'd had a fucking coronary.

D. Gerard came up the court the first time, before the Villeuranne defense was set, and threw a behind-the-back pass to Earthwind from half-court. It caught the Villeuranne players so flat-footed that even Earthwind, dragging ass the way he was by now, was two steps behind everybody. He had time to mug for the crowd with this wild-eyed, amazed look before he dunked the ball.

It was the same as it had always been with him: Hey, look at me.

Except the play wasn't about him.

It was about the pass.

While Earth was still playing to the crowd, D. Gerard was already back on defense himself, ignoring the way his pass had brought the house down, the Monte Carlo people, who'd been getting bored themselves, back into the game now.

By Eddie's count, Gerard had five assists the first six times he touched the ball. He hadn't taken a shot yet or come close to driving the ball to the basket. He just stayed on the outside and ran the fast break and seemed to find the right guy on Antibes every single time with his passes. Suddenly the charity game in Monte Carlo was about this skinny kid, whoever he was.

Eddie couldn't even tell whether he was white or black.

It was interesting, though, watching the way the kid somehow managed to keep everybody on his team involved—interesting to Eddie, anyway. He had played the point his whole life, all the way back to Christ the King High, and knew how hard that was, passing out the sugar, making sure everybody was happy, trying to let the hot guy stay hot and not pissing off everybody else. It wasn't just who you passed it to, it was where you made the pass, and when. Mostly passing was about creating angles. Eddie knew, because Eddie had always known angles, Eddie'd always figured he saw things nobody on the court could see. It was that way even now. It didn't matter whether it was college or the pros, how good the game was, Eddie always imagined he was still playing the point, that he still had the ball. A pilot friend of his said it didn't matter whether he was a passenger or not, he always felt as if he were at the controls. That's the way Eddie felt watching basketball, as if he were still out there creating the angles.

It was the way he felt now, watching this kid.

Who *was* he?

The coach, Barone, knew enough to keep him in there the last few minutes. The kid kept making plays. There was another half-court job, behind his back, not just hitting Earthwind right in stride but zipping the ball. The only guy Eddie'd ever seen who could throw that pass that way was Ernie DiGregorio, back at Providence College when Eddie was growing up.

There was a no-look to Black Messiah Lewis, back in the

game, Eddie nearly missing the pass because Gerard sold him so well that he was going left with the ball instead of right.

The crowd went nuts again and the kid just got back on defense, ducking his head, just giving a little low-five to Black Messiah as he ran by.

Eddie noticed Gerard didn't even have any tats on skin that was the color of a light coffee.

The big finish came with about fifteen seconds left, everybody in Stade Louis II on their feet by now—even the Prince, who'd just been sitting there all night like he was asleep. Antibes was ahead by a lot. Barone had taken out Earthwind with about two minutes left, but now he put him back in, as a way of getting a curtain call now that the kid had stolen all his thunder. It was like this night at the Jersey shore when Eddie was a sophomore in college, driving down there with some buddies from Queens, pounding beer at this little jazz club, and all of a sudden there's Springsteen up on the little stage, jamming with Clarence Clemons.

The Villeuranne coach had emptied his bench, but even the scrubs had lost interest by then, so only two of them were at the Antibes end of the court when D. Gerard came upcourt with the ball. Earthwind was with him—Eddie thought his name should have been Suck Wind by then—somehow managing to bust it down the right, sure that Gerard would give him one more piece of cake.

Gerard came up the middle at full speed, looking up as he did to get one little check of the clock. When he got to the key, he saw the two Villeuranne guys on defense coming to him, like, the hell with it, they weren't going to get embarrassed one more time at the buzzer.

Gerard stopped then, the ball going behind his back. From where Eddie was sitting, high up in the corner, the play coming toward him, the ball actually seemed to disappear for a second, except that Gerard had both hands showing, and neither one had the ball in it.

For the first time, Eddie thought he detected a smile underneath the Celtics cap as the kid quickly looked left, then right, like, Oops, where did the ball go?

He was in a little crouch now, like he was bending over to tie his sneaks.

Somehow D. Gerard had balanced the ball on his skinny ass, because suddenly he was ducking down a little more, reaching behind him in the same motion, flipping the ball over his head to Earthwind Morton, who dropped in a layup as the buzzer sounded and then just sat down under the basket as if he couldn't believe what he'd just seen.

Eddie looked around to see how D. Gerard had reacted, but all he could see was the back of No. 14, disappearing through one of the doors leading to the locker rooms.

Eddie had told Earthwind he'd check him out after the game so they could kick back and talk about old times a little bit, see where his head was at. But Earth was still down at midcourt, chatting up the royals, posing for the photographers, as if the night were still about him.

Only now it wasn't.

Eddie hurried downstairs and kept showing his locker room pass at a series of solemn-looking frogs, and finally came to the Antibes locker room. He was on his way in there when he saw a flash of green down the hall and realized it was D. Gerard in his Celtics cap, a big black gym bag slung over his shoulder, a hooded gray sweatshirt over his uniform, heading toward the exit.

"Yo!" Eddie called out to him. "Hold on, *s'il vous plaît.*"

D. Gerard gave him a quick look over his shoulder, pointing to himself. Me?

"Yeah," Eddie said.

The kid was still in that slouch, like he was going to throw that pass again, looking down.

Eddie said, "*Parlez-vous* English?"

The kid said, "Sure. What about you? English your first or second language?"

"When you're from New York, it's hard to tell sometimes," Eddie said. "I'm Eddie Holtz. I work for the New York Knights."

He paused, then added, "From the NBA? In the United States."

They shook hands. Kind of smallish, Eddie thought, delicate almost, but with long fingers, like a piano player's hands.

"What does the D. stand for?" Eddie said. "In D. Gerard?"

"Dee," the kid said.

Then the kid lifted his head a little and smiled, a great big one, giving him the high beams.

"Oh, for God's sake, let's stop screwing around here."

He took off the Celtics cap and untied all the hair underneath, long black hair, and let it fall down to the shoulders, giving the head a little toss at the same time.

"Short for Delilah," Dee Gerard said to Eddie Holtz. "Except I always hated Delilah. My mom liked Delilah."

Eddie Holtz just stared at her.

"You're a girl," he finally managed.

Dee Gerard smiled.

"My whole life, practically," she said.

two

Dee had started to worry at halftime that Barone wasn't even going to put her in the stupid game, which meant she wasn't going to have any fun with Eddie Holtz at all.

She knew he was in the stands. Earthwind had been bragging about it in the locker room after the other guys on the team had made her dress next door, in what used to be the coach's office at Stade Louis II. Dee would've been happy to get dressed in one of the bathroom stalls; it never took her long, she was just there to play, not to bond. But the boys didn't want her to see them naked. For all their big talk about how well-endowed they were, for all the times they acted like they had a present for you when you were alone, put a bunch of them in a room and they suddenly had an attack of modesty, because they thought you were comparison-shopping.

Dee had learned a long time ago. Most men she'd known, starting with Cool Daddy, went their whole lives without knowing how truly funny they were.

"Got a scout here, come all the way from *New* York City!" Earthwind had told her. "Want to see if I can still do it."

"Do what, eat?" she'd said.

On the way out for the second half, she almost said something to Barone, who hadn't even looked at her all night. She was going to tell him, in French if she had to, that it might be his job to sit through Earthwind's audition, but not hers.

But before she did, Earthwind came over to her and told her to make sure she got loose when they got back on the court, because he'd made sure Barone was going to put her in the game. This wasn't for Dee; Earthwind was looking out for himself, as always. The other guys on Antibes were already sick of him hogging the ball, and so they'd stopped passing it to him.

Earthwind and Dee had played a little pickup ball over the last couple of years when he'd get a few days off and come down here to gamble; he even knocked around enough to know her father. But Dee was just another guy in the game to him, out there only to make him look good. But at least he knew enough about her game to know she'd pass him the ball.

"You be ready, old man," she told him. "You don't want a pass to hit you in that cute face in front of the princesses."

"You notice?" he said. "I think the one with some mileage on her, one been a little unlucky in love, been eyeballin' me."

"Just be ready," she said.

Earthwind said, "What, bein' bossy run in your family?"

"Yeah, I got it from my old man, along with my ballhandling ability."

"I figure," he said.

Five minutes into the half, Barone finally called her name. She went right out and threw one behind her back to Earthwind Morton from halfcourt and heard a sound from the crowd she'd heard her whole life, whether they knew who she was or not, just reacting to a high note that came out of nowhere. She gave a quick look to the low stands as she went back on defense, some of the people down there in formal wear, black tie and gowns, looking at her the way she imagined Eddie Holtz was somewhere. Like: Who is *that*?

Me, she thought to herself.

She remembered Cool Daddy telling her once what it was like the first time he heard Ruth Brown at the Apollo, headlining a bill that had Miles Davis and Thelonius Monk on it, how she just went out there and got right into it, not easing herself into a song at all, almost not waiting for the band, as if she'd waited all day to blow the door and roof off the place. After that, after Dee started listening to all the records herself, she'd always imagined she had all this Ruth inside her when she was playing ball, listening to music, some crazy beat, jazz and blues and even big band sometimes, only she could hear.

She took a couple of deep breaths in Stade Louis, finding her man, trying to calm herself down, thinking she couldn't possibly be this excited after one cheer.

Could she?

Jesus, had she missed it this much?

Whatever you do, girl, don't look around.

Barone didn't wait to get Earthwind back in the game, because it was clear that Antibes needed some guys who could stay with her. The Serb kid, Oley Ovanisevic, was out of breath already, and kept motioning to his own coach, as if he were having some sort of potentially fatal asthma attack.

The third time down, she eyeballed Earthwind the whole way, showing him her right hand at the same time she back-handed a little no-look pass to Black Messiah Lewis.

Black Messiah, who'd been bitching when he came out of the game for her, gave her this little closed-fist five on his way past her, solemn-looking, and said, "You must be shittin'."

Dee said, "Keep your eyes open, baby. And your hands up."

"I hear that," he said.

It didn't take long for the Villeuranne guys to start getting pissed about her showing them up, Dee not knowing or really caring if they knew they were getting shown up by a woman, not even caring if the swells in the crowd had made the connection between the "D. Gerard" in their program and the Dee Gerard who used to be somebody. She started getting a little shove here and there, just their way of getting her attention. Dee knew they weren't going to get dirty, not in a charity game in front of this much royalty. But she knew she had to fight back, with something other than the elbow shots to the kidney that Cool Daddy had taught her, so they couldn't think they could get her off her game by putting the muscle on her.

So she did what she'd always done with the boys: made them chase.

"You ain't ever gonna be big enough to kick somebody's ass," Cool Daddy'd tell her. "So you got to wear they asses *out.*"

She did that until there was maybe half a minute left, when she decided to throw her Cool Daddy pass. Barone had just put Earthwind back in the game, as a way of giving him a curtain call. Dee was feeling it now, wanting to come down the court one more time and throw her arms out, let the crowd know she could hear them, that she'd been hearing them all along, even if she couldn't allow herself to see them.

But she never mugged for the crowd that way, it wasn't her style. Jeremy always said it was actually the height of style.

It certainly didn't mean she couldn't leave them wanting more.

Dee checked the clock as she came over half-court, not wanting the stupid horn to blow before she got the ball to Earthwind. He was waving for it, over to her right, but Dee knew if she gave it up now, she'd never get it back. So she winked at him, nodding her head as she did. Feeling prettier than she ever did in makeup or a dress or her best jewelry.

Flying.

Don't mess this up, she told herself.

Do not rush.

Keep your balance, girl.

The skinny kid who'd been trying to guard her, Plexico Burrow, whom she remembered from the Lakers, a black kid with his short hair dyed platinum blond, came up on her and tried to read her, watching the ball. That's what they were all trained to do. Follow the ball. That's how you created the angles you wanted.

Only now the ball was gone, balanced on the small of her back exactly the way Cool Daddy had taught her, balanced on what just about all the men in her life had told her, in various ways, was her shapely and adorable world-class butt.

It was really more a dancer's move, from her mother, but she never told Cool Daddy that.

The people sitting behind her, on the court and in the balcony, they could see the ball. But Plexico sure couldn't. Now she closed her eyes, picturing the move, feeling it like feeling the music, knowing where everybody was because she could always do that, take a snapshot of the whole court. Now it all happened at once, Dee leaning down a little more as she snapped the pass to Earthwind over her head, hearing one last cheer from the crowd, looking up to see Earthwind sitting on that fat ass of his underneath the basket.

While the place roared.

Before she knew it, she was heading for the door with her bag over her shoulder, hearing someone calling out to her in tourist French, somehow knowing it was Eddie Holtz.

When she took her cap off, she asked him if he wanted to go someplace and have a beer.

"Where?"

"My place," Dee said.

Right away she could see the guy's wheels turning, wondering how he could possibly have been this irresistible to her this fast.

"Relax, Eddie," she said. "I own a bar."

Dee showered in her office at DC, the name she'd given the place, wanting everything to be new. Then she threw on a short black sweater dress she'd left hanging there, so she could go to the game in sweats. She unlocked the bottom drawer of her antique desk and got the baby pearl necklace out of the jewelry box, put on some flat shoes. Her work-the-room clothes. Eddie would probably think she'd gotten all dressed up for him. She didn't take much time for her hair, even though she'd let it grow out. Jeremy, her ex, had always told her she looked better with it short. He'd been wrong about that, too.

There was no live music tonight; they were still only trying that out on the little bandstand on Mondays. Dee had gone through three piano players already, looking for somebody cool enough to remind her of Jimmy Rowles, another one of her favorites off her scratchy old records. Tonight she told her bartender and manager, Gilles, to put on *Crane's Blues* by Coltrane.

Coltrane got right into it with "Blue Train." Dee saw that most of the tables were occupied, some of them with the black ties from the basketball game, over for a late dinner of a limited menu Dee had authored herself, mostly featuring the best hamburgers and ribs and barbecued chicken in this part of the world; also the world-class steaks she demanded from butchers as far away as Nice sometimes. She loved that part of the business, too, and the trips to the bakeries and greengrocers, and the fun she would have sometimes just picking out new napkins, or new wineglasses, or the paintings she had scattered around the place.

People would ask her sometimes if she thought of DC as more of a bar or a restaurant.

What *is* it? they would ask.

Mine, she would answer.

Gilles told her the bar crowd had been good all night. He'd been born in Paris, but had gone to college in the States on a soccer scholarship at the University of Connecticut; his English was as good as Dee's French. His greatest value to DC was that Dee trusted him.

"How did you play?" Gilles asked, handing her a Chardonnay.

"Not bad for an old broad."

"How many knew?"

"That I was, in fact, an old broad?"

"Oui, madame."

"I don't really know." She nodded at her table, where Eddie was sipping a beer. She caught his eye and he raised his glass at her, and smiled. "But I certainly shocked the shit out of that guy over there."

"So you've been discovered?" Gilles grinned.

Dee tossed her head and said, "I feel so girlish and scared."

"Bullshit," he said.

"You smooth-talking French," she said. "You have the right word for everything. By the way, when Earthwind Morton gets here, show him where we are, okay? And watch the guy whose tuxedo doesn't fit. Last time he was here, he drank all the champagne and then walked on a check as fat as he is."

"Oui, big madame boss lady," he said.

"I am so the boss," Dee said.

When she sat down, Eddie said, "You really don't mind that I asked Earthwind to join us?"

Dee said, "I like the guy, I always have. He comes in here a lot, pops cheeseburgers into his mouth like they're M&M's. He likes the music, and there's always enough pretty girls. Nobody really hassles him."

"You think he's clean?"

"I forget. Are you a scout or a cop?"

"I'm his friend," Eddie said.

"I think he still smokes a little weed. He likes his wine. But I think he's off the hard stuff. I frankly don't think he'd weigh as much as he does if he were still on it. Remember how skinny he got at the end, with the Clippers?"

Eddie looked at her.

"You know our league?"

Dee smiled at him. "You've got a lot of questions, don't you, Eddie?"

Dee C. Gerard, she thought to herself, international woman of mystery.

"How old are you, if you don't mind me asking?"

"Thirty-two," Dee said. "Thirty-three in May."

Eddie put down his glass. "Look," he said. "I played ball myself."

"Christ the King High," Dee said. "St. John's. Drafted in the second round by the Nets. Started your first three years, until you blew your knee out. After that, you mostly sat next to the trainer."

Eddie said, "Okay, but I've got a couple of birthmarks I'm pretty sure you don't know about."

The front door opened, and Earthwind came in with a blonde Dee had seen him with before. Dee was pretty sure she was one of the waitresses from the Tip Top Bar, over by the Loew's–Monte Carlo. She had seen her in the second row during the game, down from where Princess Stephanie and

Princess Caroline were sitting with their father. The waitress was hard to miss, in a tight red dress barely holding in breasts that seemed to have won all of this year's implant awards. Earthwind was talking to Gilles, and she could see he was going to have a drink at the bar before he came over to lay some of his charm on Eddie Holtz. Trying to be cool.

After everything that had happened to him, Earthwind Morton still thought he could get by on bullshit alone. Dee had remembered reading on the Internet about Earthwind's hearing in front of the NBA commissioner, right before he got kicked out of the league.

"Why do you like cocaine so much?" the commissioner had finally asked him.

Earthwind said, "You mean other than for the sheer enjoyment of it?"

Now he made a motion to Eddie from the bar, like, *Give me a couple of minutes.*

Eddie said to Dee, "You must've played ball. Goddamn, you're the best woman player I've ever seen."

"I played nine years in all. It would have been ten, except I sat out one with a knee. One year in Israel, one in Japan, with a team called Nittsu. One with Club DKSK, in Hungary, which sounds like Donna Karan sponsored the team. I really didn't become a star, or at least as much of a star as you can be over here, until later. First with USV Orchies, later Tarbes Gespe Bigorre. Then Spain." She smiled at him. "If we get crazy tonight, I'll show you all the stamp marks in my passport."

"It sounds pretty interesting," he said.

"It was a way to make a living doing what I wanted to do," she said.

"How'd you end up here?"

"I quit playing after I got married. Then I quit being married and got this bar in the divorce, before my ex could close it, which is what he was planning to do." She sipped some of her wine. There were two levels to DC; you had to walk down three steps from the bar area to where most of the tables were, and the better light, not that there was much light anywhere in the place. That was Dee's idea, from all the small dark New

York places she liked best, where the bar was always something separate, more private. She saw Black Messiah Lewis
leaning against the brass railing of the bar now; he had two of
his teammates with him, and three women. Dee gave a little
wave to the new kid working the front door, Monique, and
motioned for her to put Messiah's party at the round table
near the empty bandstand. "And what about you, Eddie?" she
said. "How'd you end up here?"

"If you know the league, you know how much the
Knights suck, right?"

"Unless the Internet made the whole thing up."

"Well, we—the Knights—have got this new owner.
Michael De la Cruz? He buys the team, he pays the Knicks a
fortune to let him share the Garden with them. Nothing
changes with the Knicks. They put out a good team every year
and still sell out. We get about five thousand fans on a good
night. One guy wrote last month that men's shelters are happier places than a Knights game."

"So the Knicks are still the hot ticket in town?"

"Always," Eddie said. "You know New York?"

Dee said, "I was born there."

"Where?"

"Uptown." She smiled. "I was an uptown girl. East
Harlem, mostly. But we moved around a little bit before that,
and after. Lived in the Bronx when I was a teenager, right
around the corner from Wakefield Grace United Methodist
Church. It's how I ended up at Clinton."

"You went to DeWitt Clinton?"

"I'd take the number forty-one bus, switch to the sixteen.
Let me off near Montefiore Hospital. I'd walk from there. It
was just me and my father by then—my mother had died
when I was eight."

Eddie was just watching her, his face completely calm, not
feeling as if he had to jump in, just letting her talk.

"Wait a second," Dee said, "this was supposed to be about
you and your basketball team."

"There's not a hell of a lot to tell," Eddie said. "We've still
got the worst record in the conference, same as we did before
De la Cruz bought the team and said he was going to change

everything. Now they're calling him a loser, too, and it's making him increasingly nuts. He told me to come over and find him some ballplayers in Europe, 'cause nobody could find him any good ones in the States. Surprise me, he said. Make something happen."

"Earth is his idea of making something happen? Who's he want you to bring back next, Dr. J?"

"He thinks if the guy has anything left he can probably give us some juice for the last couple of months, draw some fans, at least get the Knights a little pub. There's some free agents we might look at after the season."

"I'll see something about De la Cruz on the Net from time to time," Dee said. "He sounds like he wants to win almost as badly as he wants to be famous."

"You want to know the funniest thing?" Eddie Holtz said. "Guy's worth a billion dollars and mostly he wants to be loved."

He sipped his drink and said, "What did your father do?"

"A little bit of everything," she said vaguely.

Including time, she thought, not vaguely at all, with great clarity. He had played ball, too. But if she told him she was Cool Daddy Cody's little girl, she was going to have to tell him all of it. And Dee didn't expect ever to know Eddie Holtz well enough to tell him all of it. She'd never told Jeremy all of it.

She had never told anybody.

The Coltrane record ended. They sat there and listened to Ella sing with Louis Armstrong. Dee was pleased when Eddie called him Louis and not Satchmo. Monique came over and told Dee that Black Messiah had ordered some champagne. Dee told her to go downstairs and break out some of the good stuff, the first bottle was on her. Finally, Earthwind Morton and his date made their way over to the table, people calling out his name and applauding as he kept saying *"Bonjour, baby"* to just about everybody in the room. He was wearing a black turtleneck and black suede jeans, a red beret.

Dee got up. She tried to turn her head, but Earthwind kissed her on the mouth anyway, then introduced her to his date, Gaby. She presented her hand to Eddie Holtz, who leaned down and kissed it, though Dee had a feeling he wanted to keep going until he could bury his head in the front of the red dress. What was it about guys and breasts? Dee always figured if she could crack the case on that one, she might even be able to figure out why they were all so hot for pro football.

When everybody sat down, Earthwind said it was champagne all around tonight, he had a feeling they had something to celebrate.

Monique brought the bottle of Moët herself, and poured.

"In the words of General Patton, I shall return!" Earthwind said, with his glass in the air.

"MacArthur," Dee said to Earthwind.

He grinned at her, showing off his gold front tooth. "Who'd he play for?"

They talked about the game. Earthwind wanted to know where Dee had learned to throw a pass like she threw at the end of the game, and she said, "East Harlem."

"Shoulda known," Earthwind said, nodding. "How come you never threw that pass when we played before?"

"I was saving it," she said, "for a special occasion."

He turned to Eddie now, as if the subject of Dee was already starting to bore him. "When you goin' home, baby?"

Eddie said, "Day after tomorrow." He leaned over to Dee and said, "Do you mind if I use your office? I promised De la Cruz I'd call him at six, New York time, and he gets pissed if he's waiting there and I don't call when I'm supposed to. Don't worry, I'll put it on my calling card."

Dee told him where her office was, past the bar, he could get the key from Monique.

Earthwind said to Eddie, "Tell the boy help's on the way."

Earthwind rose to visit the men's room. Gaby and Dee nodded at each other. Gilles replaced Ella and Satch with Betty Carter and Ray Charles singing their duet of "Baby, It's Cold Outside." Eddie was gone awhile. So was Earthwind, which worried Dee a little bit, just because when Earthwind was still using, she was sure he'd done some of his best work in men's rooms all over the National Basketball Association.

Earthwind looked a little too mellowed out when he got

back to the table, but Dee couldn't believe that he would have risked a toke, or whatever they called it nowadays, knowing Eddie could come walking in.

"You tell him what I tol' you?" Earthwind said.

Eddie said, "I did. I told him help was on the way."

Earthwind pounded his chest, the way ballplayers did nowadays to celebrate something as trivial as a free throw.

"Me," he said.

"No," Eddie Holtz.

Now he was looking right at Dee Gerard.

"Her," Eddie said.

⓪ three

Earthwind had left a couple of hours before, pissed off, saying he was going over to the Casino de Monte Carlo, still not believing Eddie was serious with this shit about a girl playing in the NBA.

Finally it was just Eddie and Dee at the table, two o'clock in the morning. Gilles was still at the bar, talking to big-busted Gaby, who'd stayed when Earthwind got up from the table and said one last thing to Eddie:

"You that hot on bringing a girlie player back with you, you should think about that Oopsie Scissor-ewksi, or whatever his skinny-assed name is."

Dee noticed that Eddie's blue eyes seemed to get lighter when Gilles turned off most of the lights. If the math she'd done on his career was right, he had to be about thirty-five by now, but Dee thought he looked a lot younger, even with his curly brown hair starting to gray a little bit around his ears.

"A guy I know once said that the test of a good idea is if it lasts through a hangover," he said.

Dee said, "I'm not drunk." She pushed her empty wine-glass into the middle of the table, closed her eyes when she saw him looking at her, then tossed a balled-up napkin into the glass. "And even if I was, what's the old line? At least I'd be sober in the morning. You're still going to be crazy."

"I'm not crazy," Eddie said.

"Where do you want to start?" Dee said. "We might as well go through the whole laundry list right now. I'm too old, for one thing."

"Since when is thirty-two too old? This isn't swimming, they don't tell you you're washed up by the time you graduate college. It ain't even women's tennis, where you reach your peak before you get a driver's license. I'd look at Magic sitting there sometimes, watching the Lakers play, and I figured he could have gotten out there and kicked some ass when he was forty."

"He's Magic *Johnson*, Eddie. Hello? I am two years out of European women's basketball. Two years. I never even got to measure my game against the players in the WNBA. You talk about kicking ass? I'd watch on the satellite sometimes and see Cynthia Cooper playing the way she did at thirty-six, thirty-seven years old, and I'd think, People have no idea; they should have seen her when she was young, when I was playing against her. You should have seen me when I was young, Eddie. I'll tell you that, straight up, no lie. I was something to see. But I'm not young anymore."

Dee looked around DC. Over at the bar, Gilles was really doing his number on Gaby in the red dress, sitting on the customer side of the bar now, on the bar stool next to her. When he got over there, he was moving in for the kill.

"There were fast guys in the game tonight," Eddie said. "You were faster."

"These were guys who couldn't even find a seat on the end of the bench in the NBA."

"But not 'cause they weren't fast enough," Eddie Holtz said. "Most of them, anyway. Because they couldn't shoot or get their shot or handle well enough. Or because they were lazy. Or just too stupid. You were smarter than anybody out there, I could see that after you were in the game five minutes."

Dee couldn't help herself, the smile came out of her.

Eddie, who didn't miss much, didn't miss it. "What's so funny?"

"It occurred to me that I'm the prosecutor here. Prosecuting myself. You sound like my defense attorney."

"My mother wanted me to go to law school."

Dee leaned forward, put her elbows on the table, rested her chin in her hands, locking her eyes on him. "The game has changed while I've been away. God, I'm not telling you anything you don't know. There's hardly any positions anymore, outside of point guard. They're all six-eight or six-nine, they're all athletic as hell, they've all got arms as wide as the court, and could defend a small country if they've got a coach who'll get them to work at defense."

"You still need a point guard to make it work. One guy out there who still understands the way it's supposed to look. That's what you do. And you know you do."

"I am a *female* point guard. A retired thirty-two-year-old female point guard who hasn't played ball in the United States of America since she was a sophomore at DeWitt Clinton High School."

Now Eddie leaned in. "Nobody's perfect," he said.

Dee said, "You saw me play for fifteen minutes in a charity basketball game. Now you want me to be Jackie Robinson."

"Nah, just Billie Jean King." He had this laid-back way about him even when he smiled, doing most of the work with his eyes. "I saw what I saw," he said.

"I'm not as good as Cheryl Miller. Nobody was ever as good as Cheryl. And even she never tried what you want me to try. Nancy Lieberman was another one of my heroes, because she came from New York and the way she could pass. She made it to one training camp with the Lakers in the old days, then she got one summer with the guys, the world-famous Long Island Surf of the United States Basketball League."

"Cheryl wasn't better, she was different. You're a point guard, like Lieberman. Cheryl was really a forward, as unselfish as she was. Her best game was near the basket or going to the basket. A lot of ways? She was really a center, that's what I saw when she scored her hundred points in that high school game. I know you think I'm nuts, but your game is like John Stockton's game. Your body—with a couple of really cool differences—isn't so different from his. And I'm not sure you're not a little quicker than he is, at least now."

The music had stopped. Dee said, "Hold that new ridiculous thought," went over to where the sound system was, and put on some Sinatra, she wasn't sure why, it just seemed like the right time of night for it. It was one of her favorites, a live performance he did at the Sands in Las Vegas when he turned fifty. She loved the music and the Basie band behind him, wanted to laugh when he did his monologue and suddenly turned into some kind of Amos 'n' Andy.

"I don't mean to be insulting," Eddie said when she came back, "but you're looking at this shit like a man."

Dee said, "Now you've gone too far, buster."

"Tell you what," he said. "Go home, pour yourself one last nightcap. Make it a brandy. Think it over a little more, then we'll see how you feel in the morning."

"It is morning."

Eddie shrugged. "You told me before you always wanted to play with the boys. I'm offering you the chance."

"I've got a business here," she said. "I've got a life."

"Let your ex-husband—Jeremy?—run the place while you're gone. How many of these did you say he had?"

"Four. London, Paris, Nice, here. I told him he could have everything else, he didn't have to give me a penny of alimony, I just wanted this one. He said it could never make money, that it was a drain on all the other ones. Now we out-earn them all, thank you. But it wasn't even about making money. It was about making something *mine*."

"What happened with the two of you?"

"He's a good man," she said. "But a very bad boy. I decided that if I wanted to keep loving him, I had to waive him."

Sinatra was singing "Angel Eyes." Eddie may have suggested it was time for Dee to go, but he didn't seem to be going anywhere. He didn't give up, but was smooth about it, making his pitch almost in a bored way. She liked that about him. Eddie had moves.

"After I talked to New York, I booked tickets for us on Air France," he said, "day after tomorrow, out of Paris. All the good parts of your life story, the ones you wouldn't tell me tonight, you can tell me on the way to New York."

Dee stood up, reached over, shook his hand, made a gesture with her head toward the door.

"It hasn't been dull," she said.

He said he would call her when he woke up, maybe they could go shoot around someplace, how would that be?

"I don't think so, scout," she said.

She sat on the living room floor for a long time when she got home, after walking the five blocks to the apartment on Avenue Princesse Grace, which sat on one of the worst curves of the Monaco Grand Prix, not too far from the Mirabeau Hotel, with her view of fishing boats in the sea, the view that made her imagine sometimes what the place had looked like when the first Grimaldi got here seven hundred years ago. Even in the best of times, she had never thought of this place as hers and Jeremy's; the first time she'd stood on the balcony, this had been hers, too, had felt more like home than anything she had ever known.

It wasn't just the apartment, and she knew it. It was her life here. It was the peace she felt. Or the fact that even when she was really alone, no man in her life, sometimes no dating at all, she felt as if everything were one *piece:* having DC and running it, being in charge, not having to count the days anymore until she was coming home off the road, from another road trip through France or Spain, because she was home, somehow feeling as if this place on the other side of the world, with its obsession with royals and what felt like a constant tourist crowd, was just a small town to her. She made pottery visits to the Manufacture de Porcelaine sometimes, or shopped endlessly on the Avenue des Beaux-Arts, where the big boys were, Bulgari and Piaget and Cartier and Louis Vuitton and all the rest of them. Or sometimes she would just wander down to the sea, where she was happiest of all, and shop down there, using the hilly streets, the ones leading to the harbor, as her exercise. She looked forward now to the Springtime of the Arts Festival and wandering through the

Musée Anthropologie Prehistorique, the whole thing feeling
and certainly sounding so much more exotic than a trip to the
Museum of Natural History back in New York.

And there was always the International Fireworks Festival,
which reminded her of one of her favorite movies stacked on
what she called the Great Wall of her apartment, *To Catch a
Thief* with Cary Grant and Grace Kelly, one of the great love
scenes in the history of the movies. Eddie Holtz had asked her
about it, saying it was his mother's favorite, not even remembering the title. Dee told him it was all right, she had it covered.

"I'm almost better at movies than basketball," she said.

And she loved all the give-and-take, the bargaining, in
French and in English, with her butchers and her bakers, and
just sitting at the sidewalk cafés sometimes, everything on the
narrow streets connected by the café tables, reading the international edition of *USA Today* and then the *International Herald Tribune,* still her favorite, sipping coffee and eating warm
bread and marking time until she'd go back to the apartment
and pick the clothes she would wear to DC that night. And
then getting to DC in the late afternoon, her day beginning all
over again, talking to the chef and the waiters and Gilles,
carefully picking out the music the patrons would listen to
that night, the music different every night.

Mine, she thought now.

Me.

The all-grown-up me.

Dee got into an old Rucker League T-shirt Cool Daddy had
given her, went through some of his scrapbooks, and then her
own, thinking about Eddie Holtz, who got it more than most
guys ever did, even the ones who knew how good she was.

Eddie didn't think she was different because she was a
woman.

He just thought she was different.

"La Franchisa," the headline writers had called her in
Spain.

She'd always known she was different, even before she
could explain it to anybody. She knew how pretty she was; it
was like she'd grown into her looks when she got to high

school, nobody could call her a tomboy after that. She hadn't cared when they said that or that her height intimidated some of them now. She just wanted to play basketball. She was interested in guys, she actually liked dating once she started. But she loved basketball. Guys thought she was making all these sacrifices, playing in two and three leagues at a time, starting when they were still on 106th Street, right before they went to the Bronx, and then Europe. Sacrifice? Were they kidding? That thinking was from off her radar. She just wanted to get better at basketball. She wanted to be Lieberman, the one she'd first seen at Old Dominion, the one who could run a team and pass like Cousy and would spit in your eye before she'd back up one inch. She wanted to be Cheryl Miller at the '84 Olympics, the first Olympics where television had paid attention to women's basketball. Los Angeles. My God, it was like the first time she'd actually listened to Ruth, or her father's old scratchy Dinah Washington records, or even the early Aretha. Like: Oh. So this is what it can look like. She wanted her hair just like Cheryl's, she wanted the same Converse shoes with the little star on the side; mostly she wanted that amazing *game*. It was always a team game, passing the ball, giving it up when somebody had a better shot, but somehow that made the whole thing even more about her. Dee watched the men that year, too, watched Jordan explode like some kind of rocket. But he wasn't Michael, at least not yet. He wasn't so much better than everybody else on the court that you couldn't take your eyes off him. That's the way it was with Cheryl.

Dee would watch her sometimes, on that little black-and-white set, and realize she'd been holding her breath.

Dee was fourteen that year. Already she knew a lot about basketball: When she was playing, when she had the ball in her hands, when she was hearing that music inside her and knew none of the other girls on the court could touch her, she wasn't a girl or a boy. She was just a kid. Basketball wasn't something that belonged only to guys. It belonged to *her*. And that didn't change when she'd go find a game with the guys, when she'd ride the subway over to Queens for a game at O'Connell Park, at 197th and Murdock, or Montebello Park in Queens, or Foster Park in Brooklyn, stuffing extra clothes inside her sweats so she'd look bigger than she was, no makeup, growing her hair only so she'd look older when she finally took off her Celtics cap, shook that hair out the way she did for Eddie Holtz. She'd sit there, waiting her turn the way you did on the playground, waiting to get *picked*, not letting on how important this was to her, not caring how long she had to wait, trying to look cool until it was her turn, until she could say what she'd been waiting all day to say:

"I got next."

She knew that once they stopped making their little comments about her being a girl, once they got through all the guy stuff—"You lost, baby?"—and she got into the game, they wouldn't let her out.

It was only one of about twelve million things that she knew that guys didn't, on the court and off.

Her dreams, about the best game, like her dreams about playing to a packed house at the Garden someday—all those basketball dreams—went back that far. Dee Gerard's fantasy life. The dreams weren't about marrying Prince Charming, even though she later thought she had done just that with Jeremy. They weren't about living happily ever after, even though that's what she thought she was doing when he swept her off her feet and they ended up here.

The big dream was the same as it had always been.

The one about playing with the boys.

She knew she still could.

It didn't mean she still wanted to.

And what about the other? Why was that going to be any different now than it had ever been? Europe had been one kind of agony for her, especially the unpredictability of it, not knowing when it was going to show up, grab her right by the heart. How much worse would it be in New York, if she made it that far?

What happened at Madison Square Garden if she couldn't come out of the locker room? She'd read about the other famous people, not putting herself in their shoes, just trying to see if there was some common ground, some thread that connected them all. Streisand. Even Laurence Olivier. What, the

coach was going to have to stuff a Valium in her mouth to
make her go on?

She sat there a long time, going through the scrapbooks,
seeing the light finally coming up over the Mediterranean.
She picked up the phone a couple of times to call Jeremy in
England; he'd called Dee a couple of days before to tell her
he had some board meeting with Sir, which is what he called
his old man. Jeremy had always been the one to tell her to
keep playing, not because he thought a chance like this
would come along someday, just because he knew how much
she loved it. You're having yourself on, he'd say. God, she'd
always loved to hear him talk; back when she was playing,
she'd call him sometimes, any hour of the night, just to hear
him talk. You're having yourself on, dear girl, if you think
you can just lock this all away forever, tell yourself you're
well done with it. Her Jeremy sounding like Jeremy Irons,
just as suave as the actor and even more handsome.

She knew this had to be some kind of gimmick with the
rich boy who owned the New York team. How could it not
be? What was left over there in the season? Thirty games?
She wasn't worried about Eddie, he was a good guy. But what
was he going to be able to do for her if this really was a stupid bullshit publicity stunt and nothing more? Who was going
to watch her very cute backside for her then?

Step right up, see the basketball babe.

Buy the official merchandise while you're at it.

Dee had decided a long time ago she wasn't going to let
any guy use her, for anything.

And what about the media? God, she hadn't even thought
about the media yet. It made her head spin even more. What
would happen when they decided they needed to know everything about her? What happened when they found out about
Cool Daddy?

All about him.

What about the headlines *then*?

No, she thought. No way she was opening herself up to all
that. She knew that's why she wasn't going to call Jeremy, because she knew he'd give her some kind of pep talk, getting
more excited than she was. She could already hear him say-

ing, But you *must*, dear girl. She'd call Eddie instead, when
he was awake, tell him one last time what she'd been telling
him all along, that this was crazy and he was crazy and goodbye.

She was asleep on the floor, the scrapbooks all around her,
when Eddie called her first, asking if they could go shoot
around someplace. She heard herself telling him that she
could scam the keys to Stade Louis II, the operations manager
was a regular at DC. She'd see him over there in about half an
hour.

She wore a gray Celtics sweatshirt that had "Cousy" on the
back in dark green letters, along with the same No. 14 she'd
worn in the game. Eddie asked her about it, and she said, "My
father was a big Cousy guy."

Eddie wore his black Knights sweats, baggy, to cover his
clunky old knee brace, the one he still brought with him wherever he went, in case he suddenly got a dumb urge to play. He
watched Dee get loose while he stretched out his bad leg,
thinking that even in workout clothes, her hair pulled back in
a ponytail, no makeup, she was the best-looking woman he'd
seen in four countries. She was way more white than black,
like Jeter, the Yankee shortstop, but with the smoothest skin
Eddie'd ever seen in his life, and what Eddie could only think
of as a perfect WASP-type nose and these huge dark eyes.

She had a guy's game, but the way she moved on those
long legs, taking these big long strides, reminded Eddie of a
girl dancer.

Eddie'd always loved the way girl dancers moved.

When he got out there himself, she said to him, "One-on-
one's never been my game. I'm the girl singer who needs a
good band."

Eddie said, "You want to talk or you want to play?"

"Winner's outs?"

"Win by two?" he said.

Dee nodded. "You sure that knee will hold up against a
younger and more talented opponent?"

Eddie looked around, as if to see who the hell she was

talking about, then snapped her a two-hand chest pass. "Shoot for it, do or die."

Her ballhandling was even better than he'd thought it was in the game. Or maybe he was just paying closer attention. What he really noticed was how fast she was with the ball, almost seeming faster, quicker, on offense than when she was trying to guard him on defense. People who didn't know anything about basketball never understood that the only thing that mattered, for a guard anyway, a point guard especially, was how fast you were dribbling the goddamn ball, that this wasn't some kind of running race, it didn't matter if you were as fast as Marion Jones. You had to be fast for about fifty feet in basketball, sometimes less than that.

Dee blew by him one time, laid the ball in, caught it before it hit the ground.

"I know what you're thinking," she said. " 'And she's a babe, too.' "

He could get his own shot, and muscle her a little on defense, make her give up her dribble before she wanted to a couple of times, and then he could use his size on her, the three inches in height and arms that had always made him play bigger, to bottle her up.

What he couldn't do, no matter how hard he tried, was get in front of her.

Sometimes Dee would beat him and, just for fun, she'd throw him a blind pass instead of shooting the ball herself, as if she wanted him to know it wasn't beating him that interested her, it was showing him, up close, just the two of them, exactly how much ball she had inside her.

"You gotta come back with me," he said when they were done, pissed off at how out-of-shape he felt. Or maybe just pissed off at how out-of-shape he looked to Dee, who'd barely broken a sweat no matter how much he'd tried to push her.

"No," she said.

She took two bottles of water out of her bag, handed him one. Eddie took a couple of sips and then poured the rest of it over his head.

"I'm getting old," he said.

"You ought to ice that knee," she said.

"Players do that," he said.

"And you're not?"

"Not anymore," Eddie said.

He sat there while he tried to catch his breath, looking around the empty arena, the ball they used underneath the basket. Eddie loved having a gym to himself, he always had. When he was at St. John's, he'd get the keys to Alumni Hall from Louie Carnesecca, his coach, and go over there at midnight sometimes, turning on the lights, having the place to himself. . . .

Dee said, "What are you thinking?"

"About lots of things," he said, stretching the bad knee out in front of him.

"Like what?"

"Like that it's taken my owner a day to fall in love with you," he said.

Which wasn't technically true.

When Eddie had gone to the phone at DC the night before, Michael De la Cruz had immediately accused him of being drunk.

"Didn't we have that talk about your drinking before you left?" he'd said, the connection amazingly good, as if he were in the next room.

"I'm cold sober," Eddie said. "You said surprise you. Here it is."

"You've found a woman you think can play in the NBA? I sent you over to look at fat Earthwind, and now you go affirmative action on me? If you're drunk, it's all right, Eddie, it's your last night, you're lonely, you probably haven't been laid the whole time you're over there. Just tell me, I'll forget you called, you sleep it off and come home."

"Listen to me," Eddie said, not with any edge to his voice, keeping in mind this was the boss, even if it was easy to forget sometimes. "I can bring Earthwind back. And we can get a little bump with him, and then I promise, he's gone after the season. His old act? It's an old act now. It's different with this girl. I call her a girl. She's in her thirties. I'm telling you, she'll knock your fucking eyes out. You said you wanted me to surprise you? How about if we shock the world?"

There was enough silence on the other end that Eddie finally had to say, "You still there?"

He looked around Dee's office. No pictures of her playing ball, just a bunch on her desk of her and some good-looking guy—*very* good-looking guy, actually—who had to be her ex-husband. Unless she was seeing some new guy, which was another possibility.

Except why did that matter?

"I'm here," Michael De la Cruz said. "Let me get this straight: You've got a girl you think is good enough to play for us?"

"Us meaning the NBA? Or us meaning the Knights?"

"Both."

"Both," Eddie said.

"And if you're wrong? And I become more of a laughing-stock than I already am with the other boys and girls who own teams?"

Eddie Holtz said, "Fire me."

There was another long pause. "Even if she can play a little, this could be a huge thing for us, just in terms of publicity and goodwill. Jesus, we'd become the soccer-mom capital of the world!"

"We might even win a few ballgames along the way."

"If we do, all the better," De la Cruz said. "But this is about something much more important than whether or not she can play, Edward."

"What's that?"

Michael De la Cruz said, "This is about being *in* play."

"You'll get a kick out of him," Eddie was saying now to Dee. "He's one of those dare-to-dream, dare-to-be-great assholes. There's no obligations here, no commitments. Shit, I know how much of a long shot this is. He says we'll work you out with the guys on a sneak, see what our coach—Bobby Carlino?—says, then go from there."

"Send me one of his motivational tapes. What do they go for over there, nineteen ninety-nine, plus shipping and handling?"

"C'mon," Eddie said, "what have you got to lose?"

"My great big fantasy life," she said. "Maybe I don't want to put that on the line. It stays a fantasy life that way."

He stared at her long enough that she looked away finally.

"You're afraid," he said.

She was in mid-drink and spit out some water, laughing her good laugh. "Absolutely."

She stood up.

"I thought about it all night," she said. "Been thinking about it all morning. And I keep coming back to: You really should've come around about five years ago, Eddie. Gotten a good look at the young Dee. She was really something to look at."

"I'll be around until tomorrow," he said. "De la Cruz told me I should keep Earthwind on the hook, in case things don't work out with you. So I gotta talk to him before he heads out on his road trip. And I want to talk to that big Serb, Oley What's-His-Name, too, about next season."

Dee gave him a low five.

"It's been fun," she said.

"C'mon," Eddie said. "We'll make history."

Dee threw her bag over her shoulder and headed for the gym door, laughing that good laugh of hers one last time.

Eddie knew it wasn't the time or the place to get distracted, but he couldn't help thinking Dee Gerard had herself one great ass.

"I've heard a lot of come-on lines in my life, Eddie, but I've got to admit, that's a new one."

He had Lebortvaillet turn in the Renault for him. Eddie'd had enough of the Grand Corniche, and decided to hire a car and a driver for the long ride back to Charles de Gaulle. He'd tried to reach De la Cruz before he went to bed the night before, but was told he'd gone to some movie opening. Eddie'd been working for the guy only a year, but already knew that De la

Cruz liked having his picture in the paper more than he liked making money.

Fuck it, Eddie thought, I'll tell him she's not coming when I get there.

He overtipped the maid, checked for phone messages one more time, made sure he had his passport and his plane ticket. The phone rang and he thought it might be Dee calling, but it was just the parking guy telling "Monsieur 'Oltz" his car was out front and his bags were already in it. Eddie *merci*-ed the guy and then said, *"Un instant, si'l vous plaît."*

He was sure she'd call.

She was as happy with a basketball in her hands as he used to be.

Hell, as happy as he still was.

Eddie didn't even attempt to figure out what the hotel bill was in American, just signed his name and looked at a number so big in francs he started to wonder if he'd busted the goddamn chandelier.

He was halfway across the lobby when he saw her over in front of the kiosk where he'd gotten his *International Herald Tribune* and international *USA Today* in the morning. She had an oversized blazer on, denim jeans, basketball sneakers, the Celtics cap.

And an old leather suitcase, covered with a United Nations of stickers.

"I've been thinking," she said.

"Yeah? What about?"

"What if you're right?" Dee said. "What if the coolest guy in the league *did* turn out to be a girl?"

⊕ four

On the way in from Kennedy, Eddie asked how long it had been since Dee had been back to the city.

"A few years," she said, in the backseat of the stretch limousine Michael De la Cruz had sent for them. "It was right before Jeremy and I got married. He had a piece of a show they tried to bring over to Broadway from the West End. In London? We came over for the opening. And the closing, as it turned out. I don't even think we were here seventy-two hours. I didn't see much except our room at the Lowell, the theater, and Sardi's."

The driver said he'd heard on the radio that there was some sort of major delay at the Midtown Tunnel, so he'd taken the Triboro, and Dee had gotten the knockout first look at Manhattan she'd always liked the best, everything off to their left as they came over the bridge, pow, there it was. This was the second limousine she'd ever taken into the city; the first had been with Jeremy. They'd come over the Triboro that day, as well, and when they passed the exit for 106th Street, she'd joked, "Tell him to let me off here, I can walk the rest of the way home."

When they'd gotten slammed on the FDR Drive in the Fifties, the driver had gotten off and gone west on Fifty-third. So now they were coming through Times Square, the traffic even backed up there at one in the afternoon. Eddie said the Knights' offices were across Eighth Avenue from the Garden, the back side, across the building from the post office — she remembered the post office, right? — and in the same building where CNN had its studios in New York.

"You believe how they've cleaned this up?" Eddie said, meaning Times Square.

"I told Jeremy when we were here he would have liked it a lot better before they turned it into a shopping mall." She was staring out the window to her left. "Is that a television studio on the corner of Forty-fourth?"

"They do *Good Morning America* there now," Eddie said. "They passed some rule while you were away that they can't do one of those morning shows if they don't have a studio on the street where you can see people from Kansas waving at the hosts and holding up signs that say, 'Hi Mom, Send Money.' "

She sat back and looked out the windows of the stretch, seeing the guys pushing racks of clothing as they got closer to the Garden, seeing a sign for Macy's on the left now, remembering when a subway trip down here to shop for clothes had felt like it did when she gave herself a couple of days in Paris now, remembering how she had come down here with the money she had saved working that summer at the Ninety-second Street Y to buy herself her one and only prom dress when she was a sophomore. She had been asked by a senior on the basketball team, her blond hero, Michael O'Neill, and realized she didn't have anything that was close to being elegant enough to wear. So she took the train down and found something in evening wear that fit her budget. The first thing she did when she got home was to cut out the Macy's label, in case anybody checked.

Wishing as she always did, in those years especially, that her mother were still around to help her.

"Where are you?" Eddie said, as they made the turn at

Thirty-third and Eighth and the driver managed to get over to
the left side of the street, where Five Penn Plaza was.

"The intersection of 1985 and the rest of my life," she said.

"You said you'd tell me your life story when you got back
here," Eddie said.

"I did," Dee said. "I just didn't tell you when."

"Here's another thing maybe you missed about the US of
A while you were away," he said. "Everybody gets to know
everything about everybody."

That's what I'm afraid of, Dee thought.

Michael De la Cruz was standing behind his desk, finishing
up a phone call, when Eddie showed her into his office, De la
Cruz holding up one finger, nodding his head at the same
time, saying, "I love you, too, Johnny, with all my heart. But
I frankly don't love you quite as much I did before interest
rates went into the old flusher."

Then he was rocking from side to side like an impatient
child, rolling his eyes, like, Please, God, wrap this up.

Dee's first impression of him was that he looked more like
a personal trainer than he did a billionaire. Or the captain of
the boy cheerleaders, maybe.

He was about six-three, his thick black hair shiny with either gel or mousse, shiny enough for her to use as a compact
if Dee wanted to check the bags she knew had to be under her
eyes. De la Cruz wanted it to look messy, as if the bangs were
falling carelessly on his forehead, but Dee knew that was just
for effect, she had a feeling those bangs were going to be in
the same place tomorrow, and probably every day for the rest
of his life. Jeremy always said there were two classes of men,
the ones who just combed their hair and the ones who
arranged it. Michael De la Cruz arranged. He was wearing a
black turtleneck sweater, tight enough to show off his pecs.
This was another thing that had changed in her life, Dee had
noticed, her adult life anyway, guys as interested in showing
off their chests as women were.

He had dark skin, darker than her own, really. Dee had read
up on him on the flight over, but must've skipped over the

part where it told whether he was Mexican or Puerto Rican or what. He had grown up in Los Angeles, she knew that, and started out peddling cell phones door-to-door in South Central L.A. when he was still a senior in high school. From the looks of him, Dee thought high school might be just twenty or thirty minutes ago.

One time, a writer from *Vanity Fair* had asked him where he'd gotten the phones to sell in the first place.

"You remember Robin Hood?" De la Cruz said. "Well, the only part of the story that was a little different was that I robbed from the rich and sold to the poor, though I must say at rock-bottom prices."

Somehow he went from there to starting a home computer business in South Central when he'd been an undergraduate at UCLA. By the time he'd graduated, he'd been trading stocks, and then he was big into tech stocks when those exploded at the end of the nineties. He walked away with nearly a billion dollars, getting out before the tech market crashed and burned. Suddenly he was thirty years old, wanting to play. He produced movies for a while, even took acting lessons himself, so he could put himself into some of his own productions. Eddie had shown De la Cruz's publicity kit to Dee, just so she could see it was exactly like the ones actors and actresses gave out. Included in it were the photographs he requested you use if you were going to write about him in a newspaper or magazine, a packet of clips, mostly from the New York tabloids, showing him with the models and supermodels he'd dated—Dee had always wondered how you moved up, if there was some sort of way points were allotted—at various movie openings and society events.

"Him and Donald Trump," Eddie had said in the car, "seem to be in some kind of weird tag-team match to see which one of them can date more Vruskas and Mariskas."

"I think I'm getting the picture," Dee said. "The biggest turn-on for guys like this is if the supermodel's country has a bobsled team."

Now De la Cruz was coming around his desk with so much energy and enthusiasm that Dee had this picture of the three of them in the office starting a fast break across Eighth Avenue and then running all the way across town.

"So this is my go-to girl," he said, bowing and kissing her hand. "Sorry to keep you waiting." Then he made a big show of sighing, either because he meant it or he wanted to pump out his chest a little more. "Bankers. Can't live with 'em, can't burn down their big houses and then pee on the ashes."

Up close he really was awfully pretty, Dee thought, though not in any way that would ever push her buttons.

She could have sworn he smelled like lilacs.

"Mr. De la Cruz," she said. "Very nice to meet you."

"Michael," he said. "Mr. De la Cruz makes me feel too old. Time slips away from us too fast as it is."

Dee tried not to smile as she said, "It's our most precious gift." That one she did remember from the clips; it was something De la Cruz said all the time, at least once he was into ten figures.

"Uh-oh," he said, giving her a boom-box laugh. "Busted. Eddie said you had a sense of humor. I *love* that. And if you've got my material down cold, that means you know my ten building blocks to a better life, right? Laughter is number two!"

"Number one is modesty," Eddie said, deadpan.

Michael De la Cruz clapped Eddie on the back so hard, she was afraid he might have busted a rib.

"I'd love to tell you Eddie only talks to me this way in private," De la Cruz said happily, "but it's much worse in public."

"He calls me his big basketball brother," Eddie said, grabbing a stack of newspapers off the desk and heading to the couch that separated Michael De la Cruz's formal office from what seemed to be the most elaborate home gym Dee had ever seen.

"Please sit down," the owner of the New York Knights said. "Bobby Carlino, our overpaid coach, just had the trainer call to say practice is running late. We'll go over to the Garden and meet him in a few minutes."

"He must be awfully excited," Dee said dryly. "The two of

us will probably be out in front of Tiffany's in the morning, just so we can be there when the doors open."

"I'm not going to lie to you," De la Cruz said. "He's not big on new things. I imagine bell-bottoms were a very, very difficult time for Bobby."

Dee said, "But you have specifically told him you're considering putting a woman on his basketball team, right?

"My team," De la Cruz said, showing off teeth whiter than snow.

"You did tell him, though," she said, staying with it. "So we don't all go across the street in a few minutes and yell, 'Surprise!' "

"I did! I did! Took him to Café Boulud last night and dropped it on him just as the Wellfleets arrived. 'Hey, Coach,' I said, 'what would you think about your new point guard being a girl?' "

"And he said?"

Michael De la Cruz leaned back on what Dee was pretty sure was a Chippendale sofa, the silk a dark green. "He said we've got enough girlie players already to qualify for the WNBA. Said we might be the first team to test positive for estrogen."

"Then you told him you were serious," Dee said.

"I did! And he told me something he tells me quite a lot."

"What's that?"

" 'I quit.' "

Eddie was sitting across the room, feet up on a coffee table, reading the *Daily News*. From behind the paper, he said, "I love when he does that."

"He dumped me before I even showed up?" Dee said. "Usually guys have to know me a lot better before they do that."

"Not to worry," De la Cruz said, "he doesn't mean it. There's as much a chance of Bobby Carlino walking away from the ten million he's got left on the table as there was that he wouldn't go pro for my money in the first place."

Dee knew all about Carlino; he'd already been a coaching star before she'd left the country. He had won his first national championship at Wake Forest when he was twenty-eight. He'd

spent ten years at Wake, then gone to St. John's and won two
more. When Dee had gotten tired of reading about Michael De
la Cruz on the flight over, she'd read up on Carlino, wanting to
know what to expect from him as much as she did an owner
who thought he could get a woman into the game. Carlino still
looked and acted like the boy wonder of college basketball at
St. John's, even though he was closer to fifty by now than forty.
He'd become a best-selling author, with one of those self-help
books that evolved out of the big-ticket motivational speeches
he gave that Eddie said cost corporations about fifty grand a
pop. "I got roped into going to one once," he said. "Close your
eyes and you could be listening to Michael De la Cruz. Funny
thing is, they think they're so different from each other. I think
it was some kind of weird self-love that brought them
together—that and a whole pile of money."

Along the way, Bobby Carlino said he would never leave
college basketball, no matter how much money NBA teams
tried to throw at him every couple of years.

Then De la Cruz overpaid for a coach the way he would for
a new summer house in the Hamptons, or a new jet.

"Don't worry," De la Cruz said to Dee. "I'll get him turned
around. Hey, turning people around is what I *do*."

He said to Eddie Holtz, "Isn't that right, Fast Edward?"

Still behind the paper, Eddie recited, "Reach for the sky.
Dream your dreams." He turned the page, showing her the
back page of the *Daily News,* which was in color now, Dee
noticed. "Your life is only a great adventure if you make it
one," Eddie said.

"You may have noticed," De la Cruz said to Dee, "our
Eddie is a bit of a cynic."

Eddie said, "My ex-wife said I was a dreamer."

Dee's head whipped around. "You were married?"

Eddie shrugged. "She said I was preventing her from
growing."

"You didn't say anything about being married."

"Oh," he said, "and I can't shut you up once you get going
about yourself."

"At least I told you I'd been married."

"Step number four!" Michael De la Cruz said excitedly, ignoring both of them. "You grow, or you go!"

All around the room were magazine covers featuring De la Cruz: *Sports Illustrated, GQ, Esquire, Men's Fitness, Details, New York.* Dee figured this must have been two offices once, because of the size of the gym, which featured not just high-tech equipment, but also the biggest television screen Dee had ever seen, showing what looked like NBA game highlights and one of those crawls she'd see sometimes on CNN International, giving scores and statistics.

"NBA dot com," De la Cruz said when he saw her staring. "It gives you all the stats you could ever want on the league. Including our stats, unfortunately.

"But," he continued, "if you're as good as Eddie says you are, we can go from being a nonfactor to the biggest story in sports!"

He punctuated the thought by giving his upper body one of those weight-lifter rips. When guys did something like that, she always wanted to go, "Oooh," just so they wouldn't think they were wasting their big manly time in the gym.

"I'm glad you brought that up," Dee said. "See, Eddie here has no idea whether or not I'm as good as he says I am. He just happened to see me shine for a couple of minutes on amateur night at the Palace."

"Comme vous voulez," Eddie said, giving her that smile again with his eyes, as if he'd gotten off a winner. He turned to De la Cruz and said, "It means 'whatever' in French. It's a polite way of me telling her she's full of shit. She knows it, too. You'll see for yourself when you see her play."

"Je partirai demain," Dee said, and then she translated for both of them. "That means I'm leaving tomorrow, if I know what's good for me, anyway."

Michael De la Cruz stood up, walked over to the mammoth window facing east. Somewhere over there was the Empire State Building. People who lived in New York thought it was only for tourists, but it had always been Dee's favorite place in the whole city, ever since she'd seen *An Affair to Remember* with Cary Grant and Deborah Kerr, another movie in the Great Wall stack back in Monte Carlo, the one where they're supposed to meet on top of the Empire State Building, only she's rushing because she's late and isn't watching where she's going and gets hit by a car. Dee got mad a few years ago when she was watching *Sleepless in Seattle,* because she couldn't tell whether Nora Ephron, the director, one of Dee's favorite writers when she was a kid, was making fun of *An Affair to Remember* or not, when the women were blubbering and saying how it was the greatest chick flick of all time. Dee had never been much for chick flicks herself, but she had always been a sucker for the part where Cary Grant finally found Deborah Kerr at the end, every single corny thing they said to each other after he finally figured out there was a reason why she wasn't getting up off the couch.

Maybe it was Cary Grant, and she was a terminal sucker for English guys.

Or maybe she was just a sucker for happy endings, even sappy ones, not that she'd had many in her life.

"Listen," De la Cruz said, a little sharpness in his voice for the first time, "you didn't come all this way if you didn't want to take your shot."

"Maybe not," she said. "I also didn't come this far to embarrass myself. I won't do that to myself, and, as my friend Earthwind Morton would say, I'm certainly not going to allow you to embarrass myself."

"You can walk away at any time," he said. "Eddie told me on the phone that he'd made that pretty clear to you."

"Abundantly clear," she said. "I just want you to tell me this isn't going to be some kind of sideshow. My father loved baseball almost as much as he loved basketball. Who was the owner he used to tell me about, the guy with the wooden leg, who sent the midget up to bat that time?"

"Bill Veeck!" De la Cruz said. "You know about Bill Veeck? He was one of my idols!"

"I'm not going to be your midget," Dee said.

"Tough lady," De la Cruz said to Eddie Holtz, giving him a man-to-man smile.

Men always thought "lady" came out sounding like a compliment when it just made them sound like condescending jerks. Lady. Babe or Baby. Chick. Girl. All in the same family, as far as Dee was concerned. She could call herself a girl the way black guys called each other nigger. She'd even let somebody like Eddie Holtz get away with it, because somehow, for reasons she couldn't quite figure out yet, she and Eddie seemed to be speaking the same language, at least when it came to basketball.

"Boy, am I not a lady, Michael," she said. "I am so not a lady, you have no idea."

"Tell you what," he said. "Let's cut to the chase here."

He got off the couch and carelessly pulled up a Chippendale chair that matched the sofa, except the green was a little lighter. Closer to the color of money, Dee thought.

"I didn't bring you over here to waste your time," he continued. "Or my time. And the part about how you don't want me to embarrass you? If I tried my hardest, if I were at my most creative best and tried to embarrass you every day for the next three years, I still couldn't embarrass you any worse than this basketball team has embarrassed me. Okay? I have never lost at anything in my *life*. Now, I am not just losing and losing big-time—losing games, losing money, losing an ass I'm told is cute enough for a cop show—people are laughing at me. I don't want people laughing at me anymore. Okay? Oh, they can laugh when they hear we're bringing a woman in to play. Let 'em. But you know what I want to hear more than anything else? I want to hear the sound of everybody's mouth shutting when they find out I was right and they were all wrong."

He leaned closer and took her hands. Dee let him. It was interesting, seeing what he was like when he thought he was going good, on a roll. She knew the show was as much for Eddie as it was for her.

Watch the master in action.

"I don't want to be Bill Veeck on this one," he said. "I don't want to be Ringling Brothers and Barnum and Bailey Basketball Circus. I want to be Branch Rickey, putting Jackie Robinson into the game. I've talked to a few people about this, people I can trust. You know Earl Monroe? The Pearl? Friend of mine, I hired him as a consultant. The Pearl told me this is going to happen sooner or later. Meaning a girl in the

NBA. I said to him, 'If it's the right one, why couldn't sooner be right now?' He said there wasn't a reason in this world he could think of, as long as she was strong enough to get through what Pearl called The Shit."

He squeezed her hands now, and Dee could actually feel the warmth of the guy, as if he were able to heat himself up as fast as a microwave. Or maybe getting this worked up, about almost everything, was just normal for him.

"Are you strong enough, Dee?" he said. "Are you strong enough to be my number forty-two for me the way Robinson was for Branch Rickey?"

She felt a giggle coming on, but managed to keep a straight face.

"Fourteen," she said finally.

"Excuse me?"

"I want number fourteen," she said. "Providing everybody in this room doesn't turn out to be completely nuts."

"Sure," he said. "I mean, sure. But why fourteen?"

From across the room, Eddie said, "She's a Cousy guy."

① five

The cover story, De la Cruz decided, was that Dee was an actress, an unknown, researching a role about a woman basketball player in a movie some friends of his were producing. He'd tell the players she'd won the part not just because of her acting talent, but her basketball talent as well, that she'd played some small-college ball out west, before she'd gone to Hollywood and taken acting classes with Julia Roberts.

"Julia Roberts?" Dee said.

"Maybe that Charlize Theron," De la Cruz. "My guys seem to have a thing for big blondes. Or I could tell them you started out with my good friend Gwyneth. Once I start with my pitch, I just like to let it happen."

The movie, he said, would be about a girl pretending to be a guy to win a bet and prove she was good enough to make the college team.

He was telling her all this as they crossed Eighth Avenue. To their right was a Garden marquee almost as big and showy as the one out front, on Seventh Avenue. The message on it kept changing, telling when the Knicks played again, the Rangers hockey team, the Knights, upcoming acts booked into something called The Theater. What was that? When she was a kid, it had been the Felt Forum; she remembered they used to have the Golden Gloves boxing there every year. Cool Daddy would get tickets; he liked the fights, there always seemed to be some kid from the neighborhood who he said was going to be the next Ali. She smiled to herself at the memory of Cool Daddy dreaming big not just for himself but for everybody else, too. They'd take the train down to Grand Central, change for Penn Station, and then they'd watch a couple of fights before he'd take her across into the Garden, on those nights when he'd been able to scam Knicks tickets off somebody, usually way up, in the cheap seats, the blue ones in those days. The mid-eighties this was, when Knicks tickets weren't hard to get because the Knicks weren't much to see. One of the first games she ever remembered was against the Utah Jazz, when John Stockton was a rookie.

Even Cool Daddy didn't know who he was, vaguely knowing that he'd gone to some college Out There, which is how he always described the West Coast, from Washington to the Mexican border. By the second quarter, though, Cool Daddy was only watching this white guard who didn't look fast enough or big enough or strong enough to dominate the game, but was doing it anyway.

"Watch the way he makes the angles," Cool Daddy said. "See that? See, little girl? They trained to follow the ball, and he knows that."

"See that, little girl? Watch how the man's mind works. That's the strongest part of his game, way it is with yours."

See that, little girl? Sounding more like *See dat*, always, with Cool Daddy. . . .

". . . what was that movie called?" De la Cruz was asking Eddie now.

"Tootsie," Eddie said. To Dee, he said, "Sometimes I know the movie, as long as it's an easy one."

"I'm sorry," she said. "My mind was somewhere else."

Eddie said, "Which year this time?"

Dee said, "Nineteen eighty-four. Was that when Stockton was a rookie?"

Eddie nodded and said, "Sounds right. You were a Stockton guy?" He grinned when he realized what he'd said. "I mean—"

Dee said, "I was a Stockton guy, too."

Michael De la Cruz acted as if he hadn't heard a word either one of them had said. "I was saying that what we're telling the players will be like our own little movie within a movie. I couldn't remember the one where Dustin Hoffman played the soap opera actress and Billy Murray played his wacky roommate."

"Well, okay," Dee said, "but I only do nude scenes if the integrity of the script demands it."

Before they went inside, standing in there on the corner of Thirty-third against a West Side winter wind she remembered instantly, like another city landmark, Dee said, "I don't mean to wear you out with this, but the coach is on board with the movie thing, too?"

"Absolutely!" De la Cruz said.

They came in through the Employees' Entrance to the Garden, around the corner from what was still the entrance to Penn Station; at least that was still where it used to be. Then the three of them walked past the security desk, down a long corridor, and took a freight elevator up to the fifth floor, De la Cruz acting as if he ran the place and not Cablevision, which Eddie said now owned the Garden and everything in it and even Radio City, too.

"What happened to Gulf and Western?" Dee asked. "Didn't they used to own the whole world?"

"They sold it," Eddie said. "Or got took over a couple of takeovers ago. I actually can't remember."

They passed some hockey nets when they came out of the elevator on five, took a right, and then they were walking into the tunnel where the Knicks came walking out for games. Dee had done it herself exactly one time in her life, her sophomore year at DeWitt Clinton, in the semifinals of the PSAL girls' tournament, the same night Cool Daddy told her they were going to Europe as soon as the school year was over and he frankly didn't know when they was comin' back, little girl. She had been last in line that night because she always was, not because she was the star of the Clinton team—which she

was—but because she had always been superstitious as hell.
There wasn't much of a crowd, most of it down near the court,
for a girls' high school game at one o'clock on a Sunday afternoon. It didn't matter to her, not even a little bit, because
she was here, in the place all New York basketball kids called
The Mecca, here in what she'd always heard the sweet-voiced
p.a. announcer say was the magic world of Madison Square
Garden. . . .

She heard Bobby Carlino before she saw him.

"You fucking *fucks*," is what she heard.

Dee turned to Eddie. "I know I've been speaking a lot
more French than English lately, but you can use it as an ad-
jective *and* a noun now?"

Eddie, still dressed from the plane the way she was, in his
own blue blazer and white shirt, blue jeans and scuffed-up
penny loafers, said, "It's sort of his trademark line, like Regis
saying, 'Final answer?' "

Dee said, "Who's Regis?"

"It would take too long to explain," Eddie said, as they
walked out far enough toward the court, the first rows of seats
on either side of them going up like bleachers. Now they
could see the Knights players, organized in a raggedy circle
around their coach at midcourt.

Bobby Carlino was five-ten if he was lucky, shorter than
every player on his team. Shorter than *me*, Dee thought. He
had dark hair, hard to tell whether it was black or brown under
the Garden lights, brushed straight back in that style Pat Riley
seemed to have made popular for coaches who still had their
hair; they all seemed to be wearing it that way when Dee
would catch an NBA game on French TV sometimes. Dee
also noticed a male-pattern bald spot in the back of the little
dude's head, which instantly pleased her for some reason she
couldn't explain. He was wearing a purple-and-black warm-
up, the same Knights colors she had seen all over the offices
across the street. Carlino was moving as he talked, like some
standup guy working a theater-in-the-round, and now as she
got a better look at his surprisingly young face, she could see
veins popping so far out of his forehead they looked like
seams on a baseball.

"You *fucking* fucks!" he said again, shifting the emphasis this time.

The players did a lot of foot shuffling, few of them even wanting to make eye contact, at least when Carlino was looking right at them. But two in back of him—a skinny black kid a head taller than Carlino and wearing a full old-fashioned Afro, huge hair, and the tallest Chinese person Dee had ever seen in her life—were grinning and rolling their eyes, as if they had heard this all before.

Suddenly Carlino's head whipped around, as if he had eyes in back of his head that could see right through the bald spot.

"Something funny there, General Tso?"

The Chinese kid was at least seven-two, but he had a sweet face on him, with some fun in his eyes, at least until Carlino got him in his sights. As soon as the coach did, the Chinese kid tried to turn his face grave and pointed to himself, as if he'd made a bad pass or taken a dumb shot in a game.

"Fucky fuck, that I, Coach," he said. "I the worst fucky fuck of all."

"No way," Big Hair said. "I'm a worse fuckin' fuck than you ever thought of bein'."

Next to him, Dee noticed a guy she remembered from European basketball, six-eight and a city block wide, Carl Anthony. She hadn't noticed him at first, but now she did when she saw he had something written in script into his haircut. She'd been playing for Femenino Tres Cantos that year, the year she was La Franchisa, and Carl Anthony was with Baloncesto Fuenladbrada Pabellon Fernando Martin, her all-time favorite name of any sports team anywhere. They loved Carl Anthony over there, even the ones who didn't speak or read English, because there was usually someone in the crowd who could translate the "Kill" he had in his hair, or "Pain," or just "Death."

Sometimes he'd put something up there about loving the baby Jesus, just to throw everybody off.

"Maybe we should take a vote," Carl Anthony said. "Decide which one of us is the biggest disgrace."

He had one of the deepest baritones Dee had ever heard. The minute he started talking, she remembered a time when he had been interviewed on television after a game and had glared at the guy interviewing him, saying, "I *said*, 'I only *hablo* the Espanish during the game, okay, Pedro?' "

Carlino said, "You guys are very funny, you know that? Sometimes I think to myself, Hey, Bobby, are they funnier at practice or when they are getting their *asses* handed to them by the Pistons?"

Dee whispered to Eddie, "Oh, can I keep him?"

Carlino glanced over to where she was standing between Eddie and Michael De la Cruz, and for a minute Dee was afraid he'd heard her.

"Now, get the hell out of here, I'm sick of looking at you," he said, making a motion dismissing them from the court, or maybe just from the whole league. But Michael De la Cruz was already through the opening in the press table and out onto the court.

"Hey, Bobby C.," he said, a hand up like a traffic cop's. "Before everybody leaves, would it be all right if I had a word with my guys?"

Carlino said, "They're all yours," and walked over and sat in the first row of courtside seats, along with three men, all dressed in the same purple-and-black outfits, who Dee assumed were his assistant coaches. When she'd first started coming to Knicks games, she couldn't even remember Red Holzman, the coach in those days, having anybody except a little white-haired trainer sitting next to him.

"I want you guys to meet somebody," De la Cruz said, motioning for Dee to join him out there.

Dee grabbed Eddie's arm and said, "You come, too. I'm not going to the mixer alone."

Half the players were sitting now, eyeing her speculatively. The rest just stood there in the same kind of slouch, giving her the same kind of attitude she always used to see on the playground when they saw it was a girl coming into the game; acting put out that they had to stay out on this court even one minute longer to listen to another asshole in love with the sound of his own voice, this one the boss asshole.

Of all the Knights out there, there were only three Dee recognized for sure: Carl Anthony; Deltha Lester, a veteran point guard with a kind of cornrowing Dee hadn't seen before, this elaborate maze that made the top of his head look like something a rat couldn't find its way out of in a lab experiment; and Jamie Lawton, everybody's All-American, the Mr. Perfect everybody had gotten so excited about at the last Olympics, his long blond hair and WASP-y good looks making him almost as pretty as Michael De la Cruz.

"I want you guys to meet Dee Gerard," De la Cruz said. "You haven't heard of her yet, but you're going to, I promise."

"You dance, baby?" Deltha said, playing to the rest of the boys. "I think I mighta had you on my lap the other night, over at The Swing."

Dee started to say something, but Jamie Lawton beat her to it.

"I keep meaning to ask you, Deltha," he said. "When was the last time you saw one of your dates with her clothes *on* before they were off?"

"You sure you want to be askin' my advice about women's clothing?"

"Good one, Deltha. No kidding. Anybody got a pen so I can write down another one of your devastatingly clever one-liners?"

Deltha started to take a step toward Lawton, but De la Cruz, smiling, stepped between them like a camp counselor.

"I hate to break up the bonding thing," he said, "but I just wanted you all to know that Dee is going to be working out with us for a few days, researching a role in a movie—"

"Aw, man, funk dat," Deltha Lester said.

"You wish," somebody said, and most of the Knights laughed.

De la Cruz waved his arms, asking for quiet. "Listen, it's only going to be a couple of days. And don't worry, Dee's played some college ball in her time. So she might surprise you."

"Oooh, I got it," Big Hair said now, affecting a high-pitched voice. "We into that you-go-girl shit."

Dee wondered how she should play it, quickly settling on modest. It was Jeremy who had once told her never to use irony in an underdeveloped country. He usually meant France, but Dee was pretty sure it applied to the modern NBA, too.

"I promise not to mess you guys up too much," she said. "If I do, I'm out of here, I promise."

"What movies you been in?" Deltha asked.

"Probably none of your favorites," Jamie Lawton said. "You know, from the hotel."

Deltha said, "The only reason I'm not tellin' you to kiss my black ass, Lawton, is on account of I don't want to put no ideas in your head."

It had always fascinated Dee, as far back as she could remember, how dumb this playground stuff sounded—even if the playground was the Garden itself now—and how important it was to guys not to lose face. When she was younger, she used to think it was all for her benefit, just because there was a girl present. But over time, after she'd witnessed enough of these scenes, she'd figured out it was a lot deeper than that. Guys would talk themselves into a corner and then they'd either have to settle things with a stupid fight, or somebody'd have to come up with a solution where nobody had to back down.

She'd been about fourteen, after a game at the Boys and Girls Club of Astoria, Twenty-first and Thirtieth Drive in Queens, over near the Astoria Houses, when she'd first heard somebody say, "If girls didn't have no pussy, there'd be a bounty on them." And she'd wondered: You mean after the bounty hunters finished with all the boys?

Now Jamie Lawton said, "Okay, okay, I'll shut up now. But before I do, you've got to let me ask one more question, Del: Who told you your hair looks good that way?"

"Guys, guys, guys," Michael De la Cruz said, his voice loud with all the Garden seats empty. "Miss Gerard is going to get the idea that we've got one of those dysfunctional families going here."

"Yeah, we nothin' like that," Big Hair said. "We more unified than the Fellowhood of Christian Ath-o-letes, or whatnot." He extended a hand to Dee. "Anquwan Posey. Number-one draft choice, University of Nevada, Las Vegas."

Dee said, "Nice to meet you, Anquwan."

"You got any dinner plans, baby?" he asked, getting a laugh out of the rest of them.

"Unfortunately, I do," she said. "I plan to devour Coach Carlino's playbook so I don't embarrass myself tomorrow."

"Your loss," the kid said.

She couldn't help it, he did look like a kid to her, even if he was out of college. Dee didn't think of herself as old, knew she didn't look old. But there was a part of her that knew she also wasn't young anymore. Especially not in basketball. Certainly not here.

Anquwan Posey and Deltha walked off together, looking back at Dee a couple of times, giggling. When they got to the tunnel, Dee saw that Deltha couldn't stop himself from making a humping motion with his hips, which made Anquwan roar.

"Well," De la Cruz said, clapping his hands together. "I thought that went pretty well, all things considered."

"Relative to what?" Dee said.

"They're just guys being guys," Eddie Holtz said. They could all hear the laughter now coming from the hallway. "Frankly, they can't help themselves."

"No," Dee said. "You can't."

Bobby Carlino's office was to the left when you came off the court, past pictures of Frank Sinatra and John McEnroe and Simon and Garfunkel and Joe Frazier standing over Muhammad Ali, even Bob Hope with Bing Crosby, big color pictures beautifully mounted on both walls.

There wasn't much to the small office: a desk, a small leather sofa, three or four folding chairs, a small blackboard on the wall, a color television with VCR. There was a plaque on Carlino's desk that had to have come from De la Cruz, saying, "Go or Grow!"

Carlino was seated behind the desk when she came in and made no move to get up, not that she cared. She noticed he was wearing some kind of diamond-studded championship ring, with a ruby setting the size of a coffee mug. It was another thing that had happened in sports without Dee noticing: Guys now were as obsessed with the size of their championship rings as they were with their favorite part.

"Which national championship?" Dee asked, pointing toward his right hand.

"The last one. St. John's. Beat Florida in the final, at the Georgia Dome." He turned around a photograph on his desk, one in an elegant sterling frame, so Dee could see it. In the picture, Bobby Carlino was on the top step of a ladder, cutting down a net. "I don't keep it here because it was the last time I won anything," he said. "I just want to remind myself there was a time in my life when I wasn't this pissed off all the time."

Dee sat down. This close to her, Carlino looked younger than he had outside when he was in his tough-guy pose, talking the way he obviously thought tough guys were supposed to talk in sports. But he looked tired, too, as if he hadn't gotten too much sleep lately. Like maybe for the last three years. There was so much dark coloring around his eyes, it looked like a bad mascara job to Dee.

"You wanted to talk to me alone," he said.

"I did," she said. "Your boss seems to mean well, but he does have this way of dominating all available air space."

"Tell me about it," Carlino said. He tried to smile, but it was clear that he didn't really mean it, so it ended up looking more like some kind of tic. "He can't make the record books, so now he's going for the history books. Like he's sending you into space instead of an NBA game."

Dee was starting to feel tired herself. She'd only been here for four hours, and it was starting to feel like four days.

"Listen, don't take this the wrong way," Carlino said, "but this is the dumbest goddamned nitwit idea I've ever heard in my life."

"Okay, then," Dee said, with a lot more enthusiasm than she was feeling, "we've found some common ground here."

She didn't know if she was consciously trying to keep things light, or if she was worried that at any second he might be calling her a fucking fuck. He was an edgy little dude, clasping and unclasping small hands on the desk, jiggling his knees underneath it.

"It didn't seem to prevent you from coming here."

"Busted!" she said, making herself sound like Michael De la Cruz for him. "Eddie talked me into it."

"Eddie Holtz is a has-been who hasn't gotten over the fact that he didn't grow up to be the greatest New York City guard since Tiny Archibald. Okay? And with all due respect, Miss Dee Gerard, Eddie didn't talk you into shit."

Dee laughed; this time she couldn't help herself, it just jumped out of her. Carlino looked at her. "What's so funny?" he said.

"Sorry," she said, "but I always get a kick out of 'with all due respect.' Nothing good has ever come after 'with all due respect' in the history of the world."

"You really do think you're in a movie, don't you? What's the one where the old guy sells his soul to play for the Yankees? Except you're selling your soul to Michael De la Cruz."

"Actually, I thought you were the one who did that, Coach," Dee said.

Bobby Carlino made a motion in the air like refs do when they're counting your basket after you get fouled. "Score the goal," he said. "There's a difference between us, though. Other than the obvious. I know my limitations."

"How do you know I don't?" Dee said. "You don't know anything about me, other than you think we're going to be in Michael's circus together."

"I know enough to know that he's kidding himself and you're kidding yourself. Do you actually think you're good enough to go from the Barcelona Big Babes, or whatever the hell the last team you played for was called, to the National Freaking Basketball Association?"

"That's what we're here to find out, isn't it? Whether or not I'm good to go?"

There was a small refrigerator Dee hadn't noticed underneath the television set. Carlino pushed his swivel chair over there, got a Diet Coke, made a motion like offering Dee one. She shook her head no. He popped the can and drank about half of it down.

"You know, I'm glad it's just the two of us having this chat. Really, I am. If the boy owner were here, I'd have to lie a little, or maybe even a lot. But now I feel I can be honest."

Dee was going to tell him honesty was like riding a bike, it would come back to him, but he kept right on going.

"You have no shot," he said.

"Thank you."

"My opinion. Okay? You in any kind of game shape?"

"No."

"When *was* the last time you played in one of those girl leagues over there?"

Girl leagues. She let it go. "Two years in the spring. But I play a lot of pickup ball and I help coach the boys' high school team at the Palace School in Monte Carlo. We don't even suit up ten, so I play all the time."

"Well, there you go. The Palace School in Monte Fucking Carlo. For a second there, I was worried you hadn't been tested lately."

"I'm sorry I didn't bring my audition tape."

He rubbed his eyes, hard, with both hands. "Why'd you quit, anyway?"

"I got married. I got tired before I got married."

"Tired of playing?"

"Tired of playing in front of no crowds. Tired of having no real future. And not nearly enough of a past, frankly."

"Somebody here did a computer sweep this morning. They said you were pretty big in Spain."

"Even when I was, I wasn't," Dee said.

"How come you didn't come back and try out for the WNBA when they started the WNBA? If you're as good as the great talent scout Eddie Holtz says you are, you could've been a star."

Dee said, "You know how we can get along a lot better? Lay off Eddie."

He put up both hands, saying, "What about the WNBA? I'm not saying you could've gotten rich, but you could have finally made some real money."

"It was never about the money with me."

"That used to be my line," Carlino said, with what actually sounded to Dee like genuine regret.

Sounding like a human being for the first time.

Dee said, "I thought it was going to be another cheap publicity stunt, coming off the way the U.S. team had played in the Olympics, built around the prettier ones. And my boyfriend, who became my husband, he's British, even though he'd been pretty much living in France for years, running his restaurants. I convinced myself my real future was out of basketball and over there."

She stopped because she could hear the smart Dee, the one inside her head always telling her to watch her mouth, asking her a question: Why are you telling this little jerk this much?

Because you think he cares?

"How'd you end up over there in the first place?" Carlino asked.

"Long story. My mother died, my father's job took him over there, he liked it, we stayed. That's the bumper-sticker version." And, she thought, technically true. Though the long version was as long as a Russian novel.

Carlino didn't press her; she could see on his face that he was moving on to his next question. She could already tell there were two things Bobby Carlino couldn't do: listen very well and care about what anybody else was saying when he did.

"So now you're running your little bistro or bar or whatever it is, according to Eddie, and you play with Earthwind and the other European brothers. And now you're going to do something Cheryl Miller never got to do, or Nancy Lieberman or Annie Meyers, even though Lieberman and Meyers both made it as far as NBA training camps once?"

"I'm only going to do it if I'm good enough."

"You're not."

"You know that already, without even seeing me play."

"I know you might be something playing against girls. I believe Eddie when he talks about how you can handle, the decisions you make, how fast you are. But I know something else: You're not fast enough, you're not strong enough, and you couldn't get your shot against me."

"Because I'm a woman."

"That's right! Because you're a goddamn woman! What, that's politically incorrect? The Giants are supposed to give you a tryout if you suddenly decide you want to play strong safety next season? After that, how about we sue because you get it in your head you want to play center field for the Yankees? Believe me, I've got nothing against women, if you don't count my second wife. But there's a *reason* why those teenaged tennis girls don't play the men. And there's a reason why Marion Jones, as fast as she is, doesn't run against the guy sprinters. And it's not because we don't believe in that affirmative-action crapola and the Equal Rights Amendment and Gloria Steinem and Billie Jean King. *It's because as good as they are, they're not good enough.* This is sports. There isn't any affirmative action once the game starts. Best guys play. Best team wins."

Dee said, "That's a very nice speech. I'm sure the National Organization of Women would be awfully proud of you. I know I sure am. But what if I am good enough, Coach? Would you play me?"

"I would. But you're not. So I don't have to."

Dee stood up. "All I'm asking for the next few days is for you not to go out of your way to sabotage me. Give me a fair shot with the other players. Will you at least make that deal?" She put out her hand. Reluctantly, he took it.

"Whatever," Bobby Carlino said.

"For the time being, we're stuck with each other," Dee said. He was still sitting and made no move to get up, even with Dee standing over him. "Maybe it's only a couple of days and then I'm back in Monte Carlo, out of your hair and out of your life. Why don't we just go ahead and make the best of it?"

"You're better off going back now."

"Practice at eleven?"

He slumped back in the chair. "Stretching at ten-thirty."

Dee got to the door, turned around. The smart Dee, the sensible one, was telling her to shut up, cut her losses, get out of there. But if she listened to that Dee, Miss Brainy, she knew she wouldn't have ended up here in the first place.

"You know," she said, "it's nice to see that some things haven't changed while I've been away."

"Such as?"

"Such as basketball coaches."

Eddie walked her out to the limousine that was waiting outside the Employees' Entrance and asked if she wanted to grab a bite later. Dee said no, but he could do her a big favor.

"What do you need?"

"Game film."

"Your first night in New York, you want to stay in your room and look at game film? Of the New York Knights?"

Michael De la Cruz was inside with Bobby Carlino, having followed Dee into his office. After that, De la Cruz had told her, he had a meeting with Marcus Betts, the NBA commissioner. But for now he wanted his go-to girl to go over to her suite at the Sherry-Netherland, where he said his own apartment was. He started to give her directions—across from the Plaza, next door to the Pierre, big clock out front— but Dee told him she knew where it was, she actually used to come downtown sometimes and mingle with the decent people.

"Just tapes of the last couple of games," Dee said.

"Can I ask why? You're practicing with these guys tomorrow."

"Information is power."

"Gee," he said, "I never heard that one."

"I'll be fine on my own," she said.

Thinking to herself: When haven't you been?

Eddie said, "Bobby give you a hard time?"

"I know you'll think this is less than ladylike, but he's one of those guys who like to bust balls, whether you have any or not."

"He can't help himself."

"He says I have no shot."

"He's wrong."

"He's wrong, I'm scared," she said. "Jump ball."

Eddie opened the back door for her. "You made it this far. There's nothing to be afraid of."

Oh, she wanted to tell him, there's everything to be afraid of.

Instead she leaned up, kissed him quickly on both cheeks. European style in the big city. "Call me later at the hotel. I'm sure you'll want to hear my observations on our team."

"Not necessarily," Eddie Holtz said.

Eddie was in the lobby of Five Penn, waiting for an elevator, when Michael De la Cruz caught up with him.

"What did you really think?" De la Cruz said.

Only one elevator seemed to be working; the other one hadn't moved from the sixth floor since Eddie'd been there.

"Bobby Carlino's a bad fucking guy," Eddie said, then started bobbing his head immediately, like some kind of doll, saying to the boss, "I know, I know. You're going to get him turned around, it's what you do."

"Bobby's not a big-picture guy," De la Cruz said. "You either are or you're not. I always have been. And if you stay with me long enough and eventually learn to watch that smart mouth of yours, you will be, too."

The only advice Eddie's old man had ever given him usually was delivered by the back of his hand. "That's for nothing," he'd say when he'd come home from the saloon with another load on, "now do something." Jack Holtz had finally gone out for a pack of cigarettes when Eddie was fifteen and hadn't come back until Eddie's senior year in college, by which time he was Big East Player of the Year. Then he'd wanted to be a dad.

But the old man had said something once that stayed with him, something he thought about a lot when he was around Michael De la Cruz for more than about five minutes.

"You're only in trouble, kid," the old man said, "when you start to believe your own bullshit."

"It occurs to me," Eddie said, "that you're trusting me an awful lot on this."

"I am!" De la Cruz said. "You want to know why? I'll tell

you why. Because you're genuinely excited about this babe. How long're you in this job now? Couple of years? This is the first time I've seen you excited about anything."

"You'll see for yourself tomorrow," Eddie said, "if our guys don't try to mess her up too much, actually give her a chance."

"It's gonna be great!" Michael De la Cruz said.

The elevator doors finally opened, and what seemed to be like half the building got out. Melissa, De la Cruz's secretary, was in the middle of the pack, probably going outside to have a cigarette. She was a tall, pretty blonde, green eyes, and had made it known to Eddie that she was there for him. She smiled, and he smiled back. Eddie used to think she was the best-looking woman in the building. Only now Dee Gerard was the best-looking woman in the building.

The elevator doors closed. It was just the two of them. De la Cruz kept shifting his weight from one foot to the other, snapping his fingers as he did. Eddie wanted to think he was more excited than usual, but it was hard to tell with him, the guy was always a bundle of nerves.

"You're not going to be disappointed," Eddie said quietly, staring straight ahead, watching the numbers change. "What I told you the first night holds. She can really play."

The owner of the Knights, his boss, turned and flashed his opening-night smile. Like Eddie was just another camera, on the other side of one of those opening-night rope lines Michael De la Cruz liked so much.

"Whatever," De la Cruz said. "I forgot already how you said it in French."

Eddie said, "What's that supposed to mean?"

"It means I trust you, Edward. I'm sure our Miss Gerard is a very nice player."

"You still don't get it. She's better than that."

Now De la Cruz was staring at Eddie, a confused look on his face, as if he'd realized the guy standing next to him in the elevator was actually a total stranger.

"Who gives a shit if she's better than that?" Michael De la Cruz said.

⑪ six

Dee told the driver to go up Sixth and then take a right on Central Park South, just so she could get a quick glimpse of the park. Seeing the park had always made her feel better, about everything. A lot had changed in New York since she'd left with Cool Daddy. The park had changed about as much as the ocean off Rockaway Beach, the only ocean she'd known as a kid.

Central Park South had been part of her long dream run when she'd started to play high school ball, as a freshman at Clinton. She'd read something about how John Havlicek, another old Celtic, used to run everywhere when he was a kid. So she'd come into the park up past the Metropolitan Museum of Art, run halfway around the reservoir, then come out on the West Side, over by Tavern on the Green. After that she'd head down Central Park West to Fifty-ninth, go east from there. Then uptown on Fifth, on the park side, past the Sherry, past the Pierre, finally knowing she had only a couple of miles back to the projects when she passed the Met again.

Someday, she told herself, passing the apartment buildings, the expensive ones, facing the park. Someday I'll live like this. . . .

She'd always unpacked first thing on the road, every hotel she'd ever stayed at when she was playing, checking to make sure the drawers were clean, calling right away for extra hangers if she needed them, always looking for some order, even for a day and a night, in her gypsy life.

Dee did that now, in the nineteenth-floor suite that even had a piano in the living room. Michael De la Cruz offhandedly mentioned he'd booked it for two months, which Dee knew was the rest of the NBA regular season, all the way to the middle of April. The big positive thinker in action. When they'd passed each other outside Carlino's office, he'd mentioned that she should think about getting herself an agent or at least a lawyer, he could recommend a couple of guys if she wanted.

"How come you haven't asked about money?" he said.

She told him what she'd told Bobby Carlino. "This isn't about money with me."

He laughed too heartily and said, "That's what all the boy players say, too."

It didn't take her too long to put her clothes away; she'd only brought about a week's worth. Then she drew herself a hot bath in the deep marble tub, a bubble bath, pouring in two complimentary bottles of the Caswell-Massey bath gel, her favorite. Then she hunted around on the FM dial for a good jazz station, and when she found one, around 88 on the dial, getting what sounded like Miles Davis, she slowly lowered herself into the water.

For some reason, the whole scene made her think of Jeremy. He had always called her his New York princess, kidding her constantly about some of her little quirks, how she always insisted on bringing along her own soft down pillow from home, no matter how expensive the hotel or the resort, just to be on the safe side. He knew why, of course, she'd explained it to him a hundred times, how hard pillows, stuffed with foam rubber, made her remember things she didn't want to remember about growing up, back when nobody thought of her as a princess or treated her like one, not even Cool Daddy.

"Am I the only one who knows?" he'd asked her once, in a suite twice the size of this one, at the Ritz in Paris, on what he called their fourth honeymoon.

"Knows what?"

They were in the king-sized bed in the middle of the afternoon, underneath a chandelier that Dee had nearly gunned down when she accidentally clipped it with the flying cork from the champagne bottle.

Jeremy ran his hand along one of her thighs, lingering on the scar above her knee, from the time Dee cut herself climbing over the high fence on the outdoor courts at the Franklin Plaza apartments, when she'd lost the gate key all the tenants got. "Am I the only one who knows you're not nearly as tough as you let on?"

She didn't feel so tough now. The long legs that Jeremy loved so much—her mother's legs—were stretched out on each side of the tub. She let her hair fall back into the water now, knowing she'd have to shampoo it when she got out, go through the whole process of getting it exactly the way she wanted, even alone here in the hotel, just planning to order in some room service and watch the Knights tape that was already on its way over.

Her hair had always been a problem. If not a problem, then at least an issue, from the time she was old enough to care how she looked. It was just the luck of the draw with a white mother and a black father. She'd gotten her mom's dancer's legs, her father's hair. It was all right when she wanted the curls. Or just got rid of the curls entirely when she wore her hair short. But when she grew it all the way out, wore it as long as she was wearing it now, that meant straightening. Straightening it always took time.

"I look like a guy," she'd told Jeremy the first time she cut it real short.

"No, dear girl, you do not. Do not, could not, will never. You just play like one."

In the last fifteen years, she'd tried everything: the kind of full Afro Anquwan Posey was wearing now, the kind that seemed to be coming back into fashion, even though he was probably growing his hair out for cornrows; modified Afro;

slicked back; high fade; flat twists; braided wrap; micro-
braids, her first summer in London with Jeremy; individual
braids; straw-set curls; kinky twist in Japan; even coils, her
last year in Spain. She'd tried her own cornrows until having
them done felt like having a second job. She'd gone a whole
season with a sort of retro Supremes look, trying that perky
bangs-and-flip thing Diana Ross went with in the sixties. One
time, in Rome, just for the fun of it, for laughs, she'd brought
along an old Supremes album cover just to show the prissy
English queen who ran the shop exactly what she wanted.

"Good Lord, why?" he said.

She said, "Because you can't make it look like my mom's
hair."

He said, "How does she wear it?"

Dee said, "Wore. She wore it long, straight, and natural
blond."

She ran more hot water into the bath. First it was Jeremy
inside her head, keeping her company, his voice. Now her
mother's. Dee knew why. She knew she hadn't run down into
this neighborhood just because she was training for basketball. There was more to it than that. It was why there would
occasionally be a detour in those days, Dee taking a right
when she got to Fifth so she could go stand in front of
Bergdorf Goodman for a few minutes, not wanting to go inside in her raggedy sweats and old leather running shoes,
happy enough to stand at the window displaying the women's
fashions of the season and remember things, the way she was
remembering things now.

Remember how her mother, between shows or working
regularly in some hit like *Chicago* or *Cabaret,* would dress
her up and they'd take the subway downtown, and they'd get
off at Fifty-ninth and Lex and walk from there. Dee was
seven; it was a year before the accident. They'd stand in front
of the same window at Bergdorf and her mother would tell her
that someday when Dee was older, when she'd met the man
who was going to make all her dreams come true, they'd
come down here and shop for the perfect outfit, so Dee would
be dressed for the part, so she could knock him right off his
feet. . . .

They never made the trip.

And now, Dee thought, putting her legs back in the water, moving the last of the bubbles around, the man of her dreams turned out to be Michael De la Cruz, though not for the reasons Marthe Wilander Cody had imagined when she held her daughter's hand in front of those windows.

She wondered what her mother would think if she knew Dee's perfect outfit had turned out to be the purple and black of the New York Knights.

She lay there until the water finally started to cool, or maybe until she started to remember too much, got out, took a fast shower so she could shampoo her hair, deciding she wanted to look nice even if it was just for herself. She dried it with the smallish dryer they gave you, went through the whole process with the expensive relaxer she'd brought with her, put on the white terry-cloth robe hanging behind the bathroom door, wondering, as she did occasionally, how much money she'd spent in her life on hair products, depending on the style she was wearing at the time, relaxer and manipulator and holding wax and molding gel and braid spray and her favorite, liquid jam—she couldn't decide whether it sounded more like a tricky move above the basket or a rock group.

"Oooh," she said, looking at herself in the full-length mirror, dropping the robe open, really checking herself out now, thinking she was holding up pretty well for an old broad, tummy and breasts and butt.

Then she was mimicking Anquwan Posey, saying, "Time for you to get into some of that you-go-girl shit."

At the Garden, Eddie'd told her Anquwan had spent only his freshman year in Vegas, majoring in what Eddie described as "guys most likely to be carrying a concealed weapon to home games."

"You still drafted him number one," Dee said.

"Michael refers to him as his work in progress. I told Michael that's what a lot of parole officers say about first offenders."

"What was his first offense?"

"He stole the Vegas coach's Mercedes."

"Wait a second, I remember UNLV," Dee said. "I thought all the players had their own Mercedes out there."

"Anquwan was looking to trade up without going through a dealer or any of what he called that red-tape bullshit."

He'd also gotten into some trouble with the NCAA when it came out that some Vegas boosters had sent two hookers to his off-campus apartment before a game against Long Beach State. Once caught, Anquwan held a press conference, where he said, "Just because I had sex with them two chippies do *not* mean I know who sent 'em."

The kid could play, though, Dee could see it in the Knights–76ers tape that Michael De la Cruz's assistant, Melissa, had messengered over. Posey could shoot and he could put the ball on the floor and beat his man off the dribble, even though he never seemed to be running the same play the rest of the Knights were running, which probably explained why Carlino spent most of the game prancing up and down the sidelines in his funny stiff-legged walk, from the end of his bench all the way to the middle of the scorer's table, acting like some sort of well-dressed chimp on crack.

Zippy the coach, Dee thought.

The Knights actually looked to be running about five different offenses for the five guys out there, as if they'd all tuned out Carlino a long time ago. Deltha was supposed to be the point guard, but apparently thought his job description involved putting up a twenty-foot jumper the first time he got a decent look at the basket. When Anquwan Posey didn't have the ball in his hands, he liked to run to an open spot and then frantically begin waving his arms, as if there were a crime in progress—the crime being he didn't have the ball.

The guy directing the game couldn't wait to show an isolation shot of Anquwan sulking when somebody else would shoot. And the color guy would jump on it every time. Dee didn't recognize the color guy's name—Jimmy Wills—but she loved his attitude.

"Look there," Wills said at one point, "Anquwan looks sadder than he did in college when somebody told him they were going to keep score in class, too."

Carl Anthony was a little short to play center against the

seven-footer the 76ers had, but he still had the same back-to-
the-basket moves Dee remembered from when he played in
Spain, though they sometimes seemed to take about as long as
his stylist must have needed to put the bumper-sticker slogans
in his hair.

Jamie Lawton played as if he'd given up sweating.

The Knights were losing 36–15 when Dee hit the Stop button on the VCR.

She thought about getting dressed and taking a cab uptown, walking around the old neighborhood a little bit, just to
see if things had gotten any better up there in fifteen years, but
it was already too cold for her by the time the sun had gone
down. She'd forgotten how much she hated New York win-
ters. Besides, Cool Daddy used to say, it was always colder
uptown, even though the fat weathermen on TV never told
anybody about that.

And what did she want to see, anyway? The landmarks
were mostly sad-making places, no matter how colorful she
tried to make them later on for people like Jeremy, as if she'd
grown up in some kind of black sitcom world. The truth was,
there was nothing she wanted to see up there.

Nothing and no one.

It was seven-thirty by now. Across the world—back over
in her world—Gilles would be closing up the place by now.
Was it a five-hour time difference, or six? She couldn't keep
it straight no matter how hard she tried. Dee stood at the huge
window in the living room, the one facing straight west on
Fifty-ninth, the traffic coming in both directions, the hansom
cabs not helping the situation very much. Even from up here,
on the nineteenth floor, she could see the little tourist people
hunched together in the backs of the carriages, freezing to
death but thinking this ride was something they were required
to do, and oh-so-glam.

Like you're not a tourist now.

What was she doing here?

Less than three days before, before the game at Stade
Louis II, before Eddie'd started working on her in his laid-
back way—*C'mon, we'll make history*—she'd considered
herself a fairly happy person. Or as happy as she'd been since

the divorce, anyway. Not dating anybody or thinking about
dating anybody, though it wasn't as if the opportunities
weren't there. She didn't think there was some rule that had
been passed that if you weren't in a good relationship at her
age then your life had turned into some kind of a horrid
wretched failure. If she did get a little restless from time to
time, missing basketball or Jeremy or both, so what? Maybe
this was the start of Act Three in what passed for the adult life
of Dee Cody Gerard.

She'd played basketball.

She'd married Jeremy.

Now her little bistro, as Bobby Carlino had called it.

So why the hell was she here?

She knew why.

She called the woman at the front desk and told her what
she wanted to do. The woman said, "Mr. De la Cruz said that
whatever you wanted is all right."

Dee went over and looked in the mirror, sadly touching
hair she'd gotten just right for the night. Now she grabbed a
handful of it and tied it up into a ponytail, changed into sweat-
pants and the Knights T-shirt Eddie had tossed into the backseat of the limo with her, laced up the high-topped,
old-school, white Adidas sneakers with the three black stripes
she'd bought after Earthwind had called her about the charity
game, the shoes still looking so new and white it was as if
she'd just taken them out of the box. Dee had always loved
the feel of new shoes, the look, maybe because when she was
growing up she used to go a whole year wearing the same
pair, sometimes longer, cleaning them all the time so they'd
look new, even buying that dab-on white stuff at Walgreens
that made her feel as if she kept putting a new coat of paint on
them.

She went into the bedroom for the official NBA ball Eddie
had tossed into the backseat with the T-shirt, went down the
hall, took the elevator down to the ballroom level.

The woman at the front desk, practically pleading with her,
said that if there was anything else she needed, *anything,*
please let her know, that Mr. De la Cruz couldn't have been

more emphatic, all she had to do was pick up the phone, she didn't even have to come downstairs.

"Just the use of the room," Dee said.

Just the feel of the ball in her hands made her feel better about everything.

Her freshman year of high school she'd done a paper for school on Bill Bradley, already a senator from New Jersey by then. Dee had read all the stuff she could find on him that didn't make her head hurt, not really interested in giving herself a civics lesson, more interested in how a slow white guy, a banker's son from Missouri no one had ever seen dunk a ball in his life even though he was six-five, had become the greatest college basketball player in the country. Not only that, he'd gone on from there to play for a pro team—the Knicks of the late sixties, early seventies—that Cool Daddy said was the equivalent of the Basie band.

"See, little girl," Cool Daddy said, "that there's the beauty of the damn game. You're good enough, doesn't matter what kind of body you got, where you come from. Willis Reed, he come out Louisiana. DeBusschere? Catholic boy out Dee-troit City. Clyde's from Atlanta. Earl the Pearl? He street. But here's the key thing, little girl: They all had the beat."

One of the things Dee had found when she was reading up on Bradley was this drill he used to do as a kid. He'd take a pair of glasses and he'd tape the bottom half of the lens, practically turning them into basketball blinders to prevent him from looking down at the ball when he was dribbling. Then, when he had the gym to himself, he'd set up all these folding chairs like some kind of obstacle course and dribble through them the way he'd dribble through the other team in a game. Bradley'd do this *after* he'd shot all his jump shots and *after* he'd taken however many free throws he'd take every day. There he'd be alone on the court the way Dee always loved to be alone on the court, not just dribbling through nine chairs, as if they were the nine other players in the game, but twenty of them, even thirty, taking what had been the weakest part of his game and turning it into a strength.

In the second-floor ballroom of the Sherry, Dee found the
folding chairs where the concierge said they'd be in a big storage closet, then positioned them all over the room, which
wasn't anything elaborate, maybe half the size of a normal
basketball court. One of the guys in maintenance had brought
her some black electrical tape. When he was gone, Dee took
off the cool amber-colored sunglasses she'd bought at Palace
Optique the day before she flew to New York with Eddie, cut
off two small strips of the tape, covered the bottom of the
lenses the way Bradley used to, put them on.

She looked at her obstacle course now, and smiled.

Not all her childhood memories were sad-making ones.

The ballroom was the Garden now. Cool Daddy said you
could make any court, even the worst one on the playground,
chain-link net or no net or anything, into the Garden if you
imagined hard enough; he was always great at imagining
things were better than they were. Now you get the beat, little girl, she told herself. Pretending, as she always did, that
the beat she was looking for started with the bounce of the
ball, coming right up from the floor into her hand.

Feel the beat.

She started slowly at first, right-hand dribble then left-
hand dribble, head up, pretending this chair was Deltha, that
one was Jamie Lawton. Anquwan over there. Carl Anthony,
glowering at her, trying to look fierce as a bear, he was the
two chairs she'd set side by side near the back door, as if they
were protecting the basket the way Carl did. Sometimes, dribbling in the traffic she'd created for herself, she'd whip a
hard, blind pass, knocking one of the chairs over.

Feel the beat.

She could hear Ruth singing inside her head, singing one
of those blues songs of hers, repeating the lyrics over and
over, the repetition becoming a thing of beauty as she picked
up steam.

Dee went faster through the chairs.

Now she was feeling good enough to take off the glasses.
She set them on one of the chairs, took off the blue paisley
bandanna she'd been wearing around her neck. She took one

more look at her court, seeing where every chair was, taking a picture inside her head.

Then she covered her eyes with the bandanna, knotting it in back.

The last look at the chairs was the look she'd take at the other players on the court before she'd start one way and then, her back to the action, fire a pass to a cutter no one could believe she'd seen. A real no-look job that would make a thousand people, maybe two thousand if she was lucky, go wild in some little gym in Lyons, or Albertville, or Marseilles.

Or in the north of Spain when she was La Franchisa.

Cool Daddy said Larry Bird, he could take that kind of picture of the court.

And, of course, The Cooz.

Dee dribbled through the chairs as if she were doing it in the dark, dancing in the dark, racing through them now, top speed, going through her legs sometimes, behind her back, mostly keeping the ball low on the dribble, so low sometimes she was sure no one would be able to see any daylight between ball and floor. She'd brush a chair sometimes, feel it against a hip or a knee, but never knocked one over—if one went over that was a turnover. When she was a kid, she'd make a game out of it: Every time she could make it all the way down the court was a point for her, every time she hit a chair too hard, that was points for the other team, until she could go up and down the court two times, three times, four times, without touching anything.

She felt that way now, as if nothing could touch her, not tired now, not scared, as if she could go all night.

She was in complete control, seeing everything, even with her eyes closed.

Now she was happy.

Dee was flying.

⑪ seven

The Knights still had the Garden to themselves, because the Knicks were on a six-game trip to the West Coast and wouldn't be back until the end of next week. Bobby Carlino had the players on the court by eleven sharp, after he'd briefly taken them through some game film of the Washington Wizards, their next opponent, finishing with what must have been his version of a rousing pep talk.

"This is a big chance for us," Carlino said. "These guys suck almost as bad as we do." Then he used the huge grease-board in the locker room to draw up some plays he said might work if anybody on his team decided to run them.

When Carlino finished, Anquwan Posey raised a hand. "You don't mind my sayin', Coach, I think maybe the way to attack them and whatnot is on the perimeter."

"Do you?" Carlino said.

His smile, Dee thought, looked as phony as a flight attendant's.

"How about this, Pose?" Bobby Carlino said. "How about you play and I coach?" For some reason, he turned to Dee then. She was sitting in the corner, minding her own business, trying to stay out of harm's way, actually paying attention to what Carlino had been doing with the X's and O's all coaches found so fascinating.

"Do you believe this shit?" Bobby Carlino said to her.

Dee sat on the scorer's table when they went outside, watched the Knights' starting five walk through the new plays. She could see that they were bored five minutes into it, as if they'd gotten tired of listening to Carlino before they even left the locker room. He'd been in a bad mood when he showed up, bitching about traffic on Seventh Avenue. Their lack of attention only made things worse. Dee could see that he was like a grenade whose pin had been pulled. He finally did explode, telling them that if they couldn't learn a simple pick away from the ball they might as well scrimmage.

He pointed up to the Garden's spoked ceilings, where they had the retired uniforms of the great Knicks from the past, Frazier and Monroe and Reed and DeBusschere and Bradley. Dee had a feeling he'd done it before.

"Watch and learn, you old Knicks," Carlino said. "The New York Knights are in the house."

Dee noticed Michael De la Cruz and Eddie Holtz sitting in the fourth row of the purple seats closest to the court. Eddie gave her a little one-finger salute, like he was a cowboy touching the brim of an imaginary hat.

Michael De la Cruz, in a white T-shirt today, gave her an emphatic two-thumbs-up, mouthing, *Good luck.*

After about thirty minutes of cursing and pouting and almost constant whistle-blowing from Carlino, he motioned to Dee and said, "Go in for Deltha at point with the first unit."

Dee said, "Anything in particular you'd like me to work on?"

"Method acting," he said. "Pretend you're a real point guard, just in drag."

"Don't the Cavaliers got theirselves one of them?" the guy getting ready to guard her said.

Dee knew from watching her tape of the Knights–76ers

game film that his name was Ray Ray Abdul-Mahi and that he was another rookie, out of Seton Hall.

"Push it every chance you get," Carlino said, hitting her hard in the stomach with the ball. "Full-court pressure on Ray Ray when it brings it up." He turned to the rest of them and said, "Anybody goes easy on her and we go an extra hour today."

Bobby Carlino stuck his whistle in his mouth and said to Dee, "You want to play with the big boys?"

He blew the whistle and said, "So play."

She came over half-court the first time, and as soon as she did, that little shit Ray Ray reached across her body, fouling her hard as he did, going straight for her tits first thing. Dee went down; Ray Ray ended up with the ball, and a dunk at the other end. He came back blowing kisses to his teammates.

Dee was looking straight at Carlino as she brought the ball back up.

"This is hardball, honey," Carlino said, in a voice louder than he needed. "Wear a helmet."

Next to Eddie, Michael De la Cruz said, "They're testing her right off the bat. That's a good thing, right?"

"He told them," Eddie said quietly.

"Told them what?"

"He told them this is for real, that it's no movie," Eddie said, his eyes not leaving Dee.

"I specifically instructed him—"

"Yeah, that always works. Look at the guys on the second team. I'm tellin' you, this is some serious shit out there."

"Could she get hurt?"

"Only if wishing makes it true for your asshole coach."

They had changed the rules the last couple of years in the NBA, trying to open the game back up to what it was in the old days, when teams used to score in the 100s all the time. By the time Eddie retired, the average score was 72–70. This year the league's Rules Committee had finally legalized zone defenses, so you couldn't put four guys on one side of the court and then have your best player isolated on the other side, going one-on-one against the guy covering him. Or having teams run one dull variation of the pick-and-roll after another, while three guys watched. What they'd really tried to do, Eddie had explained to Dee on the plane ride over, was make the NBA game more like the European game, which meant more movement, better passing, less hand-to-hand combat. They'd even made the courts in the NBA bigger, wider and longer, finally admitting that the size of the players was starting to make the sport look as if it were being played in a crowded elevator car.

Most important, they'd eliminated hand-checking of any kind. If you put your hand on the player you were guarding, the ref was supposed to blow the whistle.

Just not today.

Not when it was Dee with the ball and Bobby Carlino with the whistle.

Today was New York playground ball all the way.

No blood, no foul.

"This isn't Madison Square Garden," Eddie said to De la Cruz. "It's O'Connell Park in the summer."

"What's that?"

"One of the places where Dee learned not to take any crap from anybody."

She tried a bounce pass, in traffic, to Anquwan Posey. He was cutting to the basket, then stopped suddenly. On purpose, Eddie was sure. Jamie Lawton intercepted and started a fast break for the second team. As Anquwan ran by Deltha, who'd taken Dee's spot at the scorer's table, he slapped him a quick low-five.

"This is nice," Eddie said. "Nine against one."

It went like that for a while. Carlino allowed Ray Ray to have his hands all over Dee, foul her anytime he wanted. Dee got a step on him one time, beat him off the dribble into the lane. Anquwan's man came over to help out on her, leaving him wide open under the basket for what would have been an easy layup or dunk. Except he ran away from the play, back to the corner, and Dee threw a pass to no one, out of bounds.

Carlino just laughed. "I think that's where the photographer for the *Times* usually sets up. Sonofabitch would have been wide open for a J."

Eddie just kept watching Dee, wondering how she was going to react. She never changed her expression. Ray Ray would knock her down, she'd get up. Every time she'd try to get out with the ball on the fast break, beat the other team down the court, the guys on her team, the ones who should have been busting it to get out on the wings, purposely hung back.

One time she looked around, saw she had no help, pulled up, and took a jump shot, which missed.

Carlino blew the whistle then. "Wait for your rebounders, goddammit! If the break's not there, set up the goddamn offense."

In the stands, De la Cruz said to Eddie, "Frankly, Edward, she's not showing me one heck of a darn lot."

"Wait!" Eddie said, and it came out sharper than he intended for the boss.

Or maybe not.

"Waiting," Michael De la Cruz said, sounding like a child. *"Waiting."*

That's when it happened.

Dee's team was inbounding the ball right in front of them, on the side. Anquwan had the ball. Dee was at the top of the key, Ray Ray guarding her. Eddie knew the play. She was supposed to fake toward the basket, flash back out toward half-court, and get the ball. Their big Chinese kid, Dong Li, then set a back pick for Anquwan, who broke for the basket. If it worked right, Dee threw him a lob pass for a dunk.

Carlino blew the whistle, said, "Go." Anquwan slapped the ball hard, which was the trigger to start the play. Even though Ray Ray knew what was coming, Dee made such a good fake on him that he stumbled.

The only way to stop her from getting the pass was to grab her. Which he did. Hard, in the area of her right breast.

Anquwan threw the ball where he thought Dee was going, and it bounced all the way across the court to a laughing Deltha Lester.

Dee looked at him, then at Anquwan, finally at Ray Ray Abdul-Mahi.

Then she hit Ray Ray Abdul-Mahi with a straight left hand to the nose, generating more pop than Eddie Holtz thought she could with that short a punch, and dropped him.

"She's ambidextrous," Eddie said now to Michael De la Cruz. "Did I mention that?"

Dee stood her ground, looking down at him, as Ray Ray, shocked, got to a sitting position and stared at the blood all over his hands, the blood that was still gushing out of his nose. The sight of it managed to turn his already high-pitched voice into an air-raid siren.

"Bitch broke my fuckin' nose!" Ray Ray shrieked.

For the first time since she had gotten into the game, Dee said something.

"You sound like a girl," she said to Ray Ray Abdul-Mahi.

With that, Ray Ray jumped to his feet and started for her. Except that a huge hand appeared out of nowhere, grabbing a fistful of Ray Ray's own wild hair—it reminded Dee of Buckwheat's—and stopped him cold, snapping the little jerk back so violently, Dee was afraid Ray Ray's neck had snapped like a twig.

Ray Ray twisted around, trying to square himself enough to throw an awkward punch as he did, until he saw that it was Carl Anthony who had him by the hair.

The message on the side of Carl's head today was simple, Dee thought, and to the point:

"Hell."

Bobby Carlino stood off to the side, waiting to see how this was going to play out. Now he said, "Let him go, Carl."

Anthony looked at his coach and said, "Shut up, little man."

To his teammates, Carl said, "We play now. Anybody punks her, punks me. That clear?"

Dee saw reluctant nods from the rest of the New York Knights.

Carl Anthony, she noted, still had a fistful of Ray Ray's hair.

"As for you," Carl said to Ray Ray, "you get out of here and get your chicken-assed self cleaned up."

Now he let him go.

"She's right, by the way," Carl Anthony said. "Whoo whoo whoo. You do sound like a little girl."

They all watched Ray Ray, both hands covering his nose, walk toward the locker room. Anthony stared him into the hallway, then walked slowly over toward where Bobby Carlino stood, the coach not looking nearly as tough as he had a couple of minutes before. Dee was afraid he was about to grab him by the throat, the way Latrell Sprewell had a few years earlier with his own screamer coach. Carlino, obviously thinking the same thing, said, "Let's not go somewhere we don't want to go, Carl." But Carl Anthony was only reaching for the whistle, which he proceeded to stuff into Bobby Carlino's mouth like a crab puff.

"Use this once in a while," he said. "Or I will make you eat it."

Carl motioned to Deltha Lester for the ball he was holding. Deltha snapped him a pass. Carl Anthony came over to where Dee had been watching the show, handed her the ball. He still looked as bored as he had when he'd grabbed Ray Ray.

"Thought you looked familiar yesterday," he said, loud enough for only her to hear.

Dee just looked at him.

"How about you give these assholes some of that Franchisa shit," he said. "That be all right?"

"Why, Mr. Anthony," she said, "it would be my pleasure."

They started by running the exact same out-of-bounds play they'd been trying to run before Ray Ray got grabby. This time Dee went over to Dong Li and said, "Follow him to the basket."

"Coach say . . ."

"I say," she said.

He came running out and set his pick. Anquwan made his

cut. But the defense, knowing what was coming, did what guys always did in practice, which means they all cheated. Jamie Lawton didn't even chase Dong Li, he hung back and picked up Anquwan, who still waved for the ball. Dee, holding her dribble, shook her head, motioned for him to go through to the opposite corner. If he was open over there, Dee was supposed to pass it to him for a jump shot.

She showed everybody the ball, over her head, as though she were going to throw him a long, two-handed pass, just the way Bobby C. had drawn things up.

They all followed the ball.

Just because everybody always did.

Only, Dee didn't throw Anquwan the ball. She brought the ball down in front of her, as if closing a shade, then in the same motion tossed an underhanded lob pass toward the basket, the ball up so high at the top of its arc it must have looked to everybody on the court as if it were on its way over the backboard.

Everybody except the Chinese kid.

He was quicker to the basket than she thought, surprisingly quick for someone his size, going up in perfect stride, reading the pass perfectly, as if they'd worked on this play a hundred times, catching the ball with his hands way above the rim and dunking it home.

"What the hell was *that*?" Bobby Carlino yelled from half-court.

Dee turned. "You really want to know?"

"Enlighten us."

"It's a variation of a double back-door," she said. "My old man said some old coach named Doggie Julian used to run it at Dartmouth back in the fifties. Then he said Dave Gavitt— he used to coach Providence?—"

"Thank you for that. Dave Gavitt. Providence. I wouldn't have known that one."

"Anyway," Dee continued, "I heard him say at a summer camp one time that he used to run it with Ernie DiGregorio and Marvin Barnes, and it always works like a charm because nobody really expects a second cutter that soon after the first."

Carlino said, "We don't even run our own plays. You're putting in new ones?"

Dee said, "I just thought . . ."

Carlino gave a quick, sidelong look at Carl Anthony, huge forearms crossed in front of him. "Don't think," Carlino said. "Just play."

They played. Dee still seemed to be a step behind the action, sometimes more than that. During one stop in play, while she was desperately trying to catch her breath, she thought: If I can't keep up with the worst team in the league, how do I keep up with the best? She tried not to show anybody how furious she was that she couldn't keep up, how out-of-shape she felt. How completely overmatched. All her life, every level she'd ever played, she'd made everybody else chase her. Now she was the one chasing. Deltha Lester beat her so badly one time on a crossover dribble, she actually laughed when she ended up sitting on her butt at the top of the key. He helped her up, saying, "That's what *I'm* talkin' about." Another time she beat him and thought she was in the clear for a layup, the way she would have been playing against what Carlino called the Barcelona Big Babes. It turned out that Dream Jackson, the Knights' first forward off the bench, one with skin as light as hers, freckles, and a goatee dyed a color that Dee wanted to call cornflower blue, had a completely different thought. He came from behind to block her shot so hard it ended up in the row of seats in front of Michael De la Cruz and Eddie Holtz.

Dream Jackson leaned down after he did it, smiling so she could see all the gold in his mouth, and said, "You know what they say, baby."

"What do they say?" Dee said.

"Get that weak shit outta here."

It was clear to her by now that Bobby Carlino had told some of them or maybe all of them that this wasn't about a movie, this was the real thing. Nobody was doing her any favors. There was no joking around, the way there would have been if they believed she was an actress, no flirting.

No fun.

At least they were letting her play.

And she managed to have a couple of bright moments near the end. Even with her legs starting to go, she and Carl Anthony got together on a fast break as neat and clean as anybody had run all day. He got a rebound, made an outlet pass to Dee in the same motion. She cut to the middle and he got out and cut behind her, out on her right. Another guy faster out here than he ever looked on television. Anthony beat Dream Jackson to the basket. Dee had stopped short of midcourt, as if she were slowing the play down. But once Anthony was in the clear, she hit him with a fifty-foot bounce pass with so much steam on it she even surprised herself.

On his way back on defense, Carl Anthony looked at her with his impassive prison-yard face, then just nodded.

Dee felt herself blush, as if he'd just stopped everything and given her a bouquet of flowers.

Carlino made them all go an extra half-hour; Dee was sure it was because he could see how exhausted she was. When he finally said next basket ended it, Deltha missed a long jumper; Dong Li got the rebound and handed it to Carl Anthony, who passed it to Dee on the side. She broke to the middle, Anthony on her left now, having cut behind her, Anquwan on her right. She was looking left the whole time, leaned that way as she crossed half-court, then switched hands off the dribble and brought the ball all the way behind her back to Anquwan for a dunk.

Nobody reacted except Anquwan, who just kept running after he made the shot, toward the locker room.

"Ax you somethin'?" he called out to Dee before he disappeared into the tunnel.

"What?"

"You ever give any thought what you could do with two balls in your hand?" Anquwan said.

Dee told Michael De la Cruz she was going to shower back at the hotel, she hadn't even brought a change of clothes with her. She was sitting with him in the purple seats after practice, the court already empty, as if someone had pulled a fire alarm.

Eddie had just left, saying he had something he wanted to discuss with Carlino in his office, they should meet him there in a few minutes.

"You did fine," De la Cruz was saying.

"I was the worst player on the court." She uncapped the extra bottle of Poland Spring water she'd packed in her gym bag, poured it all over herself, then draped a purple Knights towel over her head like a shroud.

"There were some flashes," he said. "There were definitely some flashes."

"Hot flashes," Dee said. "I've already started basketball menopause."

"When we get this thing up and running," he said, "you're going to have your own dressing room, the same one Sinatra used when he did his big comeback concert here in the old days. 'Sinatra: The Main Event,' they called it. Like you're going to be the main event." Nodding to himself, the way Dee noticed he did a lot. "We'll move the Knights' Streetcorner Dancers over into the rotunda someplace. Jesus, wait till you see them. I asked for a little T and A and ended up getting girls with no clothes doing the Dirty Boogie."

"Up and running?" Dee said. "Were you watching? I couldn't *walk* by the end."

"Step number six!" Michael De la Cruz said. "Easy does it only works for drunks!"

He took her hand, helped her out of a seat he said cost fifteen hundred for a Knicks game.

"How much for a Knights game?" Dee asked.

"Make me an offer," he said.

When they walked into Carlino's office, Eddie had the coach of the Knights by the front of his purple-and-black warm-up jacket, shoved up against the wall behind his desk.

". . . your job!" Carlino was sputtering.

"My ass," Eddie said, somehow looking completely still even as Carlino tried to shake loose from him.

"Eddie," De la Cruz said, shutting the door behind him, then latching it.

"You told them," Eddie said.

Eddie wasn't a big guy; Dee actually thought he looked

smaller in street clothes than he had when they'd been on the court together. He certainly didn't have much size on Bobby Carlino. But somehow, seeing the two of them together, it was as if he had a doll up against the wall.

"So what if I did?" Carlino said. He tried to move his head back and succeeded only in giving the back of it a good rap against the faux brick wall. "What's the big goddamn *deal*? Like, they weren't going to know what the deal was eventually?"

"I don't need you to fight my battles," Dee said. "For what that's worth."

"I'm not," Eddie said. "He just thought it was cute, letting Ray Ray turn you into a tackling dummy."

"Let him go now," De la Cruz said, putting a little more snap into his voice.

"What are you, her bodyguard?" Bobby Carlino said, his face the color of a plum by now.

Eddie tilted his head to the side, a couple of frown lines appearing on his forehead, as if he were trying to decide what to do on his own. Finally he gave Carlino one more good shove and let him go.

Bobby Carlino edged along the wall until he was clear of him, straightened his jacket, which had run halfway up the black T-shirt he was wearing underneath it, turned to De la Cruz, and said, "I want to know—what are you going to do with this asshole? Players get suspended for shit like this!"

Michael De la Cruz didn't say anything. No one did. The only sound in the room was Carlino's breathing.

"First you let that lump Carl Anthony grab me, and now *him*?" he said. "Over *her*, for Chrissakes?"

De la Cruz, in a gentle voice, almost a whisper, said, "You told them? After I told you not to tell them?"

"Ah, come on, Michael, what's the difference if it's today instead of tomorrow? I told them because they had a right to know. And I made them promise they wouldn't tell anybody else."

He was back behind his desk now, trying to act as if he were back in charge, somehow trying to get his strut back

even sitting down. Only, De la Cruz wasn't playing. He
walked over, calmly placed his hands on the season schedule
Carlino used for a blotter, leaned over. He wasn't peppy
Michael now. He wasn't trying to be one of the boys.

This wasn't even for Dee's benefit.

This was just the boss, the guy who had sharp enough elbows to make all the money. This was Jeremy one time at his
place in Nice, Café Gerard, with a bartender he'd caught
stealing from him, her charming Brit husband looking and
sounding nothing like the playing fields of Oxford or Cam-
bridge or any of the rest of his good-boy Brit background.

"Let me explain something to you, Coach," he said, using
that feathery voice like the back of his hand. "The difference
is that I specifically told you not to. The difference is that
telling these assholes any kind of secret is the same as hiring
a goddamn *skywriter.* The difference, *Coach*"—giving him a
little slap every time he called him Coach—"is that this isn't
your call, it's mine. It's my show. My story. And if it plays out
the way I think it might, it's bigger than you or basketball or
even this league. So I don't want you—and I'm sure Miss
Gerard will pardon my French here—fucking this up to a
fare-thee-well. I must not have made that clear to you yesterday. But is it clear now? Coach?"

Still right in his face.

Boys, she thought, will always be boys, just about every
time, hardly any exceptions.

"I know you want me to fire you," De la Cruz said, finally
pulling back, still standing over him so Carlino had to look
up. "I know how many feelers you get every time another college coach from Dipstick U. gets fired, even if you think I
don't. I know sometimes you kid yourself thinking that I'm
just like all the other bosses you used to have, that I'm some
dipstick athletic director thrilled to be in the same room with
the great Bobby Carlino. But what you should really do is
check your contract. And see what kind of settlement you're
entitled to if I can prove you or your representative ever have
any contact with the representative of another team—NBA,
college, or the CYO. Or if you fall into some really, *really*
neat definitions of insubordination."

Carlino cleared his throat. "Listen, Michael, I was just . . ."

"Being the duplicitous cockroach you can't help yourself from being sometimes?" Eddie said, finishing the thought.

"Okay," Carlino said. "I screwed up. I apologize. You have a right to be pissed, same as I do when I tell our boys one thing and they do whatever they goddamn well please. But bottom line? It's better that we test her right away—from what you say, it's not like she's going to get a month of spring training here. Am I right?"

Talking about her as if she weren't there.

De la Cruz was sitting on the corner of the desk. "Did you tell anybody besides the players?"

"No."

"The truth."

Eddie said, "What about the lemmings who cover the team?"

Carlino snorted. "The beat guys from the papers? What, I'm going to help them because they think I'm so adorable? I told the players, that's it. You want me to tell them again to keep it in the house, I'll be happy to do it."

"You've done enough for one day," De la Cruz said. He stood up. "Let's go."

Eddie unlocked the door, started to say something to Carlino, thought better of it, and left. De la Cruz made a motion to Dee, as if saying *ladies first*. She said, "You go ahead, I want to have one more word with the coach." Michael De la Cruz, hand on the doorknob, gave Carlino a long look and said, "This better not show up in the press before I want it to."

"If it does," Carlino said, "it's not on me. You've got my word."

"You remember what I'm saying here," De la Cruz said.

Then it was just Bobby Carlino and Dee.

"You were the worst player out there today," he said. "You know that, right?"

Dee said, "You said you'd give me a fair shot. This, here, today, this was your idea of a fair shot?"

He said, "Around here, it's a man's game."

She left him sitting there.

"You got nothing" was the next-to-last thing she heard, standing in front of the star dressing room De la Cruz said would be hers.

"Bitch" was the last thing.

◍ eight

"There's somebody I want you to meet," Eddie said. They were down at the other end of the hallway from Bobby Carlino's office, outside the Knicks' locker room. Dee said she wanted to take a look, she'd always pretended she was a Knick when she was a little girl, up there in the cheap seats, which she'd noticed before were no longer that tacky blue she remembered. When they were inside, she said to Eddie, "It looks like a locker room, just nicer."

Back outside, he was saying, "You got any plans the rest of the afternoon?"

Dee told him she thought she might just walk around a little bit, see how much had changed on Fifth Avenue between her hotel room and St. Patrick's.

Dee said, "You don't think I've made enough new friends today?"

"This is worth it, I think."

"What's this about?" she asked.

"About watching your back," he said. Then he tried to give her a Groucho Marx leer as he said, "In addition to your backside."

"Are you flirting with me, Eddie?" Dee said.

"In the past," he said, "I've made it a policy never to do that with the other players."

It was a head fake, not an answer.

She said, "How about now?" Sometimes she was sure she could read him, sometimes she had no clue whether he was teasing her or not.

And what about her? Was she flirting with him? What was this, all of a sudden?

Better yet, *who* was this?

"How about I come by in an hour or so?" Eddie said, and then his cell phone was chirping and he was walking toward the court, where he said the reception was better for some reason. Or maybe because he didn't want her to hear.

She fussed with her hair after her shower, getting it exactly the way she wanted—she was going to have to find someone she trusted here the way she finally had in Monte Carlo—put on a beige lamb's-wool pullover and Joseph jeans and her new J.P. Tod's shoes, black suede penny loafers with the driving heel on the bottom that she liked.

Eddie had called to say he'd be there at three o'clock. The buzzer sounded at three exactly.

When Dee opened the door and saw who was standing there with Eddie Holtz, big as life, she burst out laughing.

"You're . . . you're Mo Jiggy," Dee said.

"And you're better-looking than Eddie said you was," Mo Jiggy said.

"Mo Jiggy," Dee repeated, shaking her head. " 'So Many Effin' Games, So Little Effin' Time.' "

"You like rap?"

"Hate it," she said, and now he laughed.

Mo Jiggy, the rap star, wore a white football jersey that said "Hawks" in front, with No. 84 underneath, and what looked like brand-new baggy carpenter's jeans and the kind of cool red suede Pumas she used to see Clyde Frazier wearing in footage of the old Knicks. He wore wraparound sunglasses that seemed to have come from some kind of space movie. His bald head was as shiny as a brand-new penny.

Mo Jiggy, friend of Eddie Holtz?

It was as if Eddie could read her mind sometimes. Because now he said, "He's a sports agent now."

Mo Jiggy said, "How 'bout we go inside and talk about how we ensure that Whitey don't hold you down, girlfriend?"

"I hate 'girlfriend' almost as much as I hate rap," Dee said.

"Figured as much," Mo Jiggy said.

Eddie hated rap music, too, but he liked Mo.

They'd met the first year the Knicks had allowed the Knights to move in from Long Island and share the Garden with them. Mo could have had all the Knicks season tickets he wanted, even in that celebrity row at courtside, but he refused once he saw Sean (Puffy) Combs, a rival rapper, sitting there, two seats down from Spike Lee, before Combs's nickname, for some dopey rap reason, progressed from Puffy to Puff Daddy, even briefly to P. Diddy.

"It's not just that the man can't sing worth a s——," Mo explained to Page Six of the *New York Post* when he was asked why he was boycotting Knicks games. "Or that he got his pansy puffy ass arrested that time in South Beach ridin' a f—— motor scooter. Turns out he can't hold on to those fat-a——ed actresses he dates on top of that. And, on top a *all* that, he turns out to be a total f——up with firearms."

Michael De la Cruz's p.r. people from Wasserman Associates were on the phone with him that same day, giving Mo four comp seats in the front row for Knights games. The first couple of times he showed up, De la Cruz had Eddie sit with him. This was about the same time Mo was making a big splash as an agent by representing A.T.M. Moore, the wide receiver who had helped the New York Hawks win their first Super Bowl.

It turned out Eddie and Mo had a mutual friend in Jack Molloy, the Hawks' owner, who in another life had owned a Third Avenue joint called Montana, where Eddie used to hang around when he was still playing. Jack Molloy hadn't been around New York much since the Hawks had won the title, turning over the running of the team to his brother and sister, but when he finally got the message Eddie had sent through the Knights, he returned the call from London.

"Jesus, they're dumping cricket matches over here," Molloy said. "I mean, if you can't trust the sissies in the white pants, who the hell can you trust in sports, that's what I'd like to know?"

In the background, Eddie thought he heard a cheer.

"Where are you?"

"Cricket," Molloy said. "I got a hundred pounds on the white pants in the lead." There was another cheer, and then Eddie heard Molloy saying, ". . . help you? The office said it was important."

Eddie said he had this special player, and was thinking about Mo as an agent.

"He's that good?" Molloy asked. "The player, I mean."

Eddie said not only good, but different.

"This is Mo's priority cell," Jack Molloy said, giving Eddie the number. "If he starts bitching, tell him I gave it to you. Here's the deal on him: He won't take any shit, he's smarter than every owner I know, including me, and he's a lot of fun to be around, once you break the ice with Regis and Kathie Lee."

"Regis and Kathie Lee?"

"His two favorite rotts."

Mo usually came to Knights games with two guys from his posse named Montell and Denzell. Eddie still hadn't met the rotts; if he had them with him today, they must have stayed inside the black Suburban that had pulled up in front of the Sherry-Netherland at five minutes to three. When Mo got out, not waiting for his driver to come around and open the door, he smiled at the doorman and said, "Yeah, baby. It's me." Then he said, "And don't bother askin' Shaheen to move the car. 'Cause he won't."

"I forgot to ask," Mo said when they were inside, moving through the Sherry's small lobby on their way to the elevators, the reception desk on their left, a side entrance to Harry Cipriani's restaurant on their right. "This girl of yours? What color?"

"Kind of in between. Closer to white."

Mo Jiggy nodded. "She can bring it, though?"

Eddie said, "Oh yeah."

"Up to now," Mo said, "I thought Jack Molloy the cra-
ziest white man I ever met, all that shit he pulled when he
was running the Hawks."

"I got him beat easy now," Eddie said.

Mo said, "But I'll tell you something I've been thinking on
since you called me. This all definitely got possibilities."

"Only if she can bring it."

"Always comes back to that in life," Mo said. "Don't it?"

Eddie was wondering how Dee would react when she saw
Mo. She laughed right away when she saw him standing
there. Really laughed. Eddie hadn't heard her laugh like that
yet, not one time, here or back in Monte Carlo. It was a bigger sound than he expected coming out of her, the way she
was always playing things so cool, on and off the court, as
though it snuck out of her, one of those belly laughs you could
hear all over a movie theater. A fat-girl laugh.

Dee showed them into the living room. She picked up the
house phone and ordered a setup for coffee and tea from room
service. When Mo saw the piano, he sat himself down and
played the opening bars of something Eddie knew sounded
familiar.

Dee said, " 'Rhapsody in Blue'?"

Mo banged the keys as he finished that and went right into
one Eddie did know, "Blue Skies," finishing his little riff by
throwing his hands in the air. "Went through a whole blue period at Juilliard one semester," he said.

"You went to Juilliard?" Dee said. It came out more surprised than she intended.

"Two years." He turned around, pushed his sunglasses
down to the end of his nose, looked over them at Dee. "You
gotta watch yourself, looks can be deceiving sometimes.
Don't you think?"

Dee said, "I hear you."

Mo Jiggy pointed at her shoes. "Those Tod's?"

She told him they were.

"I love those. They got a store over on Madison, around the corner. Got their winter sale going on right now."

They made small talk until the room service waiter arrived. Mo asked what her first impression of Michael De la Cruz was. She said he reminded her of a male model who'd come into some money. Mo said pardon his language in front of a lady such as herself, but come was what he always seemed to be on the verge of doing. Mo said Eddie'd told him Dee came from someplace uptown and he asked, Where exactly? Dee said they moved around a little bit, but the place she most thought of as home was the Franklin Plaza apartments, on 106th, between Second and Third. Mo said they were practically neighbors, he grew up at 109th and Second, across from Jefferson Park Junior High.

It was after the room service waiter left with the crispy fifty-dollar bill Mo had given him as a tip that Mo turned to Dee, all business, and said, "Okay, who the hell are you?"

Dee took a deep breath, looked at Eddie as she answered.

"Well, for starters, I'm Cecil Cody's daughter."

Eddie spoke first.

"You're Cool Daddy's girl?"

She smiled, imitating the old man even if they didn't know it. "I am all of dat."

And told them.

Even Mo Jiggy knew, all this time later, that Cecil (Cool Daddy) Cody once had been one of the most famous New York City playground players of them all, up there—at least in Cool Daddy's version of things—with Pablo Robertson and James Barlow and Herman (Helicopter) Knowings and Connie Hawkins and even Earl (The Goat) Manigault, who'd had a book, *The City Game*, written about him; up there with little guys like Joe Hammond and Tiny Archibald, who would come along later on, and Kenny Anderson, out of Lefrak City, and Stephon Marbury, out of Coney Island, who would come along much later on.

"Book on The Goat was by Pete Axthelm," Mo said. "There was some stuff about the Knicks in it. But Goat was the star of it, the character people remembered. Did a paper on him when I was averaging twenty-two a game for McBurney."

Eddie said, "Best basketball book ever written."

Dee said, "Cool Daddy always used to say, 'Yeah, Goat was the book, but was my life should have been the feature film.' "

He came out of Boys High in Brooklyn, same as his man The Hawk, Connie Hawkins, had before him, in the early sixties. Cecil Cody was a six-one point guard, but he still averaged thirty points a game his sophomore year and at least ten assists a game, even though nobody paid too much attention to keeping assists in those days. The college recruiters were already starting to come around. Cool Daddy would tell her later that if you could've gone straight from high school to the NBA in his day, if he'd known that he was only looking at two more years of school instead of two more of high school and four in college, his whole life might've been different.

"Coulda gone pro when I's sixteen," he told Dee. "You know why I couldn't? 'Cause I's always ahead of my time, that's why."

He went to the Green Correctional Facility, medium security, just south of Albany, instead.

It was March of 1964, the PSAL championship game between Boys and Benjamin Franklin High. Cool Daddy's team from Boys won, but that's not what everybody would remember about the occasion; what they would remember for years to come was the vicious fight that broke out afterward between fans of the two teams. The seats at the old Garden on Fiftieth Street were slashed by the kids carrying knives. The stands would be littered with broken bottles and bloody clothing. Dee had read up on the whole thing one long afternoon when she was a sophomore at Clinton, on microfilm at the New York Public Library, where she always loved going to research school papers. She decided to find out for herself how it all started for her father on St. Patrick's Day, 1964.

There was his version and the police version.

There always seemed to be two versions of everything with him.

Sometimes more than that.

Her father's version was that the girl he was dating at the time got roughed up by some punks from Franklin once somebody had identified her as Cool Daddy's girl; this was at the Garden right after the game. Cool Daddy and some of his friends found out who they were and went looking for them that night, finally found them at a party on 155th Street. Now another brawl broke out, this one smaller than the one at the Garden but even more tragic. Cool Daddy and a friend, Rumeal Roosevelt, chased down the two Franklin kids. The four of them ended up in an empty lot between 158th and 159th. Cool Daddy would swear afterward that he was walking away from the fistfight that had blackened both his eyes and cost him three teeth when he heard the shots ring out from behind him. One of the Franklin kids, seeing the .22 Rumeal had pulled from the Boys letter jacket Cool Daddy had given him, had already run by then. The other one, Marky Price, was dead, a single shot to the head.

The police version was that Cool Daddy knew Rumeal had a gun, that he had brought Rumeal uptown with him as a bodyguard and, if necessary, as a shooter, and that made him an accessory after the fact, no matter how innocent he said he was. Rumeal, who had already gone down for second-degree murder, said he lost his head and shot the guy, that Cool Daddy had nothin' to do with nothin'. The jury didn't believe him. The judge in the case gave Cool Daddy five years at Green Correctional and told him he was getting off easy.

Cool Daddy always told Dee, easy his ass, the judge should have tried to be Prisoner No. Whatever Number He Was at Green Correctional. He always said it was basically the story of his whole damn life, wrong place at the wrong damn time.

He got out in the summer of 1969. There were still a couple of colleges willing to take a chance on him, Dee said, but it was a different time in college sports, in all sports, really, before anybody who still had the talent got a second chance, and a third, as many as they needed sometimes. Cecil Cody had passed his high school equivalency courses at Green Correctional, even his SATs, though Dee always figured he'd had help. Al McGuire, the old Rockaway Beach guard who was coaching at Marquette then, who remembered Cecil Cody from all the summer ball he played, offered him a partial scholarship. "I'll be his parole officer," McGuire said, and told people that he wasn't in that alley off 158th Street that night, and didn't pretend to know what really happened, but that you had to say that Cool Daddy had been a victim, too.

He lasted one month at Marquette. During that time, he told Dee, he went to six classes. "And two of those was 'cause of a girl," he used to say. He went back to New York, worked odd jobs, played in every church league and semipro league and playground league he could find. In the summers, he was as much an attraction in the Rucker League as any of the New York City pros who played in it, any of the hotshot local kids from high school and college. He got a tryout with the New York Nets of the ABA, Dr. J's old team; the third day of training camp, he showed up with a broken hand, from a fight the night before outside the Apollo after an Aretha Franklin concert. "It was just one of those things," he told Dee later. "One thing led t'another."

"One thing always led t'another," she said to Eddie and Mo. "There was always another piece of bad luck or bad timing holding him back. None of it was ever his fault, of course. Not according to him, anyway. He used to tell me his woe-is-me stories like they were fairy tales."

"He was what we called an Ida, I was growing up," Mo said.

"Ida?" Eddie said.

Mo said, "Yeah. If Ida practiced, I would've been a great player. If Ida had a few more breaks, I wouldn't be on this here street corner, telling you everything Ida been able to do, if only I worked a little harder."

He ended up with the Harlem Wizards, a second-rate version of the Globetrotters, toured with them for a couple of years. It was in Chicago one spring that he met a dancer named Marthe Wilander—"Like the tennis player, no relation," Dee said—on tour herself that year with a revival of *Hello, Dolly.* She was tall, blond, Swedish, a flower-child sixties hippie at heart. Cecil (Cool Daddy) Cody was the same handsome smooth talker he'd always been. "I's *always* catnip to the ladies, little girl," he would proudly tell Dee.

Marthe Wilander called him her Sammy Davis, said that she was his Mai Britt, the blond actress Davis had married back in the fifties. Their affair started up that first night in Chicago, after they met in a bar on Rush Street. She told Cool Daddy she was on the pill, but when he did the math afterward, when they were both off the road and living together in her apartment on Eighty-sixth and Third, he figured that Dee had to have been conceived that first week they spent together in the room Cool Daddy had sprung for at the Drake Hotel.

He told Dee these things when he decided she was old enough, which meant one night when she was fourteen and he finally decided to warn her about bad boys exactly like him.

"My mother and father waited until I was three to get married, as it turned out," Dee said. "Even though they'd discovered by then that the only thing they had in common was the thing that produced me."

Her mother came off the road for good, working only Broadway shows, when she could get the work. Cool Daddy took a couple of years off from the Wizards, working as the greeter at a jazz club some friends of his opened in the Village, not too far from the old Village Gate.

The place was called CD.

The marriage between Cool Daddy Cody and Marthe Wilander, who always kept her maiden name, at least professionally, lasted until their daughter was eight years old.

"They split up then?" Mo asked. "That's about when it happened between my old man and old lady."

"She got shot to death buying me a quart of whole milk," Dee said.

Cool Daddy had Dee with him at a playground on 108th, a few blocks away from their new apartment. Her mother was the only customer in the bodega run by an elderly Puerto Rican couple when a hopped-up kid robbed the cash register of $78.25 and then shot the Puerto Rican couple and her mother dead.

"After that," she said, "it was just the two of us. I was Cool Daddy's girl."

Mo had asked who she was, after all.

Somehow her father worked out an elaborate day-care center with the women, mothers and grandmothers and sisters, who lived in their building. The Harlem Wizards folded about that time and Cool Daddy decided to put together a team of his own, the New York Apollos. They didn't travel too far, mostly playing games in the tristate area, occasionally getting a game in Pennsylvania, or even Washington, D.C. Dee went with them on weekends, riding an old blue-and-white Academy bus that should have been condemned long before. Cool Daddy rented it from a friend for practically nothing; he always had this elaborate network of friends somehow managing to supply him with whatever it was he needed at a particular moment, a bed or a ball or a bus or a court or a couple of hundred dollars. If he needed baby-sitters, he came up with them, too. The Apollos usually played Friday nights and Saturday nights, occasionally a Sunday afternoon. During the week, he worked as a custodian at Hunter College. He'd go early to work in the morning, when the gym was still empty, and work on his game; a couple of mornings a week, he'd take Dee with him before school. She was in junior high then. Already falling in love with basketball herself.

This was the one thing she had in common with Cool Daddy Cody.

Everything he knew about basketball he gave to her. If he'd really wanted a son instead of a daughter, he never let on.

"Watch this, little girl," he would say.

"Try this, little girl."

"Check *this* one out, little girl."

He used to laugh, this big laugh, she said, much bigger than he was, and tell her, "There ain't gonna be no money when I pass on. But I'm gonna leave you with the beat, little girl."

There was never much money, even when her mother was alive and they were both bringing home a paycheck. She didn't care that she was being raised by apartment 10B and 7A and 3C. Dee Cody didn't care that the other girls in school, in eighth grade and ninth, seemed to be speaking a different language, about boys and clothes and hair and drugs and even sex. She had no clue.

She just wanted to play ball.

She started to go looking for the best game, even if it was just her and nine boys playing. She told Eddie about Foster Park, over in Brooklyn, being her longest subway ride. He nodded and said, "Went there, too." She didn't care how long she had to wait to get into a game on West Fourth Street on a summer night, with what felt like the whole Village watching the pickup games, or even the Summer League games, through the chain-link fence.

"I'd wait all night to get picked," she said.

She told them about going as far away as Jersey in the summer, if she could hitch a ride with somebody.

Eddie said, "You ever play White Eagle Hall? In Jersey City?"

"Are you kidding?" Dee said. "You could get yourself killed on the side walls of that stupid bingo parlor."

It was when she was a sophomore at Clinton, halfway through her first season on the varsity, people just starting to talk about her, that Cool Daddy came home to the apartment on Penfield Ave. they were living in by then and told her he had a couple of guys, two more friends from that bottomless reservoir of friends, who wanted to bankroll the Apollos on a barnstorming tour through Europe. Magic Johnson and Larry Bird were the stars of the NBA by then, the commissioner of the league, David Stern, was starting to market his sport over there, and basketball was beginning to take off like a rocket in France and Italy and Spain.

He told Dee she could stay, he hadn't saved a lot of money, but with her mother's insurance money and a little bit he'd saved, there was enough for boarding school for a year, maybe two, depending on how things went with the Apollos.

Or she could go with him, they'd figure out schools when they got over there.

I'll think of something, he told her.

Don't I always think of something, little girl?

She could picture it now, the two of them sitting in the little kitchen on Penfield, with the family next door, the other side of the attached house, having their nightly yell practice through walls as thin as Saran Wrap.

"I told him I'd seen enough of Harlem and the Bronx, I'd just as soon see the world," she said.

He made Paris the home base for the Apollos, somehow got her into the American School there. "Don't ask," he'd said when she asked him how. There were a lot of things she never asked. He found them a small apartment a couple of blocks away. Of course, she made the basketball team, making trips with it to play the American Schools in London and Germany and The Hague, in addition to Department of Defense schools in Europe. She had said she was going to see the world, and she did. When Cool Daddy went on the road during the school years, he somehow found the same network of mothers and grandmothers on whatever *rue* they'd lived on, as he had back on 106th Street.

In the meantime, the New York Apollos became a hit, playing exhibitions against Division I teams, or Olympic teams from the various countries, sometimes even the best women's teams, drawing big crowds. The one year they were going to stay over there became two. They had planned to go back to New York the first summer, and then they picked up some extra games, and so they stayed. It turned out they never went back.

It was during that first summer that Cool Daddy came up with the idea of Dee playing with the Apollos a few minutes a night. Like it was a basketball duet. He was pushing forty by then, not even close to what he'd been. He was only playing a few minutes a game himself.

But when he was out there with his daughter, the two of them making the same moves sometimes, doing the same sleight-of-hand tricks with the ball, he would shine.

"He never changed, not really," she said. "He was never completely in shape. Even in games where he was supposed to be putting on a show, clowning it up, he'd get into beefs with players on the other team, or with the refs. There was always a part of him that was the hothead who'd gone looking for Marky Price and the other guy on St. Patrick's Day night.

I'd hear the stories from the other players about how he was still getting into bar fights, still going after somebody else's girl. I remember something my mother told me about him once, after they'd had some fight about what time he came in. She said, 'If you're born round, you don't die square.' "

There was some talk about Dee coming back to the United States when it was time for college, but by now she knew two things: She just wanted to play ball, and the best women's ball was in Europe. The French promoter who used to book the Apollos' games, Louis L'Ami, became her agent. He got her a tryout at an open camp for the European League. Within two months, eighteen years old but considering herself a cool expatriate woman of the world by now, she was playing in Hungary.

"Eddie knows the travelogue," Dee told Mo. "A team in Hungary. One in Japan, which was paying the best money in those days. Even Israel. That was a thrill. We played three-hundred-seat arenas in a kibbutz. The people showed fan support by banging on the pots and pans they brought with them to the games."

She came back to France and became a star. Spain came calling after that. There were scouts from the WNBA all over Europe at the time, knowing there was as much talent there as there was back home at places like the University of Connecticut, the University of Tennessee. But Dee had married Jeremy Gerard by then, at a party thrown by her Spanish owner at Jeremy Gerard's first hot restaurant, the one in Nice.

"I got to Europe in the first place because Cool Daddy said I had to decide, go or stay," Dee said. "I decided to go. Jeremy basically told me the same thing, told me he'd support me even if I wanted to go back home. I told him I was staying."

She said, "You can talk yourself into anything. Even a happy marriage."

And now, she said, big drumroll, here I am.

"On account 'a Eddie," Mo said.

Dee bowed in Eddie's direction. "Of all the gin mills in all the world, he walked into mine."

"Wait," Eddie said, grinning slyly. "I know that one."

Dee looked at her Swiss Army watch. She had been talking for more than an hour and knew she hadn't even told them half of it, thinking of all the good parts she'd left out. And the bad ones.

Now it was Mo Jiggy who seemed to be reading her mind.

"What happened to your father?" he said.

"He died a couple of years ago," Dee said.

"What of?"

"A ferryboat sunk in Greece one night," she said. "He was on it."

Mo Jiggy noticed Dee's basketball lying on the floor. He picked it up. "This regulation?" he asked. "Girls play with a smaller ball, right?"

Dee said, "It's regulation."

He sat down on the edge of the couch and twirled the ball perfectly on his middle finger.

Eddie said, "It's the finger his fans know best."

Mo snapped a pass over to Dee.

"So how do you do it, exactly?" Mo said.

Dee had already noticed that his I'm-bad accent seemed to come and go.

"It?"

"It. This. The whole deal. How do you make it work? Because as far as I can tell, the only person who thinks you can do it is Eddie, and when you ask Eddie how he knows, he says, 'Because I know' or some shit like that. I'm s'posed to feel better 'cause he knows whatever the fuck he knows. The guys in the league are going to want you to fail, and the girls in the girls' league are going to want you to fail. Especially the girls in the girls' league. You'll be showing them up as much as the guys if you actually make the grade."

Now Dee spun the ball on the index finger of her right hand, then switched to her left hand, keeping the spin tight. Then back to her right, her hand facing her now, so she could bring it around her back and switch it back to the left hand. The ball still spinning. Mo looked as if she'd just pulled a quarter out from behind his ear.

She snapped a pass back to him.

"I've got to find a way to run the offense and stay away from the physical play," she said. "That's one. I've got to have a godfather on the court, which I think I may have found today in Carl Anthony. Right?" she said, turning to Eddie.

"He acted like Ray Ray had said something bad about his momma," Eddie said.

"What else?" Mo said.

"I've got to show them I can laugh when I screw up. But at the same time, I have to let them know I'm serious, which I might have accidentally done today when I had my Cool Daddy moment and clipped Ray Ray."

"She dropped him with one punch," Eddie explained.

"You lyin'," Mo said.

"If I am, I'm dying," Eddie said. "Broke his nose."

Mo whooped with delight. "And I thought the only excitement of the girl's first day was going to be when the coach called 'Shirts against Skins.'"

Dee said, "I was ready for him if he did. I remember something Nancy Lieberman told me when she was giving a clinic at Queens College one summer, about when she went to training camp with the Lakers in the old days. Pat Riley had just started coaching them. The players started yelling for shirts and skins and Riley was saying no, no, no, but as he did, Nancy said, 'If that's what they want, fine with me,' and whipped off her practice jersey, only it turned out she had a bathing suit on underneath."

Dee told Mo that maybe the biggest break of all for her, providing the other things she'd mentioned fell into place, were some of the rules changes while she'd been away, especially the league bringing back zone defenses.

"When Lieberman played one summer in that United States Basketball League, back in the eighties? They needed her as an attraction, so they made sure they allowed zones, just so the other team couldn't post her up every single time down the court."

There was quiet in the room. Dee could hear traffic sounds from the street, even all the way up here; she had forgotten how traffic was the real background music of New York, no matter how high up you were. There was the muted blare of a horn every ten seconds.

Mo said, "Gun-to-the-head time—"

"Wasn't that one of your albums?" Dee said.

"—can you really be better than a guy?"

Before Dee could answer, Eddie did. "That's not the point." He looked right at Dee. "Is it?"

Dee said, "I can't ever be better. I just want to be *even* with some of them. As good as some of the good guys, not embarrassed by the great guys. I can out-think a lot of them, I'm not worried about that. Guys like Deltha Lester and Ray Ray, I'm not expecting them to write how-to books when they retire. I know I can outpass most of the guards in the league, with a few exceptions. And beat the slower ones down the court. But that's it, that's as high as I can raise the bar. They're too big, too long. They can get their shots anytime they want to. I can't. I've got to do enough of what I do on the floor—the way somebody like Stockton always did—so it won't matter that I'm not even in the game when it's played in the air."

Mo ran a hand over his shiny head. "How long has she got before your owner wants her out there?"

"I don't think he'll wait more than a week," Eddie said. "He's already like a kid trying to keep a secret you know he can't keep."

Mo said, "Not better than the guys."

"As good," Dee said. "Just for a little while."

"Why?"

She gave it a beat and then told him the truth. "Because I've got to know."

He said to her, "What about me? Don't you want to hear about what I'm gonna ask for, my brilliant marketing plans if this thing takes off, how we play it?"

Dee smiled, at the rap star who was a lot smarter than he let on. Maybe that's why he wore the sunglasses, Dee thought, even indoors sometimes. Because when he took them off, you could see the intelligence in eyes the color of amber. The fun and the sparkle in there. Then his cover was permanently blown.

"If you're okay with Eddie," she said, "you're okay with me."

She nodded toward the piano.

"Forget blue," she said. "You know anything by Ruth Brown?"

⓪ nine

Harold Wasserman was Michael De la Cruz's personal public relations man, and spokesperson, on those increasingly rare occasions when the Knights' owner didn't want to speak for himself. Occasionally that happened after Michael had played one of his favorite media games, leaking something to the newspapers and then acting outraged afterward at this breach of security, as if someone inside his operation was selling Los Alamos–type secrets to the Chinese.

To the rest of New York, Wasserman was simply the most powerful p.r. man in the business, bigger than Rubenstein or Klores or any of them. He was the founder and CEO of Wasserman Associates, and had represented everyone from disgraced former U.S. presidents to gangsters to the heads of tobacco companies, even Arafat for a while. Michael had asked him once how he could reconcile his supposedly devout Jewishness and a business relationship with someone Michael liked to describe as a "scarf head."

"What can I tell you, Michael?" he said with a cherub smile. "His checks certainly look kosher to me."

He wasn't much more than five-two, a tall midget as far as

De la Cruz was concerned, with ridiculously thick black glasses always perched at the end of a beak nose. Not once in all the time Wasserman had represented him had De la Cruz ever seen him dressed in anything other than a blue suit, white shirt, plain red tie, clunky wing-tip shoes, no matter what the temperature outside was.

Harold Wasserman was legendary for speaking in a voice not much more than a whisper, except when standing on courthouse steps with one of his crooked clients and wanting to be heard by the reporters in the back. But anybody who did business with Wasserman Associates knew the deal, which is why they were in business with him in the first place: The mere sound of Harold Wasserman's voice could reposition a big story, even in *The New York Times*.

Or, if need be, kill the story entirely.

People paid a vulgar amount of money to hear what this poodle had to say, even if he made them all feel as if they needed to run out and buy a Miracle Ear.

Wasserman was in Michael's office along with Reg Taylor, the former Lakers great of the 1970s and '80s. He had been one of Michael's sports heroes when he was growing up, and now held the title of general manager with the Knights, even if both he and Michael knew Reg's real job was hood ornament, like he was a bigger and more famous version of one of the adorable jockeys out in front of Michael's favorite power restaurant in New York, 21.

"Is this a great country or what?" Michael told him one time. "A poor kid like me can grow up to have a six-time All-Star as his walkaround guy!"

Reg still had his famous Little Richard hair, but the lithe body that could once defy gravity by hanging in the air when all the other players near the basket had returned to earth had gone soft and doughy. His garish clothes, something out of a time warp, only drew more attention to what a slob he had become, at least in Michael's opinion. On this particular afternoon, an awful three-piece suit the color of the jacket the winner of the Masters golf tournament gets to wear made him look like some sort of stuffed green pepper.

Michael had discovered long before that the last team Reg

was able to assess intelligently had been the '85 Lakers. But he invited him to meetings like these because he knew how much it would hurt his feelings if he didn't feel as if he were still part of what the owner called his "inner ring."

When it came to any kind of decision, from changing the team logo to a new look for the uniform to a No. 1 draft choice, Michael did more polling, put together more in-house focus groups, than a Beltway politician. All Knights executives like Reg Taylor understood by now that whoever was in the room with him at a given moment, that's whose opinion—or opinions—he trusted the most. Michael actually was aware enough to know this about himself. Even temps at the Knights' offices knew that he had more rings than a two-hundred-year-old redwood.

"When the time comes," Harold Wasserman was saying now, "we're going to have to ask ourselves a very big question."

"I think we've got to go with the Knicks game, next Friday," Michael said.

Patiently, like a teacher talking to a slow student, Wasserman said, "I meant, do we go with Barbara or Diane?"

"Can't we do both?"

There was an ambulance racing up Eighth Avenue, so even though Wasserman kept talking, it was as if Michael had muted a TV set suddenly and all he could see were Harold Wasserman's thin lips moving.

"Jesus, speak up, will you, Harold, you sound like you're on a fucking respirator."

Wasserman was sitting on the Chippendale sofa, tiny feet not quite reaching the floor, his hands clasped together on his chest.

"We've gone over this before, Michael. Remember when Jamie had to choose whether or not to actually dignify the gay thing with a comment? Barbara and Diane are both dear, dear friends, but they're more competitive than two hockey players going after the puck in the corner."

Reg Taylor said, "Aren't we getting a little ahead—"

Michael turned to him, smiling. "Hel-*lo*? Harold and I are talking here, Reg."

"We need to have a game plan in place right now," Wasserman said. "Right across the board. The only no-brainer is Matt and Katie get first crack in the morning, and then Larry King gets her the second night, after we decide about which magazine show gets her first the night before. Whenever that night is."

"You're right. There are a lot of decisions. Like *Rosie* or *The View.*"

"Or Regis and that little soap opera girl who replaced my friend Kathie."

"And it's not just ABC," Michael said. "What happens if we bypass both Diane and Barbara for the first go-round, and just go with *Dateline*? We could just tell them that NBC's a partner with the NBA, and Commissioner Betts said they had to get first crack at her."

"I might convince Barbara," Harold said, "just because we have a longer relationship. But if I go the other way, Sawyer—and I love her like a daughter—will be all over me like a rat."

Reg said, "Boss, I don't mean to disrupt with an interrupt—"

He still liked to rhyme things sometimes, from when he was doing color commentary for the Knights on television. This time Michael put up a hand, feeling like a school crossing guard stopping some slow kid from crossing against the light.

"Reg," he said, "we'll all talk basketball in just a second."

"I thought this was s'posed to be *about* basketball," he said.

"It is," Michael said. "But only up to a point."

"If we could get *back* on point," Wasserman said, "I have to say I was thrilled to discover, even from where I was sitting today, that she is every bit as attractive as you told me she was."

"I told you," De la Cruz said. "If she'd been a dog, she would have been on the first plane back to the Riviera."

Wasserman, eyes twinkling, said, "Blond and blue-eyed would have been even better, of course."

"I know," Michael said sadly. "I know."

"Well," Wasserman sighed, the sound more like a squeak, "you can't have everything."

"The color thing frankly doesn't bother me that much. I actually wish she had slightly bigger tits, something you could actually see in the front."

"You think she'd be willing at some point . . . ?"

"Bigger tits through technology? Forget it, she's not the type."

"Well, maybe down the road," Harold Wasserman said. "People surprise you sometimes. You think you can't work with them, and then they turn out to be team players after all."

Michael said, "Like the governor, with the fake cancer scare that time."

Wasserman shyly held up a hand of his own now, as if stopping applause. "You really only need one doctor to be a good sport," he said.

Reg Taylor, getting huffy the way he did sometimes when he felt as if he was being ignored, said, "You know, I *am* the general manager of this basketball team, even if I didn't get so much as an e-mail on the female 'fore you brought her over here."

"Reg," Michael said, "I'm begging you to lose the couplets."

"All I'm sayin' is, I watched the same practice you did. And even though I could see her playing her way into it a little bit at the end, swishin' and dishin' a little bit, she still didn't look like nothin' special to me."

He can't help himself, Michael thought, it's the world's weirdest speech impediment.

"She didn't look special, huh?"

Reg said, "No, sir."

Michael said, "Well, you'd know, wouldn't you, Reg, since you've drafted and signed so many special"—Michael made a quotation-marks motion around the word "special"—"players for me?"

"You're tellin' me you think that in a week this girl can be ready to play in an NBA game?"

"She might not be ready," Michael said. "But I will."

"You ever think about who Bobby's gonna sit, he wants to put her out there?"

That one made Michael bark out a laugh. "Jesus Christ, Reg. We're not breaking up the old Knicks. When people want to see our record, they have to drag the standings, like they do the river for bodies."

Michael looked at Wasserman now. "Who sits?" he said. "I've got a better question: Who the fuck *cares*?"

Wasserman said, "Here's what I care about: our timetable."

"We've caught a break in the schedule, just because it's soft right now," Michael said. "After the Wizards we don't play until Monday night in Boston. Then the Knicks next Friday night, at the Garden, our home game, which means I control the tickets. That's the one. If she plays that night, I've got to announce it no later than Tuesday, because that gives television two days to beat the drums."

Wasserman said, "When did you tell her you were going to make the announcement?"

"Not until she was absolutely, positively sure she was ready."

"She bought that?"

"Harold," Michael said innocently, "you know the only person who lies better than me is you."

Wasserman turned the corners of his mouth up just slightly, which meant he was happier than a hard-on. "And people wonder why you're my favorite," he said.

"You mean it's not because I call you on your birthday?"

"Remember one thing, Michael, at all times," Harold Wasserman said. "Everybody else is going to think this is about her. You and I know differently, don't we?"

"Yes, Daddy."

"This is about you, Michael."

Reg Taylor looked at his watch eventually and said he had some business to take care of across the street at the Garden. At this time of day, Michael De la Cruz knew he just wanted to get over there and watch the Streetcorner Dancers rehearse in outfits that made ring girls at Garden prizefights look over-dressed.

"Keep me in the loop," he said. "So's I don't look stupid later on."

"The last thing you need," Michael said, "is someone to make you look stupid."

"Later, gator," Reg said.

When he was gone, Harold Wasserman said, "We've got to be the ones controlling the information streams, at all times. You know my thinking on this."

"Presentation is everything."

"Good boy."

"Have you thought about whether we break it on television or in the newspapers?"

"Newspapers, I think," Wasserman said. "If it ends up on television, even with Brokaw or Rather, you know the kind of hissy fit the sportswriters will throw. And we're going to want them, or at least the majority of them, on our side."

De la Cruz said, "We could take the easy way out, and just call a press conference."

"No," Wasserman said. "An exclusive is better, it feels more like a bombshell that way. This is all about size, every step of the way. Size matters here as much as it ever has."

De la Cruz walked over to the coffee table in front of where Wasserman was sitting. Spread all over it were the morning papers. *Times. Daily News* and *Post.* The Queens edition of *Newsday.* Two New Jersey papers. The *Journal-News* from Westchester. *The Wall Street Journal. USA Today.*

And, of course, his favorite, *Variety.*

He picked up the *Daily News,* opened to the first page of the sports section. "Check this out," he said, then counted the pages out loud as he turned them, working his way back into the section, getting up to ten before he found the page with the Knights' off-day story on it, a feature about Jamie Lawton and how he was coping with all the losing after being such a big winner in college, and with our Olympic team.

"They even play our stories behind fucking hockey," he said.

Wasserman said, "Yes, but that's all about to change.

We're about to be front-page news all over the world. You know who's going to lead the network news next Friday night? You, Michael. You and your basketball team and your basketball girl."

"You really don't think we should draw this out a little more?"

Harold Wasserman said, "A few days will be enough. Look at how tired people get of all the bullshit before a Super Bowl football game, and sometimes that's only a week. If Mrs. Wasserman's son Harold does his job properly, and you say your lines, seventy-two hours from the announcement until she plays should be more than enough to whip the country into a small frenzy about our girl."

Michael said, "People only thought they knew how well sex sells."

"And in our case," Harold Wasserman said, giving his mouth that happy twitch again, "it's almost better than sex. Do you know why, Michael?"

"Why?"

"Because for our purposes, she's the same as a virgin, Michael, that's why."

With that, Michael De la Cruz jumped to his feet, raced over to his desk, held his liter bottle of Poland Spring in the air like a trophy.

"To the fair sex!" he shouted.

Wasserman said, "I don't want to get ahead of myself. But this woman could make you Man of the Year."

After Eddie and Mo Jiggy had left the day before, Dee had gone out for a run, nothing special, up the thirty or so blocks to the reservoir and once around, then out onto Fifth and back to the Sherry, just to put a little burn in her legs, work on her wind a little, sprinting sometimes. Clearing her head. Wiping practice away the way she would a play on Bobby Carlino's greaseboard. Maybe she'd be the worst player on the court again tomorrow, and the day after that. But she knew she was better than she'd shown.

When she'd come back to the room, she saw that Michael

De la Cruz had arranged to have the treadmill and StairMaster she'd requested installed in the smaller of the two bedrooms in the suite; with them came a box of free weights in different colors. De la Cruz had asked if she wanted him to send over one of his personal trainers as well, making it sound as if he had a small army of them on call. Dee said she'd be fine on her own, she knew her own body and how to get it in shape and that is exactly what she was doing now, seven the next morning, listening to Aretha on her headphones, twenty minutes on the StairMaster, another twenty on the treadmill, fast-walking mostly, pumping her arms up high with the ten-pound weights.

She had just taken the headphones off, was on the floor doing some stretching, a few yoga exercises that made her feel as if she were rinsing out her lungs, when the phone rang. It was Eddie, on his cell.

"After you hang up this phone, do not answer it again," he said.

The phone cut out a little bit. ". . . until I get there" was all she heard.

Dee said, "Eddie? It's not even eight o'clock in the morning. What's wrong?"

". . . wrong," he said, "is that . . . front page of the goddamn New York goddamn *Daily News* . . . what's wrong."

So she was, an old team shot of her from Spain, a little grainy, looking more like some kind of basketball Most Wanted picture, her hair in those tight braids she'd worn only a couple of months, the sight of them making her cringe now.

Just not as much as the headline over the picture:

Knights' Mare?

There were a couple of columnists from the *News* whose names she actually remembered. She used to read a young guy named Gil Spencer when she was in high school, just because he seemed to be the only guy in town she thought made any sense about the Knicks. The other star of the sports section, then and now, was Walt Ransome, whose column was called "Ransome Notes."

The story about Dee on page three was under his column picture, which showed Ransome in a tight Marine crew cut, mustache, and scowl, reminding Dee somewhat of Jack Nicholson in some of his later movies, when he started playing fat weird cops.

The column began this way:

> Well, Pretty Boy De la Cruz, owner of the Knights, has finally gone off the deep end, though with him it will be pretty hard to tell. In an act of sheer desperation, and one that shows how all the boy owners like him are destroying sports as we know them, the News has learned that De la Cruz is about to sign a woman to play for his pathetic loser team.

Out loud in the suite, Dee said, "Well, *yeah,* but what do you really think about me?"

There was some brief biographical stuff on her career in Europe, giving some of her stats from France and Spain, talking about how she'd been out of basketball the past couple of years. There was no mention of Cool Daddy, maybe because Dee had stopped talking about him a long time ago, no mention of New York, or how she ended up in Europe in the first place. It was a sloppy piece, all over the place. Dee didn't know anything about newspaper deadlines, but it looked as if it had been thrown together in a hurry.

Or maybe this kind of scatter-shooting was Walt Ransome's A game.

> It is a nice little résumé for someone of what we called the fair sex in my day, even though I am too polite to tell a lady what she should do with that résumé, or perhaps where she should put it. So I'll tell her this instead: You go, girl. Back to Monte Carlo. Back to what I'm sure is the adorable little bistro you were running there.

Little bistro.

Dee thought: Bobby Carlino.

I would tell her to go back to the kitchen where she belongs, but of course I am much too modern for that. And
way too in touch with my feminine side. Besides, I
don't want the Thought Police to come down on me the
way the rest of the league is going to come down on
Miz Gerard, whoever she is, for as long as this circus
lasts.

He ended by saying that he had talked about the whole
thing with an anonymous Knights player, who described in
great detail Dee's dreadful performance at her first practice.

" 'Girl does have a cute a—on her,' " this player told
me. "Maybe that's why Mr. De la Cruz signed her. What
me and the guys can't figure out is how people are
going to see it with her sittin' down there at the end of
the bench."

The buzzer sounded then, like some sort of bizarre punc-
tuation to Ransome's column. Dee looked through the peephole, saw it was Eddie, opened the door, saw he was holding
his own copy of the *Daily News*.

"What bullshit," Eddie said.

Dee said, "You talking about old Walt's prose? I think
you're being awfully generous."

"It's got to be Bobby," he said, walking past her. "You got
any coffee?"

"In the kitchen," she said. "I put some on before I worked
out. Bought it myself yesterday. Man, how long has this
Starbucks thing been going on? I got in there and told them
I wanted everything that had 'mocha' or 'chino' in the
name."

"You're acting pretty calm," Eddie called from the tiny
kitchen, "considering this just turned into Pearl Harbor
Day."

He came out with two mugs, handed her one. Dee noticed
he hadn't had time to shave properly. She hadn't asked him
where his apartment was, but it must have been close by,
because his hair was still wet, and there was a little bit of

shaving cream under one of his ears. Maybe it was the stress. Or maybe it was something else. But Dee suddenly felt this urge to lick it off as if it were whipped cream.

"Hey, you had to know it was going to get out once Bobby told the players."

"Ransome is Bobby's guy," Eddie said. "About the only one left who feels sorry for him, like he's some kind of political prisoner at five million a year."

"Maybe it was a player."

"You see that part about the bistro? It sounded exactly like him."

"He could have used the same words with the players when he told them this thing was for real. 'You know where the bitch has been training for the chance of a lifetime? In some little bistro she runs.' Something like that."

She was leaning against the fireplace, sipping her coffee. Over the mantel was a huge mirror. She turned her head discreetly, checked herself out, saw how sweaty she still looked from her workout. She used to come home from practice at Clinton and Cool Daddy, if he happened to be around, would tell her she looked as if she'd been rode hard and left out wet.

"This has Bobby's fingerprints all over it. Are you kidding? You've seen him in action now. He's the kind of snake gives copperheads and water moccasins a bad name."

"My money's on Ray Ray," Dee said. "He's not exactly the brightest diamond in the setting, but this could be his way of hitting back. He must have an agent. Maybe his agent put him up to it."

Eddie's cell phone made its bird noise.

"Yeah," he said when he answered, nodding. "No, actually, I'm already here. No, the Sherry. Her room."

He snorted, shook his head in a disgusted way.

"No," he said. "I mean I'm here because I just got here."

He jabbed at the buttons, stuffed the phone back inside a side pocket of his jacket, a gray tweed today. But he was wearing jeans, as usual. "Michael," he said. "He lives here, remember? He's on his way down. And he's on the fucking warpath."

"Okay, but what's the good news?" she asked Eddie.

"Remember what Earl Monroe told Michael?"

"You mean about The Shit?"

"This is pretty much how it starts," Eddie said.

⊕ ten

Most of the time, Eddie knew, Michael De la Cruz was starring in the show he imagined his life to be. A one-man show. Somehow he had invented himself young, back in Los Angeles, created this vision of himself as someone the world wouldn't be able to ignore, whose name everybody would know sooner or later. Eddie never thought of himself as any kind of deep thinker, but he knew that it didn't matter how guys like De la Cruz made their big fortunes, their real career was being famous. Michael De la Cruz actually admitted to Eddie one time that he just wanted to be a rich kid, even after he grew up.

And the guy just stayed with that.

"I want to be the cool guy with his own car in high school," he said. "The one with the money and the babes."

Eddie was sure that De la Cruz's childhood couldn't be the colorful place he made it out to be now, but that was the story he stuck to with the magazine writers and *60 Minutes* and Larry King, the rest of the media people Michael De la Cruz let run his silly goddamn life. He'd joke that everything that had happened to him was like some kind of movie script.

Only Eddie, watching the guy up close the way he did, knew it was no joke.

This morning he was the shaker and mover who had to act fast, come out of the gate kicking ass and taking names.

He looked as if he'd skipped the elevator from his penthouse apartment, the one with the garden on top, and taken the stairs. He was in workout clothes, too, sleeveless sweatshirt, baggy satin gym shorts, with the two-toned Nike basketball shoes, completely white on one side, violet on the other, that about half the Knights were wearing this season.

He was carrying a tall covered mug that Eddie knew had some kind of voodoo power shake inside.

"Bobby swears it wasn't him," he said, pacing now in Dee's living room, occasionally hitting a couple of keys on the piano. "Says I can give him a lie detector test if I don't believe him."

"*Do* you believe him?"

"Who the hell knows? Even if the little bastard didn't do it, he started the ball rolling by telling the players."

He reached into the satin shorts, pulled out a cell phone, which had an earpiece and a microphone. He'd gone to the earpiece when the stories started coming out about cell phones causing cancer. De la Cruz was more afraid of disease than about not being able to get it up.

He started bobbing his head immediately, the way he did. "Uh-huh, uh-huh . . . My office, Harold . . . I'm aware you have other clients, Harold. Just not today."

He had just taken the earpiece out when he said, "Shit," and started talking again. "Extra guys on the back door. Yeah, on Thirty-third. Where the hell else, Kevin? And make sure you've got guys at the bottom of the ramp, where the players come in with their cars. If nobody's there, you can just flash a Press card and walk right up to the court. . . . No, you tell him this isn't a *Garden* decision, this is a Mr. De la Cruz decision."

He smiled and nodded and said, "Well, if he tries to go there, tell him to shove those league rules up his ass."

"Sorry," he said to Dee. "You okay with all this?"

"The last time I was on the front page of a New York rag

was the Clinton school paper. We beat Lehmann. I scored all our points in the second overtime."

"Yeah," De la Cruz said. "Right." He took a slug from the tall mug. "I'm going to have to hold some kind of press conference after practice," he said. "It would be stupid to deny this now that the cat is out of the bag. That way we can turn this back into a positive right away."

Eddie knew they were really just props, he was mostly talking to himself.

"That's what you do, you make the negatives work for you." He seemed to brighten for the first time since he'd come charging into the suite like a cab trying to make a light. "You know what Step Seven is, don't you, Edward?"

Eddie said, "A plus is just an intersection of two minuses."

"There you go!"

Dee said, "Golly, I feel better already! Let's put the show on right here!"

"You know something?" Michael De la Cruz said. "A lot of this today, a lot of this whole thing, *is* a show. We just have to make sure we hit the right notes in responding to what most reasonable people are going to think was an antiwoman, mean-spirited piece of crap. I just stand up there today and tell the truth, that we aren't sure where this is going exactly, we're all along for the ride, but basically we just think this is an idea whose time has come."

"Not according to old Walt Ransome," Dee said.

Eddie noticed she had somehow found time to comb out her hair, switch into a plain white T-shirt and tight faded jeans without him even noticing she'd been out of the room. She looked good, he thought. But Eddie'd thought she looked good the moment he'd walked in the door.

"Are you ready to play *Meet the Press*?" Eddie said to her.

"You mean full-court press, don't you?" Dee said, smiling.

Eddie looked at the antique Rolex his ex-wife, Susan, had bought him the Christmas they got engaged. She'd admitted to him afterward that if he hadn't come across with an engagement ring, he would have gotten a stainless-steel Hamilton, about a third of the price.

That was way before Susan's career path veered away from acting and simply became Bitch.

It was still just 8:15. Eddie was already exhausted.

Dee said, "I want to say one thing. I think Walt Ransome has the sensitivity of a prison guard. But I have to admit, when he lays things out the way he does, when he puts my so-called career up against some of the women from the WNBA—Sheryl Swoopes, Lisa Leslie, Chamique Holdsclaw—who've never made a run at this, it does sound like the world's silliest publicity stunt."

She was talking to De la Cruz. Eddie saw her doing the thing she did with her eyes, widening them as if something in the conversation had just surprised her, when she got serious.

"Tell me one more time this isn't the world's silliest publicity stunt."

"We've gone over this," Michael De la Cruz said.

"Humor me."

"It is not a publicity stunt. Sometime next week—provided you tell me you're ready—you're going to be on the front page of the *News* and every other paper in the world because you were good enough to play in the NBA."

De la Cruz resumed pacing again. For some reason, he reminded Eddie of a dog marking his territory.

"I'll handle the press today," he said. "Dee, you just keep your eye on the ball. You go to practice, even if we might have to smuggle you in."

"Like counterfeit goods?" Dee said.

"Like the one woman in New York everybody wants to know today."

The buzzer made them all jump. Eddie said he'd get it, in case somebody figured out a way to get upstairs.

It was one of the bellmen, carrying a fruit basket as big as he was.

"For Miss Gerard," the kid said.

When Eddie came walking in with the beast, Michael De la Cruz burst out laughing.

"Oh goody," Dee said. "Somebody sent me a whole farmers' market."

De la Cruz said, "Babs."

Dee looked at him, curious. "Excuse me?"

De la Cruz said, "Barbara Walters. Fruit baskets are her m.o. when she's after somebody."

Eddie said, "It's not even nine o'clock. What, she's got Baskets R Us on twenty-four-hour call?"

Michael De la Cruz said to Dee, "Open the card. I'll bet you anything it's her. And people say that old girl has lost a step."

Dee read the card, handed it to Eddie.

" 'Dee—I can't wait to meet you. Your new best friend. Barbara.' "

Eddie handed it to De la Cruz, who clapped his hands together and said, "Let the games begin!"

When it was time to go to practice, a few minutes after ten o'clock, Mo Jiggy showed up in front of the Sherry, as if the clock there were his personal parking meter, in what looked like a shiny black tank. Eddie told her this particular SUV was a Suburban, and you saw as many of them in Manhattan now as yellow cabs.

"Suburban," she said to Eddie.

"Cute, huh?"

"Good," she said. "We can use them if we invade Connecticut."

Mo rolled down the smoked window on the passenger side.

"Get in, girlfriend," he said, winking at her.

"I thought we went over the 'girlfriend' thing."

"You shouldn't've told me you didn't like it," he said. "Rookie mistake."

She and Eddie climbed into the backseat, which was roomy enough to have a picnic. Mo introduced his driver as Shaheen.

"You remember a couple of years ago?" Mo said. "When that pantload Puffy or whatever he's callin' himself now got arrested leaving the scene?"

Dee told him she vaguely did, but it finally got too hard for her to remember which rap star was in trouble with the cops and which one had gotten picked off in a drive-by. "No offense, of course," she said.

"None taken," Mo said. "My point is, if it'd been Shaheen driving him away from the club, cops could've chased his ass to Santa Monica, never caught up with him. Just in case some of the media gets, you know, ambitious with they pursuit and so forth later on when we leavin' the Garden."

Michael De la Cruz had offered his own driver to take her over to the Garden, just to get her safely through the media crowd he was sure would be waiting at the usual players' entrances. Eddie said he'd take care of it and called Mo when De la Cruz was gone to his meeting with Harold Wasserman at the Knights' offices. Mo bitched that Eddie had awakened him, but then Eddie quickly told him about the *News* and what time practice was, and Dee saw Eddie grinning, not looking so edgy and tight, for the first time all morning.

He handed Dee the phone.

Mo said to her, "You more high maintenance than Chelsea."

"Who's Chelsea?"

She heard a woman's voice mumbling from what sounded like the bottom of a tunnel. "Not a morning person, that's for damn sure," Mo Jiggy said.

Mo told her in the Suburban he'd purposely dressed down. That meant a plain khaki cap, "NYPD" sweatshirt, understated shades. He said when you were trying to slip in the side door, you didn't want to be playin' no games of hey-look-at-me like the ballplayers did.

Shaheen went first when they walked up to Four Penn. He was small, young-looking, in jeans so baggy they looked like a long denim skirt and fleece vest that was about three sizes too big for him. It was the same here as it had been the last few years in Europe, young guys dressed like pup tents.

Mo said to Shaheen, "No matter what today, you keep that thing in your pants."

Dee whispered to Eddie, "I don't mean to pry, but what does that mean, exactly?"

Eddie said, "I expect he's packing."

"Oh."

"Hey," Eddie said. "It *is* the NBA."

On the court Michael De la Cruz told the players, "Anybody screws around with her today is screwing around with me. That clear, fellas? I'm not going too fast for anybody? Not hurting anybody's feelings? Messing with their manhood?"

He pointed to a tall skinny white kid underneath the basket at the Eighth Avenue end of the Garden, head shaved as clean as Mo Jiggy's.

Dee was starting to wonder what happened to guys' hair while she was away, she hadn't ever noticed this many bald heads in Europe.

Guys wanting to be bald on purpose.

"That's Darrell. Wave, Darrell." Darrell waved. "Some of you guys may recognize him from our games. He's going to shoot today's practice. I may want to let out a little footage afterward, I haven't decided yet. But just play ball today, okay? I know there's some kind of rule that got passed that you have to play to the camera, *any* camera, but see if we can give that shit a rest today."

Dee thought: Look who's talking about playing to the camera.

De la Cruz clapped his hands. "Guys, today is the beginning of a great adventure. Just go with it!"

Behind her, Dee heard Anquwan mutter, "Great adventure like a fuckin' *theme* park."

She could tell right off that she felt more into the rhythm of it today. Felt like she had her legs more. She couldn't relax for five seconds, that hadn't changed. Every time, every *single* time she made a mistake, offense or defense, even chasing the ball out at the top of Bobby Carlino's 1-3-1 zone defense, somebody would make her pay. If she was a step late, Deltha or Ray Ray—wearing what looked like a tiny plastic windshield to cover his broken nose—would hit the open jump shot.

She was still seeing what she thought were good passes getting picked off and turned into layups at the other end. But little by little, she started to feel less like the wallflower at the school dance. Carlino had her with the second unit, and she got them running every chance she got; Dee'd always thought pushing the ball was the best way to beat any zone defense, beat them down the court before they set up.

Whether you were playing with the girls or with the boys.

One time she heard applause from where De la Cruz and Mo and Eddie were sitting. She ended up out on the wing, a set play. The ball came to her from the corner at the exact same moment Carl Anthony came flashing across the lane. She knew it must have looked as if the ball never touched her hands, she tip-passed it to him that fast, and Carl turned for an easy jump shot.

"Now we're playing some ball," she whispered to Carl on his way past her, as much for herself as for him.

She always talked to her teammates on the court, never yelling, never loud enough for the other team to hear, just little pep talks, admonitions. *Come on. You gotta be there. That's the way to run it.* Cool Daddy told her that Fred Astaire used to talk to his Gingers when they were dancing, it's just nobody could hear him or even see his lips moving.

"You know something, little girl?" he'd say. "Sometimes the coolest move is the one they don't even know they just saw it or not."

She still messed up too many fast breaks, fast breaks always being her bread and butter, at least playing against other women, because of her speed, because of the way she could see the court. Because of the way she could pass the ball. Sometimes Jamie or Carl would end up with the basket anyway, but Dee would know she'd made the wrong pass, or the wrong decision.

Two plays before Carlino whistled them off for the day, she snuck out on the break the way she told Carl Anthony she would. He got the rebound, turned almost without looking, flung the ball out to where she said she would be at half-court. When the rest of the players saw how wide open she was, with a clear path to the basket, they stopped running.

Not Carl.

"You get the ball, follow me," she'd said in his ear.

She slowed up just enough to give him time, until she saw him coming without even looking back. Cool Daddy always said she had what he called that peripheral eye shit, same as Cousy did. And it was true. She could always see things the other ones couldn't.

She saw Carl Anthony now.

She made it look as if she were just going up for a regulation layup, straight stuff, push off the left foot, gently put it off the board with the right hand. Only, instead of using the backboard, Dee gave the ball a little punch with her left hand, like she was underhand serving in volleyball, punching the ball straight overhead, floating it above the basket until Carl Anthony caught it and dunked it in one ferocious motion.

On her way past her cheering section, she caught Mo Jiggy's eye, and winked.

"You da man," she heard him say.

She stayed on the court when practice was over, shooting midrange jump shots, fifteen feet, twenty, trying to get her feel back. Her shot had been off since the first time she stepped on the court with these guys. And she knew why: She was rushing. Outside shooting had always been the weakest part of her game; she'd never averaged more than eighteen points a game, even in her glory years in Spain and France, and out of that, maybe three baskets a game were jumpers or old-school set shots; the rest she got in transition and at the free-throw line. Only now she was more gun-shy than ever, worried that if she was even a little bit slow releasing the ball, whoever was guarding her was going to smack it back in her face.

It's why she was out here now, looking not just for feel but a quicker release, because she could already see how they were daring her to shoot.

One more dare.

One of the Knights' trainers, Joey Shahoud, dark and slight, Lebanese-American he told her, was rebounding the ball for Dee, snapping crisp bounce passes to her. Joey doubled as the team's traveling secretary, and occasionally their p.r. man on the road. "Up to now," Joey told her, "we've actually tried to discourage any publicity for the team."

Dee moved around the perimeter, catching, shooting, imagining a guy right on her, moving the other way now, doing the same thing again, then again. She was so focused on the drill, on the routine, deep into it, she didn't notice Anquwan Posey behind her until she heard him say, "You better than I thought."

Dee stopped, breathing hard, ball cocked on her hip. Over Anquwan's shoulder she could see Michael De la Cruz, Eddie, Mo. They had been joined by a tiny man in thick glasses who reminded her of the old Keebler elf from television commercials when she was a kid, and a fat guy in a cornflower-blue suit who looked as if he used to be Reg Taylor of the Lakers.

Dee said, "Why, thank you, Anquwan, that's very nice of you to say."

He looked down at his sneaks.

"Wanted to personally 'pologize and whatnot, for the way I tried to mess wit' you yesterday. Me and the other guys, we was just playin' and then shit got out of hand. The way shit does sometimes."

"No apology necessary. I'm sure you can think of a lot of guys without jobs in this league who are better than me."

He shook his head. "No," he said. "I'm not playin' now. You can see the ball. See the court. Damn, you see the court."

"Thanks again."

"So," he said, "you want to go out?"

She felt a smile coming on, but managed to get it under control. "I'm too old for you."

"Older than I'm used to, but that's my problem. Be fun. We can kick back, have some wine. I got an apartment in that new Trump? Over to the West Side? Even Jersey looks good."

"Well, it's a very nice offer, I must say. But I've got enough on my plate right now without adding a social life."

Anquwan Posey frowned, as if trying to figure out just how much of a rejection this was. Dee had been around good players her whole life. She knew that if you were good enough to make the NBA, as this kid had, if you were one of the blessed, chosen few, it meant you hadn't heard the word "no" one whole heck of a lot.

"You a lesbian?" he asked.

Dee pretended to cough, as a way of trying to get her whole fist inside her mouth.

"I mean, I know how many lesbians they got in that WNBA. We like to call that one the Want No Booey Association."

"Booey?" Dee asked.

"You know," he said. "The bad."

"Booey," Dee repeated.

"All I'm sayin' is, if you are a lesbian, I'll understand."

"That's very generous of you. But no, Anquwan, I'm not a lesbian. It's just that right now I don't want to go out with you or anyone else. Of any particular sexual persuasion."

"I don't want you thinkin' I got somethin' against lesbians. 'Cause I don't."

"Me neither."

"Just so's we clear. Anquwan Posey don't discriminate against no deviations of any kind."

When he was gone, Joey Shahoud, who'd heard the whole thing, came up to her, grinning.

"You know what I was impressed with?" he said. "He went with lesbian instead of some of the more common alternatives."

Dee said, "What, you don't know a smooth talker when you hear one?"

Dee and Eddie and Mo watched Michael De la Cruz's press conference on ESPN News. They had snuck out of the Garden the same way they had snuck in, Shaheen waiting for them in the same spot where he'd dropped them. Now they were back at the Sherry, watching De la Cruz make a brief opening statement about how he had been hearing for years, from people who knew a lot more about pro basketball than he did, people like Walt (Clyde) Frazier, the old Knick now doing television, that someday a woman would play in the

NBA. Which Eddie actually said was true, he'd heard Clyde
Frazier say the same things himself.

"We think someday has arrived," De la Cruz said. "If
we're right about Dee Gerard, and we just *know* we're right,
someday is actually going to arrive sometime before the end
of the month."

Dee said, "If he says someday his princess is gonna come,
I'm out of here. I mean it."

Eddie and Mo both told her to shush.

He said he was sure there were women in the WNBA de-
serving of a chance like this. Golly, Michael De la Cruz said,
he loves the WNBA to death.

"It's just that, well, fate literally dropped Dee Gerard into
my lap," De la Cruz said.

"Powerful imagery," Mo said.

"Laps," Eddie said.

"Okay, guys," Dee said. "What guy thing am I missing
here?"

"Lap dancing," Mo said. "Guys in the league—hell, *all*
leagues—like 'em better than they do tattoo parlors."

Eddie sighed and said to Dee, "You are *so* not a guy."

De la Cruz showed a few highlights from practice then, finally told everybody they could meet Dee Gerard in person
before the Knights-Wizards game the next night at the Garden, good seats still available.

"I'm just asking one thing," Michael De la Cruz said,
being earnest now. "Just please keep an open mind about this
the way I have, the way my basketball people have, especially
Coach Bobby Carlino. . . ."

"Gag me," Dee said.

"And one more thing," De la Cruz said.

He was talking to the camera now, not the reporters, even
leaning forward a little bit.

"If you are lucky enough to sit close to the court once Dee
Gerard gets out there, stay loose. Because if she thinks you're
open, she will pass *you* the ball."

Pointing at the end. Like a recruiting poster:

Uncle Mike Wants You.

Dee watched then as the Keebler elf from practice introduced himself as Harold Wasserman. She couldn't tell whether he was just mumbling, or if Mo, who had the remote, had accidentally lowered the volume. Wasserman was saying that all his good friends in the media should save their questions for Miss Gerard. Mo aimed the remote at the set now, and the screen went to black.

"You're right about him," Dee said to Eddie.

"The owner or the munchkin flack?"

"The owner. He does want to be loved."

Mo Jiggy said, "Sad, ain't it? You want a sexual analogy?"

Not that much, Dee said.

She told Mo she didn't want this to come as some sort of bombshell, but she only wanted to be one of the boys up to a point.

In the backseat of Harold Wasserman's stretch Mercedes, Michael said, "I frankly don't see why I couldn't've taken a few more questions. I was on a roll today, Harold."

"Leave them wanting more," Wasserman said. "Sometimes I get the feeling you're not listening to me."

"I am! I am! It's just that I can't hear you if there's any significant background noise."

"You're almost as cute as you think you are, you know that, right?"

"Seriously," Michael said, "you thought it went all right?"

They both knew this drill. Even if Wasserman didn't think so, he was supposed to lie a little.

"You know I don't usually like it if you deviate from the script. But I thought the ending, about them staying loose at courtside, was quite a nice touch, actually."

"And I think your instincts were right about throwing the dykes from the WNBA a bone."

Wasserman's eyes twinkled. "I'm not sure my dear friend Ellen DeGeneres would have put it exactly that way."

"I forget," Michael said, "which tennis player did she go out with?"

Harold Wasserman hit the intercom switch and told his driver to drop him at his office, which was on Fiftieth and

Park, and then take Mr. De la Cruz wherever he wanted to go. But Michael told him, no, he'd get out on Park, too, he could walk the rest of the way to the NBA offices, in the Olympic Tower.

"Marcus has called me ten times today already," Michael said.

Marcus Betts, the commissioner who'd succeeded the guy who'd succeeded David Stern, basically had his job because the players had finally decided they wanted a brother in there instead of somebody who looked like their accountants.

Michael said, "If I don't get over there, he's going to shit a bowling ball."

"I could come with you, if you want."

"I'll be fine. He's just going to want to know why he wasn't consulted, what this does to his precious WNBA, what a field day the media is going to have if she falls on her face, blah blah blah."

"Marcus doesn't understand that you're not supposed to let the media run your life," Wasserman said. "It's the other way around."

"It's why you get the big bucks, my little friend."

"Call me afterward on my private line, in case the secretaries have gone home. I've got a couple of hours before the first-edition deadlines. I want to work the phones a little bit."

De la Cruz saw a look from him he'd seen before, as if Wasserman had already moved on to the next thing he was going to do.

"What are you plotting, Harold?"

"I'm thinking about trying to finesse your friend Mr. Ransome a little bit."

Michael said, "What do you mean *my* friend? Did you read the column? The guy cut me up into more pieces than Russia."

The car had come to a stop on the west side of Park. The driver had the door open at warp speed. Wasserman made no move to get out, just stared at Michael. "You're saying you didn't leak it to him?"

"I just assumed it was you."

"Did you, now?" Harold Wasserman said, trying to sound mysterious.

The two of them sat there, like a couple of kids waiting for the other one to blink first.

Finally Harold Wasserman said, "We all need our secrets."

"Don't we, though?" Michael said.

⏱ eleven

Dee Gerard had a secret.

The first shrink she had ever seen, a Brit friend of Jeremy's with a practice in Paris, had referred to it as a floating anxiety disorder, telling Dee she should think of it as a different kind of cramps, brain cramps, ones that only showed up out of the blue, instead of every month. The shrink, Dr. Asprey, finally recommended yoga as a way of building up what she referred to as Dee's "theatrical immune system."

"I'm a basketball player," Dee told her on their last visit, "not Barbra Streisand."

"You are a performer, same as she is," Dr. Asprey said, getting huffy the way she would when Dee would disagree with her. "As you requested, I came to watch you play, even though I know next to nothing about basketball. But you are most assuredly a performer, Dee, the same as you say your father was. You talk constantly about all the ways he found to sabotage himself, do you not?"

Dee said, "You're saying that's what this is all about?"

"What?"

Dee loved it when she did that. Question with a question.

"That I'm trying to sabotage myself somehow."

Dr. Asprey smiled. "Did I say that?"

Floating anxiety disorder. The other shrink she saw, in Spain, a cute Spanish guy who spoke perfect English and clearly wanted to go out with her, called them random panic attacks. Different wrapping, same package. Dee knew everybody was talking about stage fright. She read up on it, found out about Olivier and Streisand, and Carly Simon, a singer she'd loved in high school because of her voice, and because she was as tall as Dee. They weren't opening-night jitters for Olivier. They weren't every-night jitters, as bad as he could get sometimes. He was well into his run with *Othello* in London, one of the stage triumphs, maybe *the* stage triumph of his whole career, when the director really did have to stuff a Valium in his mouth, literally shove him onstage when it was time to make his entrance.

Dee started telling her teammates she had to be alone before every game, just as a way of hedging her bets if she felt an attack coming on.

"Bill Russell used to throw up before every single game," she told her coach with USV Orchies once. "I just think I'm going to most of the time. But it's not pretty either way."

They'd leave her alone. When it was time for the game, somebody would just come and find her, sometimes in a storage room, if that was the only place where she could get the privacy she needed to go one-on-one with herself.

She got through it most of the time. Once or twice a year, tops, she'd lie about back spasms, just because she had been bothered by back spasms all the way back to DeWitt Clinton.

It wasn't necessarily big games that brought it on, or big crowds. She'd been fine the night Eddie "discovered" her in Stade Louis II. The attacks, her brain cramps, had always blindsided her, from the beginning. It would be a half hour before the game, and all of a sudden there would be one of the trigger things: cotton mouth. Or she'd feel as if somebody had turned up the temperature in the locker room about twenty degrees. Or she'd start to feel as if her legs had fallen asleep. Or her arms.

Sometimes it was as simple as this: She felt as if she'd need a forklift to get her out of her chair in front of her locker.

And no one in the locker room, no one in the whole building, would know that the greatest play she would make all night would be doing just that.

Getting up.

Over time, she started to believe the yoga was really helping, that somehow learning to breathe the right way helped her on those nights when she felt as if she couldn't breathe at all.

The way she couldn't breathe now, fifteen minutes before she was supposed to play what she'd come to think of as *Meet the Full-Court Press*, an hour before the Knights were going to play the Wizards at the Garden.

"I need to take a little walk, get myself together," she said to Eddie in the dressing room that was going to be hers, the one from which the Knights' Streetcorner Dancers had been evicted about an hour before by Michael De la Cruz.

She wondered if her voice sounded as weak and tinny to Eddie as it did to her, as if it were coming from the referees' room next door.

"Sure," Eddie said. He was wearing his usual uniform, except that tonight he had added a knit tie. "We can walk around the back of the court, over to the rotunda on the other side. The Knicks use it when they have an overflow of press sometimes, but it's empty tonight. It's always empty for us, though that may be about to change."

Dee said, "Just give me a couple of minutes alone. Okay?"

"Are you okay?"

"I'm moving up on okay," she said weakly. "I just made a big move off mildly hysterical."

She took a left out the door, walked past the room where she knew they were going to hold the press conference, walked behind the court at the Garden. There was an insanely long limousine parked right there. The vanity plate read "MDLC." For some reason it looked like the name of a rock group, not De la Cruz's initials. She kept the court to her left and then walked through a small door into the dark expanse of the rotunda, which looked big enough and wide enough for another basketball court.

I could set up some chairs, dribble around for a while, she thought.

She was starting to feel dizzy.

Sometimes it was dizzy.

It's what Cool Daddy had always called her mother. Big damn dizzy blonde.

Dee thought: Please, not tonight.

It had happened only with basketball before. No, that wasn't exactly true. It had actually happened on the street in front of the lawyer's office in Nice, before she went up to sign the final divorce papers. When she finally got up there, Jeremy had asked, "What took you?" She'd told him the cab-driver had gotten lost, and she knew he knew she was lying.

Breathe.

She walked past some blue curtains, walking slowly, a drunk trying to walk a straight line. She pictured herself moving like a guy on stilts at the circus. There was an usher coming from the other direction, taking the last puffs of a cigarette. He was wearing a maroon-colored sports jacket that had "Garden Staff" written across the front pocket. Underneath that it said, "John." He nodded at her, smiled. Dee tried to smile back, though even getting her mouth to work right now felt pretty ambitious.

She said, "Ladies' room?"

"Through that door at the end, then take a left."

She walked for what felt like about an hour, found the right door. The room was empty. She walked down to the end of a line of stalls, went inside, latched the door, put the seat down. Sat down.

I'll just spend the rest of the evening in here.

She could see somebody saying across the hall, "Where's this Dee Gerard we've heard so much about?"

"Oh, her? Bathroom."

"When's she coming out?"

"Well, funny you should ask, we're not exactly sure."

Her heart was going like one of those Grand Prix race cars she used to watch in Monte Carlo, turning the postcard town into a video game. She looked down at her clothes: cashmere turtleneck, gray, the sapphire necklace Jeremy had given her for their first anniversary, darker gray slacks, just the bottom of her high black Prada boots showing.

"Dee?"

"Hey, Dee, you in here?"

Eddie. Just by the way his voice sounded, she could tell he was poking his head inside the door, not wanting to come in.

"I'm not here," she said.

The stall door opened.

"I can see that," he said.

"Maybe," Dee was saying to Eddie now, "I finally took a step back, the way a sane, normal person would, a girl with both her feet on the ground, and saw just how absurd this whole thing is. I'm going to play a regular-season game in the NBA in a few days. Right."

He had taken her down a corridor and down some steps, she couldn't even remember how many flights, then through an unmarked door into The Theater, which she couldn't believe was the old Felt Forum, a place that she remembered as smoky and dumpy. Now it looked like some plush, elegant, off-Broadway place. She and Eddie sat on the edge of the stage, legs dangling over the side. Eddie had gotten her to drink a Coke from the concession stand across from the ladies' room. He'd asked if she wanted him to go get something from Joey Shahoud to settle her down. She said no, the last thing she needed was a pill, the way she was wired now there was no telling how her body would react.

So he took her by the hand and said, "C'mon."

She'd noticed the first day, just the way he moved around, that the Garden was like some sort of secret clubhouse for him, full of shortcuts and backdoors and hiding places that only he seemed to know about.

All she knew now was that she just generally felt better about things holding his hand, the way she'd held Cool Daddy's hand when he first started bringing her to the Garden.

On the stage with her, Eddie said, "You got scared. Big deal. It used to happen to me sometimes, especially after I hurt my knee. Even though I was the only one who gave a shit whether I did well or not."

"You didn't get scared like this. This kind of scared and you feel like you're moving about as well as Lady Liberty."

"You're moving fine now, lady." He grinned, trying to keep things light. "Look at you, walking and talking just like a big girl."

Dee said, "I can't do this."

"Which this is that?" Still grinning.

"Any of it. How do I get on that court if I can't even walk across it to answer some stupid questions?"

He picked up her cup and drank some of her Coke. "You'll be fine."

"Do I look fine?"

Eddie said, "I like a sweaty girl. Always did."

She saw him look at his watch, some kind of small-looking antique.

"Think about it," he said. "What's the worst thing that can happen?"

"Other than I make a fool out of myself in front of the whole world?"

"Yeah. Other than that."

He reached inside his jacket, brought out a white handkerchief, made a *May I?* gesture, and gently dabbed at her forehead.

Eddie said, "Say the first question goes something like this: 'Tell us, Miss Gerard, why you of all people, of all the women who have ever played basketball, think you can be the one?' Okay? You can handle that one, no problem. In fact, what you do is, you make a joke out of it. Say Mr. De la Cruz and some dipshit scout, I forget his name, told me we could all make history. What girl wouldn't be a sucker for a line like that?" He shrugged. "I'm just spitballing here, of course."

"And what about this?" Dee said. "What happens if I get one of my little episodes some night when we've got a packed house?"

"We'll do just what we did tonight," Eddie said. She noticed him flexing his knee, grimacing a little. "We'll come over here, and we'll sit awhile, and I'll tell you the story of my life. It's like a mild sedative, I've seen it work on my dates."

He carefully jumped down, extended a hand up to her. "C'mon, we gotta get going."

Dee took his hand, and when she was standing next to him at the base of the stage, he put his arms around her. She put her head into his shoulder. "The story of your life," she said. "Is it any good?"

"There's a few gaps in it."

"Name one."

Eddie said, "I never played the way you're going to, not in the big time."

She pulled back and looked at him.

"Okay, then," she said.

"Okay what?"

"Okay, let's go."

He said, "Not for nothin'?"

Dee waited.

"You smell pretty damn good for a point guard," Eddie said.

The first question came from out of the lights and faces in front of her, so Dee didn't know who asked it. Michael De la Cruz was on her left, Bobby Carlino was on her right. They had both made brief opening statements before De la Cruz introduced Dee.

She pulled the microphone closer to her, looked out at the crowd, and said, "Shoot. But only if you're open."

"I've got to ask you one question right off," the male voice said. "Why do you, Miss Gerard, out of all the women who have ever played basketball, why do *you* think you can be the one?"

A few feet away, Eddie Holtz was leaning against the wall. He looked at Dee and shrugged, trying to act innocent, as if he hadn't set up the first question like a coach setting up the first play of the game.

Dee said, "Michael De la Cruz and Eddie Holtz told me we could all make history. Now let me ask you all something: What girl wouldn't fall for a line like that. . . ?"

There was some laughter in front of her. More flash cameras exploded. She heard what sounded like ten questions shouted at once, saw hands somewhere between the flashes of light and the row of cameras in the back of the room.

Dee thought: Oh, so *this* is what the bottom of the rabbit hole was like for Alice.

◎ twelve

Her first game was network instead of cable.

It turned out there was a clause in NBC's contract with the league that gave them prime-time rights, even during the week—which usually belonged to either TNT or WTBS—for what were described as "extraordinary circumstances and events."

"That would be you, cupcake," Eddie said to her when they read about it in the papers.

They were walking down Fifth Avenue, four o'clock in the afternoon, four hours from when she would make her debut against the Knicks at the Garden. Eddie had called in the morning, asked what time the car should be there. Dee told him she wanted to leave at four and he'd said that was awfully early, it gave her way too much time to sit around and stew on things. She'd said, Stew? And he said so sue him, it was one of his mother's expressions.

"Let's walk over," she said.

"You sure you want to?" Eddie asked. "You're famous now."

"I'll have to risk it."

So they walked. When they got tired of walking on Fifth, past the big Presbyterian church on Fifty-fifth, past a huge NBA store she didn't even know existed, what looked like the Bloomingdale's of basketball, they took a right on Forty-seventh Street. At least the diamond district was still where it had always been.

"I just want to see where my teammates like to shop," she explained to Eddie.

If anybody recognized her, just off all the coverage of the past few days, they didn't let on. Besides, Eddie had told her the strict rules of celebrity strolling in New York City. One, keep moving. Two, no eye contact ever. Dee said she thought she'd have it down by the time they got to Seventh. She was wearing her new camel topcoat over her sweats; she'd bought it at Bergdorf the day before, since the temperature had refused to move out of the thirties since she'd been in town. She'd bought herself an old-style Brooklyn Dodgers baseball cap at the New York Yankees clubhouse store a couple of blocks from the Sherry, a pair of new Armani sunglasses.

They had eluded the media waiting out in front of the hotel by coming out the service entrance of the Sherry on Fifty-ninth Street, a little door next to one of those places where you bought airline tickets, facing FAO Schwarz. It didn't hurt that Eddie had Melissa, Michael De la Cruz's secretary, dress up in Knights sweats, a Knights baseball cap, her own wrap-around sunglasses, then come out of the Sherry's revolving doors about a quarter to four and start sprinting north on Fifth like a hotel guest out for her afternoon run. Melissa didn't look anything like Dee, but the Knights cap was pulled down tight enough to the sunglasses and she was the right size; Eddie knew some of them would follow her for at least a few blocks.

"Follow the ball," he said when they came out the service entrance and walked the other way on Fifth.

Dee said, "That's my game."

She had made it to game day somehow, as if she'd washed up on it after some wild storm that had begun nine days ago at Stade Louis II. The last forty-eight hours, Mo Jiggy had run most of the interference for her, even with Michael De la Cruz when it came time for her to sign her contract. Dee had originally thought she wanted to sit in, just out of curiosity, when they did that in De la Cruz's office, the day after her press conference. But then she watched, nearly in horror, as the two of them, her new agent and her owner, turned into a couple of dogs in heat.

Bitches in heat, she thought, even if she knew it would kill both of them to hear that.

De la Cruz wanted to sign her to a contract for the rest of the season, one that gave him an option on next season as well.

Mo laughed and told him they just wanted one of those ten-day contracts NBA teams used on scrubs from the minor leagues when somebody got hurt.

"This is my show, dammit!" De la Cruz yelled at Mo.

"Yeah," Mo said, "I can see that would be your thinkin'."

"You don't trust me? That hurts me, Mo, I just want you to know that. That hurts my heart."

"That's what your white record producers always told me."

"What, I'm The Man all of a sudden?"

"Just looking out for my wo-*man*," Mo said.

"I'm not . . .*white*!" De la Cruz sputtered. "I'm practically from . . . *the barrio*, for God's sake."

Dee left them there. When she and Eddie got to Forty-seventh and Sixth now, she giggled, remembering De la Cruz trying to act as if he and Mo were brothers of different colors.

Eddie said, "What's so funny?"

"Men, bless your hearts."

"At some point, you've got to get past that."

"I'm trying," she said. "God knows I'm trying."

She made them take a right, go out of their way, because she remembered she hadn't been past Radio City Music Hall. Eddie asked if Mo had finally settled the fight between *60 Minutes, Dateline, 20/20, and PrimeTime*, which had gotten uglier in the newspapers than a border war.

"We went with Barbara Walters, whatever of those shows she's on," Dee said. "The agreement is that we don't have to do the interview right away. But they do get to follow me around with what they say will be a small crew. Though I have to admit, I don't know what small crew means, exactly."

"Me neither," Eddie said. "But I hear these big network women always lie about the size of their crews."

Mo had also negotiated a preliminary book deal with Putnam, though he said that the shylocks from a couple of the other important houses weren't throwing in the towel just yet. Dee said she couldn't believe they would just sign her to a contract on spec, she hadn't even played yet. Mo said to her, "What's that shit got to do with anything?" Dee wanted to know if she'd have to keep a diary of her innermost thoughts, and Mo said, "Hell no, we'll hire a guy to give you some deep-type thoughts later."

They had walked the three blocks to Radio City by now. Dee stood under the marquee, smiling from ear to ear like a tourist posing for a photograph. She told Eddie she had only been inside once in her life, for a concert featuring Ruth Brown, Sarah Vaughan, Aretha, Gladys Knight, even Ella for a couple of songs at the very end.

"If you were writing today up in your diary, what would you say?" Eddie said.

"If I wrote today," Dee said, "the page would look like some polygraph test gone horribly wrong."

"It's like I keep telling you. Scared is okay, as long—"

"As long as I don't turn into Carrie at the prom."

"It's not exactly the movie I would have gone with."

"How about we talk about something else?" Dee said.

They crossed over to Seventh on Forty-second Street, a huge billboard of Chris Rock facing them as they came up on Times Square, the big ESPN restaurant on their right. Then they took a left on Seventh and walked south on the parts of it that still looked to her like Fashion Avenue until they could see the Garden marquee between Thirty-third and Thirty-first. The very first message Dee saw was this:

DEE GERARD
TONIGHT
8 P.M.
SOLD OUT

They walked past the marquee and down to Thirty-first so they could enter once again through the Four Penn entrance. Mo was waiting there for them with a TV crew of his own, one he said was from his production company, Toe Tag, Inc. There were also two posse guys Dee had only heard about, Denzell and Montell.

Montell was holding the leash on two rottweilers.

"Regis and Kathie Lee, right?" Eddie said. "I've heard of them."

Mo said, "We had to put Kathie Lee down, she was so damn mean she was even starting to scare the other dogs. And Regis, he nearly was another dog sent to heaven, after that episode at the Grammys."

"What episode?" Dee asked.

"Don't ask," Mo said.

"The cop provoked them, is the last thing I'm gonna say," Denzell said.

"Anyway," Mo said, "these two here are Bill and Hillary."

Dee said, "I thought the only authorized crew was from *20/20*. Isn't that what you said you and Michael agreed to?"

"Michael's not the boss of me," Mo said.

Bill and Hillary led the way into the Garden. Mo and Eddie and Dee were behind them.

"So," Mo said to Eddie, "how the girl doin'?"

Eddie Holtz said, "Oh, right. Today's the day I finally learn how to read women."

She put on a gray T-shirt, kept her warm-up slacks on, went out to shoot around by herself about six o'clock. Anquwan and Dream Jackson were already out there, practicing long jumpers at the Eighth Avenue end. Even two hours before the game, the court was completely ringed by media, two rows deep. When Dee made her way through them, she was instantly greeted by the Fourth of July light show that had been greeting her for days, at least when she wasn't able to give them all the dodge the way she and Eddie had leaving the hotel.

Up in the crowd, she saw signs being held up already, every one of them by what looked to be teenaged girls.

You Dee Wo-Man!

Go, Girl

You are woman, hear the Garden roar

You've Got Ball!

A girl, almost Dee's height, skinny as a swizzle stick in her blue Nike warm-up suit, very pretty, somehow had wedged herself in between a couple of camera crews under the basket with a sign that simply read: "My Hero."

She caught Dee's eye and held up a Magic Marker. Dee motioned her to come out to where she was at the free-throw line. A security guy she knew already, a green blazer instead of the maroon the ushers wore, started to gently put an arm out, but Dee said, "Jimmy, it's okay, let her come."

The girl walked out slowly, one small step at a time, as if walking through some kind of minefield.

Which, Dee thought, she probably was.

"Hey," Dee said, shaking the girl's free right hand, "Dee Gerard. What's your name?"

"Sharmayne. Sharmayne Brown."

"You must be a player."

"Varsity," she said. "Clinton."

Dee smiled. "Hey! I was Clinton, too."

Sharmayne, showing her the whitest of white teeth, said, "I know." Ducked her head and said, "I mean, I know, like, everything about you now."

Dee signed the poster. "How'd you get tickets? I heard this thing is sold out."

"Our coach got 'em somehow, through the Ticketmaster, I think." The girl looked down shyly and said, "Play good. We're counting on you."

"We?"

Sharmayne Brown said, "All the girls."

A male television reporter, his blond hair piled on top of his head like lemon pudding, called out from under the basket, "Hey! Hey, Dee? Could you and the kid pose in this direction?"

Dee repositioned Sharmayne so that her back was to the guy and then said, "No, thank you," motioned to Anquwan for the ball, swished a little push shot, told Sharmayne she'd do her best, and jogged toward her dressing room.

Keep moving, she told herself.

No eye contact.

Dee had actually seen the dressing room on television first, the night before, on *Access Hollywood*. Michael De la Cruz was conducting a tour for a blond woman who looked like one of the Streetcorner Dancers De la Cruz had kicked out of their digs so they could remodel the place for Dee; it reminded Dee of that old show she used to think of as "Lifestyles of the Rich and Incredibly Lame." De la Cruz was showing off the giant-screen television, the tiny Jacuzzi, the matching antique sofa and chair that looked exactly like the Louis XIVs Dee had seen in his office, in the same shade of green; and the private shower, walk-in closet, massage table, laptop and printer, stereo system.

None of which Dee had asked for, though that never came up in the interview.

"Turned this broom closet over in three days!" De la Cruz said. "Of course, things go pretty smoothly when your construction foreman is the guy we like to call The Donald!"

"The Donald who?" Dee had said to the television. "Duck?"

The reporter then said in a breathless voice, "How do the other players feel about this star treatment for Miss Gerard?"

De la Cruz said, "Bambi, they all feel the way I do: Anything that makes Dee feel as if this is her new home is fine with them."

Dee decided she had met a lot of bullshitters in her life, most of them male, but that they were all going for the silver medal from now on. De la Cruz had locked up the gold.

Back inside what she was already thinking of as her personal massage parlor, Dee popped a cassette of the Knicks' last game, against the Cleveland Cavaliers, into the VCR attached to the big screen, wanting to see a little more of their offense, checking out the tendencies of their point guard, Pooh Bear Moriarty, who brought whole new dimensions, she thought, to the expression "black Irish," even if he did have orange hair. Pooh Bear liked to go to his right, would never make a simple pass when he could turn the play into some kind of elaborately choreographed dance video, and was a worse jump shooter than Dee. He also had quicker hands than the guys she used to see dealing cards outside The Legal Aid Society building, across the street from the Franklin Square Apartments.

Back when she first dreamed about playing here, she'd imagined herself wearing a Knicks uniform. Or maybe Celtics green, when her father first got her worked up about Cousy. Tonight it would be the old-school Knights home uniform, white with deep purple numbers and letters, No. 14 on the back underneath "Gerard," just "New York" and a smaller 14 on the front. She turned off Pooh Bear and the Knicks now and got into her white sports bra and uniform jersey and shorts. She liked the shorts baggy, just not as baggy as the young guys in the league did these days, their shorts looking more like old-fashioned bloomers. Joey Shahoud had made sure they were exactly right, bringing in a couple of different sizes he said he'd ordered special for her.

Once she was dressed, she sat down on the floor, assumed the lotus position she used for yoga, as dumb as it made her feel, closed her eyes, breathed deeply and slowly, imagining the air pouring into her as slowly as syrup, letting it out just as slowly. Then again. Thinking good thoughts now. Basketball thoughts. Thinking of the look on Sharmayne Brown's face. Dee had been on red alert all day, waiting for the first signs of the yips, even a full-out attack of them. There was nothing, not all day, not now, just the good pregame jitters she got most of the time; she just hadn't had them in a while because she hadn't played a real game for a while.

These were good nerves, she thought.

Good girl.

Cool Daddy's girl tonight, for better or worse.

His basketball girl.

Eddie had told her he was going to leave her alone, he'd see her after, he'd be sitting with Michael De la Cruz right next to where the radio announcers called the game, to her right and right above her as she came out of the tunnel to the court. Dee told Eddie to tell De la Cruz she'd see him after the game, as well, just not before, she didn't need any pep talks or any of his motivational speeches. Eddie said he'd pass that along in a slightly edited version.

At seven-fifteen there was a knock on the door. Dee said it was open, and Joey Shahoud poked his head in.

"You ready?" he said.

"Number fourteen in your program," Dee said.

Joey said, "Number one in the hearts of decent people everywhere. Most of them being of your female variety."

"What about the boys on the other team?"

"Are you kidding?" Joey said. "They probably plan to treat you with about the same respect they do sportswriters."

"Well," Dee said. "Screw 'em if they can't take a joke. Isn't that what you guys like to say?"

"Close enough," Joey said.

In the hall, he extended his palm discreetly, and Dee slapped him a smooth low-five. Up ahead, Dee could see the rest of the Knights waiting near the entrance to the court, banging chests and various body parts. Even back here, she could hear the *thump-thump-thump* of the rap music blaring over the Garden sound system.

"Good luck," he said.

From inside, she could hear the p.a. announcer yelling, "And now . . . yourrrrrrr New York Knights. . . ."

"Just a game, right?" Dee said, taking one more deep, cleansing breath.

"Well," Joey Shahoud said, "not exactly."

She got into the back of the line her teammates had formed. The back of the bus, she thought briefly. Then Dee ran into all the light, all the noise.

⚪ thirteen

It was halftime, and the Knicks had a 57–50 lead on the Knights.

She hadn't played yet.

Other than that, the evening was going swimmingly.

Diana Ross, looking pretty good for a woman of ninety, Dee observed, had sung the national anthem. Then, after the Knights' starters were introduced, the p.a. announcer asked for a big Madison Square Garden welcome for the "the newest—annnnnnnnnnnd prettiest—member of the Knights' family . . . Deeeeeeeeeeeee Gerard!" Sounding a lot like that game show announcer who used to tell contestants to "Come on dowwwwwwwwn!"

Maybe this was some kind of weird game show, more than just a game, where she was the contestant who'd been selected from the studio audience, the one trying to win valuable prizes.

Dee took a couple of steps toward half-court, where she was greeted by an ovation that seemed to swallow her up, one the newspapers would say lasted nearly two minutes. She made a couple of quick turns, smiling, waving to both sides of the court, then finally put a finger to her lips and pointed toward where the players were lined up, waiting for the ref, a small red-haired guy she'd heard some of the players call Buddy, to throw the ball up and start the game. A nice way of saying, Enough already. Then she sat down at the end of the bench, where the anonymous player quoted in that shit Walt Ransome's column had said she would sit.

And stayed right there.

Joey Shahoud was down there with her, making a constant stream of observations as he kept track of fouls and time-outs, as funny and bitchy about everybody as if they were sitting under adjacent dryers at the hairdresser's.

Occasionally the crowd would start chanting her name— *"Dee! Dee! Dee!"*—as if only using the first half of the famous Garden chant she remembered, the one about *DEE-fense!* The chants, she noticed, got a lot louder when the Knights fell behind by ten points early in the second quarter, against the Knick team currently leading the division they shared, the Atlantic. The Knights were in fifth place in the Atlantic. Dee never even bothered looking at how many games they were behind; she knew the number would actually make her teeth hurt.

She heard the first boos for the Knights when Pooh Bear Moriarty stole the ball from Deltha Lewis for the third time, boogied his way in for an uncontested shot, elevated in an amazing way on his short bow legs, and resoundingly dunked the ball. When Deltha picked up his third foul a minute later, frustrated at getting beaten by Pooh Bear again, Dee could feel herself start breathing faster—these were the good nerves, she told herself now, no problem, *normal* ones— thinking Carlino was going to call her name when he leaned forward and looked down the bench.

"Ray Ray," he snapped, "get in there for my dead-assed point guard."

"Now, goddammit!"

Eddie was afraid Michael De la Cruz was going to burst into tears if Bobby Carlino didn't get Dee into the game soon. Or De la Cruz was going to do what he occasionally did on the rare occasions when the Knights attracted a decent crowd, maybe even gave one of the league's better teams a decent game: run up and down behind the bench in the black Knights sweatshirt he liked to wear to games, and start jumping around like the team mascot, exhorting the fans with a lot of hyper arm-waving at the same time.

When he got really juiced, he would make sure the ushers and waiters down near the court would give him enough room, usually during a time-out, then give himself a running start to do the kind of cartwheel the pasty-faced midget girls did in the Olympics.

He wasn't doing any cartwheels now.

Deltha Lewis, back in the game for only a couple of minutes, had just had the ball stolen from him for what seemed like about the twentieth time, and both Eddie and De la Cruz could see how twitchy Bobby Carlino was.

De la Cruz said, "He's got to put her in now, doesn't he?"

Eddie didn't say anything right away; he was watching Dee watch Carlino from where she was still sitting at the end of the bench. You learned early in basketball, starting with the first team you ever played on at the Y, that you couldn't beg your way into a game with your eyes, that it wasn't cool even to try. But even Dee was leaning forward now, as if sure this had to be the time.

Now, Eddie said to himself, not wanting to encourage De la Cruz, get him more agitated than he already was.

Put her in the game, you stubborn, evil little shit.

Only, both he and De la Cruz watched as Ray Ray Abdul-Mahi, adjusting the new fiberglass mask for his broken nose that made him look like a scuba diver, stood up, casually stepped out of the warm-up slacks that unsnapped on the sides as soon as you gave them a little pull.

Next to Eddie, Michael De la Cruz stuck out his lower lip and blew up a jetstream of air, actually making his bangs move a little. Usually that would only happen in some kind of gale-force wind.

"Okay, that's it, he has to fucking die," De la Cruz said. "The only question is whether I kill him fast or torture him first." He nodded. "We could talk to Mo. Right? Those rap stars know more shooters than there are in war movies."

Eddie said, "He must be saving her for the early part of the second half, that's the only thing I can figure. If it's close, he's not going to wait and throw her in there in the fourth. It's gotta be a couple of minutes into the third."

"You're sure of that, huh? Maybe I just go into the suck-up suite at halftime, make an announcement to Oprah and the Whoopster and Rosie and *Senator Hillary* that I am not the asshole they are probably thinking I am and that they have not wasted a trip over here because my shit-for-brains coach might actually put in the *only player they want to fucking see* in a little while. If we're lucky, that is."

He grabbed his purple towel then, the one he liked to wave when a ref made a call against the Knights, or just to draw even more attention to himself, and started chewing on it, a baby with a pacifier. As he did, Eddie could see him doing that little eye-dart thing he did, seeing if there were any roving cameras in the vicinity.

A voice behind them said, "There be some kind of Metropolitan Opera–like grand design here from that cocksucker that nobody told me or my client about?"

Mo. He had made his way over from the other side of the court, once he realized Eddie had his cell turned off.

De la Cruz said, "I have nothing to do with this, believe me."

Mo Jiggy said, "You know that dumb-ass song they play at games now, 'bout letting the damn dogs out? Your coach don't get my girl in the game soon, I'm gonna let *my* dogs out."

Eddie said he'd hold Bobby Carlino down for Bill and Hillary, Mo could apply the steak sauce.

With Ray Ray running the offense, the Knights proceeded to cut the Knicks' lead down to five points and could have gotten to within a basket right before the first half horn sounded, except that Jamie Lawton, part of the group that brought the Knights back, missed a wide-open three-point jumper from in front of where Dee noticed Whoopi Goldberg cheering wildly between Dan Rather and Alec Baldwin.

Michael wanted to go down to the locker room at halftime, or at least wait in the hall for Bobby Carlino to come out, just so he could ask him—calmly and rationally, he promised Eddie—just what his thinking was here, exactly.

Eddie told him the last thing they needed at this point was a shot on television of him and his coach looking like they were getting ready to tango.

The two of them were in a private room off Suite 400, where the celebrities came to schmooze before the second half started and do so much hugging and backslapping it reminded Eddie of all the banging the players did to each other and with each other during the player introductions, when they looked as if adrenaline had turned them into human bumper cars. Michael was a toucher, but not like some of these people. Christ, wasn't Diane Von Furstenberg married again?

Michael knew Eddie couldn't possibly be as composed, as put-together, as he was trying to act, but this was part of their routine, the big-brother routine they'd tried to explain to Dee, Eddie was the cool older brother. The sensible one. Even though Michael was the one with all the money.

Eddie said, "If I take a step back and look at that big picture you're always talking about, it's fair to say that one of the things we're trying to do with Dee is generate some goodwill. Am I right?"

"I don't want to be overly dramatic . . . ," Michael said.

"Right," Eddie said. "We wouldn't want that."

"But we happen to have the *eyes of the whole frigging world watching this basketball game!*" Michael said. "They want to see a girl play with the boys. Only, one of the boys won't let her play."

"I'm aware of that."

"Are you?" Michael said. "Are you really? I've got crews from Japan here. I've got more celebs in the house than the Knicks get for the playoffs. I've got Brokaw, Rather, and Jennings *in the same room.*" Michael started to say something else, then took a couple of deep breaths because his heart rate suddenly felt as if it should have commas in it. He put out his hands, as a way of showing Eddie he was trying to stay calm. "I am more in play with this team than I have ever been."

"It's the biggest night we've ever had," Eddie said.

"Not if she doesn't fucking play, it's not!"

"He'll play her eventually. He's got to play her. Bobby's pigheaded. But he's not suicidal, at least not that I've noticed."

"You're telling me he'll put her in this quarter?"

"That's what I'm telling you."

From outside, they could hear the blast of the horn that meant the second half was about to start. They walked past the door to the press room. Walt Ransome, built like the water cooler right behind him, came out wearing a black sports jacket and black shirt. Matching the color of his soul, Michael decided.

"Hey, owner," Walt Ransome said. "You know I'm no literary type, right?"

"Gee, Walt," Michael said, smiling as if this were some kind of joke between them. "I hadn't noticed."

"But when did this big promotion of yours turn into *Waiting for Godot*?"

Was "God-it" the way you pronounced it? Michael couldn't remember. He'd have to ask Melissa at the office tomorrow, she'd majored in theater arts at NYU and had always acted snooty around him, until the first time he'd asked her to lock the door, he had something he wanted to show her.

It was funny how many of them loosened up with the boss when the door was locked and both sex and career advancement made the air in the big office so thick and heavy.

Ransome got no reaction out of Michael, so he just made the snorting sound that passed for laughter with him, as if he'd cracked himself up with the God-it line, then walked off, shaking his head. Michael and Eddie continued on down to their seats, some of the fans calling out Michael's name, others reaching out from aisle seats to slap him five. "When's she getting off the bench?" a suit yelled from the next section over from theirs.

Michael said, "We wanted to make sure she made an entrance."

The suit, a tall plastic glass of beer in his hands, looking to Michael like a Wall Street asshole for sure, said, "Just make sure it's before we all start heading for the exit."

Michael thought: Or you could head out now, dickhead.

Bobby Carlino was fairly subdued at halftime, surprising Dee, reminding her somewhat of an animal who had been sedated as part of a lab experiment.

He told the Knights their effort was better than they'd shown him in a month, wondering out loud if they'd all gotten off the weed at once.

"It must be the big crowd and all the cel-*eb*-rities," he said in a singsong voice, "getting you guys more excited than fairies in the school play."

Then he showed them a couple of plays he said might help them break the press against Pooh Bear, whom he called "that toilet plunger" because of the orange hair.

Right before they went back out to warm up, he said, "I'm going to make one change, at point."

He paused before wiping the greaseboard clean and then said, "So it's the same five who started, 'cept for Deltha. Ray Ray, you stay out there, we've got a little momentum going."

The Knights stood up, Dee along with them.

"Hey!" Bobby Carlino said. "In case you've forgotten, we haven't beaten these pantloads in two years."

He looked directly at Dee then. "How about we show them tonight's *our* night?" he said. "How would that be?"

Midway through the third quarter, the Knicks, led by Pooh Bear Moriarty and the team's All-Star forward Shlomo (Bad) Levine, had stretched their lead out to fifteen points, 80–65. It was here that the people in the Garden, as if on cue, rose to their feet and began to chant, *"We want Dee!"*

They chanted through a television time-out, kept chanting even as the Knights scored eight points in a row to get back into the game, Anquwan Posey making a couple of steals and

Carl Anthony getting a couple of put-backs after Jamie Lawton missed shots.

"We want Dee!"

Michael spotted a cameraman and sound guy from the Madison Square Garden network coming right for him, stopping in the aisle about three feet from his seat, putting the camera and boom mike on him like spotlights.

His good side, too.

Michael jumped up and began chanting along with everybody else.

On the other side of the court, he saw that Mo Jiggy, flanked by two of his hoody rap gunsels in their wool stocking caps, had turned his back to the game and was waving his arms like an orchestra conductor, using his rolled-up souvenir game program as a baton.

Now the Knicks called a time-out, trying to slow the Knights down, trying to get the crowd out of the game a little. But this wasn't about the game now. The Knights were going good and the place was alive and they wanted it all to get better now, get a real look at Dee Gerard. See what they'd come to see. Michael mugged for the camera a little more, pumping his fist with every word, as if throwing hooks into his heavy bag.

"We . . . want . . . Dee!"

Down below him, he saw Bobby Carlino step out of his huddle, look up in his direction, smile at him, and nod.

Michael hadn't seen any contact of any kind between his coach and Dee Gerard all night, but now Carlino walked over to her, seemed to be whispering something in her ear.

Finally, Michael thought.

Finally, finally, finally.

"You know what's great?" Carlino said to Dee, gesturing toward the stands. "These assholes always think they can coach better than me."

She didn't say anything, or even look at him, wondering where he was going with this.

"Hip New York basketball fans, my *ass*," he said.

She had figured out by now, without him saying anything, without any of the other players saying anything, that he wasn't going to play her. Even knowing how important this was to Michael De la Cruz. Even after the ridiculous, insane buildup of the last couple of days.

Now Dee turned, saw Carlino smirking at her, as if he'd been waiting for her to see the look.

"Some night, huh?" he said, then pushed his way into the circle of players, shouting to be heard, telling them to keep doing what they were doing, the Knicks were getting tired. Then he clapped his hands together and told them he was staying with the same five who'd been out there—Carl, Anquwan, Ray Ray, Dream Jackson, Jamie Lawton.

Through it all, the fans in the Garden kept chanting, the way she'd heard them chant for the Knicks when she was a kid.

Only, now it was for her.

"We want Dee!"

When she sat back down, Joey Shahoud said to her, "Well, it's always nice to be wanted by someone."

Michael De la Cruz was on his way down to the court before Eddie realized what was happening.

I never was quick enough, Eddie thought, even with good knees.

"That's it" was the last thing Eddie heard from him.

Eddie Holtz watched now, fascinated, not having any idea what was coming next, as De la Cruz took the last three steps before the courtside seats in a leap, ran down the aisle behind them, then took the steps down to the court level, the place where the players came out of the tunnel, in another leap.

Everything seemed to happen at once then. The chanting for Dee stopped briefly. There was a brief roar from the crowd, a thunderclap, there and gone, as Carl Anthony took a backdoor pass from Dream Jackson, up-faked a couple of times, banked home a layup, bringing the Knights to within four points, 82–78.

The press table at the Garden was in three sections, the

biggest opening at midcourt where the players entered if they didn't want to walk all the way down to the bench areas. De la Cruz made his way through that opening, the p.a. announcer on his right, the stat crew on his left, all of them looking up now, surprised to see him, ignoring the action on the court.

Eddie Holtz figured that was all right, since Eddie was pretty sure that the real action now was Michael De la Cruz.

Dee saw him coming before Bobby Carlino did.

"Call a time-out," De la Cruz said, making sure he was heard over the crowd.

Carlino was standing up in front of his chair, arms folded, watching the Knights run the set play he'd just called at the Seventh Avenue end of the Garden, down to his left.

"Bobby!" De la Cruz said. "Look at me. I said call time."

Carlino did what Dee thought was a rather classic double take, turning and seeing De la Cruz, quickly turning back to the court, then turning back to the owner, as if he couldn't believe his eyes.

In a quiet voice, Dee said to Deltha Lewis and Dong Li, "Would you guys mind if I just skooch down a little here?"

"What is the skooch?" Dong said.

"Move, spring roll," Deltha said, and the two of them got up and Dee slid behind them, closer to De la Cruz and Bobby Carlino, so she could hear.

"What the fuck?" was the first thing she heard Carlino say.

De la Cruz took a step closer and poked him in the chest. Off to her right, Dee saw all this movement underneath the Eighth Avenue basket, as all the photographers suddenly shifted their cameras away from the game like it was all one synchronized move, and focused on what was happening at the end of the Knights' bench.

Bad Levine had just fouled Anquwan, who was stepping to the line to shoot two free throws.

"Call time, or I will," De la Cruz said. "We're officially done screwing around here."

"I'm coaching a goddamn game here, for Chrissakes!" Bobby Carlino said.

The redhead ref, Buddy, holding the game ball under his arms, came walking over.

"Um, I hate to interrupt," he said, "but owners on the court during games is sort of frowned on over the league office. They sort of decided that a few years ago with that perky Mr. Cuban of the Mavericks."

"Back off, Sparky," De la Cruz said.

"Buddy," the ref said.

"Whatever. I need a second here."

"You're gonna get fined for this, Mr. De la Cruz," Buddy said. "I just want you to know that."

"I've got a billion dollars in the bank. Buddy, is it? So I'll just have to risk it, if that's okay with you."

Buddy made a little circle with his thumb and forefinger and said, "Ten-four."

Dee noticed it had gotten very quiet at the Garden all of a sudden, after the runway sound of the last few minutes.

"First you call time out," De la Cruz said. "Then you put her in the game, you worthless piece of shit."

"I told you I'm working here," Carlino said, not backing down at all, getting up in Michael De la Cruz's face the way he would with Buddy the ref.

De la Cruz turned away from him and yelled out toward where the Knights were standing in a group, as mesmerized by the scene as everybody else.

"One of you guys call a time-out."

"I'm the coach!" Carlino was yelling out there himself now. "I . . . am . . . the . . . coach. I call the time-outs."

When Dee replayed the whole night in her mind afterward, she decided her very favorite part came next.

De la Cruz said to Carl Anthony, "What's your contract status there, Carl?"

"Dollars or years or both, yo?"

"Both."

"This year at four-five."

Dee actually thought she detected a tiny smile crack Carl

Anthony's prison-yard face, there and gone, like an almost imperceptible shift in a rock formation.

Tonight Carl's hair read "Lethal," and what seemed to be "Injection" underneath in much smaller script, though Dee couldn't say for sure.

"Plus an option," Carl added.

"Whose option?"

"Yours."

"How about you call time out for me?" De la Cruz said.

Carl Anthony turned to the ref closest to him, a fat little black guy with Uncle Ben white hair, and made an emphatic time-out motion, slamming his right palm into the upraised fingers of his left hand.

Everybody on the bench stayed put. The five on the court came walking slowly over, giving a wide berth to the owner of the Knights and their coach, as if the two of them were standing in the middle of an oil spill.

De la Cruz said, "Dee, go in for Ray Ray."

"Ray Ray!" Carlino said. "Stay where you are."

De la Cruz said to him, "Why are you doing this? Can you at least explain that to me?"

"All I am doing here," Carlino said, "is giving *my* team its best chance to win *this* game. Which is exactly what my contract says I'm supposed to do."

"Put her in."

"Fuck you, you don't tell me who to play. I figured tonight was as good a night as any to remind you of that."

"Uh, either one of you can handle this one. I'll just throw it out there," Buddy the ref said. "Would this be a full time-out or just a twenty-second?"

"You're fired," De la Cruz said to Carlino. Then he smiled and said, "With cause, of course."

"What cause?"

"Insubordination," De la Cruz said. Smiling even more broadly now, as if a great load had suddenly been lifted from him.

"You can't fire me during the game," Carlino said.

"Watch me. Either leave on your own or I get security to drag you out," Michael De la Cruz said.

Then added, "You fucking fuck."

Dee heard the crowd start to clap rhythmically now, the way crowds did sometimes in Europe when there'd be an unexpected delay in a game, a malfunction with the clock, or something wrong with the basket. Down at the other end, all of the Knicks players had stepped away from their own bench area, moving out onto the court far enough so they could get a better look at Michael De la Cruz and Bobby Carlino.

Next to her, Deltha Lewis let out a low wolf whistle. "New Yawk, New Yawk," he said. "Sound so nice they named a bitch twice."

Carlino turned to the players on the bench and said, "You believe this shit? Over *her*?"

"Last time," De la Cruz said. "Beat it, or we give everybody more of a photo op than they already have."

Dee knew what was happening here, because it was the same thing that always happened when it was boy on boy. Bobby Carlino was figuring out a way to make his exit and save face at the same time.

Finally he said, "Go ahead, asshole, coach the team yourself if you want. It's what you've always wanted." Then he put out his arm, moving De la Cruz out of the way even though he had the whole court to his right, acting like a little hard guy to the end.

A little hard something, anyway, Dee thought wickedly to herself.

Carlino walked down, shook hands with a couple of Knicks players, waved one way to the crowd, then the other, getting a small cheer. A couple of fans behind the Knicks bench shook his hand. Then he took a right turn, heading toward where the locker rooms were. But before he did, he managed to do something that would give both the *News* and *Post* pretty dramatic back pages the next day.

Shot Michael De la Cruz the finger.

Joey Shahoud had wedged himself in between Dee and Deltha Lewis. Dee turned to him and said, "I can't believe how much this reminds me of Jane Austen."

It was Carl Anthony, the team captain, who finally stepped forward, urged by Buddy the ref, and put a hand on Michael

De la Cruz's shoulder. De la Cruz's circuits were running so
hot and exposed, he actually jumped.

"Need a coach, yo," he said. "You want to go with one of
the assistants, just for the rest of the game?"

"Nah."

It had gotten quiet again now that Carlino was gone, everybody wanting to see what was going to happen next.

De la Cruz turned to where his seats were, up there next to
Bert Sharp, the ancient play-by-play man he'd hired away
from the Lakers, somebody so loud Dee could actually hear
him during the game occasionally, no matter how raucous the
crowd, or how loud they were playing rock-and-roll music
during a time-out.

"Hey, Eddie!" he yelled. "You busy for the next hour or
so?"

⚾ fourteen

In the huddle, Eddie calmly said, "Okay, floor show's over. Same five."

Ray Ray said, "Which five, yo? Man just said—"

"The five that was out there," Eddie said. "But Anquwan, you switch with Ray Ray and play up top on the zone. Ray? If they stay in man, which I think they will, next time down, run that isolation play we've got, whatever the hell it's called. And Carl? If Pooh Bear does get past Anquwan, makes that little crossover move he's been using to pinch to the line? Before he makes the pass to the wing, knock him on his fuckin' ass one time, okay?"

"Pleasure," Carl Anthony said.

Dee thought: He acts as if he's been coaching the Knights since the first day of training camp. Or maybe his whole life. Dee was afraid it was going to be like a substitute teacher showing up in the bad-boy class, but there was something about him, the way he got right down to business, none of the bullshit they were used to from Bobby Carlino, that seemed to make them all shut up and listen.

She figured he'd get around to telling her when she was

going to play, but now wasn't the time to ask. Eddie, knowing he had their attention, was busy coaching his team.

"Wouldn't it be a kick in the ass if we won this sonofabitch?" he said.

Dee would find out the next day that the real-time delay in the game, from the time De la Cruz showed up on the court until play resumed, was eight minutes. Eddie would tell the press afterward that it seemed longer to him than college.

Anquwan still had two free throws coming to him. As Buddy the ref reminded everybody of that and shooed them back down toward the Knights' basket, he said, "Okay, everybody promise to play nice the rest of the way?"

Eddie motioned for Dee to sit next to him. They both watched as Bad Levine, one of the few white guys since Larry Bird to average twenty points and ten rebounds a game, even Dee knew that, missed a long jumper. Jamie Lawton got the rebound. Ray Ray immediately called for the play Eddie had told him to run. He threw it to Anquwan, who turned on Pooh Bear Moriarty and made about a ten-foot jumper and the game was tied.

"I'm putting you in with two minutes left in the quarter," he said.

Dee looked up at the giant scoreboard hanging over the court like a spaceship. He was talking about two minutes of game time from right now. "You okay with that?" Eddie said.

"Me?" Dee said. "Oh, I'm fine. You can't believe how many times we fired coaches during games in Europe. It was practically a regular feature over there. Until, you know, they started to run out of coaches."

In front of them, Carl Anthony and Bad Levine went for the same rebound and Bad Levine ended up spray-painted to the basket support.

Dee said, "How about you? You good and loose here?"

"You know me," he said, "I just try to go with the flow."

Dee said she had noticed that.

"This wasn't part of some script, right?" she said.

"You think that?"

"No," she said, "I don't."

"Be very careful around Pooh Bear," he said. "Take care of the ball like you're guarding your virtue."

Dee started to say something back, about how her virtue had gone the minute she signed on for this duty, except the Knicks called time now and she looked up at the clock and saw there was 2:05 left in the quarter and Eddie was saying to her, "Showtime at the Apollo."

Dee managed to stay on her feet for almost ten whole seconds.

Eddie told them to stay in the 1-3-1 zone they'd been using, with Dee chasing out at the top. So she chased as Pooh Bear threw it over her head to Bad Levine, who then passed it right back to Pooh Bear. Dee followed the ball back to him. Pooh Bear then made the crossover dribble, left hand to right, Eddie had talked about in the huddle. As soon as he did, Dee was on him, moving with him, trying to beat him to his spot at the foul line, the place where he'd been breaking down the Knights' defense every chance he got.

Maybe it was because she couldn't hear anything, not even the sound of her own breathing, over the sound of the Garden, maybe that's why she didn't hear anybody call out the screen that DuWapp Piersall had come up to set behind her.

Or maybe her teammates just didn't bother, wanting to know what it would look like if DuWapp Piersall used the girl in the game for a crash dummy.

But she ran into him now the way she would have run into a tree and went down in a heap while Pooh Bear fed Bad Levine for an open jumper in the left corner.

"Woman down," she said weakly to Carl Anthony when he helped her to her feet. "I'm hit."

"Rub some dirt on it," he said.

She looked at him blankly.

"One of those dumb-ass expressions from baseball," he said.

Anquwan inbounded the ball to her. She tried to block out all the noise around her—for her—and just concentrate on the basics now, the feel of the ball, the bounce of the ball.

Nothing fancy, she told herself.

Make the easy pass.

She made it all right, not just made it but telegraphed it, a stupid simple entry pass to Carl in the post that DuWapp Piersall saw coming a mile away and batted over to Pooh Bear, who started the fast break that Billy Phalls, the other Knicks guard, finished with a dunk.

With fifteen seconds left in the quarter, Knights ball, Eddie stood up and told them to hold for one shot. Even now, slowing things down, Dee still felt as if everything was going way too fast for her, as if the game was being played at fast forward, a different speed—warp speed—than she'd watched from her seat next to Joey Shahoud.

The play was for Dream Jackson in the low blocks, to her right. But Billy Phalls fought through a pick and the thing broke down right away. Dee ended up with the ball, the time the same on the 24-second clock as it was on the game clock, only four seconds left. Pooh Bear backed off, even made a showy, flourishy motion with his hand like a bullfighter waving his cape, finding time at the end to give his crotch a little squeeze.

"C'mon, bad girl, give it to me," he said.

She let the shot go with one second left, heard the horn end the quarter while the ball was still in the air.

That was right before it fell about three feet short, and her first career shot, the first a woman had ever taken in an official NBA game, officially became an air ball.

"Damn," Pooh Bear Moriarty said, putting his arm around her, "the Hindenburg landed softer than that shit."

Dee played the first eight minutes of the fourth quarter, at which time Eddie called her over, said, "That's enough," and told Deltha Lewis to go back in there.

Her stat line in the papers the next day would show her with ten minutes played in all, 0-for-3 shooting, 4-for-4 from the free-throw line, and three assists. She turned the ball over twice, once on that first pass, the one DuWapp knocked away, and another one that really wasn't her fault. She beat Billy

Phalls, who had her in a switch, got inside, got both DuWapp and Bad Levine to come up on her. Anquwan was open on her right, Jamie Lawton to her left. She was convincing enough looking at Jamie, as if she were going to telegraph another cream-puff pass, that even Anquwan bit.

Because when Dee fired a pass to him with her left hand, right off the dribble, it hit him in his pierced ear and bounced out of bounds.

"Oops," he said casually.

Like, no big deal, girl.

She told him what she'd told just about every teammate she'd ever had, from all the girls and women she'd played with in her life to Earthwind Morton himself that night in Stade Louis II.

"Keep your goddamn eyes open," she said, surprising him with her tone. "And your hands up. Got it?"

Three possessions later, the kid showed her that, yeah, he got it. The Knicks had stayed with their man-to-man, even though Pooh Bear hadn't abused Dee the way he thought he would at the start. As she came past half-court, he flashed in, going for a steal, but Dee saw him coming, went behind her back, saw him stumble as he went past. Five-on-four. She thought briefly she had a clear path all the way into the lane, but Bad Levine, who was the best defender the Knicks had by far, jumped out again and so did the Knicks' power forward, an African kid named Kunta Kunta who was built like Penn Station. Kunta Kunta slapped at the ball, briefly knocking it away, but Dee had faster hands, reaching down, picking it up before either one of them could get the steal. As she did, twisting her body to the left to keep herself between them and the ball, she saw a flash of white behind them that turned out to be Anquwan, Bad Levine's man. Somehow Dee reached around Kunta, who was closest to her, reached all the way around his big butt, and threw a two-hand no-look pass that one of the sportswriters would say reminded him of a guy on an airport runway directing a pilot to his gate.

Anquwan made a sure catch, not even trying a flashy dunk, laid the ball gently into the basket.

On the way down court, Dee put her hand out so he could slap it and said, "That's what I'm talkin' about."

You just had to pick your spots being one of the boys. She'd figured that out a long time ago.

The Knights were down six points when she came into the game and fell behind ten right away when she screwed up her first couple of plays. But they were down only three when she left to a standing ovation.

She sat back down next to Eddie Holtz, who without looking at her said, "You didn't suck."

"Stop it," Dee said. "You're making me blush."

She sat there and watched as the Knights tied the game with thirty seconds left, watched as Bad Levine flopped after he'd missed a little baby hook in the lane, got two gift free throws from Buddy the ref with eight seconds left, made them both; watched as Deltha Lewis, who'd made a couple of shots down the stretch and decided he was going to be the hero, ignored a wide-open Carl Anthony and forced up a jumper with two seconds left that harmlessly grazed the side of the rim before bouncing all the way down to where Dee saw Tony Bennett sitting between Reggie Jackson and Harrison Ford.

They brought Dee into the same interview room where she'd first talked to everybody a couple of days before, the one just up the hall from her dressing room. She'd asked for about twenty minutes after the game, deciding how she wanted to play it, even how she wanted to look, whether or not she wanted to shower and change into the sweater and slacks outfit she'd left hanging in the closet after practice the day before. She finally decided to stay in her uniform, just throw on the long-sleeved white shirt that players wore under their warm-up jackets. Her hair was still tied in a ponytail, and that's the way she left it, frizzes and all.

There was a knock on her door and she thought it was Joey Shahoud, telling her they were ready for her, but it was Mo Jiggy instead, looking as worn out as if he'd played the game.

He looked her up and down and said, "You gonna go like that?"

"I don't want this to look like I'm posing for the cover of *Vogue*," she said.

"Don't worry your head none," Mo said. "You don't."

"I'm a ballplayer," she said, "even if I wasn't much of a damn stupid ballplayer tonight. I always hated it when those tennis girls would go change right after the match and come into their press conference looking like Lolita."

"Shit movie," Mo said. "No wonder it went straight to cable."

When they went across the hall, Walt Ransome, sitting front and center, asked the first question.

"Well, congratulations there, Miz Gerard," he said.

"Thanks," Dee said. "I guess."

"I'm not talking about the game," he snapped. "I meant congratulations on getting your coach fired. Was that what you and your owner meant when you talked about making history together?"

Dee put a hand over her eyes, shielding them from the glare of the television lights, getting her first good look at the man. In person, his face reminded her even more of a pug's than it did in the picture they used with his column. His lips were pulled back in a fake smile, and even from the podium Dee could see that his teeth were the color of a legal pad.

He had small, dark, pig eyes.

Dee said, "Is this that soft feminine side you were talking about in your column the other day?"

"Were you able to make it through the whole thing without bursting into tears?"

Dee smiled, brilliantly she'd see on the late news, when they ran the back-and-forth between her and Walt Ransome.

"Poor syntax actually doesn't upset me the way it does some people," she said. "I'm just more tolerant that way."

Bad girl, she thought.

Bad Dee.

"So that's your smart-mouth answer to Bobby Carlino being fired in this outrageous manner because you were shoved down his throat," Ransome said, giving it a beat before he said, "So to speak."

"I don't hire and fire people," she said. "I'm just a player."

"And not much of one, at least off what I saw tonight." He

folded his arms in front of him, trying to look fierce and dangerous, as if Dee was supposed to faint.

"Well," Dee said, "we've finally found some common ground, haven't we? If I can't do better than I did out there tonight, I'll be out of your retro hair before you know it, Walt."

Before he could say anything back, the bad Dee added, "Retro, of course, means old-fashioned, out of another time. . . ."

The people behind Ransome laughed. He got up, his chair making a loud scraping noise, and said, "You be funny in here, missy. I'll be funny for seven hundred thousand readers in the morning."

And walked out.

Dee sighed and said, "Boy, I've had bad first dates before." There was another ripple of laughter. "What else?" she said.

A female voice, somewhere in the back of the packed room, said, "Can you describe your response to the crowd's response tonight?"

Dee said, "Biggest cheer I ever got. But then, this is the biggest room I've ever worked."

A male voice said, "Dee, did Bobby Carlino ever tell you flat-out he wasn't going to play you?"

"No."

"Do you think he would've played you if Michael hadn't come down there?"

"You'll have to ask him."

"Michael or Bobby?"

"Both," Dee said.

Another male voice, with a thick New York accent. "You ever had two guys fight over you in public before?"

Now Dee laughed. "Not like that," she said.

A woman in the front row stood up, identifying herself as Vicky Dunne from Fox Sports. She had spiky hair the color of a stop sign and wore a sweater tight enough to show off what Dee always thought of as pool-toy breasts.

"Dee," she said, "how would you evalutate your performance tonight, in light of expectations?"

"Whose expectations?"

Vicky Dunne seemed to freeze for a second, as if one question was all she had in her.

"Well," she managed finally, "*everybody's* expectations."

"Off what you saw tonight," Dee said, "I can only quote what the noted basketball scholar Pooh Bear Moriarty said after my first pathetic shot attempt," and then she told them what Pooh Bear had said about the Hindenburg.

She stayed in there about fifteen more minutes, continuing to deflect all the questions about Bobby Carlino, giving a sanitized version of what went on between them at the end of the bench. When she finished, Mo ran interference for her along with Montell and Denzell, who had just appeared out of nowhere, both of them wearing black Oakland Raiders jackets and matching wool caps. They took her out to the right, to the area behind the court where Michael De la Cruz parked his limo. The limo was gone but the Suburban was there. Shaheen was standing next to it, with the backseat door on the driver's side open for her.

Dee noticed Barbara Walters—whom she'd seen in the first row of seats—standing off to the side with her crew. Dee gave her a little wave, made a motion like she'd call. Mo went over, bowed dramatically from the waist, kissed Barbara's hand. Dee couldn't hear what Mo was saying, just saw Barbara nodding, and then laughing as she shooed him away.

As Shaheen eased the car down the ramp toward Thirty-third Street, Mo said, "I just told her not tonight, my girl got a headache."

They met Eddie at a joint on Second Avenue he said he liked called The Last Good Year, Eddie calling the car and telling them Joe Healey, the owner, had cleared the back room for them, because New York radar had already informed the people in the joint that Dee was on her way over.

Once she was in the back room, Dee discovered it was like some kind of shrine to old-time baseball things, all of them meaning absolutely nothing to her. Dee knew how much Cool Daddy loved baseball, the Mets especially, explaining that by saying they was National League and Jackie Robinson was

National League, and by God that was good enough for him. But for the life of her, Dee had never been able to understand why guys got more emotional over baseball, talking about some stat from some game that happened in 1951, than they did over their first cars.

Or talking about their moms.

They had talked about having burgers at The Last Good Year, but halfway through a glass of wine, Dee said she was tired, she was ready to go home. Mo said Shaheen was out front. Eddie said he was ready to go, too. Mo said for them to tell Shaheen to come back for him, that he was going to watch the end of the Lakers-Blazers game and then go meet Chelsea and chill a little down at this place he had a piece of, one called Beef.

Dee and Eddie had Shaheen drop them at the corner of Fifty-ninth and Madison, they said they'd walk from there.

Dee said, "I want him to make you the coach."

"I told you," Eddie said, "we're meeting at eight-thirty, his office. I'll find out then."

"He didn't give you any indication?"

"Nope."

"You want it?"

"Yup. I told him there was only one condition, which he had no problem with. I told him Reg gets sent off to Europe for the rest of the season to scout over there like I did. And no more inner-ring committees running the team, it was just me and him."

Dee pulled up the collar of her coat. "Old Michael loved this tonight, didn't he?"

Eddie said, "I really don't think he planned it, but somehow he made it as much about him as it was about you."

When they were in front of the Sherry, she said, "I hope I see you at practice."

"I'll be there," he said. "One way or another."

She leaned forward, the way she had at The Theater, and put her head on his shoulder. Then Eddie had his face in her hair, as if somehow he knew that's what Jeremy used to do, when Jeremy used to tell her how good she smelled, before he was telling her how good she felt and tasted, and then Dee

Gerard, the first woman ever to play an official NBA game—
an official woman at last! she thought—and the man who had
coached her were foolishly making out on Fifth Avenue like a
couple of teenagers in the back row of the movies.

He was a good kisser.

You always wondered, every single time, what the first one
would be like, how he would taste and smell, whether he
would slobber or get too pushy, whether he'd know it was
supposed to be a first kiss and not a grab fest, whether he'd
know this was just supposed to be a beginning, like a switch
being thrown, let's not get carried away here.

Dee was the one who started to get carried away, which is
why she suddenly pushed back like a plane leaving the gate.

"Now I'm the one who wants a time-out," she said, "not
Michael."

Eddie, with that fun in his eyes, said, "Twenty or full?"

"How about we say good night now?"

"You sure?"

Dee said, "Not even close." She kissed him lightly now
and said, "You smoked some cigarettes tonight."

"I have one in moments of great stress," he said. He
brushed some hair out of her eyes. "Or after great stress, de-
pends on the setting."

"My life's complicated enough right now," she said.
"Maybe you've noticed."

"I've noticed."

"This should be good night," Dee said.

"Then good night it is."

He kissed her again, with even more follow-through than
before.

Neither one of them thinking about what they were doing,
or where they were doing it, neither one of them noticing
anybody watching.

⚾ fifteen

RANSOME NOTES
by Walt Ransome

Bill Russell never did it. Neither did Wilt the Stilt. Or Oscar. Or Michael or Magic or the great Larry Bird. Willis Reed never did it in this town. Or Clyde. Or Earl the Pearl. Or Senator Bill.

Not one of them ever got a coach fired before they'd ever played a minute in the NBA.

Dee Gerard, though, a woman in a man's league, did that last night before the first sellout crowd in the history of the New York Knights and the national television audience that turned in for a look-see at what should have been called the National Babe Association.

The Knights lost more than a game last night. They lost a coach—and a damned fine one, despite his record—and gained a point guard who I'm frankly not sure could make the varsity at St. John's.

Men's or women's team.

I heard a lot of silly chanting at the Garden last night. "We want Dee!" was the message.

It must have been coming from the guys without dates, because it certainly couldn't have been coming from real fans of basketball, and the Knights.

All week long Michael De la Cruz told us that this game between the Knights and Knicks would be like a big Broadway opening. Fair enough. He had his opening. Now he can just go ahead and close the show. It was a flop last night and will be a flop for as long as it lasts.

The only thing more outrageous than the notion that this uppity woman can play in the league of Russell and Wilt, Magic and Michael, is the way De la Cruz fired Bobby Carlino. . . .

It went like that, longer than a normal newspaper column, Dee thought, reading to her like some bad epic poem. The *News* had gone with Bobby Carlino's obscene gesture on the front page, underneath this headline:

Dee's Number One!

The back page was the shot of Dee sitting on the floor after running into DuWapp Piersall's pick. The headline back there, even bigger than the one in front, was tied to Walt Ransome's column:

Butt Out!

The coverage of her first game made everything leading up to it seem like some sort of overture. Dee now had an idea of what would happen if World War III broke out in the middle of Central Park. There were stories about the press conference Bobby Carlino held after the game on the stage at The Theater, which still featured some of the set from a revival of *The Wiz*, which meant Carlino talked to everybody with the festive yellow-brick road behind him.

There were reaction stories from coaches all around the

league, one of whom, Howie White of the Hawks, said, "I knew they were bringing in a woman. I just didn't know it was Lizzie Borden."

The coaches all attacked De la Cruz and Dee. But in the separate reaction story about owners in the *News,* she thought Michael De la Cruz came off fairly well. The woman doing the piece had even managed to contact Mo Jiggy's friend Jack Molloy, the owner of the New York Hawks football team, at the Connaught Hotel in London.

"Good for Mike," Molloy told the reporter. "I fired that gasbag Vince Cahill on the team plane one time, and that was only after my general manager talked me out of tossing the b—— at thirty-seven thousand feet. I wish I'd thought of doing it at the fifty-yard line during a game."

"That's really the deal here," Molloy concluded. "Michael De la Cruz basically did what we've all thought about doing."

NBA commissioner Marcus Betts—with whom Dee was meeting before practice—regretted that what was supposed to have been such an historic occasion for his sport and for women all over the world had been marred by what Betts described as "bad reality television, which frankly might be redundant."

The commissioner of the WNBA wasn't much help, either. *USA Today* had had one of their basketball writers watch the game with Kit Norwood in Knoxville, who was there for a women's game between the universities of Connecticut and Tennessee the next afternoon. Kit Norwood was a former Tennessee star herself and had played one season against Dee in Israel, for the Tel Aviv Kibbitzers.

"I've always liked Dee's style," Kit Norwood said. "Everybody—at least everybody abroad—always thought she had a nice little game. But with all due respect, if she's good enough to play with the men, so are about half the point guards in my league."

In the coffee shop around the corner from the hotel, right next to the big show window for Eddie Bauer, Dee said, "You liked my nice little game a lot better that night you tried to come on to me in the bar of the Tel Aviv Hilton."

She called for her check, drank the last of her tea, left some money on the table, and headed for the door. Her waiter, who'd recognized her the minute she walked through the door, had given her a back booth next to the kitchen, so she could sit with her back to the room and not be bothered.

The waiter said, "Hey, Dee, you're forgetting your newspapers."

"Only if I try really, really hard," Dee said.

She didn't know what the commissioner wanted to talk about, she didn't know who her coach was going to be at practice, she didn't know if the guy who hired her was about to be suspended, she barely knew when the next game was, or against whom.

Yeah, she thought, I'm number one.

If she was a guy, she could tell herself she had the world by the balls.

Marcus Betts, commissioner of the National Basketball Association, stood at the bay window in his office, the spires of St. Patrick's Cathedral behind him looking close enough to touch, and reminded Dee of the little black actor, fat cheeks like a cartoon chipmunk's, who used to be in *Diff'rent Strokes* on Saturday nights.

The NBA commissioner was bigger than that, perhaps five-six with the lifts Dee was betting he had in those pointy black shoes that looked as if they'd be too small even for her. But Betts had the same kind of fat cheeks, though hardly any neck to speak of. His hair was in tight gray curls that matched the color of his double-breasted gray suit. He was wearing one of those shirts Dee hated and guys seemed to love, dark blue with a spread white collar.

All in all, Dee decided, he looked like a well-dressed black Hobbit.

Michael De la Cruz was already in the office when Dee showed up, yabbering away on his cell phone. He was on a long sofa that took up most of the wall across from Betts's desk, seated next to Harold Wasserman, whose feet, Dee noticed, didn't quite touch the carpet.

If they had a quick game of two-on-two afterward, the only fair sides would have Harold guarding Marcus Betts.

Mo Jiggy was perched on a corner of Betts's desk. He wore a black suit, white shirt, navy tie with subtle stripes, small knot.

Betts came over and shook hands with Dee, but she was staring at Mo.

"You're all dressed up," she said.

"Court appearance."

"Not your own, I hope."

"Shaheen. He was over to Club New York about six months ago, then he had a problem with the same old thing."

"Wait, I can get this one," Dee said. "Someone disrespected him, right?"

"Was the word 'no.' Used to turn his whole world upside down, till we got him into that anger management deal."

"I'd love to hear more about your own version of the Von Trapp family," Marcus Betts said. "But I know you're on a tight schedule, as are the rest of us, so let's get started, shall we?"

"Tell me again why we all here on a Saturday," Mo said.

Dee had seen this before. When others in the room wanted to sound like the English department, Mo went street on them.

Betts, back to posing in front of the window, hands clasped behind him, said, "I just thought this would be as good a time as any to convene a short meeting of Dee's support group."

"Short is good," De la Cruz said. "I've got to get to the Garden before practice."

"Along those lines," Marcus Betts said, "I assume you've decided on a coach for the rest of the season?"

"Eddie Holtz," De la Cruz said.

Yes! Dee thought.

"You're not worried about the possible—how shall I put this—innuendo?"

Dee blurted out, "What innuendo?"

Betts said, "About you and the coach?"

Dee said, "There isn't any innuendo about me and the coach."

"You're sure of that?"

"Well, of course," she said. "We *must* be having sex. That's what us girls do when we have a chance to advance our careers. We sleep with the scouts just on the outside chance that they'll become coach eventually."

"Shit," Mo Jiggy said.

Marcus Betts said, "You and Mr. Holtz have spent an awful lot of time together since you arrived in town, there's no secret about that."

"How you know that, exactly, my brother?" Mo said.

"We have an interest in all our players," Betts said evenly, "especially the ones with a higher profile."

Dee said, "Eddie found me, Commissioner. He's the one who talked me into this. I didn't *know* anybody else when I got here. Have I leaned on him? You betcha. Does that mean we're an item all of a sudden? I'm not going to even dignify that with an answer. You sound like Walt Ransome."

"Low blow," Betts said, smiling.

"How else she gonna get a good shot in on you?" Mo asked. He casually leaned over and wiped off a spot on the square toe of his buckled black loafers.

"I'm just trying to anticipate problems here," Marcus Betts said.

"Or," Mo said, "you could just take a flying funk with your in-nu-en-do."

"I beg your pardon?" Betts tried to raise an eyebrow in an aristocratic way, but just looked as if he had some sort of twitch.

Mo said, "You say you part of my client's support system, whatever that is. Then you waste her time and my time worrying that somebody might think she doin' it with the new coach."

Michael De la Cruz said, "C'mon, guys, we don't need any melodrama today, we had enough of that last night."

Mo said to Betts, "I'm just askin' the man if he talk about sex with the guy players he bring in here?"

In a voice just audible enough for Dee to hear, Harold Wasserman said, "Well, that one time with Jamie Lawton."

Mo said, "What's the deal, he queer or not?"

Betts said, "Let's just say I accepted his explanation about what he was doing in the bathhouse, and leave it at that."

"Dee," Michael De la Cruz said, "Marcus just wants to make sure that we are, all of us, on the same page."

He was wearing a copy of the same T-shirt he'd left for Dee at the Sherry the day before.

"Boys Annoy Me," it said.

"It just sounds like the gossip page to me," Dee said.

"I was telling Michael and Harold before you and Mo got here," Betts said, "that we cannot have a repeat of last night, because then the whole thing really will degenerate into burlesque. And even though you, Dee, were an innocent bystander, there will be people who blame you anyway."

"Even though I'm the one he's talking about suspending," De la Cruz said. "But I tried to explain to him that he can't suspend me, we're only talking about a twenty-five-game season here. Plus playoffs, if we make a run."

Mo said, "What planet you from?"

The Knights were currently 21–36: for this point in the season, their best record in years.

Betts said, "You should have thought about what a short season Dee is playing before you ran out on the court."

De la Cruz said, "Check the tape, I never set one foot on the court."

"Michael, Michael, Michael," Betts purred. "I've told you this before. Don't plead your case like this is some kind of hearing. There's no Players Association for owners. If I say being on the sideline is the same as being on the court, then it is the same as being on the court."

Harold Wasserman leaned back in the sofa, forgetting how soft it was, and his feet flipped up in the air, catapulting him back into the cushions. When he regained his balance, he said, "But you really don't want to suspend him, do you, Commissioner?"

"And why is that?"

"Because getting a bedbug like Bobby Carlino out of the way is a good thing. Because a coach who appreciates Miss Gerard's skills is a good thing. Because if this works out the way we think it can, Miss Gerard can do for you what she is going to do for herself, the Knights, for Michael."

"And what is that, exactly?"

"Make everybody look like a winner."

"Tattoo's talkin' some good shit now," Mo Jiggy said.

"You remember *Fantasy Island*?" Dee said.

"Remember it?" Mo said. "We livin' on it now."

Harold Wasserman said, "Marcus, you know and I know that the league has been in the Dumpster pretty much since Michael retired. The ratings are down across the board, network and cable, the public has clearly grown tired of young players who frankly make our friend Mr. Jiggy here look wholesome enough for one of those 'Got Milk?' ads."

"Turned that shit down," Mo said. "Fuckin' dairy products will kill you."

"Anyway," Harold Wasserman continued, "we are fast approaching the point where your league— our league— becomes the same marginal entertainment buy it was before Magic and Larry came along to save the world."

Betts said, "Excuse me, but our tracking numbers . . ."

Sweetly, Harold Wasserman said, "You know what you can do with your tracking numbers."

Dee decided it was like watching one squirrel let the other know who was boss.

Harold said, "There's no more point in suspending Michael this time than there was the last time."

Michael turned to Dee and explained. "It was an accident, I swear. I never thought I had a chance of hitting the ref with my gum from where I was."

Wasserman, standing now, trying to take the room, said, "A suspension just sidetracks us here. We are here today to decide what's the best way to proceed with the one basketball player everyone is talking about right now, everyone wants to see, everyone wants to know."

"There are already sellouts next week in Miami and Orlando," De la Cruz said. "Same thing after that in Cleveland and Chicago."

"The Knights are getting fifty interview requests per day,"

Wasserman said. "And I bet your p.r. people are getting the same."

"More, actually," Marcus Betts said.

Michael De la Cruz said, "Every girls' basketball team around here, from CYO to college, wants at least one block of tickets before the end of the season."

"If we play it right," Wasserman said, "it's a rocket to the moon."

Mo said, "Soccer moms of the world hoop it up."

"I've been saying that from the start!" De la Cruz said.

Dee was sure they'd forgotten, at least for the moment, she was even there. It didn't bother her. She was fascinated by the amount of testosterone in the room, that they were all somehow going to be bigger than they already were—even the short ones—because of her. She knew it was true even for Mo Jiggy, who wanted you to think he didn't take anything seriously. This was all as exciting for them as sex, not the imagined kind with her and Eddie, but the real thing.

Big guys acting big.

Maybe this *was* sex for them.

"I have to fine you something, just for the sake of appearances," Betts said to De la Cruz. "I can't even remember, what did we go for last time?"

"Quarter of a million."

"Half a million okay for this one?"

De la Cruz said, "No problem."

Dee said, "Half a million *dollars*?"

Betts said, "You think it's not enough?"

He's serious, Dee thought.

"I'll just shut up now," she said.

They talked about an interview schedule for road games, one formal deal after the morning shootaround, then nothing until after the game. Mo said he had set the date for a sitdown with Barbara Walters, then Matt and Katie the next morning, then Larry King the next night; he said he'd told them all that he just wanted to wait until she had five or six games in the books.

"Okay, then," Marcus Betts said. "Thank you all for coming." To Dee, he said, "You know, all things considered, I thought last night went pretty well."

She said, "I can do better. If I can't, I really *am* history."

"It would be nice," he said.

"I know," Dee said. "You've all got a lot riding on me."

Dee left with Mo, who said he'd drop her at practice on his way downtown to the courthouse. Michael wanted to know what court convened on Saturday, and Mo said, "The court where the judge say he tired of which sideman pointed which gun at who in the club, he wish everybody got shot and died instead of just winged." Mo said he'd see Michael at the Garden tomorrow, Knights against the Phoenix Suns, first game of NBC's tripleheader.

Harold Wasserman said he had some paperwork to do at his office, even though it was Saturday, and then he was gone.

It was just Michael and Marcus Betts, who shut the door behind Harold Wasserman and said, "I know he can be trusted, but what about the pictures?"

"Relax about the pictures."

Betts said, "We're in uncharted waters here, Michael. Let's not go out of our way to make more trouble for ourselves. Or for our girl."

"Trouble isn't always a bad thing, necessarily."

"Please don't tell me about two negatives making a plus." Michael put his hands up. "Fine with me."

"We've got enough story here, Michael, we don't have to go around looking for more angles."

"We have to be the ones to move the story along. We ride it. It doesn't ride us."

"What about the father's past?"

"Still looking into it. Beyond the arrest when he was a kid, I mean."

Betts said, "The ex-husband?"

"It doesn't sound like he wants to come out and play. From what I hear, the guy's still about half in love with her."

"What about the coach?"

"This is his big chance," Michael said. "He'll be fine."

"You say he's very loyal to her."

Michael put an arm around Marcus Betts, gave him a squeeze, and said, "Aren't we all, Mr. Commissioner. Aren't we all."

⏀ sixteen

She had played fifteen minutes against the Suns, the second-place team in the Pacific Division, but operating somewhat shorthanded that day because of one DWI arrest to their starting power forward; the misadventures of their willowy shooting guard, who'd ignored a restraining order from his ex-wife—starting an oil fire in their Olympic-size backyard swimming pool—for what a Phoenix judge said was a third and last time; and a raid of an after-hours topless bar in Tempe two nights before that had effectively eliminated both the Suns' starting point guard and his backup for the first two games of the Suns' six-game East Coast road trip.

The Suns' lack of depth pretty much explained why the Knights had managed to stay with them, neither team ever more than four points ahead, since the game's opening tip.

Dee had scored her first NBA basket—it came on a goal-tending call against the Suns' All-Star center, Silicon Fusco—handed out four assists, even made her first outside shot, a wide-open twenty-footer behind a Carl Anthony screen. She had also left the court briefly in the third quarter with a twisted ankle, getting tangled up with Dream

Jackson diving for a loose ball. But Joey Shahoud retaped her as if she were timing him and she came right back to the bench.

As she did, Ray Ray Abdul-Mahi was in the process of getting himself ejected from the game.

Silicon Fusco had lost his man in a switch on the baseline; Ray Ray had got down there to cut him off, and seemed to set himself before Silicon ran him over. The ref, Tony Vazquez, called it a blocking foul on Ray Ray, and awarded Silicon two free throws.

"Tu madre es una perra!" Ray Ray snapped at Vazquez, using a phrase he'd say he'd learned from Carl Anthony.

Dee didn't even have to be as proficient in Spanish as she was to know that Ray Ray was telling Tony Vazquez his mother was a dog.

Vazquez blew his whistle, called him for a technical foul.

"Shit, man," Ray Ray said, going after him, "you can't tee me up for somethin' I said in Mex-cin."

"Just did," Vazquez said, walking away like the refs did when they wanted something to be over.

"Well, then, how about this in English?" Ray Ray said. "Eat me, Taco Boy!" and then Ray Ray was done for the afternoon.

Deltha went in at the start of the fourth quarter with the Knights ahead now, 84–82. With two minutes left, the game was tied, 100-all. Eddie looked down the bench, saw Dee all the way at the other end. "Dee," he snapped. "Get in there for Deltha."

She crabbed her way past the other players, sat down next to him.

"Are you sure? My ankle's still a little stiff."

Eddie said, "Deltha's exhausted, he must have been out all night. Run the offense. And stay out of the goddamn double teams better than he did."

There was a whistle, a rebounding foul on the Suns after a Jamie Lawton miss, Carl Anthony on his way to the free-throw line. Before she took off her warm-up jacket, which she knew would get the crowd excited, just because the crowd got excited if she stood up to refill her cup of Gatorade, Dee said, "You sure you're sure?"

"You've got to stick around till the end of the game anyway," Eddie said. "You might as well make yourself useful."

The Suns' third-string point guard was Sam Cook, who Eddie told her was a Brooklyn kid, Thomas Jefferson High, and had played for the Knights a couple of years after very nearly graduating from Iowa State. He was thirty now and had kicked around the league until ending up at the end of the Suns' bench. Today, though, because of what Eddie called the police raid on the Suns' roster, he had played all forty-six minutes of the game so far.

"He's tired, too," Eddie said.

"I'm a girl with a sore ankle."

"Bitch, bitch, bitch," Eddie said.

Cook was six-four, the kind of length Dee knew she had no answer for; in women's ball in Europe hardly anybody, even the centers, was six-four. Now she was up against a point guard that big. Big and fast and younger than she, even though thirty in the NBA meant you were getting up there.

Her ankle had stiffened more than a little while she'd been sitting on the bench, it was actually throbbing like hell, but she wasn't going to let Eddie Holtz see. She bounced off the bench, spiked her jacket, heard the explosion of noise from the crowd, went and kneeled in front of the scorer's table. After Carl Anthony made the first free throw, the horn sounded and Tony Vazquez waved her in.

Anthony missed the second free throw, but Anquwan knifed past Silicon Fusco and kept the ball alive, finally collected it, and threw it way back outside to Dee. Sam Cook and the wing man on the right side, Varney, a white kid about Cook's size with a Mohawk haircut and tattoos of various jungle animals covering his entire upper body, went right after her, forcing her toward the sideline, then trapping her there before she could get rid of the ball.

All Dee could see was Sam Cook on one side of her and what looked like the daddy from *The Lion King* close enough to bite her, so she called one of the two time-outs she knew the Knights had left.

"Goddammit, Dee!" Eddie snapped when she got to the huddle. "I told you not to get pinned."

Dee said, "I didn't exactly plan to get surrounded quite that quickly."

Eddie said, "Pay attention out there. If you see the wing guy coming up on you, reverse the goddamn thing."

He was right and she knew it. She had been a step slow. She hated being a step slow. After the time-out, they came after her again, same two guys, but before they did, Dee reversed the ball, threw a pass over the top of the zone to Dream Jackson in the opposite corner. Dream didn't like his shot, went back outside to Lamar Sheet, a backup guard Eddie liked. Lamar made a motion like he was coming back to Dee with the ball, as Dong Li, just in there for Jamie Lawton, flashed across the lane. "C'mon," Dee said, motioning for Lamar to make the pass. He did. The replays everybody would use that night showed the ball barely touching Dee's hands as she touch-passed to the Chinese kid. He turned and used his favorite shot, half jumper and half hook. It went in. Now the Knights were ahead by three.

Sam Cook came back up the court, pulled up right in front of Dee, hit a three-point jumper, saying "Sweet"—it came out sounding like "Thweet" because of his pronounced lisp—before the ball dropped through the net.

It was 103–103.

"All day, girl," Sam Cook said on his way past her. "Gonna give you that thweet thit all day."

She had learned a long time ago not to answer back, the trash talkers always found a way to get in the last word, even if it was something truly awful, even when—as tough as she liked to think she was—she heard things that made her sick.

"Give it to you good," Sam Cook said.

Dee thought: The game, girl.

Shut this jerk up by winning the damn game.

Twenty seconds left. Eddie was standing in front of the scorer's table, arms crossed in front of him. She dribbled up the right side, in his direction, looking right at him, thinking he might want to call their last time-out, set something up.

In a casual way, looking like the most relaxed person in the house, he shrugged and said, "Play."

She could feel the Garden as well as she could hear it. This had always happened to her in the heat of the last minute, the heat of a packed house, when she was lucky enough to get a packed house. Somehow all she could hear were basketball sounds. Bounce of the ball. Screech of sneakers. Grunts and slaps of flesh on flesh. Players on both teams calling out to each other. An occasional "Fuck."

Quiet gym sounds, no matter how loud the place was.

When was the last time she'd been here, with a game on the line?

The answer flashed through her head, briefly, a streak of light:

You've never been here.

The Suns were trying to cross them up, going man-to-man for the first time since the first quarter. Dee called the back-door play, Ohio, that they were supposed to have run that first day at practice.

Ten seconds.

She caught Dong Li's eye.

He was supposed to curl to the weak side, away from the ball, while Lamar Sheet, his dreadlocks flopping wildly, broke for the basket.

Dee looked at Dong and mouthed, *Go.*

The kid gave her one nod.

Lamar ran through, after faking to the outside.

Sam Cook, who had backed off Dee, turned his head and saw Lamar go and yelled in his lisp, "Wath the backdoor!"

Dee sold the pass to Lamar, only pulling the ball back at the last moment.

Dee always made sure she knew where the game clock was, up in the stands behind the basket.

Five seconds.

Dong followed Lamar to the basket like Lassie used to follow little Timmy.

Dee didn't lob the ball the way she had at practice, just threw it hard and high above the defense and the kid caught it

and dropped it through the basket like he was dropping another coin in the meter.

Knights 105, Suns 103.

Ballgame.

Some of the Knights huddled at midcourt for what Dee
thought looked like some sort of drive-thru prayer service.
Dee and Eddie walked past them toward the locker room. A
short, dark-haired woman with a microphone in her hand and
a cameraman behind her, came running up to them, introducing herself as Hallie something, NBC Sports, putting a death
grip on Dee's right forearm at the same time.

"Can we get you for just a minute, Dee?" she said, even as
she was already motioning frantically to the cameraman,
showing him where she wanted him to set up.

Hallie was nodding vigorously, talking into the mike, saying, "I've got her now, for Chrissakes. Let's go, let's go, *let's
go*!"

Dee calmly reached down and removed Hallie's hand
from her arm.

"Oh," Hallie said. "Sorry."

"I was just afraid we might have to call for the Jaws of
Life," Dee said pleasantly.

Hallie smiled vacantly, doing what Dee had noticed just
about all television reporters did: not listening.

"Okay," Hallie said to Dee, "here we go." Then she turned
to Dee and said, "Well, Dee Gerard, what does it feel like to
be the first woman to win an NBA game?"

"I didn't win anything," Dee said. "I threw a pass to a talented kid who made a great move. You ought to be talking to
him."

Hallie said, "But you're the one America wants to hear
from! All in all, how did you think you played today?"

"Until the last play I'd pretty much played like crap,
Helen."

"Hallie."

"Sorry. I thought I played like crap, *Hallie*."

"Well, there you go," Hallie said. "Back to you, Marv and
Bill."

•   •   •   •

Eddie was waiting for her in her dressing room after she'd finished with the press. Dee rolled up the pant leg of the sweats she'd worn in the pressroom today, put her sore left ankle in the whirlpool. Eddie racked up the tape of the game that had already been made for him, and the two of them went over the sixteen minutes she had played against the Suns.

It wasn't just her ankle that was sore, her whole body felt as if she'd been run over by a cement mixer, but she wasn't going to tell her coach that. Her friend Eddie, she might have told him.

Eddie the good kisser.

But not Eddie the coach.

Ruthie Brown used to sing about how the men in her life, they kept changing, but not her, it was only her stayed the same.

She wondered if Eddie would change now that he was the coach, how things might change between them. Whatever things there were between them. Dee thought: No matter how old you are, no matter how much you think you know, there were parts of the boy-girl stuff that never changed, once things changed with that first kiss. You ended up feeling like a teenager, as if you should pass a note to somebody after psych class, trying to find out if he likes you as much as you like him.

Eddie the coach.

She'd just have to see how that played out. Be careful what you wish for, Dee thought to herself. Even the good stuff, Eddie replacing Bobby Carlino, somehow made it all a little more complicated.

Every once in a while, he would freeze the picture on the big screen. He was doing that now, saying, "Why'd you wait there?"

"I didn't react fast enough."

"Yeah."

He fast-forwarded until she was back in there and stopped the tape again. This time he said, "You see Dream down on the baseline, I know you do. What the hell are you waiting for?"

She started to say something, and Eddie said, "I'll tell you what you're waiting for: You're waiting to make a safer pass."

Finally, they were watching the last play of the game, the pass to Dong Li, and he said, "You played scared the whole game until here."

Dee said, "This just in: I *am* scared."

Eddie pointed the VCR remote at the screen, which made a whirring sound and went to black. He had worn a suit to his first official game as Knights coach, dark gray, a shirt almost as dark, and his usual old-school knit tie.

Old-school like she was old-school.

The way they both were.

Eddie went over to her refrigerator and got a bottle of Samuel Adams beer.

"Everybody else thinks you did good today," he said, "but you and I know better." He took a long swallow of beer, then another one. "You gotta be the player I saw the very first night in Monte Carlo," Eddie said, "the player I know you are."

"It's going to take a little more time than two games."

"There's twenty-four games left in the season after today," he said. "You don't have a lot of time. And neither do we if we're gonna make a run at the last playoff spot."

Dee took her ankle out of the whirlpool, dried off, went over to her coach, and stuck the ankle in a bucket of ice.

"You think this team—our team?—can make the *play-offs*?" she said.

"I do," he said. "Wait," he said, giving her that little smile, "let me be the kind of born leader Michael says I am." He straightened up in his chair and said, "I do!"

"I checked the conference standings today, the one where they combined both divisions in the East," Dee said. "It's not just the Heat we're chasing. We've also got the Cavaliers and the ever-popular Tampa Bay Nets between us and the Heat."

"We can do it," he said. "But not without you. Not if you're going to do just enough to get by. That's not enough for me, and it sure as hell shouldn't be enough for you."

He stood up, came over and sat down next to her, serious now. "Listen," he said, "I think I know what you can and can't do against guys, especially guys of this caliber. And the more you play, the more they'll try to exploit your size, your lack of strength, blah blah. You'll learn as you go. The shit you don't know about the league, you can pick that up. But the things you can do, the change that comes over these bastards when you're in there and the ball is actually moving? That's shit you gotta be born with."

"I'm feeling my way," she said.

"You're trying not to screw up. You can't play that way."

"I need a little patience, from you of all people."

Eddie said, "That's a cop-out and you know it. This isn't about me being patient with you, or being behind you, 'cause if I wasn't, you wouldn't have been out there in the last minute today." He looked away now as he said, "You know I care about you."

Dee didn't say anything.

"I know this is all on you. I can only imagine what it must be like to *be* you right now. But this isn't about the hype or the bullshit. This is about playin' *ball*." Making it sound, as always, like some kind of sacrament. "When you're out there on the court, you can't be afraid to trust the ball you got in you. I hear you talk about baseball sometimes. You know what you are right now? You're like a batter squeezing the bat too hard. You can't hit that way."

"But you put me back in today."

"I took a shot," he said, "that you'd get swept away by the moment, or whatever, and let your instincts take over."

Dee said, "Stop with all the sex talk, you're making me hot."

"I'm serious."

Dee stared at him. "I know," she said.

Eddie the coach.

They were very close on the couch, but now he stood up. "So," he said, "you ready for your first official road trip?"

"This whole thing is a road trip," Dee said.

"I'm gonna play you a little more in Florida."

"Because Michael wants you to?"

"Because *I* want to. But every time I see you holding back, playing it safe, I'm gonna sit you down the way I would anybody else." He leaned back down, kissed her on the top of her head. "Even if you are the most famous woman in America."

"I'll bet that's not what little Hallie of NBC thinks. I'll bet little Hallie thinks I am a bitch on wheels."

Eddie Holtz said, "Well, let's face it, you can only resist the pull of your gender so much."

"That's fairly sexist," she said, "for an evolved guy like yourself."

He shrugged.

"Unfortunately," he said, "the key word is still 'guy.' We hardly ever resist the pull of our gender."

Dee said she'd noticed.

For her whole life, practically.

Anquwan Posey made another run at her on the flight to Miami the next afternoon.

They were sitting in the middle cabin of the 737 Michael De la Cruz had purchased for the Knights from his friend Harvey Weinstein of Miramax Films. According to Eddie, De la Cruz had then spent $10 million renovating the inside of it for his guys.

The front cabin, where the coaches generally sat, was called The Ralph. As in The Ralph Suite. For Michael's close personal friend, Ralph Lauren. It looked like some kind of suburb of Santa Fe, with a definite Southwest motif, the cabin of an airplane actually having the feel of a real cabin.

She thought of some of the puddle-jumpers she had flown in Europe, all the planes over there that she called Amelias, for Amelia Earhart.

The second cabin, where some of the players had their private sections, all of them with pullback drapes, was called The Calvin.

Klein.

This one had a lot of beige and white, a more modern feel than The Ralph. Joey Shahoud told her she'd be in there, along with Jamie, Carl, Dream Jackson, Lamar Sheet, Anquwan.

Behind that was The Tommy, for Tommy Hilfiger, this one with more flags in it than a Veterans Day parade. The rest of the players were in this one, slightly roomier than the other two, with a lot more tricky track lighting.

Behind The Tommy was the video arcade, which the guys used if they got tired of playing games on the DVD players Michael De la Cruz had provided all of them. Back there were individual stations for Nintendo, Nintendo64, PlayStation, PlayStation 2, Dreamcast, old-fashioned Pac-Man games, a vintage Star Wars pinball machine. And behind the arcade was the screening room where players could watch game film if they wanted to, but generally, according to Eddie, watched movies instead, most of them having "Secret" or "Forbidden" or "Suburban Housewives" in their titles.

"Go back there at your own risk," he said. "Even the flight attendants try to steer clear. Emotions tend to run a little hot when the guys get to the good parts."

"You don't go back and watch with our kids?" Dee said.

"I haven't traveled with the team a heck of a lot unless Michael wants me to make a trip with them," Eddie said. "When I do, I just tell them to come get me if there's a car chase, or a building being blown up."

Behind the screening room was the trainer's room, with two massage tables, a small whirlpool, sauna, shower.

They flew out of a little airport in White Plains that Dee didn't even know existed, and were somewhere over North Carolina when Anquwan Posey opened the drapes of Dee's compartment, where she had her ankle wrapped in ice and was watching game film of the Heat on her own DVD.

Anquwan was wearing cream-colored cotton trousers and a long-sleeved silk shirt, a little too tight, that Dee thought was the color of a Creamsicle. His hair was different, not wild today, in a cornrow pattern that looked almost as complicated as a grid of the New York City transit system. He had three diamond studs in his left ear, two more in his right, and one in his left nostril. Dee was also troubled by something poking out of his shirt in the area of his right nipple.

He smelled as if the perfume counter at some big department store had exploded all over him.

"Been thinkin' on something," he said, plopping down into

the roomy swivel chairs across from her. "And whatnot," he added, by what Dee already knew was force of habit.

Dee hit the Pause button on the DVD, offered Anquwan some of the Lemon Zinger iced tea she had in a pitcher on the table next to her own seat. He shook his head, so she just waited.

"It was like you and me, we stepped out on the wrong feet," he said.

Dee said, "Don't worry about it, Anquwan. This has been a difficult and awkward situation for everyone. You guys are trapped in another losing season, and now you have to deal with a girl on the team."

Anquwan rubbed hard on his goatee, as if trying to create some kind of friction.

"Wasn't talking about the bassetball," he said.

"Oh," Dee said, "I just assumed . . ."

"I meant, when we was talkin' on the booey," he said. "The bad."

Dee smiled. "How could I forget?"

"Anyway," he said, "that was then, this isn't. Now we playin' together and whatnot, you helpin' me, me helpin' you, one hand rubbin' the other's back. So to speak."

"Like a real team," Dee offered.

"There you go," he said. "That's why I'm thinkin' maybe it's time to, you know, *reset* our situation."

"You mean like we'd reset our offense."

He brightened. "One play don't work, you regroup, try another."

"Make an adjustment," Dee said. "So to speak."

"Now that we know each other a little better, I don't see no reason why we can't go ahead and do it."

"The bad," she said.

He nodded solemnly. "And if we do do it, get booey with each other, I just want you to know you don't have to worry."

"Well," Dee said, "there's a relief."

"Because," he said, "and this here be the key . . . *it don't mean nothin'."*

Dee bit her lip, frowning, even put a hand over her mouth in case it wouldn't behave and tried to smile.

Trying to look instead as if she were in deep, deep thought, assimilating this crucial information.

"Check it out," Anquwan said, leaning forward. "There is shit that do mean somethin', everybody know that. Your contract, for example. Or tryin' to get your agent off his four percent, get him down to two or three."

Now Dee nodded.

"Takin' care of yo momma," he said, "that mean somethin'. And havin' the right boys around you."

"On the team, you mean?"

Anquwan gave her a look. "Boys you hang wit."

"What else?" she said, fascinated.

"You want one more? Makin' sure some bitch you meet on the road don't set you up and get herself knocked and then come back nine months later tryin' to lay some of that DNA bullshit on you."

"I can see how that would mean plenty!" Dee said, trying to sound enthusiastic.

"Fuck," Anquwan said. "You don't believe me, ask Deltha."

The captain came over the p.a. system then and announced that they were still at their cruising altitude of 36,000 feet, and would be touching down in Miami in about an hour and fifteen minutes.

"Say tonight," Anquwan continued, "after we checked into the Grand Bay, got ourselfs settled, and you come over to my room or I come over to yours, it don't hardly matter, and we go end-to-end . . ."

"Like a fast break."

"Uh-huh," he said. "We get right to the bad, killin' some time, havin' some fun, maybe put one of them Specter-vision movies on." He closed his eyes, smiled, as if trying to create the perfect mental picture. "Chillin'," he said.

"And whatnot," Dee said.

"But the whole time, we both got ourselves– what the word I'm lookin' for?– *liberationed,* because we both know that *it . . . don't . . . mean . . . nothin'.*"

He reached into the pocket of his slacks, pulled out a tin of

Altoid mints, popped one triumphantly into his mouth, put the tin away without offering it to Dee.

"So," he said, "what you think about that, say, nine o'clock?"

He'd been so patient with her, she felt at least she owed him a soft landing.

"Actually, Anquwan, I've already got dinner plans."

"Be in all night," he said. "Call when you get back, you feel like it."

"I'll probably be late."

"Okay," he said. "But you change your mind?"

"I probably won't. We couldn't get a reservation at the place we wanted until late . . ."

"Just says you do," he said. "You get back, you had a little wine, you got urges, you know, like you all do?"

Dee put her fist up to her mouth again, coughed. "Wine will do that," she managed finally.

Anquwan said, "And you call my room and you maybe a little surprised to hear a girl answer? *Do not hang up.*"

"If you've got another girl in the room, it don't mean nothin'?" Dee asked.

"There you go," he said.

⏺ seventeen

Eddie was moving the minute her head hit the floor.

Sometimes he was quick.

Second game of the Knights' two-day Florida trip, Orlando now, the TD Waterhouse Centre. Dee had played like crap again the night before, not just her opinion but Eddie's, too. The Knights had still managed to come back in the last five minutes and win. Twelve minutes for her, four turnovers, four fouls, three assists. The Heat had shot lights out against the Knights' zone from the outside, got themselves back into the game doing that in the third quarter, so he'd gone man against them in the fourth. Ray Ray was back in New York, suspended for five games when "Taco Boy" found its way into the newspapers and then across the two sports-talk radio stations in New York, WFAN and WNUT, like a fucking grease fire. Ray Ray had issued an apology to all Hispanic-Americans through his agent, saying he loved them all the same, Mexicans, Puerto Ricans, Spaniards, Caribbeans, though he frankly found some of their bean foods a bit rich. But the damage was done and Commissioner Betts's suspension held.

"Our league doesn't stand for intolerance in any form from any of our players," Betts told WNUT, "whether they actually intended to sound like a complete f– – moron or not."

Deltha had played the entire fourth quarter against the Heat, but Eddie wanted to get Dee in there early against the Magic. So when Deltha picked up his second foul just three minutes into the game, Eddie told Dee to get in there and push the ball every chance she got, he didn't think either one of the Magic's guards, both converted small forwards, could keep up with her.

It happened with her pushing the ball.

It happened the way Eddie had been afraid it was going to happen some night, the way his own players said it was going to happen: once the novelty was starting to wear off, some punk on the other team who didn't want girls in the league and didn't care how bad he looked was going to lay the bitch out.

The punk in this case was Pryor (Priors) Gaines, a six-eight and 270-pound forward who had started out as a linebacker at the University of Illinois but switched sports after punching out the back judge after a controversial call that went against the Fighting Illini in the Michigan game his sophomore year.

"They done destroyed my enthusiasm for the game I love," he'd told the *Chicago Sun-Times* at the time. He'd transferred to Fresno State, led the nation in rebounding for Coach Jerry Tarkanian, ended up a lottery pick for the Magic.

During his two seasons in Fresno, he had been arrested six separate times for assault, and once for driving his Subaru hatchback through the front door of his girlfriend's sorority house, but because of his prowess on the basketball court had escaped with probation each time, though he did acquire his new nickname in the process.

Eddie had met him his senior year, at the rookie camp the NBA ran in Chicago, and asked him about all the arrests.

"Same old same old," he said. "Blame the black man."

Priors Gaines was back on defense when Dee came flying

up the left side of the court on a fast break, Dream Jackson on her right. When Priors moved to his left as a way of cutting down Dream's angle, Dee went to a left-hand dribble, looking as if she was going to take the ball all the way to the basket herself, even against Priors, who was leading the league in both flagrant fouls and ejections.

Priors didn't bite. He gave her room, taking away the pass to Dream at the same time. Dee slowed up slightly, reacted to what she was seeing from him, gave a little extra burst of speed, pushed off on her right foot, and started to lay the ball up with her left hand.

She didn't know how quick Priors was.

Eddie did. Eddie could see Dee was the one who had been faked out, even though she was the one with the ball.

She was committed to shooting, that was obvious. When she saw Priors Gaines standing there in front of her, she tried to pull the ball back down, shovel it to Dream somehow.

Too late.

Way too late.

Priors Gaines had sold out on trying to block her shot, and when she pulled the ball down, it was too late for him, too— or maybe it wasn't—and he hit Dee across the side of the head with a right hand the size of one of Catherine Holtz's old oven mitts, and even though Dee got one hand out to break her fall slightly, her head made a sound on the floor at the Waterhouse Arena that was like an egg cracking against the side of a frying pan.

Her eyes were wide open when Eddie got to her, after first giving Priors Gaines a good shove on the way by.

"You're a tough guy, Gaines, you know that?"

Gaines said, "You go to the rack against me, you goin' down, I don't care what kinds of underwear you got on you."

He walked away, saying, "By the way, Coach, we hear you gettin' some of that. That true?"

Eddie let him go and knelt next to Dee. Joey Shahoud lifted her head slightly, slipped a white towel underneath it.

She was smiling what Eddie's uncle Sid, a Golden Gloves boxer back in the fifties, used to call a Queer Street smile.

Eddie said. "You okay, kiddo?"

Dee shifted slightly and grimaced. "Never better."

Eddie said, "Loved the move."

"I love you, too, Jeremy," she said.

They were supposed to fly out after the game, but a wall of thunderstorms had blown across Florida in the late evening and the forecast said there were more on the way after midnight. Rather than sit on the runway for three or four hours, Eddie told the players just to go back to the Marriott where they had stayed the night before, and check back into the rooms they'd checked out of at five-thirty— the front-desk people had told Joey Shahoud they still had plenty of vacancies.

Before her teammates left the locker room, Dee saw them all with their cell phones pressed to their ears, presumably talking to some of the women who'd been waiting for them in the lobby when the Knights' bus had pulled in the day before, these women— girls, really— looking exactly like the ones she had seen when they had gotten to the team hotel in Miami.

In both places, the lobby had resembled a baby-sitters' convention.

Dee heard Anquwan say into his phone, "She say when she be back?" He nodded a couple of times and then said, "Well, what you look like, baby?"

Joey told them to be in the lobby by nine, the plane was leaving at 10:30, when it landed they were going straight to practice. The Knicks were in town for a game against the Lakers, so the Knights would bus over to Mamaroneck, the *House Beautiful* practice facility Michael De la Cruz had built for them at the site of an old firehouse a few miles from the Winged Foot golf course.

The Magic team doctor, a short perky blond woman, not bad-looking, who'd introduced herself as Anne Garten, poked her head in one last time to see how Dee was feeling.

"More drugs," Dee said, "that's how I'm feeling."

The side of her head where Priors Gaines had clipped her was still throbbing, but once they'd established it wasn't a concussion, Dee had just put it into the category of a bad headache. She still got woozy when she moved around, but she wasn't going to tell Dr. Anne Garten that, or Eddie, or Joey Shahoud. She was going to show them she could play hurt, even if the game was already over.

Dr. Garten said, "If there was a game tomorrow, I'd encourage you to sit it out."

"But there's not," Dee said.

"So take it easy tomorrow, and then have back at them." She shook Dee's hand and said, "Good luck with this."

"Thanks."

"And next time, maybe you could think about pulling up for a mid-range jumper."

Eddie said there was a cab outside. Dee told him it was about five hundred yards to the hotel, and she could use the air. They came up a long ramp and into the what felt like a summer night. There were still some kids, most of them girls, waiting to get her autograph, see how she was feeling. She signed until there were no programs or caps left to sign and then she and Eddie walked in silence back to the Marriott, through the lobby, picking up their new keys at the front desk.

Her suite was on the tenth floor. Eddie was on eleven.

When the elevator stopped at ten, she said, "I think I can make it the rest of the way without further incident."

Eddie reached over, took the envelope with her key in it, one of those plastic cards, checked the room number, said, "I just want to make sure you're okay."

"I'm okay," she said. "Would you give Ray Ray this kind of treatment if he'd been the one got whacked upside the head?"

"Absolutely," he said.

Mo had arranged with Michael De la Cruz that Dee got a suite on the road. "Why?" she'd asked. "Because I can, that's why," Mo said, as if that were the most obvious explanation in the world. This particular suite at the Marriott wasn't anything special, small living room, small kitchen, bedroom with a king. When Dee reached over to turn on the lights, she felt a sudden wave of dizziness, put a hand on Eddie to steady herself.

"Whoa, girl," he said.

"The last aftershock," she said weakly.

He put an arm around her, walked her slowly over to the black fake-leather sofa, sat her down, went into the bedroom, came back with a couple of pillows, put them behind her head.

"You want me to give that doctor a call?" he said. "She gave me her cell."

"I'll bet," Dee said.

"Seriously."

"Seriously, a hard head is one of my very best features."

"Actually," Eddie said, "it's not even close."

He put on ESPN—watching the highlights would be like returning to a crime scene, he said—reached into the side pocket of his blazer, and came back out with a couple of the Tylenols with codeine in them Anne Garten had given Joey. He came back with a glass of ice water, sat down next to her on the couch, made her take the pills. Then she put her head on his shoulder and they watched SportsCenter.

When she woke up in the night, she was in her bed, under the covers, wearing an oversized Knights T-shirt.

When she went into the bathroom to get a drink of water, there was a note taped to the mirror:

You think Phil Jackson gives this kind of turndown service? Love, Coach Holtz.

When they landed in White Plains, the team bused over to Mamaroneck. Dee was driven into Manhattan by the stretch limo ABC had sent for her, for the official sitdown interview with Barbara Walters that she'd completely forgotten about until Joey Shahoud passed on the urgent message from Michael De la Cruz reminding her, as if forgetting Barbara Walters would be a like a diabetic forgetting insulin.

They shot it in De la Cruz's opulent, surprisingly tasteful apartment at the Sherry. When Dee walked in, she said, "Now I don't feel so bad that I never took the Versailles tour all those years I lived in Paris."

The highlight of the interview, Dee felt, was when she was asked if any of the players had "come on" to her.

"Come on," Dee said.

Barbara Walters said she meant, had any of her teammates made advances.

"No," Dee said, smiling, "I mean, come *on,* Barbara."

Then Barbara, leaning forward, wanted to know how they were all treating her.

"The good news," Dee said, "is that they're treating me like one of the boys."

And the bad news?

"They're treating me like one of the boys," Dee said.

They ran it that night on a show called *PrimeTime*, ten o'clock. Dee watched only the beginning. Mo Jiggy said she had to see how pissed Diane Sawyer, the host of the show, would be introducing an exclusive by her hated rival Barbara.

He was right. Diane Sawyer seemed as happy as if she'd just swallowed razor blades.

The next morning on *Today*, Katie Couric leaned forward about halfway into the interview and asked if playing in the NBA was Dee's ultimate fantasy.

"No," Dee said.

Well, then, she wanted to know, what *is* your ultimate fantasy?

"Having guys do a heck of a lot more for me than just hit open shots," Dee said.

That night Larry King asked more questions about what it was like being Cool Daddy Cody's daughter and the way her mother had died and then tried to pin her down about her plans after this season.

But you *will* be back, right?

"I didn't say that," she said.

But, Larry King said, you're still young enough to have a long career in this game.

Dee said, "Who said anything about having a long career?"

Larry then leaned forward—it must have been some sort of required interviewing move—and asked if she was trying to sound this mysterious on purpose.

Dee leaned forward and said, "How about we take some

calls." Raising her voice to imitate him, she said, "Topeka, you're on the air with Dee Gerard!"

When she got back to the hotel, she called Gilles, as she did every couple of days, to see how business was at DC. It was the middle of the night, but she wasn't worried about it, Gilles had always kept vampire hours, she knew he'd be up.

He said he'd watched her with Larry King on CNN International.

"Two words," he said. "More sleep."

"That's it. Not, nice outfit. Or nice pearls. Or you actually got your hair right for once? Just, more sleep?"

"Okay, other than the little smudgy things under the eyes, you looked *très magnifique*. How's that?"

"You sound very peppy. We have a good night, did we?"

"What can I tell you? It's good being king."

Then: "Wait."

Dee heard a voice in the background and then Gilles exclaimed, "*Bonjour*, Gaby!" and told Dee he'd talk to her soon.

After practice at the Garden the next afternoon, her first hard practice since she'd hit her head, she pronounced herself good to go for the Pistons game on Sunday. Eddie said he planned to give her a few more minutes. Fine with me, Dee said. The Heat had lost twice since the Knights had left Florida, and now were only six games ahead in the loss column.

Dee started to think that maybe Eddie wasn't so crazy after all, talking about the playoffs.

He walked her out to Thirty-third Street when practice was over. There were kids there waiting, because there were after every practice now, especially the ones on the weekend. As usual, there were more girls than boys. Dee signed everything they wanted her to sign, posed for pictures, laughed with a couple of teenaged girls taller than she was, wearing "Boys and Girls High" warm-ups.

When she was done, she asked if Eddie wanted to have a bite to eat and he said he had to be a good coach and go look at film, there was a rule that had been passed that you were supposed to look at film until your eyeballs melted.

"Be ready tomorrow," he said.

She told him she was.

It was the day after she wasn't ready for.

The front page of Monday's *Daily News* was not about the Knights' 94–87 victory over the Detroit Pistons, or about the fact that Dee had gotten her first start because Ray Ray was still sitting out his suspension and Deltha Lewis had shown up at the Garden suffering from severe back spasms.

The front page wasn't about the mayor's song-and-dance number from *La Cage aux Folles,* in drag, at the annual Inner Circle dinner.

It wasn't about Bill Clinton—the ex-President, not Mo Jiggy's prize rottweiler—being photographed outside a downtown club with a young woman who was definitely not his wife Hillary—the United States Senator, not Mo Jiggy's other favorite rott.

That picture got bumped back to page five.

The picture on the front page was of Eddie Holtz kissing Dee Gerard in front of the Sherry-Netherland underneath this headline:

Office Romance

⊚ eighteen

RANSOME NOTES
by Walt Ransome

Well, at least we understand now how Dee Gerard won
her starting job with the Knights.

Now the only question I have goes something like
this:

Where do they keep the casting couch in the NBA?

I've watched every game the Knights have played, in
person or on television, since this circus came to town.
The next morning I've turned to the stats page in the
News and checked out the box score. And because I
thought sports was still run on the merit system, I never
dreamt she was working her way up to a start.

I didn't see how any coach—even one getting on-
the-job training the way Eddie Holtz is (getting that and
a whole lot more, apparently)—could even think about
giving her more meaningful minutes.

Any coach still thinking with his brain instead of
something else.

At least I didn't see that until now.

Like you, I wasn't reading between the lines. I've frankly never had a head for numbers, which is why people always have to practically draw me a picture.

Or show me one worth at least the 1,000 or so words I'm giving you today.

And giving Eddie Holtz's new sweetie.

Right between those eyes of hers that looked so cute closed the way they are on the front page.

Michael held his press conference in the screening room he'd had built on the second floor of the Knights' offices at Five Penn. The Knights were practicing in Mamaroneck before their flight to Cleveland for a game the next night against the Cavaliers. He picked a time when he knew the players met with the media, usually on their way to the bus.

When everyone was in place, he read a short statement about how outraged the entire organization was about this invasion of Miss Gerard's privacy, even in what he described as the peep show culture of New York newspaper journalism.

At the end he said people were always going to draw their own conclusions before all the facts were in, but there shouldn't be the usual rush to judgment because of one angry newspaper columnist's antiwomen agenda.

Michael didn't add the last part until he had Harold Wasserman's assurance that Walt Ransome wasn't in attendance.

"You know me, Harold," he said. "I'm only confrontational up to a point."

The last line of his statement, which he added to Harold's original text, was that the photograph was out of context.

"How can a picture in the paper be out of context?" a male reporter from Channel 5 asked.

Michael smiled. "Rock," he said. "We're all adults here, with the possible exception of me. A kiss doesn't mean they're having a romance, as the headline suggests. They're *not* having a romance. Sometimes"—he shrugged here in what he hoped was a man-of-the-world way—"a kiss is just . . ."

"A kiss?" Rock said, trying to be helpful.

"My coach tells me he was just saying good night," Michael said.

A girl reporter Michael didn't recognize, a cutie with the kind of long black hair Michael loved, stood up behind Rock and said, "Does he say good night to Carl Anthony that way?"

A voice to Michael's right murmured, "Jamie Lawton would be a better bet," and there was a brief ripple of giggling.

"Gentlemen," Michael said. "And ladies. Is this the best we can do to shoot down what is such an important statement on my part, on the team's part, on the league's part, and most of all on Miss Gerard's part? Aren't you all better than that? Aren't we all?"

"What does Dee Gerard have to say about all this?" the cutie asked.

"Her response is that she isn't going to dignify it with a response." Michael paused and said, "Which makes her a better man *and* woman than me."

He noticed that, as always, the television lights made him hot in more ways than one.

"She has more grace than I do," he said, just the way Harold told him to, really selling it. "She has more grace than the people attacking her for sport, who wanted this to be more about cheap sex than about someone of her sex trying to do this monumental thing." He paused and said, "Dee's better than this."

Michael turned to a beaming Harold Wasserman, then back at the crowd in front of him.

"In the grand scheme of things," Michael said, "this doesn't mean a thing."

"It don't mean nothin'," Dee said in her suite at the Ritz-Carlton of Cleveland, practically next door to the Gund Arena.

"Beg your pardon?" Eddie said.

Dee said, "He sounds like Anquwan."

The two of them were watching the highlights of Michael

De la Cruz's press conference on the 6:30 SportsCenter, along with Joey Shahoud.

Dee muted the sound. "Who took that picture?" It was the same question she'd been asking Eddie all day.

Eddie said, "I think my question is better."

"Once they had it," Dee said, "why'd they hold it?"

"I was on-line before," Joey said. "The *News* won't say who took the picture, just that it was a, quote, freelance photographer, unquote."

Joey was wearing his Knights warm-ups, the same he wore for practice, for games, on the team plane. It occurred to her that she'd never seen him in any other kind of clothing.

"So somebody waited for us outside The Last Good Year, followed us in the car, saw us get out, then snapped the picture of us making out when we got to the hotel?"

"Or was just waiting at the hotel," Eddie said, lighting another cigarette.

Dee noticed he was even smoking on the team plane now.

She said, "I'm not doing this."

He looked at her. "Doing what?"

"*This*," she said, pointing with the remote at the television set, which now showed ESPN going to some sort of panel discussion with the front page of the *News* as a backdrop, dropped in like a chandelier behind them. "This . . . shitty *shit*."

She could feel the tears starting to come, got up and walked over to the set and shut it off even though she had the remote in her hand, just to buy herself some time. When she turned back around, she saw Eddie staring at her and she knew he knew what she really wanted to do was cry.

But she didn't.

She said in a tiny voice, "No crying in baseball."

"A League of Their Own," Joey said.

"Like you," Eddie said to Dee.

"Like me, what?"

"You're the one in a league of your own."

She said, "I'll bet you say that to all the girl players you kiss."

She was wearing the same lemon-colored cotton sweater

she'd worn on the plane, the black jeans. Eddie and Joey each had a chair in the sitting room. Dee stretched out on the couch. She'd set up her portable stereo and Ruth Brown was singing "I Can't Hear a Word You Say."

"I feel holed up like a rock star," she said. "Afraid to go down to the lobby. Extra security on our floors."

"You are a rock star," Eddie said.

"I didn't expect this."

"What did you expect?"

Dee said, "I knew I'd be a big deal, I'm not that naive. I knew I'd be the flavor of the month. Do they still even have a flavor of the month, by the way? I knew I'd be asked about Cool Daddy getting sent up when he was a kid and my mother dying the way she did. I expected silly pieces out of the London papers about my ex-husband. The rubbish, as he'd call it."

"Absolute rubbish," Eddie said in his bad British accent, which he generally liked to use when the subject of Jeremy came up.

"But after that," Dee said, "I thought they'd let me play, if I actually could play, that is."

"Maybe it's like the owner says," Eddie said. "This is really about being *in* play." And lit another cigarette.

"How many is that for you today?" Dee asked.

"You sound like a wife."

"That is an ugly thing to say," she said, and felt herself want to smile for the first time since she'd picked up the stupid *Daily News* outside her door at the Sherry.

"Once you're in play," Eddie Holtz said, "you're fair game. Except the part they don't want you to know is that hardly anybody plays fair."

Joey said he was going downstairs to have a bite to eat, he'd call her later. Dee stood up, went over to the big picture window facing out to what Joey had informed her was the Rock and Roll Hall of Fame across the street, and then Lake Erie beyond that. She'd had to ask which lake. It was the first Great Lake she had ever seen. It was the first time she'd ever been to Cleveland, which Eddie said used to have about the same charm as East New York in the downtown area but was now one of the nice stops in the league.

She had never been to Cleveland the way she had never been to Miami or Orlando, where there had been mouse ears on everything.

I've seen the world, she thought, just not the country.

What was that book by Anne Tyler she'd liked so much, the one she'd bought at duty-free that time and couldn't put down? *The Accidental Tourist.*

That's me, she thought.

One accident after another.

She stood there, her back to the room, watching the last of the afternoon light, a spooky winter glow, leave Cleveland, replaced by streetlights. Off to her left, across from where Eddie'd told her the Indians' ballpark was, she saw a rush-hour crawl of cars make its way across a bridge over the Great Lake she hadn't seen until today.

Ruthie sang, "Why Me?" It was one of her all-time favorite CDs, *Miss Rhythm.* Dee knew it the way she knew all Ruth Brown recordings, old and new, knew that the next song was "I Don't Know."

Eddie came over without Dee hearing him and put his arms around her from behind, and kissed her hair.

Dee turned, put her arms around the back of his neck.

Thinking: I don't want to be a rock star now.

I don't want to be the most famous girl in the world.

I don't want to be Front-Page Dee.

Or the smart Dee, the one who knew she shouldn't be like this with Eddie in this hotel suite, not on today of all days.

She didn't care.

She wanted to be held.

She felt herself starting to move a little, side to side, with the music, pressing herself closer to Eddie Holtz as she did.

"You dance, Coach?"

His eyes were bright, serious, alert, alive, all at once.

"I won't," he said. "Don't ask me."

"Don't worry," Dee said. "I'll lead."

They slow-danced in Cleveland with the lights of the city behind them and then they were kissing in the way that had put them in the newspaper, and then Dee was still leading, toward the bedroom now.

Eddie stopped, still holding her hand.

"You sure about this?" he said.

She said, "Of course not."

Eddie said, "Just so we're clear on that."

"Crystal," she said.

They were standing near the bed then, Ruth Brown's voice suddenly sounding far away, and Dee was unbuttoning Eddie's shirt, pulling it open a little bit, putting her hands on his warm, smooth back.

"You know what they say?" Eddie said.

"What do they say?"

"If you're going to do the time, you might as well do the crime."

Dee said, "Is that what they say?"

Dee had always found that her first reaction, first thing the next morning, pretty much told the tale for her.

If she thought about making a run for it—even if it was her place—that was a very bad sign.

Or: If it was his place, and before she even brushed her teeth she was already composing the cute note she was going to leave him?

Much, *much* worse.

Dee had never been enough of a drinker that she couldn't remember what happened. And the truth was, there hadn't been that many guys to begin with. She always brought it back to a line from another of her all-time favorite movies, *Pat and Mike*, the one with Tracy and Hepburn where the Hepburn character was vaguely modeled after Babe Didrickson, one of Dee's heroes, from way back, when Dee first started playing ball with the boys. Probably from the time she found out that Babe Didrickson, the greatest female athlete of them all, in about nine sports, had been the first woman to play with male golfers back at the Los Angeles Open in 1938, and that a few years before that had even pitched an inning in an exhibition game against the Brooklyn Dodgers without giving up a hit.

"Not much meat," Tracy had said about Hepburn's body, talking about her as if she were a racehorse. "But what's there is *cherce*."

Dee always felt that the men in her life, the few she had been intimate with, the ones she had allowed to be intimate with *her*, had been *cherce*.

Even the ones like Jeremy who had tried to break her goddamn heart.

She'd always told herself that she was the one who had been *cherce*, with her choices.

Now it was Eddie Holtz, who occasionally talked softly in his sleep during the night, not that she could make out what he was saying.

She lay there with her eyes open, saw the back of his head, saw more gray in his hair this close, heard his steady breathing, no snoring, remembered everything that had happened in the night, and then happened again, the second time so soon after the first, even better than the first, surprising both of them, Eddie more than her. She slipped quietly out of the huge bed then, on her way to brush her teeth. The clock on the nightstand on Eddie's side of the bed said 7:32 when she came back wearing one of those white robes places like the Ritz always thought were such hot little numbers.

She had run a brush through the tangle that her hair had become once Eddie was done with it, brushing it hard; she knew she was a nut about the way her hair looked first thing in the morning, and about her breath, which is why she had not only brushed like the dentist was watching, but hit her Listerine hard as well.

Eddie was still sleeping, so she went into the kitchen and poured some Starbucks House Blend into the filter—Mo made sure it was waiting for her in every new hotel—and turned the coffee machine on; when the coffee was made she poured herself a big mug of it and went back into the bedroom and sat in the chair across from the bed, next to the cabinet with the television set in it, and watched Eddie sleep a little

more, officially wondering how things were going to change
between them now.

Whose idea was this, anyway?

She knew.

It was hers.

Hers all the way.

I'll lead, she'd said.

She was tired of worrying how everything looked, tired of
watching every move she made. She had wanted to make this
move on Eddie. She had wanted this to happen for a while,
even before they kissed in front of the Sherry. She had really
wanted something to happen with somebody—not just
falling into it—for the first time since Jeremy, and now she
wasn't going to analyze this, try to play it all the way out. This
is where they were now. Here. Cleveland. Eddie in the bed,
her making the coffee. Game tonight, flight home right afterward. They'd go from here. She felt herself smiling again,
thinking, Just because we're making history doesn't mean we
can't make out.

Eddie turned over now, blinked his eyes open, saw her in
the chair, her legs curled underneath her, watching him.

"Hey," he said.

"Hey yourself."

Eddie sat up a little. "How *you* doin'?" In the thick New
York accent that was almost as bad as his Brit.

Dee said, "You know, I've been sitting here asking myself
the exact same question."

"You come up with an answer yet?"

"After much consideration," she said, "I have decided I
am quite fine."

He gave her his crooked grin, said, "You know, sex the
night before a big game is supposed to be bad for you. That's
what guys have always been told, anyway."

Dee said, "Not being a guy, as you've clearly noticed by
now, I decided to chance it."

"Of course, the morning *of*," he said, "I've never heard
much discussion on the merits of that, one way or another."

Dee said, "Would you like some of my delicious House
Blend first?"

"Sure," Eddie said. "And on your way back?"

"Yes."

"You could think about losing the robe."

It was after that morning's shootaround, Dee on her way to the interview area behind the court at Gund Arena, that Deltha Lewis came over and told Eddie that he and some of the boys wanted to have a meeting with him.

Eddie asked which players and was told Deltha, Anquwan, Dream Jackson, Ray Ray, and Thruston B. Howell, the six-six swingman who'd been on the injured list with a bad hamstring but had made the trip to Cleveland and was eligible to play that night. Thruston B. Howell was known in basketball as Sea Lion. He was, Eddie had decided long before, the blackest black man he had ever seen, shaped remarkably like the seal family that had given him his nickname, with the same kind of whiskers and tiny ears, and a tendency to flap his arms, seal-like, when he walked. But he had what the players called hops when it was time to jump, and was deceptively fast for someone with his body, about 250 pounds stuffed into a six-six frame.

They all went into the visitors' locker room, the rest of the team on its way back to the Ritz through the indoor shopping mall that separated the arena from the hotel.

Eddie said, "You guys want to wait for Dee?"

"This *about* Dee," Deltha said.

It was fifty degrees outside, a day one of the weather girls on the morning news had called a false spring in Cleveland, but Deltha was wearing a black wool Yankees cap, the kind downhill skiers wore, pulled down nearly to his eyes, a thick black hooded sweatshirt with "Reebok" in huge letters across the front, jeans hanging halfway off his skinny ass. Deltha had untied the laces of his new Nike high-tops, which Eddie thought had some patent leather in the tips, as soon as the Knights had stopped walking through their plays.

Eddie had never understood the untied-shoes things with these kids, but that was just one more thing he didn't get, along with the tats, the pierced body parts, the shit with their posses and their boys, the dope he knew a lot of them smoked in their free time, as if grass were legal and having a fucking beer was against the law now. But Eddie wasn't kidding when he said he had to go with the flow. As young as he still was, he knew he was just another old white guy to the black kids on his team. On top of that, he knew it was their game now, not his. If Eddie wasn't hip to the fact that Deltha was the face of basketball now, and Anquwan with his crazy-ass hair, and Ray Ray with so many flying fish tattooed on his arms and even his stomach, he looked like one of those dolphin theme parks in Florida, then he better get the hell out of the way and let somebody else try to coach them.

Chuck Daly, who Eddie thought was the coolest of the modern coaches, the one who communicated the best with these guys, once told him, "You gotta understand something: These guys *allow* you to coach them."

In the visitors' locker room in Cleveland now, Deltha Lewis said, "You startin' her tonight?"

There was no reason to bullshit him, or buy time. "Yeah," Eddie said. "I am."

He nodded at the rest of them, who'd grouped their chairs together in the middle of the room. Ray Ray, Eddie noticed, was wearing a blue baseball cap that looked like a replica of the old Brooklyn Dodgers', but the logo was "BC."

"What's the BC stand for, Ray?" Eddie said, just to say something.

"Brooklyn Cyclones. Is a new minor league team over to Coney Island. Got a girl works with them, over in that Park Slope."

Deltha said, "He bangin' her, Coach. Maybe she thinks it will improve her situation, the way bitches do."

"She ain't one of my bitches," Ray Ray said. The commissioner had decided to shorten his suspension, which meant he could play that night. "It ain't like that."

"I don't mean nothin' by it," Deltha said.

"You know where we goin' with this?" Dream Jackson said.

"I believe I do," Eddie said.

Dream—his goatee was hot pink; Eddie noticed he switched it every couple of days—was one of the guys Eddie genuinely liked on the Knights, the one who hated losing the most, even more than Carl Anthony. Dream said, "Ax you something, Coach?"

"Sure."

"You know how bad it looks for Deltha and Ray Ray—who play the girl's position—you put her ahead of them?"

Before Eddie could answer, Deltha said, "We want you to know that just because you fuckin' her don't mean you can fuck us."

"There it is," Thruston B. Howell said.

"Uh-huh," Dream said.

Eddie said, "Anybody else?"

Anquwan raised a hand, as if he needed permission to speak. He hadn't done his cornrows yet today, so his hair was in a full Buckwheat Afro. "You don't care about lookin' like some booey-whipped fool . . ."

"Booey?" Eddie said.

"The bad," Anquwan said gravely.

"Oh," Eddie said.

Another thing he didn't get. You needed subtitles now to keep up with a conversation about getting laid.

"Was sayin'," Anquwan said. "Just because you don't care about lookin' bad, we do."

"Which all springs from the fact you've all decided I'm doing the bad with Dee," Eddie said.

Now there was a chorus of "Uh-huh."

Eddie pulled up a chair of his own, facing them, crossed his good knee over his bad one, and said, "Anything else?"

"We think you get our meaning," Deltha said.

Eddie smiled. "You know who really gets fucked here if she can't play? Me."

Deltha leaned forward. "This ain't about—"

Eddie held up a hand.

"You know how much time I've got to show I can coach in this league? About twenty games, or whatever it is now. That's my season, that's my shot—you guys know that, right?"

They stared back at him. It wasn't just snotty French guys who practiced not giving a shit, he thought.

"I didn't make it as a player. I don't know what would've happened if I didn't blow out my knee. But I did. So there's one more thing I'll never know. What I do know is this: I fucking *scouted* to stay in this fucking game. Before I took the scouting job, they talked to me about doing color with that old man who does our play-by-play on the radio. Then Michael De la Cruz decided he liked having me around to explain shit to him. Only, now shit happens and I'm the coach. I got eleven guys on this team and one girl and this bullshit cockeyed notion that all twelve of you, playing together, can get that last playoff spot in the East."

Once again Anquwan raised his hand, like a student at one of the classes he didn't attend at UNLV.

"We clear on that," he said. "We want to win, too."

"I thought you said there ain't no W's and L's on your paycheck, mon," Thruston B. Howell said.

"Was before we actually won a few games," Anquwan said.

"Hey," Eddie said sharply. "Let's wrap this up."

He went from face to face, taking his time, making sure he had their attention.

He said, "I frankly don't give a rat's ass what you think about Dee and me, what you think you know, what you hear on the radio or what you read in the goddamn newspapers. But if you're gonna play for me, if I'm gonna *get* you to play for me, I do care what you think about me in here. And I'm telling you something straight in here: I'm playing her more because right now I think that gives us a better chance. Deltha? You and Ray Ray might not get the minutes you want, but you gotta trust me to get you in there, use you both in a way that might help us shock the shit out of the rest of the league." He shrugged. "And if I'm wrong, you're here next year and I'm gone."

He stood up.

"People talk about you guys being selfish all the time," Eddie said. "Shit, there's nobody in the world more selfish than a coach. I'll do whatever it takes to get the best out of her, same as I will the rest of you. Because it helps *me*. Because it makes me look better. I'm the guy with guts enough to play the girl and make it work. Auerbach never did it, Wilkens never did it, or Riley or Phil Jackson. But Eddie Holtz did. You guys want to think I'm doing this for her, go right ahead. But I'm not. I'm doing it for *me*."

He walked out and left them there, wanting a cigarette, wondering how much of it was true. From behind him, he thought he might've heard Dee call his name. Eddie kept going, through the double doors into the mall, as if he didn't hear. He was tired of talking.

⚾ nineteen

Dee remembered the first one.

An All-Star Game at the Olympic arena in Barcelona, the arena where the Dream Team with Michael Jordan and Magic Johnson and Larry Bird had played in the '92 Olympics. The best players from Spain against the best from Division I in France. Cynthia Cooper was in the game, all the top girls.

Another charity game she knew she'd never forget.

Dee had gotten a message from Cool Daddy that day, saying he was in town, maybe she could leave him a ticket to the game, popping back into her life the way he did in those days — before he was gone for good — saying he wanted to see his little girl, which always meant that he needed money.

Dee had gotten dressed in her uniform that night, cute little blue stars all over it, done her yoga exercises, simple stuff, more to get her loose than anything else. Pillow under her head, knees pulled up as close to her as she could get them, holding that pose for two minutes. Then two minutes over on her stomach, weight on her elbows, until she felt the knots start to come out of her lower back. Then up into a sitting position, looping a belt around the balls of her feet, pulling hard on it for two more minutes.

She had just gotten the belt out, was sitting in front of her locker, all the other players on the French team still out shooting around, Dee having told them she'd be out in ten minutes.

It was maybe an hour before the game.

Suddenly she couldn't move.

No one else in the room, not even the coaches, everything perfectly quiet.

Perfectly still.

Including her.

She would try to explain it to Jeremy later, before she ever tried explaining it to a shrink, how she actually felt like she'd been *invaded* somehow, not by another person, not like that, but by this mass, a block of ice not just on top of her but all around her, freezing her there in place in front of her locker, the belt still in her right hand.

Her mouth had turned to sand; she desperately wanted something to drink, just to show herself she could swallow. She could see the plastic bottle of water next to her on the chair.

Only.

Only, she could not reach over to pick it up.

The best she could do was open and close her eyes, like she was communicating in some kind of code. Except no one was there.

When the first players started to come back from the court, she closed her eyes, ashamed of the terror she was feeling, hoping they would think she was in some kind of meditation. She could hear them talking now, laughing occasionally, but the sounds seemed to be coming from another room. Everything was muffled that way, like the music she would hear from inside the arena when the door would open and another player would walk in.

Help, she thought, even the voice inside her head sounding weak and far away.

She knew no one knew what was happening. How could they? She hadn't known, not the first time, not until Kym

Wells, a kid she liked, new to European ball, a South Philadelphia kid who'd been a star at Temple, had seen something when she opened her eyes, that's what Kym would tell her later, saw the panic Dee was feeling, came over and sat down on the carpet next to her, as if there was no problem, and quietly said, "Can you move?"

"No."

The sound surprised her, escaping from her in a whisper.

"You can," Kym said softly. "You don't think you can, but you can."

Dee remembered tears starting to come out of her eyes then.

"I've been there," Kym said. "You've got to trust me now, girl. It'll pass. It . . . will . . . pass."

"When?" Dee said.

Another whisper.

"When it's ready, girl. When it's ready. And I'm gonna sit here with you till it does, even if it takes all night."

Kym told the trainer Dee was having back spasms, she needed help moving her, and then a couple of the other women, two of the bigger ones, two sisters from the Samoa Betera team in Valenica who'd come by to say hello to some old friends on the French team, came over and helped pick her up, Kym telling them to be careful, can't you see my girl's in pain here? They got her up on a massage table. By then Dee could move her arms and legs, even if they felt the way they did when you slept funny and something went numb on you. Right before the start of the game, the fans already in their seats, Kym took her outside, the two of them walking out a side door to the arena, a jacket over Dee's uniform, Kym saying she was going back inside but that Dee should just keep walking around the arena in the cool night air, which is what she did, walking slowly at first, then picking up speed, then started to jog a little bit, feeling the life slowly start to come back into her legs.

She actually came back and played the second half somehow, not that she remembered anything except that she had gone out there. . . .

It was happening to her now in Cleveland.

In the small dressing room with the blue walls and blue carpet that usually belonged to the male coach of the Cleveland team in the WNBA.

He needed to be separate from the girls, Dee from the boys.

She sat on the couch in the white buttoned-down shirt she had worn over here from the hotel, in her new Lucky jeans, in the Arche loafers she'd bought in the mall after she'd bought the jeans, having gone shopping after she'd just missed Eddie at the end of practice, trying to catch him before he left so the two of them could have lunch.

Dee sat there with her heart beating a hundred times faster than it had when this had happened to her in the Garden that day, before her first press conference. None of them were ever the same. What was she calling them these days, she forgot? Episodes? Attacks? She could move this time, she knew that. Oh, boy, she sure could move, her legs shaking no matter how hard she tried to press her knees together, her hands shaking so badly when she tried to get a cup of tea to her lips that the cup fell out of her hands and smashed on the coffee table in front of her.

It was happening to her again, and she wanted to cry.

Or scream.

She knew she wouldn't.

Scream.

Oh no, she was much too put together for that.

At least that's what everybody thought.

Please, she thought.

Not tonight.

She had kidded herself, coming into this, thinking that maybe the shakes and the frights had forgotten her over the last couple of years, moved on from Dee Gerard to somebody else, some singer or actor or ballplayer. Somebody more important than an old women's basketball player.

Dumped her, like a boyfriend would.

She didn't want to understand them anymore, what brought them on, where they came from, if they were somehow tied up in all the mixed-up feelings she had for Cool Daddy, the colorful character she tried to make him out to be for the rest of the world, the slob he really became. Or always was. Or if they were tied up somehow in the memories of her mother. Or with both her parents, because both of them had been performers, always dreaming about being bigger than they really were. One had the skill, not the will. That's the way the shrink in London had put it to Dee one time. The other, her mother, had never stepped out of the chorus, no matter how much she wanted to.

Dee was the one who had stepped out of the chorus, been bigger than both of them, maybe even *showing* both of them, even as she kept telling herself it was for the love of the game.

Round and round.

A million thoughts flashing inside her head while she sat there, the same old light show. The deep Old Vic voice of the London shrink telling her that some people never found out what brought on attacks like hers.

Okay, Dee thought.

Okay!

She just wanted them to go away.

Now.

Please.

There was a soft knocking on the door.

"Dee?"

Joey Shahoud.

"Dee, you in there?" he said.

Well, she thought, I am and I'm not.

"Hey, you better be decent, kid, 'cause I'm coming in."

He cracked the door open. Poked his head in carefully, saw her on the couch, saw the teacup in pieces on the coffee table, the puddles of tea spilling onto the blue carpet.

Looked at her and clearly didn't know what to say.

So she said something.

"I can't."

Fingers locked together, because if she separated her hands, he'd see the shakes, understand that she was about to come flying apart like the goddamn teacup.

He said he was going to get Eddie, that Dee should stay right there, if anybody but them knocked on the door to tell them to go away.

Where am I going? Dee thought.

To powder my nose?

Michael looked at Eddie as if he'd started speaking Chinese all of a sudden, the way his big goofy Dong Li did when he wanted to call the ref a cocksucker.

"What do you mean she can't come out of her dressing room right now? Jesus, I've been around enough actresses. They've usually got to have more bitch in them than Dee before they refuse to come out of their trailers."

Eddie said, "It's not like that."

Michael's new Gulfstream X—Ron Perelman, who'd told everybody he was going to have the first one, could kiss his ass, okay?—had landed him in Cleveland forty-five minutes before. He had decided at lunch that day, Le Cirque, that he wasn't going to miss a single game the rest of the year, had called Teterboro and told them to crank up his baby and point it toward Lake Erie, he'd be there after his facial.

Miss one game, he'd decided, and you might miss an opportunity. If he'd been in Orlando, it would have been him who'd gotten to Dee first. More important, *much* more important, it would have been Michael kneeling over her in the newspapers the next day.

Harold Wasserman had held up the front page of the *Times* to Michael like a rebuke and said, "If you don't mind a stand-in doing your big scene, Michael, I guess I don't either."

Mini-Me was right, as usual.

"I should have told you about this before," Eddie said.

They were standing just inside the door to the Knights' locker room, maybe ten minutes before the opening tip, the music in Gund Arena sounding loud enough to be part of a concert starring Michael's good friend Sting.

"Told me what?"

"She has these . . ." He could see Eddie searching what Michael had always thought was a fairly limited jock vocabulary—Eddie never understanding the power of words—looking for the right way to say it. "She has, like, stage fright sometimes."

"Her?"

Eddie nodded.

"You're shitting me," Michael said.

"The way she explained it," Eddie said, "it's not techni-cally stage fright, since it doesn't happen all the time. Or even regularly, the way I understood her. Random attacks, that's the way she described them." Eddie held up a finger, like say-ing, *I've got it*, and said, "Floating anxiety disorder."

Michael couldn't believe his ears.

"Like Tony in *The Sopranos*? Going to pieces because his old man chopped off the butcher's pinkie, or whatever the hell it was. This is a joke, right?"

"Not to her."

"Let me talk to her. Getting people to do things they think they can't—who's better at that than me?"

"No," Eddie said.

Michael cocked his head a little, looking at him. He'd no-ticed a change in Eddie since he made him coach. It was more than his demand that he wanted Reg, the doorstop general manager, out of the way. Michael knew how people from the outside looked at him, like he was some kind of New Age preacher sometimes, Anthony Robbins, just much better-looking. As if all that money had made itself. But Michael knew he was a good judge of people, he had good instincts about most of them, even if you couldn't tell so far by the bas-ketball assholes he'd hired before Eddie.

Eddie Holtz wasn't one of those assholes. People thought it was some kind of heat-of-the-moment deal when he'd zipped Bobby C.—the king of the assholes—but it wasn't that way at all. Michael had been thinking about making the move from the moment Eddie showed up in his office with Dee Gerard.

But there was no question he'd changed. None. And now Michael would have to take a step back, see how things played out before he knew if that was a good thing or not.

"You're telling me I can't see her?" Michael said slowly, like he was putting each word in a measuring cup. "Or, and I am *sincerely* hoping this is the case, you're telling me you don't think it's a good idea I see my girl right now."

Eddie stood his ground, Michael had to give him that.

"Either way. I calmed her down once before, but this one is much worse. She's shaking like she's got the fucking DTs."

"Well, then you tell her to snap out of it, for Chrissakes!" Michael exploded, feeling that high heat he sometimes had in the back of his neck when the world wouldn't do what he wanted it to do.

He said, "There's a sellout crowd out there, which is something they haven't had in this town since the ugly lake came back from the dead. And besides, TNT bumped the Lakers to put us on tonight."

Eddie said, "They're gonna make an announcement she's got back spasms and she still might play."

"Who told them to do that?"

"Me."

Him.

The new Eddie.

Maybe it really was the girl giving him this kind of stick all of a sudden, maybe he really was banging her.

"What if she doesn't play?"

Eddie shrugged. "We hope it doesn't happen again."

Michael opened the door, and the two of them stepped outside. Michael jerked his head in the direction of Dee's dressing room. "The rest of this, whatever happens the rest of the night, goes through me. Understood?"

Jesus, you even had to remind the smart ones.

Sometimes even Eddie, whom he liked, acted like a court jester who thought he'd turned into royalty.

"I gotta go coach my team," Eddie said.

"My team," Michael reminded him.

When he was gone, Michael reached into the pocket of his windbreaker for his cell phone, grateful as always that he had Harold Wasserman on speed dial.

Michael wasn't the only one who could turn minuses into a plus.

Michael thought: Maybe another opportunity had presented itself.

*   *   *

Dee played.

She played after Joey mixed her up a pot of what he called his special "tranquillity tea."

She played after Joey made her start her whole pregame routine from scratch, making her undress—after he left the room for a couple of minutes—and take a hot shower and get back into the clothes she'd worn to the arena and wait for him while he ran back through the mall to the hotel and got her music for her, the *Miss Rhythm* CD she told him she'd left in her machine from the day before.

Before her and Eddie.

Dee played after Joey balled up pieces of paper from a program he found in the Knights' locker room and challenged her to a game of horse, shooting the balled-up paper into a wastebasket he set up near the door.

After he made a second pot of tranquillity tea and shared some with her and told her he was starting to feel so loose he felt as if he'd smoked a joint.

"What's in this, anyway?" she asked.

"Nothing illegal, lady, if that's what you're asking. Other than that, I'm not saying another thing until I talk to my lawyer."

"You promise it's all natural?"

Joey said, "You want to split hairs here, or you want to get yourself right?"

"I still don't think I can."

"Sure you can," he said cheerfully.

"Maybe it would just be better for everybody if I fought again another day."

Joey fired a piece of paper that bounced off the door and went in. "Can I ask you something?"

"Make it something easy."

"You more worried about Eddie or about starting?"

"What about Eddie?"

"Right," he said. "What about Eddie? Wherever did a question like that come from?"

Dee sighed. "I've paid a fortune in my life being analyzed. I'll pay you *not* to analyze me. Okay?"

"I'm as qualified as anybody else you've ever talked to. I watch a lot of afternoon talk shows when we're on the road."

Dee said, "You want an honest answer? I don't know what it is. But I've never known."

"The other times? Did you play?"

"Sometimes." She paused. "Not all the time."

"So play tonight."

"You make it sound simple. It's not. It's the complete total opposite of simple, believe me."

Joey said, "I believe you. Let's see the hands."

Dee put them out in front of her, studying them as if they belonged to somebody else, noticing just a slight tremor now, like a soft breeze blowing through curtains.

Not anything like before.

"I blew my start," she said.

"Hey," Joey Shahoud said, "you know what they say. It's not where you start, it's where you finish."

"Is that what they say?" Dee said.

Sometimes she only heard what she wanted to hear from guys. No matter which guy, no matter what the situation.

Sometimes she couldn't tell who was leading at all.

Three minutes left in the third quarter, Sea Lion Howell at the free-throw line, Eddie heard this cheer go up at Gund Arena, turned and saw Dee and Joey Shahoud making their way between the first row of the stands and the Cavaliers' bench.

He told everybody to move down and make some room for them.

When Dee sat down, Eddie said, "Are you okay?"

"God," she said, "you've been asking me that all day."

He thought he could read her pretty good by now, but he wasn't sure. She still looked shaky, as if she might start crying if he said the wrong thing, even used the wrong tone of voice.

Where was there any-goddamn-place left where you didn't have to watch what you said with women? Or how you goddamn said it?

"You can play?" he asked.

Dee said, "My contract says I gotta stay till the end of the game. I thought I might as well make myself useful."

Ray Ray Abdul-Mahi was down at the end of the bench and might as well have been in Siberia as far as Eddie Holtz was concerned. Ray Ray had smarted off to Eddie earlier in the quarter, Eddie telling him to run one play, Ray Ray ignoring him, then motherfucking him all over the place when Eddie pulled him from the game. He was through for tonight and maybe for a few more; maybe he'd suspend him the way Marcus Betts had, it would depend on how Eddie felt after the game.

Meanwhile Deltha, who had turned an ankle in the first half, was getting eaten alive by the Cavaliers guards. One was Jere Nolan, a Queens kid who reminded Eddie a little of himself the way he played. The other was Mephisto Morton, Earthwind's kid brother, one who'd made headlines recently because of a promotional deal with Milky Way candy bars that had him put a colorful tattoo of the regular Milky Way bar on his right biceps and the new low-fat Milky Way on his left biceps.

"Myself was able to do this without violating the integrity of my existing body art," Mephisto said at the press conference announcing the deal.

Dee had been seated next to Eddie for about a minute of game time when Jere Nolan stripped Deltha in the backcourt and fed Mephisto for a layup, after which Mephisto pointed to one of the Milky Way bars, then flexed his arm.

Just like that, the game was 76-all.

"Go in for Deltha," Eddie said to Dee.

He felt her eyes on him, but she didn't say anything.

Eddie said, "Knock my socks off."

"Been there," Dee said quietly, turning her head toward Eddie so only he could hear. "Done that."

When she was kneeling in front of the scorer's table, waiting to go in on the next whistle, Eddie said to Joey Shahoud, "How you'd get her out here?"

"Well," Joey said, "I gave her some of my tranquillity tea for starters."

"What the hell is that?"

"Lipton decaf," he said, "with a couple of packets of Sweet'N Low."

She felt as if she were playing the game underwater at first. She wouldn't even remember the one shot she made, a little scoop shot right in front of the basket, until she saw it on the highlights the next morning. Mostly she'd remember the noise the Cleveland fans would make every single time she touched the ball, whether she did anything good with it or not. She knew the deal, as shaky as she was: They had been told this was an Event, a Happening, that this was the only time they'd get to see her play in person, and she could feel how determined they were to get their money's worth, whether she actually delivered the goods or not.

The third time down the court, she found Lamar Sheet loose underneath the basket after Carl Anthony had set him a wrecking-ball screen away from the ball, and she hit him with a pass that went through such a narrow opening Lamar would describe it for the writers afterward as a credit-card slot. His basket put the Knights ahead by two as the quarter ended.

Nobody got ahead more than a basket after that; finally, in the last minute, the game was tied. Another close game. Eddie said the Knights weren't good enough to blow anybody away. Dee had played the whole fourth quarter, eventually finding her legs, running the plays that Eddie called out to her. Halfway through the quarter, during a time-out, Eddie had said to Deltha, "I'm gonna stay with Dee. You cool with that?"

Deltha thought about it and finally said, "Yeah."

Then Deltha turned to Dee and said, "They stay in they man? That hedgehog they got in at small. Jervis? He act like the pick-and-roll got invented tonight. Don't run it every time. But you can beat his ass with it when you do."

Dee waited for a punch line, thinking that Deltha hadn't gone out of his way to help her since the first day she'd shown up at practice playing the part of Dee the actress.

Only, there wasn't a punch line.

"Thanks," Dee said.

The first play after the time-out, Eddie called for the pick-and-roll with Thruston B. Howell. Jervis never saw it coming. Dee hit Thruston with a bounce pass for an easy layup. On the way down the court, she looked over at Deltha Lewis and made a little fist. He nodded his head slowly, then looked away.

With twenty seconds to play, Jere Nolan hit a three-pointer when Dee was way slow getting out on the wing to cover him. She was already saying "Shit" as he released the ball because he hadn't missed anything he'd looked at in about half an hour, and he didn't miss this one now.

Cavaliers by a basket.

Jamie Lawton missed a jumper that would have tied the game again. The Cavaliers rebounded. Dee could hear Eddie from the bench yelling "No foul, just get the goddamn ball." Mephisto Morton swung it to Nolan. Dee knew he'd try to run clock here, that he wouldn't shoot, even as hot as he'd been. She acted as if she were scrambling to get over to cover him in the zone, but then stopped suddenly, and when Nolan tried to throw the ball back to Mephisto, Dee stepped in front and intercepted the ball and called time with .5 second left.

In the huddle, Eddie grabbed his greaseboard from Joey Shahoud, started to draw up a play that was like a Hail Mary pass in football, all the Knights in the lane, Anquwan trying to go up and tip the ball into the basket behind a Dream Jackson pick.

Suddenly, a voice said, "I've got a better idea."

Dee was as shocked as any of them to realize the voice was her own.

Eddie was seated on the folding chair Joey had pulled up for him. He stopped drawing his X's and O's and looked up at her, grinning, and said, "Really?"

Now they were all looking at her.

Maybe, she was thinking now, it was whatever Joey had used to spike the tea talking.

I've got a better idea?

Who *was* she tonight?

But she reached down, grabbed Eddie's board, cleared his scribbling away with her forearm, and started drawing up her

own play, describing it as she did, talking fast, the words running into each other, knowing the time-out was almost over.

When she was finished, Eddie said, "I like it."

Thruston said, "I think I saw this one with the Globies one
time."

Dee said, "They stole it from the Harlem Apollos."

She took the ball from the ref at half-court. Tony Vazquez
again. He blew his whistle, telling them to play. The Cavs
didn't put anybody in front of her, deciding instead to drop
five guys back on defense, covering the four other Knights.
Dee faked a two-hand chest pass to Anquwan, who'd come
running straight for her. Then she turned and threw the ball
like a football quarterback, not the high-lofted Hail Mary
Eddie had talked about, but straight on a line at the Knights'
backboard.

Just about everybody on the court except Thruston B.
Howell was on the left side. His man, Cheeca Jones, turned
his head just long enough when he saw Dee put the ball in the
air, and that was all the time Thruston needed to go flying past
him to where Dee had promised him the carom would be.

She did throw it a little higher than she meant to, for a moment afraid the ball was going over the top of the backboard.
But it kissed the top of it, bounced to the right, bounced right
into Thruston (Sea Lion) Howell's hands. The clock wouldn't
start until a player on the court touched the ball, but with just
.5 left, the rules said you couldn't catch the ball and still have
time to get a shot off. So Thruston just tipped it through the
basket in the same motion, and by the time the ball was
through the net, the game was over.

Thruston did the drive-thru prayer with his teammates, did
a one-minute interview with television, caught up with Dee in
the tunnel.

"Yo," he said.

By now Dee had figured out that with her teammates "Yo"
could be used as a question mark or a period or a comma,
could mean hello, goodbye, what's up, what's happening, nice
pass, got a question, need to talk to you, you're full of shit,
your momma, nice tits on that one, I'll raise you a hundred,
pass the salt, or kiss my black ass.

She just went with it now.

"Yo," she said.

Thruston smiled and said, "You throw like a girl." Then he gave her a high five and walked toward the visitors' locker room, shaking his head.

Michael De la Cruz was posted by the door, giving out high fives of his own, having to give a little jump sometimes as he did. Dee thought she could give him the dodge, get down to her dressing room without having to talk to him, but as soon as he spotted her, he came running after her like a happy Lab.

"It just gets bigger and bigger for my All-American girl!" he said.

"That's me," Dee said. "The fun never stops."

"Come on, kid, it's all right to be happy once in a while."

"You be happy for both of us tonight. How would that be?"

"Hey," he said, "I heard what happened. You know, before? Don't let a little case of the heebie-jeebies get you down."

"I'm just a little tired right now," she said. "I'm gonna go sit down for a minute before I have to do the interview room."

"Well," Michael De la Cruz said, giving her arm a squeeze. "I'll be the one in the back of the room beaming like a proud papa."

Dee almost laughed, but not for the happy reasons he wanted her to.

They all want to be your daddy, she thought.

Not in any weird, hinky way. Probably not in any way they could ever explain to themselves—guys—or understand, or even communicate to each other, when they sat around and talked about how great they were with babes.

But they really, really wanted to be your daddy.

Even Mo Jiggy, whom she loved to death.

Even Eddie.

When she went back over everything later, she knew it was Cleveland where she first thought about quitting.

⊕ twenty

By now Dee was into the rhythms of the season, the routine of practice and morning shoot the day of the game and back to the hotel, at home or on the road, her walk in the afternoon, sometimes a long one, then a nap if she had time. It seemed there was always another bus ride to the airport, when the Knights were going on the road for a game the next night, or coming back home. Then a car ride into Manhattan in the middle of the night, or a bus ride into the next city, another city she didn't know; then the next hotel. Chicago was another Ritz-Carlton. And Chicago was Michigan Avenue, which Eddie said was his favorite walking street in the country, even better than Fifth Avenue. So in the afternoon before the Bulls game, played inside the arena with the statue of Michael Jordan outside, Dee put on the disguise she needed now on the road — another new pair of Oakley sunglasses, the Chicago Bears cap she'd bought in the same shop next to the hotel, new cashmere topcoat — and walked up Michigan Avenue and then down, spending about a thousand dollars in Marshall Field's.

She hadn't slept with Eddie since Cleveland, not back in New York, not on the road.

He didn't try, and neither did she.

There was something between them, they both knew that. Something good, something pretty powerful, she thought, but now something else, a wall of some kind. If the guys on the team watched them, the players and Joey and the one assistant coach, Bill Flynn, the old Seton Hall coach Eddie had kept from Bobby Carlino's staff, they probably couldn't tell that things had changed between Eddie and Dee.

Changed again.

But they had.

On the plane ride from New York to Chicago, he had come back to her compartment, where she was listening to Sarah Vaughan and reading the new Carl Hiaasen novel Joey had recommended.

"Listen," he said, "I just wanted you to know that if there's anything you want to talk about, I'm here."

"You're more here than you know," she said. "I just needed a little time-out, is all."

Eddie gave her a long look. "Twenty or full?"

Dee made the motion you used for a twenty-second time-out, hands reaching up to tap her shoulders.

There was an awkward silence, and then he got up, saying, "Okay, then."

"Okay," she said.

When he pulled the curtain shut behind him, Dee thought: Perfect. You hang around guys long enough, you start to act like them.

Don't talk about anything.

Except right now she didn't know what she wanted to talk *about*.

Mostly she just wanted to get to the next city and the next game and play her ball.

Three weeks left in the regular season, twelve games left, and now there was no one between them and the Miami Heat, still in eighth place—the last playoff spot—in the Eastern Conference. The Heat had a record of 32–38. The Knights were 28–42. Even if the Knights could catch them, Dee knew it would be no bargain making the playoffs, because number eight in the conference had to play number one in the first round, and number one was the Knicks, whose record was 55–15. Dee had never been great at math, but she knew enough to know that in a season where her team had won just 28 games, they were 27 behind the Knicks in the standings.

That wasn't the point, and Dee Gerard, starting point guard of the Knights, knew it.

The Knights had never made the playoffs; that was the point, that was the object of the game the rest of the way, and they all knew it. She had her dreams, Eddie Holtz had his, as crazy as it had sounded when he first mentioned the playoffs, but not nearly so crazy now. He didn't mention the playoffs too much, before practices or games when he'd talk to them individually a little bit on the plane. You play, he kept saying, I'll worry about everything else. But they all knew where they were, and then the papers started to pick up on it once the Knights passed the Magic to get into ninth place in the conference.

The Knights beat San Antonio at the Garden that night, ending a three-game losing streak, and now were three and a half games behind Miami. When Michael De la Cruz knew the rest of the players were dressed, he dragged Dee into the main locker room, mostly for the benefit of the *60 Minutes* crew that had been following him for the past week. Once inside, he hugged everybody in sight, including, Dee observed, the NBA columnist from the *Times*.

"It's like Yogi said with the '69 Mets!" Michael De la Cruz said. "It ain't over till it's over!"

Joey Shahoud quickly moved in next to him, leaned up, and whispered something in his ear.

"And the '73 Mets, too!" Michael said.

After a few more hugs, he took Dee's hand and led her back into the hallway, saying to the *60 Minutes* producer, an attractive young woman, "We can clean up the baseball shit in the editing room, right?"

Dee was starting every game by now. Against the Spurs, she had scored six points, had eight assists in thirty-two minutes. As she walked toward her dressing room with De la

Cruz, his arm around her, Dee feeling like some kind of prop, a boom mike hovering over their heads, the owner of the Knights gave her a squeeze and said, "You were great tonight, baby."

Dee stopped, reached up, pulled the boom mike down, and loudly said, "Earth to Michael: I'm not your baby."

She left him there as he began to explain to the woman producer what a cutup Dee was, and they weren't planning on leaving that in the piece, were they?

Mo Jiggy said, "You don't seem to understand. I got the man in the doggy position, begging me to spank him."

Dee said, "There must be a better way for you to put that, especially you being the kind of dog lover you are."

"Good point," he said. "All I'm sayin' is, we've already reached the point I used to reach with my whitey record producers, where they start out trying to screw me and then end up sayin', 'Please take my money, Mo. How much a my money you want?' "

Dee felt herself smiling, the way she always did when Mo Jiggy came walking into the room, or when she just heard his voice on the telephone.

"You're a genius," she said. "But you don't need me to tell you that."

"Don't try to use that girlie-girl jive on me," he said. "You sound like that Amber, I tell you about her? Showing up nine months and two weeks later that time, tryin' to tell me how wonderful I am, how much she missed me, how she never met a man like me in her whole life, and, oh, by the way, the baby's mine."

"Sorry," Dee said.

" 'Mikey,' I say to him, 'this shit with ten-day contracts turns out to be more boring than Celine Dion. How's about you and me look at the big picture?' "

"That must have made him hot. The big-picture part, I mean."

They were having a late room-service breakfast at the Sherry. The Knights had four games in the next five nights, and so Eddie had given them their first day off from practice since he'd become the coach. Dee had called Mo when she knew he was awake and asked him to stop by and he'd said, damn right he was gonna stop by, they had important mogul-type shit to discuss, for her to go ahead and order him an egg-white omelette with maybe some of those asparagus tips he liked cut up in it, maybe some mushrooms.

And maybe they could brew him up some of that herbal tea with the fresh mint leaves?

"He love the big-picture part, hate Mikey more than people not payin' him enough attention."

Dee said, "You bring any of the guys with you? I love it when you do that."

"Darnell," Mo said, eating a small piece of omelette.

Dee said she didn't think she knew Darnell.

"Boy been away," Mo said.

"Vacation?"

Mo said, "You could call it that, not that he was pickin' up any American Advantage miles where he was at."

Dee said, "Back to what we were talking about? I don't want to sign anything past the end of this season."

Mo speared a tiny piece of asparagus with his fork. Dee had noticed before that he had the eating habits of a model; sometimes he even asked her if she thought he was putting on weight. She loved it when guys were this vain about their appearance. It somehow seemed to level all kinds of playing fields, making them seem as silly about silly things as any woman Dee knew. When she got inside the Knights' locker room, she'd sometimes sneak a peek into some of the lockers and see enough hair-care products and body lotions and colognes to build a whole new wing at Saks.

Mo said, "You know what I got on the table soon as you turn me loose on some of these damn endorsements? I know you don't like hearin' about this all, but I'm gonna tell you anyway."

"Thought you might, big fella."

"I got that thing I don't like to talk about, the new Tampax deal looks like it could fit inside a thimble, then pops up?"

"I get tingly just thinking about it," Dee said.

"I hear you." He dabbed at the corners of his mouth with his napkin. "I got that, I got that new Bud Lite they think can be as cool for a girl on the go as a glass of Chardonnay. I got the new sports bra from Reebok, one they say gives you all the protection you want and still pushes those babies up."

Dee was looking at the headline above Walt Ransome's column, which read "Not Great, But Not Half-Bad."

Mo said, "I got J. P. Tod's, once I told them how much you like those new blue mules. I got any SUV you want, foreign or domestic."

He paused. "But I don't got shit if you won't commit past the end of the year."

"I want my options open. All of them."

"Let me see if I understand you, girl," he said. "You did all this, went *through* all this, to play twenty-odd games? Well, excuse me for being such a cynical motherfucker, pardon my dirty mouth, but I ain't buyin' that."

"I'm not saying I won't be back," Dee said. "I'm just alerting you to the possibility. You don't have to tell Michael. You don't even have to tell Eddie. It's just something I'm thinking about."

"You're only gonna get better."

"You sure about that?"

"I see what I see."

"Me, too," Dee said. "And you know what I see? These guys are better than I thought. I've been reading all this stuff on the 'Net the past few years about how the league went straight to hell after Jordan quit the Bulls. And guess what? It's baloney. Maybe the old guys were smarter, I'll give them that. I can't believe how little some of these kids know about the game, the way it's supposed to be played. The fundamentals. But when they get going up and down the court? It's like when I was little, watching Secretariat run. And that is gonna catch up with me, sooner rather than later. You think I'm fast? The next girl after me is gonna have to be faster. And a better shooter. And stronger. Maybe I'd feel differently about all this if I were ten years younger. But I'm not. So I don't."

She knew he sometimes listened about as well as a TV guy,

but this time he let her go, and when she stopped, he said, "So what's this all about with you? Really?"

Another time when the jive accent disappeared.

Dee said, "I told you before. I have to know, once and for all. And one thing I can promise you: I won't bail out until I do know."

"You don't yet?"

"No," she said. "I don't."

He was wearing new starched jeans, black Adidas sneakers with white stripes, and a cap that said "The Imus Ranch" on the front. Mo loved Don Imus's radio show, which Dee knew they now ran on television as well. Mo even went on as a guest sometimes, ever since he'd started representing athletes.

Dee knew Imus had been defending her from the start, even after games when he'd say she looked more out of place in the NBA than a white guy.

"I'm gonna make him pay big-time for the rest of the year," Mo said. "With a playoff bonus that kicks in as soon as the Knights make it, if they make it."

"Knock yourself out."

Just like that, he was back to playing the part of Mo Jiggy.

"And you got to give me one endorsement," he said. "Let me pick one of them out the line, so they can give it up to the Mo."

Dee laughed. "Enough about me," she said.

"At least I'm honest about it," he said. "Your boy Michael De la Cruz want the world to think he cares more about sisterhood than Oprah."

"Honesty like that should be rewarded," she said. "You can have the sports bra."

"Why that?"

"I've got one on right now," she said. "Want to see?"

"I thought you was lookin' a little chesty today," he said, and went into the bedroom to make a couple of phone calls, because the battery on his cell was running low. By the time he came back, Dee had finished reading Walt Ransome's column, which ended this way:

I still don't think she belongs in a man's game. I don't even think she's close to being the best woman around, and if you don't believe me, just ask some of the gals from the WNBA. But somehow the Knights keep winning. And Dee Baby is the one with the ball.

Dee showed Mo the column and said, "You see this?"

Mo said, "I figured he might lighten up on you a little bit, after we had our talk."

"Uh, what talk would that be, exactly?"

Mo waved a hand dismissively, as if getting rid of flies. "One we had the other night, after we both left Elaine's."

Mo said it was him and Shaheen and Darnell having a late dinner, waiting for Chelsea to finish with her acting class. Montell and Denzell had the night off, to attend the opening of the new Jet Li martial arts movie. Mo said he was their favorite now—hardly any dialogue to worry about, just two straight hours of ass-kicking.

Anyway, he said, they noticed Walt Ransome a couple of tables down, having a drink with Harold Wasserman, the munchkin p.r. guy. Mo waited until Ransome paid his check, at which point he decided to do a little p.r. work of his own.

As he was telling Dee this, she crossed herself.

Mo asked what she was doing, and she said, praying, just a couple of fast Hail Marys.

"Figures," he said, "go with the girl."

When Ransome was outside, Mo sent Darnell out to talk to him.

"About what?" Dee said.

"About get in the car," Mo said.

He poured himself more herbal tea.

"I just wanted to talk to him about his female problems," Mo Jiggy said, making it sound, Dee thought, vaguely gynecological.

Shaheen drove, Darnell rode shotgun, Mo and Ransome were in the backseat of the Suburban. Mo told Shaheen to take it slow through the park. He said Ransome was pretty cool about the whole thing once Mo told him about Shaheen's anger issues, and how they were nothing compared to the rage

Darnell was still feeling about what he said was a stone setup on the felony assault.

Dee said, "I don't suppose you could have mentioned something to me—the client?—before you went off to play Big Strong Man, Helpless Little Woman?"

"Was a spur-of-the-moment thing."

"Oh."

Mo asked him who leaked the original story about Dee. Ransome said forget it. Then Mo asked him who gave the *Daily News* the picture of Eddie and Dee. Ransome said he didn't know and, by the way, he wouldn't tell the Notorious T.H.U.G. even if he did know.

"He called you that?" Dee asked.

"Actually made me start to warm to the guy," Mo said. "Sittin' in my car. My boys in the front. Callin' me a thug and lookin' at me like, *Now what, assface?* Boy showed me some rope."

All Walt Ransome would say about his sources, Mo told her, was that maybe some of Dee Gerard's close personal friends weren't as close as she thought they were.

"I told him, was a time I could have made him tell me everything," Mo said, "but that was before bein' a close personal friend of yours put me in touch with my nurturing side."

"So you not shooting him is why he was almost nice to me today?"

"Fuck, no," Mo said. "Was *Beef* did that."

"That boys' club downtown you told me about."

"When we was done talkin', I took him down there, introduced him to a couple of new dancers we just hired, call themselves Thelma and Louise. Then Thelma and Louise took him up to one of our Do-It Rooms."

Dee told Mo that sometimes you could almost have too much information. Mo said, Shit, tell me about it, I found that out at Shaheen's trial.

"Anyway," Mo said. "It turns out Thelma and Louise give me a breakthrough on my man Walt Ransome."

He smiled.

"Old Walt likes girls fine," Mo Jiggy said, "he just honestly don't think they should be playin' ball with the boys."

• • •

"Patience, Michael," Harold Wasserman was saying. "Though I know it can be a more painful concept for you than modesty."

They were having an early dinner at Il Cantinori, east of Fifth on Tenth Street, before the Knights played the Boston Celtics that night at the Garden. The game had officially become a sellout a few hours before, which meant that the Knights had sold out every game, at home and on the road, since Dee Gerard had joined the team. But as happy as the crowds made Michael, as much as they confirmed that signing the girl had been a stroke of pure genius, he knew that Mo Money, which is the way he thought about Mo Jiggy now, would use them as a negotiating point against him.

Mo Money, Michael had decided, wanted to sound blacker than a squeegee guy, but was whiter on the inside than the chairman of the Federal Reserve.

In their meeting at Five Penn earlier in the day, Mo had told Michael what it was going to cost to sign Dee for the rest of the season—with no guarantees for next season—and Michael had been in a pissy mood ever since. Not about the money. The money was nothing, a way of keeping score, as real to Michael as Monopoly money—just more chips in the game. No, it was this smiling punk who had gotten rich writing rap songs that all seemed to be about shoot-you, stab-you, gimme-your-wallet, acting as if the two of them were equals.

As if putting Dee Gerard in the NBA had been Mo Money's idea.

It technically hadn't been Michael's idea, either, both he and Eddie knew that, but by now Eddie knew there was a way to tell the story in the press that made it sound like it was.

Mo Jiggy sitting there in his office, dressed like a player for Chrissakes, telling him, This is the way it's gonna be. . . .

Now Harold Wasserman sat there across the table, picking at his endive like the rabbit he was, telling Michael he had to be patient.

"I want the front page every day!" Michael blurted out suddenly.

They were in the back room, which was even darker than the front, even this early. Michael didn't care, there weren't enough people in the restaurant yet so that he had to worry about the proper positioning for him to be seen. He sipped some sparkling water, then pushed his own salad around.

Harold said, "You know it doesn't work that way."

Michael slapped the table now. "When you do this right, it does!"

"This?"

"The game," Michael said. "The real game. Jesus, Harold, you helped invent it. The one where you play everybody like they're a goddamn Steinway and they all end up talking about *you*. Nobody sees you doing it, they don't even notice as you start moving up to the head of the line. But all of a sudden, it's not Tom and Nicole splitting up, or who's the father of Jodie's baby, or what's happening with Bill and Hillary. . . ."

Harold Wasserman shook his head, saying, "I hate those dogs."

"The *real* Bill and Hillary," Michael said. He leaned forward. "You know what I'm talking about here, Harold. I've finally got the stage now. And I sure as hell don't want to give it up."

"Michael," Harold said, "you do what you do, and then you have to let things play out a little bit."

"I just want to make sure we stay on top of things, Harold. Missionary style."

"Michael, you are drawing the biggest crowds you've ever had. For the most part, you're getting wonderful press. Your team might actually make the playoffs. Doesn't all that make you a little bit happy, bubby?"

"It does." Michael says. "It does. Even though I'll believe the part about the playoffs when we're actually in the play-offs." He felt the tiny StarTAC phone in the pocket of his jeans buzzing, ignored it until it stopped. "But you yourself have said it from the start, Harold. The basketball is about the girl. The history is sort of about the girl. But we constantly have to remind them that I'm the *man*. I'm the hero, her big defender. That's why we have to keep tweaking the story a little bit as we go, don't we? Isn't that what you said?"

Wasserman took a birdlike sip of his red wine, then dabbed at the corners of his mouth with his napkin.

Michael knew Harold was happily married to the woman he called His Selma, but God almighty, he acted like a flamer sometimes.

"Oh, it's been more than tweaked," Harold said. "Sometimes we have grabbed it right by the fucking balls."

He took another sip of wine, as if to rinse out the naughty words.

"Not enough," Michael said.

He felt frustrated, the way he did when he felt people only *thought* they were seeing the big picture, when they said they could see Michael's grand vision of things but were seeing only bits and pieces.

I'm an impressionist! he wanted to yell sometimes. Take a step back so you can really *see* me. Maybe that was Harold Wasserman's problem, if Michael really thought about it. Maybe even he got too close sometimes to fully appreciate what a piece of work Michael really was.

Michael said to him now, "I just don't want us to lose our momentum, is all." The cell phone was buzzing again. He slapped at it like a bug to shut it off. "You know what I really want, Harold?"

"Do tell."

"I want this to be like a soap opera. Tune in tomorrow! Don't miss a single episode! Remember what it was like in the old days with my man The Donald when he was splitting with Ivana, when we found out he'd been banging the Maples girl? Shit, it was better than *Dynasty* or *Dallas* when I was a kid. *That's* what I want."

Harold leaned back carefully in his chair, making sure his feet were still grounded, clasped his tiny hands across his red tie, closed his eyes, smiled an elf smile.

"You want more surprises from Mrs. Wasserman's son, is that what you're really telling me?"

"I just want one more," Michael said, in what he knew was a sad voice.

"I want, I want, I want," Harold said.

Little did either of them know.

⊕ twenty-one

Dee didn't tell Eddie she was thinking about quitting. There wasn't much of an opportunity for that anyway, not the way things were between them these days, which meant strictly business. When they did have a conversation, it was about basketball. He was putting more on her, giving her more minutes, more responsibility; more freedom with the ball, especially since Ray Ray Abdul-Mahi had gone down, for the season and maybe longer than that, with a torn Achilles tendon.

It had happened the week before, against the Celtics at the Garden, a game the Knights ended up winning in double overtime. Ray Ray had been looking to drive against the Celtics' center, a seven-two load from Oklahoma State named Whup Griffin who reminded Dee of a grain silo, just not as smart. It was Ray Ray against him on a fast break, Ray Ray coming hard from the right side. But when he crossed over on his dribble to his left hand, one of his sneakers got tangled up on one of Whup Griffin's size 22½ Converse All-Stars, and when Ray Ray went down, his Achilles made a sound every player on the court knew, a pop that made it sound as if he'd stepped on a plastic soft drink bottle.

Dee instantly knew what they all knew. It was just as if the popping noise were somebody firing a small-caliber bullet into the back of Ray Ray's ankle.

She was out of the game with four fouls at that point, Eddie saying he was saving her for the end. But now he put her back in for Ray Ray and she played the last nine minutes of regulation and both the overtimes, scoring in double fig-ures for the first time — sixteen points — and handing out ten assists.

She also got her first technical foul.

Actually, it was part of a double technical with Whup Grif-fin, who had let her know his attitude about women in the NBA right before he went for the opening tip against Dong Li.

Dee made it a habit to shake hands with all of the other team's players, trying to read body language a little bit, get a sense of which one might be the first to take a shot up in the area of her new Reebok sports bra. Or which one might try to grab her butt, as more than a few of them had.

All in all, another subtle way of trying to cover that butt.

Whup Griffin had given her a limp, disinterested hand-shake, then said in a twangy, farm-boy voice, "Ma'am, you know'n what we used to think was the best form of exercise and so forth back on the farm. For a girl'n, I mean?"

"What was that, Whup?"

She pronounced it "whoop."

"Whup," he said.

Rhyming with "yup."

"Sorry. So tell me, what did you think was a good exer-cise for a girl?"

"Reachin' for another can of peas," he said.

They were standing at midcourt, waiting for the refs to straighten out a problem with the 24-second clock.

"So you don't think I should be here?"

"Only if you're wearin' one of them skimpy outfits the cheerleaders and them wear."

The Bad Dee said, "You know what I think, Whoop?" And

motioned for him to lean down so he could hear. "I think the cow just called to say the calf is yours, you fat goober."

And gave him a pat on his butt as she went over to take her position, and that was her last meaningful interaction with him until there were three minutes left in the game. Griffin set a pick that Anquwan told her was coming, but when Griffin saw that Dee was going to get past him, he stuck out a forearm that caught Dee so hard across her neck her immediate reaction was that she was drowning.

When she went down, she immediately put her head between her knees so no one could see her trying to choke some air into her lungs. Her teammates were all around her, asking if she was all right. She would absolutely have loved telling them she was. But talking was pretty much out of the question until she licked breathing. She gave them a little wave of the hand as if she were.

Hi, guys.

She sat there, head between her knees, trying to look as if she were just collecting herself, elbows on knees. She stayed that way awhile, until she started to breathe again, small breaths at first, then great big hungry gulps of air, like a swimmer who'd finally broken the surface.

Carl Anthony was the one closest to her. He voiced his concern as deeply and passionately as he could. But maybe this was a sensitive night for him. Dee had noticed in the locker room that his hair for the Celtics read, "Give."

"Yo," he said now.

"I'm okay," she said, in a voice she felt had a dusky Lauren Bacall quality to it now.

Whup Griffin was standing next to Carl, trying to look concerned. When he could see Dee starting to get up, he made a show of extending a hand to her.

Dee made a motion to him, like, *One moment,* giving herself a chance to gather herself for what she planned to do next.

There'd be some question later, no matter how many angles people saw on television, about her intent. But there wasn't much question about what *did* happen as Dee, all in one motion, almost like a choreographed dance move, took Whup Griffin's hand and sprang to her feet like a pop-up doll.

As she did, she kneed him squarely in the balls.

Just like that, it was Whup Griffin on the ground. Once he got there, Dee told him he sounded more like a hen than one of those cows she was sure he'd done it with back on daddy's farm.

Forgetting his manners, and the pain he was clearly suffering, Whup Griffin reached up and awkwardly took a swipe at her.

Dee reached over and took the ball from the ref standing next to her before the ref realized what was happening, and bounced it off the top of Griffin's desktop-size, crew-cutted head.

Whistles all around now, and the double technical, one for Dee, one for Whup. The problem for Whup, quite apart from the searing, intense pain he was still feeling in his groin, was that it was his second technical of the game, which meant an automatic ejection; he'd picked up his first in the first quarter when he'd called Buddy the ref a "gerbil pimp homo" after a disputed call had gone Dee's way.

With Whup out of there in the second overtime, Dee fed Carl Anthony for three straight easy baskets and the Knights pulled away.

In the interview room, the first question was about whether or not Dee had, in fact, meant to knee Whup Griffin in the balls.

"What balls?" Dee said sweetly, in a way she imagined a Junior Miss would.

She'd played forty minutes in all against the Celtics. So it wasn't just the most points she'd scored, it was the most minutes she'd gotten. A little over two weeks left in the regular season now, the Knights still three games behind the Heat for that last playoff spot. The numbers weren't great with so little time left. But they still had a chance, more chance than they'd ever had, including a game with the Heat at the Garden to end the regular season.

Now they were flying to Minneapolis for a game against the Timberwolves the next night. When the pilot announced that they'd be landing in ten minutes, Joey Shahoud came back to her compartment and pulled up her shade.

"Pay attention," he said.

She had been sleeping on and off, listening to Ella with her headphones.

"Check out the big water down there, between Minneapolis and St. Paul," Joey said.

Dee leaned forward and said, "It looks like the Hudson, only wider."

"It's the Mississippi, dummy."

"Up here?"

"Yup."

"Those bridges down there? I can walk across the Mississippi if I want?"

"Like walking across the Fifty-ninth over to Queens."

"Cool," Dee said.

When it came to geography, Joey talked to her like she was in the sixth grade. "Next season," he said, "you even get to go all the way to California."

Right, Dee thought.

Next season.

Wherever they went, there would always be some new body of water she'd only heard about or read about or seen in books. It would only make her miss her water, the Mediterranean, even more than she did already, the view of the water from her apartment, the boats, the way the sun looked on it in the late afternoon—that time of day when she'd start to feel that excitement, a rush she'd only ever gotten from basketball, knowing she was on her way to DC, where she was the boss, she was the one calling the shots.

It's good being king, Gilles kept telling her on the phone.

Tell me about it, she wanted to say. . . .

They were staying at the Radisson Plaza, across the street from a Marriott, the two hotels connected by a skywalk that Joey explained was one of about a thousand skywalks downtown, connecting all the places where people liked to shop, turning the city into one huge mall for when Minneapolis felt colder than Greenland in the winter. The Target Center, where the Timberwolves played, was just a couple of blocks up.

Dee was used to the scene at the hotel by now. And it was pretty much the same scene, every city, every hotel, even when they arrived in the middle of the night. Sometimes Dee even thought they were the same girls, most of them looking way too young to be dressed the way they were, dressed up this big, with big hair and big makeup, trying way too hard to please Anquwan or Dream or Deltha, the guys on the team she knew were out there the most, trying to screw themselves into the record books, talking about every new girl in every new city incessantly, usually on the bus, not caring that Dee could hear. Maybe wanting her to hear. If Carl Anthony, the one she liked the best out of all of them, the one she thought was the most solid, was out catting around, he didn't want anybody to know, and certainly didn't talk himself up with the boys on the bus. Or, more likely, he just didn't cat around, since both Eddie and Joey had told her that Rita Anthony, Mrs. Carl, was the only person in the world, male or female, that Carl Anthony seemed to be truly afraid of.

Plus, Rita did Carl's hair.

The really young girls in the lobby, when the team'd arrive in the middle of the afternoon like this, right after school had let out, were waiting for Dee. Their teeth were in braces sometimes, skinny things in sweatshirts and warm-ups, all arms and legs and bright eyes like Sharmayne's that night at the Garden, Sharmayne Brown from DeWitt Clinton High School. Here in Minneapolis, Dee noticed, the names on the fronts of the jerseys and jackets all seemed to have "Olaf" in there somewhere. She would sign their autograph books, the sweatshirts themselves, pose for pictures, sign the posters of her in her white No. 14 that were already out there, even hand out the dozen or so tickets to the game that Joey would always have ready for her, before he finally came over and rescued her, always saying there was a team meeting starting in a few minutes.

He did that now in the small lobby of the Radisson as Anquwan passed by, on his way to the elevator, two girls with him, a tall blonde and a shorter black chick all in black leather, head to toe, short jacket and pants. Dee could hear Anquwan saying, "Charrisse, you get the ice. I got enough of them small bottles from the plane we could play us some dominoes. . . ."

Joey handed her the envelope with her plastic keys in it. Dee usually checked in under a fake name, just so she didn't have to take phone calls from drunk fans in the middle of the night, or local radio stations just wanting her to "pop on for a couple of minutes" with some host who always seemed to be nicknamed after some sort of furry animal. She had taken to using the names of famous women's players from the past, Cheryl sometimes, Lieberman, Carol Blazejowski, Anne Donovan. Today she was Cheryl Cook, University of Cincinnati in the 1980s, the one they called the female version of Oscar Robertson, the Big O himself.

Joey told her that if she wanted to get a bite later, there was a Morton's steakhouse around the corner.

"Room service," she said.

"I figured. You're getting a rep, you know."

"Ooh," she said. "As a bad girl? I want so much to be a bad girl."

"Antisocial," he said. "I'm told in Hollywood they call it LLD."

"LLD?"

"Leading-lady disease."

"I vant to be alone," Dee said in a deep voice.

"You sound like Whup just got you in the neck again," Joey said.

It was when she went back to the front desk to pick up a local paper, the *Star-Tribune,* that Dee noticed the pretty white-haired woman in the blue down parka, almost as dramatic a blue as the woman's eyes, cobalt blue, fixed on Dee, as if they were trying to hold her in place.

"Been waiting for you," the woman said to Dee.

"I'm sorry," Dee said. "I just signed—"

"I don't want your stupid autograph, missy," the woman snapped.

"Oh, I just thought—"

"I *meant,*" the woman said, "I've been waiting for you about forty years."

Dee said, "Do I know you?"

"Maybe you do, maybe you don't," she said, putting out

her small hand, giving Dee a big handshake with it. "Ellie Ryan."

Now Dee stared.

"Ellie Ryan of Nashville Business College?" she said.

"So," Ellie Ryan said, "you're not one of those ditz-head girls think they invented basketball."

"You played with Nera White," Dee said.

"It was her team," she said. "I just passed her the ball."

"So I heard, Miz Ryan." Dee felt herself smiling. "So I heard."

"Call me Ellie," she said. "You think your room has one of those minibars? I could use a little something to warm these old bones of mine."

"Do you live in Minneapolis?"

"Montana," she said. "Drove halfway yesterday. Came the rest of the way this morning."

"You came all this way to see me?" Dee asked.

"No, missy. I wanted to get one more look at the Mall of America over there in Bloomington before I went toes up. See how many Gaps and Banana Gaps and Eddie Gaps and Abercrombie and Gaps they've got now." She made a snorting noise. "Of course I came all this way to see you."

Nera White, by all the accounts Dee had read or heard, was the greatest women's basketball player who had ever lived, even if hardly anybody had ever seen her play when she was at her best in the 1950s and 1960s.

Dee had read up on her in high school, on microfilm, in her usual nook at the New York Public Library; even there she was shocked to discover how little a record there was of what White had accomplished in her AAU career with the team sponsored by the Nashville Business College. Later on, after White had finally been inducted into the Basketball Hall of Fame in Springfield, Massachusetts, Dee was able to learn a lot more about her on the Internet, and by accessing information from the Women's Sports Foundation, as that became a bigger and bigger deal back home.

The pictures of Nera White that Dee now saw on her com-

puter were the same as the grainy ones she remembered from
the public library. White's face still reminded Dee a little bit
of Amelia Earhart, and perhaps that figured, since Nera White
was the first woman in basketball, even nearly fifty years ago,
who made the people watching her believe she could fly.

At the summer clinic when Dee had first met Nancy
Lieberman, that summer before Dee and Cool Daddy left for
Europe, Lieberman had told her about how she had finally se-
cured a phone number for White, years after Lieberman had
played AAU ball and first started to hear the legend. White
was twenty years retired from basketball by then, living on
her Kentucky farm. Nancy Lieberman told Dee she finally
had the courage to call her one Easter Sunday.

Lieberman stammered something after "Hello," the words
tumbling out, running into one another, about how White had
always been her role model.

Nera White said, "You're the first ever thanked me."

Then Lieberman, the Rockaway kid who'd really learned
to play with the boys, who would be the first person to tell
Dee that someday a woman would make the NBA, nearly
twenty years before she did, asked White, "So, did you really
have game?"

"Did I have game?" White yelled into the phone. And then
she was telling Nancy Lieberman about a famous move
Michael Jordan had just made in the NBA finals against the
Lakers, hanging in there for what seemed to be about five
minutes, switching hands as he did, still making the shot.

"I was doing that move in the fifties," White said.

Dee could still remember Lieberman laughing as she told
the story. "She blew me off then, saying she had to go break
some horses."

White was a six-one player—a six-one Kentucky white
girl—with no real defined position; she was as good playing
center or guard, could shoot and dribble and handle the ball.
And fly. She came out of Macon County, Tennessee, in the
days before there was any real women's college basketball to
speak of, certainly no scholarships for women, no Title IX to
shove down the stupid throats of college presidents and athletic directors. If you wanted to play at the highest levels of

women's ball—what women's ball there was in those days—
you played AAU. And that is exactly what Nera White did.

The team was sponsored by Nashville Business; all Nera
White did was lead the team to ten national AAU champi-
onships across the fifteen or so seasons of her prime. By now,
Dee knew the numbers on her better than she knew her Social
Security number. White graduated from Macon County High
School and joined the Nashville Business team the next year,
1955, and she was named the outstanding player in the AAU
tournament ten times between then and 1969.

Her nickname was "Queen of the Hardwood." She was an
AAU All-America fifteen times, and twice was MVP of the
AAU World Championships, in '57 and '58. She played, Dee
knew, in Russia and West Germany and France and Brazil and
England, long before the best players from the States ended
up playing in Europe, because that was where the only real
pro ball was for women, and the only real money. Or any
money at all.

Nearly forty years after she had broken in with Nashville
Business, they finally got around to putting her in the Hall of
Fame; Dee read a tiny item about it in the *International Herald Tribune.* She remembered being surprised that whoever
had written the wire service story even mentioned that around
all the history she was making, Nera White had somehow
found the time to get her college degree from the George
Peabody College for Teachers in Nashville.

She was the first true legend of women's basketball, and
still the biggest in Dee's mind, since Dee had always believed
that the best legends involved things you had heard about,
rather than seen, almost as if they came out of some grand,
epic novel.

And what you really heard about Nera White was this:

The only ones who had really seen her were the ones who
played against her.

Or with her.

"She was a little bit like you, if that won't go to your silly
head," Ellie Ryan was saying now in Dee's suite on the four-
teenth floor of the Radisson, drinking bourbon out of a wineglass. "I'm talking about all those years when you must've

felt like you were singing for your supper over there in Europe. The only ones really knew about you were the ones on the court with you."

Ellie Ryan said she was four years younger than Nera White—"Do the goddamn math yourself if it's that goddamn important to you!" she said before Dee even thought to ask how old she was—and had grown up on a ranch outside Bozeman, Montana. By the time she was in high school, she said, she figured she was the best basketball player from the Mississippi to Puget Sound. "No brag, missy, just fact." She had started hearing about Nera White when she was in high school, the same as Dee would later. Ellie Ryan enrolled at the University of Colorado in Boulder, started playing AAU ball there, and after two years, decided she was moving to Nashville, just like that, and see if she could hook up with the team from Nashville Business College.

"I loved basketball the most," she said. "I never worried about my hair or my clothes or my looks. Basketball made me feel pretty. You know what I'm talking about."

More than you know, Dee thought.

Ellie Ryan said, "I could do two things better than any girl around: ride a horse and pass a basketball. Used to dribble circles around those farm boys in my high school. And you surely know what I'm talking about with *that,* don't you? I knew in my heart that if I was gonna play some real ball 'fore the world took my dreams away from me, I was damn sure gonna play with the best."

Ellie Ryan moved to Nashville, took some courses at Nashville Business, got herself a secretarial job at the Grand Ole Opry and a tryout with Nera White's team.

"Of course, it was a nice team already, built around her. I made it nicer. Way you've made those tattooed kids with their hair—when did the boys start taking more time with their goddamn hair than us?—nicer. I knew when to get it to her, where she liked to be, how to wait for her while she got herself there, no matter how many girls they had covering her. You know Stockton and Malone? Of course you do. Well, let me tell you, Nera White was better than Malone, she could do more things than him. But I was her Stockton."

They played ten years together and then Ellie Ryan said she'd goddamn well seen enough of two things: the inside of a bus, and the world. She'd moved back to Montana, met a rancher she called Mr. Right, settled down in a farm just outside Big Sky.

Dee said, "So you're the one who actually found Mr. Right."

"What the hell are you talking about?" Ellie Ryan snapped again. "W-R-I-G-H-T. Earl Wright."

Ellie Ryan said that she had really begun watching basketball again on the television after Earl Wright passed on. She loved women's college basketball, especially when it was Tennessee versus Connecticut, hated what the NBA had become, and had vaguely been interested in the WNBA as long as Cynthia Cooper and Sheryl Swoopes were in the game.

"Sheryl was Nera on that Houston team," she said. "Cynthia Cooper was me."

Finally, Ellie Ryan said, holding out the wineglass to Dee and saying hit me, she turned on her TV one night and there was Dee Gerard doing what Ellie had done all the way back at Bozeman High when she was the girl with the fancy game, dishing with bigger boys.

"You're not half-bad," Ellie Ryan said, "for a rookie. I figure if you keep your head out of your butt and your eyes open so you don't keep getting knocked around like a goddamn piñata, you might actually be something to see next season. 'Stead of just a novelty, and a way for men to act like they actually give two shits about what happens to you."

"You mean if there is a next season," Dee said, knowing exactly what she was saying.

Knowing the one thing she wasn't going to do today was try to kid Ellie Ryan for even one minute.

Ellie Ryan, who had been talking almost nonstop since they got inside the room, didn't say anything, just fixed Dee with those blue eyes, those amazing blue eyes that up close were the same deep, deep blue as the color of the sea, back home.

But how could that be home? Dee asked herself now, as if

the question had floated into the room from the picture window facing out over all the downtown skywalks.

How could that be home if she'd come home to play ball?

"You better get me one more drink, missy," Ellie Ryan said. "And this time let's not get so damn generous with the ice."

Dee opened up to her.

In this case—with this incredible old woman—maybe it was a woman thing.

Or just plain old-fashioned girl talk.

She told Ellie Ryan, the spitfire cowgirl who'd once played ball with the best, everything she'd held back from the people who had become the men in her life. Then more truth after that, about the men who'd been in her life before, like Cool Daddy and Jeremy Gerard.

More truth than she'd told anybody lately.

Including herself, maybe.

Ellie Ryan, wearing faded jeans and a heavy ribbed navy turtleneck and boots with little flaps on the toes that looked as old as Ellie. With her surprisingly short legs stretched out in front of her on the couch now. With her white curly hair looking as soft as a snowdrift. With her beautiful face, despite all the wrinkles, from what looked like it had been a whole life spent outdoors once she'd gotten out of the gym. With those eyes, hot and bright as a blue flame sometimes, making her look younger.

Ellie Ryan taking it all in, as Dee told her about the crazy six weeks since Eddie had talked her into it.

When Dee finally stopped talking now, took a sip of the cold beer she'd gotten for herself, Ellie Ryan said, "That must have been real hard."

"What?"

"Talking you into it."

The old woman smiled for the first time, her whole face, which she'd tried to make tough as a saddle, suddenly softening, making her look even younger.

"Bet you played real hard to get," she said.

"At first I wasn't coming," Dee said.

"Sure you weren't."

Dee let that one pass, then told her the rest of it, about Eddie and Michael De la Cruz and the pictures in the paper and what Walt Ransome had written and what she'd hear on the radio sometimes, when she was in Mo's car.

"I listen sometimes to that ESPN radio network," Ellie said, "when I'm out in the truck. Those callers are dumber'n yard dogs."

And then Dee told her about how she'd been thinking more and more lately about how happy she'd been just running her bar, over on the other side of the world, in what was starting to feel too much like another life.

There was another silence. Ellie Ryan's glass was finally empty. She'd set it on the floor next to the couch. Now she had her hands behind her head, staring up at the ceiling fan spinning at low speed directly above her.

"Oh, woe is me," she said finally.

"Excuse me?"

"Let's have a pity party for Dee Gerard," she said.

"Listen . . ."

"No, *you* listen," Ellie Ryan said, the one who'd had enough spunk in her once to tell Nera White to go over there, she'd get her the ball when it was time.

"I'm on that Internet myself now," she continued, sitting up. "Maybe we could get together a buddy list, e-mail all the other girl basketball players in one shot, organize a special day when everybody could log on and tell how sorry they feel for you."

Dee said, "That's not what I meant. I'm not looking for sympathy."

Ellie Ryan ignored her. "I'm sure Lieberman, who didn't have a pot to piss in when she was growing up, who couldn't even have *gone* to Old Dominion if they hadn't started giving girls scholarships right then, she'll probably feel her heart breaking when you start talking about the pressure you're feeling, poor thing, to sign for however many millions that pretty-boy owner of yours is willing to throw at you."

She bounced off the couch like a cat. "And Annie Meyers, who got drafted as a publicity stunt but then had the guts to try out for the Pacers, she'll want to hear all about your problems, too. And little Dawn Staley, who didn't let being five feet six inches — my size, for Chrissakes — keep her from being one of the great goddamn college players of all time.

"And Miss Cheryl Miller, who was too old by the time the WNBA came around, Cheryl Miller, one of your heroes, she'll probably want to get together with you for a great big cry. And then after that, I'll have to put you together with Nera, who used to *hate* that we played six-on-six in the old days instead of five-on-five like the boys, making it feel as if we were playing a different sport from them, I'll bet Nera would want to hear all about how the bad men in the newspapers aren't being nice to you. How they're not treating you like — what? Some kind of delicate goddamn flower?"

"I'm not like that," Dee said weakly, knowing as soon as she did how lame she sounded.

"Actually, I don't expect you *are*," she said. "But it happens to be the way you *sound*. You want the truth?"

Dee said, "I'm thinking I don't have much of a choice."

Ellie Ryan said, "You sound like some big baby who doesn't deserve that chance that the rest of us would have sold everything, including our goddamn *dignity*, to get."

She sat back down now, a splash of pink around her eyes, as if she were suddenly out of breath. "I get tired," she said, sounding old for the first time, her voice suddenly frail.

"I didn't mean to upset you," Dee said. "I mean, it's been such an honor meeting you."

"Oh, don't give me that crap," Ellie said. "I'm the one wanted to meet you. I'm the one came all this way to see you do this thing with my own eyes. What I don't want to hear is what a tough time you're having being the one. You want to know what the real honor is here? That out of all of them — all of *us* — it was you who turned out to be the one."

Dee asked her where she was staying. Ellie said she had a reservation at the Marquette, where she'd stayed once with Earl Wright.

Dee said, "I've got two bedrooms here." She smiled. "If you promise to be nice, you can stay here."

"I'm too old to be nice."

"I know," Dee said. "You can stay anyway."

"Okay, then." She asked which bedroom, and Dee told her to take the one with the king in it. Ellie Ryan said she might take a little nap, and then maybe they could order some room service, see if there was some game to watch on the cable. Dee said that would be fine with her.

Ellie Ryan turned in the doorway and said, "You haven't screwed this thing up so far."

"Thank you. I guess."

"So don't screw it up the rest of the way," Ellie said. "Because if you do, I think you know now who you'll be letting down."

"All those people you mentioned?" Dee said.

"Me," Ellie Ryan said.

⚾ twenty-two

Ellie Ryan sat behind the Knights' bench the next night and watched Dee score fourteen points and get ten assists as the Knights beat the Timberwolves 110–102 at the same time the Heat were losing to the Hornets in Charlotte.

The Knights were two games out of the last playoff spot, six games left.

Ellie Ryan sat in Dee's dressing room after the game, sipping bourbon she'd brought with her from the hotel. When it was time for the bus to the airport, she scrawled out her phone number and even an e-mail address, though Dee told her she wasn't putting in much time on her laptop these days. Then she told Ellie Ryan to use the suite at the Radisson, she'd already arranged that with Joey Shahoud, hugged her, and said she'd be in touch.

The old woman said, "Remember, missy. I'm watching every move you make."

Dee said, "I'll try not to let you down."

"Do more than try," Ellie Ryan said.

Two days later, a Saturday afternoon game on NBC, Dee fouled out early in the fourth quarter and the Knights lost to the Hawks at the Garden. But they didn't lose any ground, because the Heat cooperated by losing in overtime to the Nets in Tampa. Still two behind, both the Knights and Heat knowing they would face each other one more time, the last game of the regular season at the Garden. The two teams had split the four games they had already played. Whoever won the last game would win the season series between them. It meant that if they ended up with the same record, the winner of that game would go to the playoffs.

After the loss to the Hawks, Dee tried to explain the whole playoff situation to Gilles on the telephone, as a way of telling him she still wasn't exactly sure when she'd be coming back.

When she heard giggling in the background, then what sounded like a champagne cork popping, she told him to say hello to Gaby for her.

"Giselle," he said. He lowered his voice and said, "The other you mentioned was stifling me."

"You mean she dumped you."

"You women," he said, "all stick together."

"How's business?"

"May I be perfectly honest?"

Maybe there was just something about her, everybody feeling the need to be perfectly honest with her. But it was usually the same as them giving you "with all due respect."

Whatever came next wasn't going to be too great, one way or another.

"Business, *chérie*," he said, "has never been better."

"But you still miss me, right?"

"Desperately."

"You men," she said, "are all despicable lying scum."

She asked about the trio she'd hired right before she left, and Gilles said, funny she should ask, he'd been waiting for the right moment to tell her, but he'd had to let them go a couple of weeks earlier, the girl singer was so loaded some nights she was forgetting more lyrics than Sinatra did at the end. But, he said, the good news was, he'd replaced them with a female singer and a very cool trumpet player.

"Trumpets?" she said. "In my intimate little club?"

"I said he was cool. You know that record you like so much, with Clark Terry and the white girl?"

"Carol Sloane."

"They remind me a little of them. And, *chérie*, the customers seem to love them."

There was a silence, and Dee could hear more giggling, before it sounded as if Gilles had his hand over the phone.

"But you miss me, right?" she said.

"I count the days until your return," he said. "But may I make one more observation along those lines?"

Dee sighed. "Go ahead."

"Go, Knights!" he shouted into the phone, gave her a double shot of *au revoir*, and hung up.

She was such a lucky girl. Wasn't she, though? Doing this kind of booming business on two continents? Making the guys she worked for as happy as the ones who worked for her?

Sitting there in the quiet hotel suite, staring at the lights of the city on Central Park South, the line of Saturday night traffic heading west, the sound of the car horns as loud as in the middle of a weekday afternoon . . . alone on Saturday night, she thought:

Really, now.

How *can* one girl be so lucky?

Little Dee, happy at last.

So how come the guys seemed so much happier about things than she was?

"Two out, five to play," Eddie said to Michael De la Cruz. "In the immortal words of Bobby Carlino: You believe this shit?"

They were sitting in the lobby bar of the Four Seasons in Boston, just back from the team's shootaround at the Fleet Center, another new cookie-cutter arena, this one having replaced Boston Garden, which was gone now, the way Madison Square Garden would be gone someday when the Knicks and Knights moved to their own new basketball palace a few blocks west.

The replacement, even if it did have all the Celtics' retired

numbers and championship banners, was just one more basketball mall.

"I didn't come to do the math," De la Cruz said to Eddie.
"I came to talk about next season."

Eddie sipped some of his weak Bloody Mary. "Talking
about next season before this season is over," he said. "Isn't
that what we used to do when we sucked?"

De la Cruz said, "She still won't commit."

"I know."

"What did she say to you?"

Eddie lit a Winston Light, knowing his smoking pissed De
la Cruz off, also knowing that if he didn't have a smoke about
every ten minutes these days he felt as if he was going to jump
out of his goddamn skin.

It scared the shit out of him, frankly, how much he wanted
this, how much he wanted to make the fucking playoffs.

How much he wanted to coach his fucking team.

"We were just talking on the plane coming here," Eddie
said. "We really haven't had much time lately to talk about
anything except winnin' the game."

"No pillow talk, you mean?"

Eddie thought, Eat me. But all he said was "No."

"Did she say she's definitely not coming back?" Michael
De la Cruz said.

"No. But when *I* said something about how all this will be
easier next time around, she was, like, 'If there is one.' "

" 'If there is one.' That was it?"

Eddie grinned, remembering. "Then she asked if I thought
we should go with my tricky new matchup zone against the
Celtics instead of our one-three-one."

"You know what this is like?" De la Cruz said. "It's like a
cocktease." He sipped his own Bloody Mary, a rare drink for
him in the middle of the day.

"I don't think it's like that with her," Eddie said. "I believe she honestly doesn't know whether she wants to put
herself through this again."

He patted the inside of his jacket for his cigarettes, then
remembered he had another one still going in front of him.
Jesus Christ, he was going to be on the goddamn patch be-

fore he knew it. "I don't know," he said, "maybe she thinks she's proved whatever point she wanted to prove to herself."

Michael De la Cruz slapped the table so hard some of his drink spilled on the white tablecloth. Eddie knew he was always a table-slapper when he wanted to make a point, hit what he thought was some kind of big note in the conversation. "This bitch is not just going to walk away from me!" he said in a voice even he had to know was too loud, especially in a room where most of the people having a quiet late lunch probably didn't have any idea who the hell he was, or give a shit if they did.

Eddie thought: This guy really does think of Dee like she's some airhead he's dating.

One who is not going to break up with him, oh no, not on her life.

A billion in the bank, Eddie Holtz thought, and he really is like some rich high school kid, the one girl he might not be able to have getting his balls in an uproar.

"Why're you assuming she is going to walk away?"

"I'm not," De la Cruz said, putting his hands out like he did sometimes, palms down, as if getting a grip. "I'm not. I just want to make sure *I* do everything possible to make sure *she* doesn't. And I want you to do the same thing."

"How am I supposed to do that, exactly?"

De la Cruz said, "Talk to her, Fast Edward. Work on her a little bit. No offense, but do whatever you did to get her in the sack. I frankly don't give a rat's ass. I just know that you're the one who got her to come here in the first place. Now I want you to get her to come back." He smiled. "She trusts you. And you know what Step Ten says about trust, don't you?"

Eddie said it with as much enthusiasm as a waiter giving you the specials. "It's a weapon or a curse, depending on how you use it."

"Of course it is," De la Cruz said, leaning forward suddenly to give Eddie's hand a squeeze.

At least he didn't come around the table for a hug.

"Because I have to be honest with you, Eddie." He took a

crisp fifty-dollar bill out of his money clip, dropped it on the table for the two Bloody Marys. "What's that cute New York expression of yours? Not for nothin'?"

"That's the one."

"Not for nothin'," Michael De la Cruz said evenly. "But if your girlfriend doesn't come back next season, neither do you."

People had started to recognize her more and more when she'd try to take her afternoon walk before games, even when the Knights were on the road. But she'd walk anyway, telling herself this was the time of day to turn her mind off, focus on a new set of streets, new stores, new landmarks, a new skyline, lose herself in all the newness so she could stop thinking, at least for a couple of hours, about how important these games were, about her future.

About Mr. Eddie Holtz.

She had also talked herself into believing that the walks kept her from losing it the way she had in Cleveland. Joey was the one who'd suggested it, saying it could be the perfect combination of shopping and meditation. You couldn't tell it by the warm-ups he always wore around the team, but Joey Shahoud pretty much thought that shopping was a potential cure for cancer.

All Dee knew was that she hadn't had an attack since Cleveland.

So she walked.

On this day she came out the front door of the hotel and crossed the street and was in the Public Garden, which was like some miniature version of Central Park, that and the Boston Common to her right, Dee asking the doorman which was which. She wore her old Celtics cap, her Cooz sweatshirt, her sunglasses, hoping it would be a good Boston disguise for her; just wanting her quiet time without having to stop and keep thanking people for their support, telling them all, men and women and children, the same thing, that what she was doing really wasn't such a big deal; wanting to be alone inside her own head, where Jeremy always said she liked it best.

She really could keep things bottled up inside her as well as any guy.

She eventually walked toward where the doorman told her Newbury Street was. The doorman, an old Irish guy, white hair, Jimmy Monahan according to his name tag, said she could get herself good and tired shopping on Newbury, which he figured might help his Celtics out later on.

"Hey, Jimmy," Dee said. "You give the guys on the team shopping tips, too? Or just the girl?"

Jimmy Monahan reddened. "I guess you could say they're looking for tips on where to shop," he said. "But usually only when it's dark out."

It was officially spring in Boston, the first week of April, the temperature nearly seventy degrees. Dee walked down Newbury, a side door to the Ritz on one side, a Brooks Brothers—looking like the home office for all Brooks Brothers—down on her left, covering ground in her long strides, for some reason suddenly remembering the time she'd been six or seven and gone out with her mother on a spring day like this. They were living in the Franklin Plaza apartments by then, the surprisingly big two-bedroom, the best apartment they'd had by far. Her mother was working in the chorus of *Chicago*, as one of the bad-girl dancers. Cool Daddy was making pretty good money with the Magicians, or so he said, Dee only finding out later that he'd had a few of his normal hustles going on the side, just because he always had hustles going on the side. She and her mother were walking west on 106th, on their way to Saverama to get her a new lunch box. And out of the blue sky, her mother had said, in a mean way, "Walk more like a girl!"

Dee remembered those words, that tone of voice, as if it had happened this morning, remembered pulling her hand out of her mother's and looking up at her, not really understanding. "What's wrong with the way I walk?"

And her mother said, "Take shorter steps. You walk too much like a boy."

They were at the corner of 106th and Third, near the front

door of Saverama, but when the light changed, Dee ran across the street and down 106th toward their apartment building, the one in the back that looked down on the well-tended gardens they had in those days, and the small basketball court behind 225 East 106th, ran into the lobby for the basketball she had left down there, so she wouldn't have to go back upstairs when they returned from shopping.

Later that night, at bedtime, it had to have been a Monday, the theaters dark, her mother had come in and apologized, telling her she loved the way Dee walked, that Mommy was just having a bad day. But for weeks after that, Dee would practice taking shorter steps when no one was watching, until Cool Daddy caught her one day, wanting to know, What you doing, little girl?

She told him, getting it all out before she started to cry. And it was one of those times when he surprised her, when she loved him even more than she thought she could, one of those times when it wasn't all about him, and his scheming and dreaming and ballplaying, when he gathered her in his arms and said, "It ain't ever gonna be about the way you walk, Dee Cody, little girl of mine. It gonna be about the way you *run*."

He wasn't ever a great father, not really, not even after Marthe Wilander Cody was gone. Even then he treated it as if he were moonlighting from his real job, the job of being this character he had created for himself, this larger-than-life Cool Daddy Cody, the character he wanted to be, not the small-time scammer he knew he really was.

But he was pretty good that night, Dee remembered.

She started playing more and more basketball at that age, she remembered that, too, all the hours she would spend on that court at Franklin Plaza. And then after her mother was gone, she played even more, feeling as safe there as in her own apartment; she could run up and down and nobody cared about the way she walked, or about whether she was a boy or a girl, just that she was better than any kid her age in any of the apartments.

In there, she knew.

All you had to do was play.

And if you played well enough, everything would be all right.

Right?

Her walk had taken her halfway down Newbury Street and then back up Boylston, both of them killer stretches of shopping if she'd been as interested as she normally was. Usually Joey got her all worked up about some new territory he seemed to know as well as he did Advil and Tylenol and icepacks and deep-tissue massage and wrapping ankles. But she wasn't into it today. She just walked. I must be thinking about this playoff deal even more than I thought, she told herself, before settling down into a bubble bath that set records in both bubbles and duration, even for her.

Eddie knocked on her door right after she finished, before she did any preliminary work on her hair, which she knew needed cutting as soon as she got back to New York. When she saw who it was through the peephole, she told him just a minute, ran into the bathroom, and quickly wrapped her hair up in a towel. She was also wearing her nifty complimentary bathrobe, this one actually worth stealing, it was that soft.

He grinned at her, the way he used to when they were sharing some kind of private joke, before there'd been a sea change.

Eddie said, "You look ravishing, in a steam room kind of way."

"I wasn't planning to entertain anybody," she said, "except maybe the room service waiter."

"Dressed like that?"

"Wouldn't you like to know."

He came in. Before Dee closed the door, she checked both ways in the hall, like some kind of reflex, to see if anybody was out there. Ever since the front page of the *Daily News* with her and Eddie kissing, she'd sometimes feel as if she were constantly on the wrong side of a peephole, not knowing who was looking at her. Or them.

They sat in the living room, Dee on the couch, Eddie slouched in some kind of antique chair that went with everything else in the perfectly decorated room; they had stayed in a lot of Four Seasons in what she occasionally thought of as Dee Gerard's Tour Across America, but this one put them all away. She could always tell, all the way back to Europe, when she was on the road: The nicer the room, the more she felt herself picking up after herself, neatening things, even when she was alone.

Eddie made himself busier than he had to lighting a cigarette. Not for nothin', she said, smiling, but this is a no-smoking room. He gave her a funny look when she said it, then he said, Yeah, and blew a smoke ring that floated lazily toward the chandelier.

"I miss you," he said.

"You can't miss me," Dee said, not sure she wanted to have this conversation today. "We spend more time together than most married couples."

They sat there staring at each other, as if this were some kind of weird first date. Or—because she found herself comparing most things to basketball these days—as if he were guarding her. Or she was guarding him. Whatever. Somebody waiting for somebody else to make the first move.

Eddie held her with those steady eyes, those great-looking eyes. "I spend that kind of quality time with Anquwan and Dream."

"Well," Dee said breezily, a lot more chipper than she was feeling, "at least you don't have to kiss them afterward and tell them you care."

He set the cigarette down on the edge of the coffee table, giving the burning part plenty of room, and got out of the chair suddenly and came over, lifted her out of the lotus position she'd assumed on the couch, had her in his arms before she knew it, and now they were kissing the way they had in front of the Sherry, the kissing that had ended them up in the newspaper.

When they both came up for air, she said, "Can I ask you something?"

"Anything."

Dee said, "You think I walk like a boy?"

Eddie said, "Absolutely. It was that and your ballhandling

ability that made me want to tear your clothes off the very first night."

"I *knew* it!" she said, and put her hand behind his neck and pulled him down to her and they were kissing again.

They were trying to make it work on the couch, Eddie Holtz half on top of her, half on the side, when he suddenly burst out laughing.

The towel that had been on top of her head was long gone. Dee brushed some of her wet hair out of her eyes, briefly imagining what kind of Swamp Creature quality it had by now. *"This,"* she said, "is funny?"

"I was just wondering," he said, choking out the words, really cracking himself up now, tears in his eyes, "if this is what they really mean in sports when they talk about a playoff push."

Then they were both giggling like kids, Eddie tumbling off the couch when he tried to move off her a little bit, Dee rolling right over on top of him.

Eddie crawled around to the other side of the coffee table, where he'd left his cigarette before he made his move. He held it out to her. "Where there's smoke," he said.

It occurred to her that she hadn't seen him this loose, not just the kissing but this kind of fun in him, for weeks. Maybe not since he'd become Eddie the coach, even with what had happened between them that day in Cleveland.

Eddie the coach, consumed with making a real playoff push with his basketball team.

"We can't do this today," Dee said. "You know that, right?"

"I do," he said. "Coaches know everything."

"Do they?"

He walked into the kitchen, blue shirt out of his jeans, hair mussed. Dee could hear him running water into the sink. When he came back, the cigarette was gone.

"We're gonna make it," he said.

"I know," she said. Knowing this was about basketball, not them. She ran her hands through her hair, which felt like seaweed. "I didn't a month ago."

"I did."

"I know," she said again. "I just want to know how."

"I know what I know," Eddie Holtz said.

He sat down next to her on the floor, put an arm around her, tucked some hair behind her ear.

"You can't quit," he said.

"Who said anything about quitting?"

"Yeah," he said, "you've made such a state secret out of the fact that you might not want to come back."

She put her head on his shoulder.

"I don't want you to," he said.

"I'm glad you don't," Dee said. "Sometimes I don't, either. But for the sake of a conversation that might help us not turn the rest of the afternoon into one of those Specter-vision movies, as the guys are always saying, what would be so terrible about me leaving when we finish doing whatever it is we're going to do?" She leaned up, kissed him under the ear. "Did that question take up the whole twenty-four-second clock?"

"This can't be enough for you," he said. "It *shouldn't* be enough."

"For who? Or is it whom? I know I learned this at the American School."

She could tell he didn't want to play.

"For yourself," he said.

"You sure about that, Coach? You're kind of a hot property yourself all of a sudden."

He looked off. For all the things that had changed between them, or at least what Dee felt had changed, one thing that hadn't was this: He was as hard to read as ever. He wanted you to think he was easy, that he was right there for you, this jock guy who knew or cared only about basketball. But she knew he was more complicated than that. Oh, he was pure about basketball, no question, with his own vision of the way it should be played, the way it should look. He had this way, from the first night as coach of the Knights—that first huddle, really, after Michael De la Cruz fired Bobby Carlino—of getting the players, all of them, to do things. Getting them on the same page. Getting them to do what he wanted, mostly. He loved to give you that routine, from Chuck Daly, over and over like it was his mantra, telling you modern players only *allowed* you to coach them.

But she knew better.

Eddie Holtz coached them.

It was as if he had been waiting his whole life to coach them, all the years, even before his knee injury, when he was kidding himself, or so he said, that he was on his way to being a great player.

He could even make Dee believe that somehow it had been his destiny all along to coach her.

He didn't say anything, and neither did she. From the start it had been one of the things she liked best about Eddie Holtz, something that cut him away from the pack, almost every man she'd ever known, starting with her old man.

He never talked just to talk. Not holding back. Just waiting until he had something to contribute to the conversation.

She pulled away a little, leaned back so she could put a hand up and rub his cheek. By now she knew he didn't shave on game day until right before it was time for him to go to the arena; she'd see some quick hit on the evening news from after the morning shootaround, and he always had a little bit of a beard. Eddie told her it was his only superstition, but Dee knew there had to be more, starting with the same knit tie that had been showing up since they'd started going well.

He gave you pieces of things.

Of himself.

"What I'm trying to say here," he said, "is that we're just getting started."

"The NBA we," she said, "or the us we? So to speak."

"All of the above. We meaning the team. And we meaning you and me."

"I see."

. Eddie said, " 'I see,' meaning I'm right?" He pushed the coffee table away so he could stretch out his bad leg. "That kind of 'I see'?"

"No."

He grinned. "I see."

Dee said, "If you want a definite answer right now, today, I can't give that to you." He reached over and carefully rubbed the bad knee. "Even though I could probably be convinced to give you something else later on tonight, in light of this afternoon's festivities."

"No turnovers against the Celts?" he said.

"That too, Mr. Needy."

Eddie said, "To play just a couple of months after waiting your whole life, that can't possibly be enough. Any more than it's enough for me." He looked at her, dead serious, saying, "You told me once that you never thought you'd get over the thrill of getting picked for the boys' games. Well, now you've got picked." He took a deep breath, let it out, frowned as if trying to find the right words. "See," he said, "we're alike, you and me. More than either one of us wants to let on. I can't tell you I knew my whole life that this is where I belong. But you want to know something? This *is* where I belong. And I know you weren't going along all those years in Paris or wherever the hell you were, thinking, 'Jeez, am I ever gonna get my chance to play in the NBA?' Except that's the way it shook out. And now you know this is where *you* belong." He walked over to the minibar, poured himself some ice water. "I read in the papers now about how the Knights are doing this, how Holtz tweaked the lineup, how Anquwan's with the program now, about all this team unity we're supposed to have all of a sudden. You know what the big thing is? We pass now. Okay? It sounds like the simplest goddamn thing, but that's it. We pass. 'Cause *you* pass. The other stuff is all true. You can see now how much player Anquwan's got inside his crazy-ass self. But you got the ball and you started passing, and then the other guys started passing. And that kind of passing did what it's done in basketball since the first goddamn peach basket: It made us smarter, and it sure as hell made us better. The sportswriters'd laugh their asses off if I ever explained it this way, but it starts with the first pass. It was that way with Bird and the Celtics, it was that way with Magic. People talk about how their rivalry changed basketball. That was just a part of it. An element. Those two guys brought the *pass* back to the NBA. You put the pass in this team."

She had never seen him this revved about anything. Certainly not her. And maybe not ever her. Or anybody else. He was pacing the suite now, spilling water sometimes as he used his hands to talk to her, trying to get her to understand.

"I'm not sayin' you're the only one who can do this," he said. "I don't know who the next girl will be, or if there is gonna be a next girl, and—don't laugh—even what's to prevent guys from saying they want to play in the WNBA if they're not good enough to make it here. What I do know is this: The only place you can't go is *back*."

"Didn't say I was."

"Didn't say you weren't."

"Why do you have to know this minute?"

He said, " 'Cause I want to?"

Dee said. "Yeah, yeah, yeah. I want what I want when I want it."

"I am *such* a guy."

"Not always."

"Hey."

"Don't worry," she said, mussing his hair even more as she stood up. "That's a good thing, actually."

She walked over to where she'd set up her CD player and her portable speakers on the mantel of the fireplace, not even remembering what she'd been listening to during her bath, flipping open the top and seeing it was Joshua Redman. She hit the Play button and the machine skipped a little, the way it sometimes did, and so this incredibly gifted saxophone kid was halfway into "Hide and Seek."

Sometimes Dee thought her whole life had turned into some jazz riff, no sheet music to speak of, no arrangement, no plan, the music just blowing her around like a cool breeze.

"I'm sorry I can't give you what you want today," she said, "in more ways than one."

"I'm pretty sure that was supposed to be my line."

"But I will make you a promise," Dee said. "When I know, you'll know."

"Know what, exactly?"

"What all you men want to know," Dee said. "Just how much us girls need what you got."

"I see," Eddie Holtz said.

He was close to her again, in front of the fireplace. He took her hands, gave her a long look, a sad look, she thought, as if there was something he wanted to tell her, or had been holding back.

He kissed her on the forehead and left instead.

Dee stood there in front of the fireplace, towel in her hand, standing there exactly where he'd left her, listening to "One Shining Soul" now, Redman skipping across it like a stone skipping across water, thinking this about men in general and Eddie Holtz in particular:

One of these days I might have to think about finding another hobby.

⊕ twenty-three

They beat the Celtics, mostly because of Carl Anthony. He told Dee during warm-ups that he still had a score to settle with Whup Griffin. "Me and Gomer Pile of Shit got unresolved issues" is the way he put it. Carl went out and had his best game of the year, scoring twenty-eight points to go with nineteen rebounds. He also blocked four of Whup Griffin's shots. The last one came with three minutes to go and the Knights ahead by twenty points. Whup Griffin tried to dunk the ball. Carl smashed the ball so hard into Griffin's face that he broke his nose. It took the floor staff at the Fleet Center ten minutes to clean up the mess.

Dee stood next to Carl Anthony while they cleaned and said, "Yuck, all that blood."

Carl, no expression, none, said, "Not my blood."

The next night, the Knights lost to the Wizards in Washington. Three nights after that, Dee had fifteen assists, a personal best, against a 76ers team slower up and down the lineup than fishing, and the Knights won. The Heat, who had upset the Suns in Phoenix the night before, lost to the Maver-

icks in Dallas. So the Knights had a record of 36–44. The
Heat had fallen to 37–43.

One out, two to play, one of them against the Heat.

No matter what happened, if the Knights won two, they
were in the playoffs. Both games, against the Knicks and
against the Heat, were at the Garden. Michael De la Cruz had
announced that they would celebrate "Dee Gerard Night" during halftime of the Knicks game. It was a way, he said in the
press release issued by Harold Wasserman's people, of hon-
oring what she had done for men's basketball, and women
basketball players everywhere.

De la Cruz didn't run it by either Dee or Mo Jiggy, but
once the press release was out there, it was too late for anybody to do anything about it.

"Is there some way Dee Gerard can take Dee Gerard Night
off?" she asked Mo on the telephone.

That same day, the day after they'd beaten the 76ers in
Philadelphia, Eddie got them all together in their locker room
at the Garden before practice. When he stepped away from his
greaseboard, they could all see what he'd written there, in huge
purple script:

To-Do List:
1. Beat Knicks' Ass
2. Beat Heat's Ass Worse than Knicks

"Yo," Anquwan Posey said, politely raising a hand the way
he always did. "Shouldn't that there be the plural of ass,
Coach?"

"Yeah," Dream Jackson said, "ass*holes.*"

Jamie Lawton, sitting in front of them, turned and said,
"I'm telling you guys, you give me just one peek at both your
college boards, you can name your price."

Thruston B. Howell said, "Whyn't you take a peek at *this,*
Barbie?"

"Yeah," Jamie said, "that's my mission in life, to commune
with a body part you actually refer to as Mr. Boo."

He couldn't see Thruston (Sea Lion) Howell lean close to

his ear and yell, "Boo!" making Jamie Lawton nearly fall out of his chair.

"Boo-*eeeee!*" Thruston yelled now.

"The bad," Dee said.

One of the boys.

Jamie Lawton was shaking his head, saying, "When I retire, it's the relationships I'm going to miss the most, no shit."

Dee had discovered on the middle-of-the-night flight home from Minneapolis the previous week that Jamie Lawton wasn't gay.

Most of the guys were sleeping, in either The Tommy or The Ralph. Eddie was playing cards with Bill Flynn up front. Joey had told Dee he was going back to the screening room to watch a bootleg tape of the new Steven Seagal movie.

"What," he said to Dee, "I can't like watching the ponytail guy take the whole Russian mob with one hand?"

A few minutes later, Jamie Lawton poked his head into her compartment, carrying a bottle of Kendall Jackson white wine. Dee, still much too wired after having one of her best games—and having it with Ellie Ryan in the house—was wide awake, reading the new *Vogue*.

What came next, Dee decided later after much reflection, as tough a grader as she was about guys trying to score—she thought of it as her own personal Guy-Q Test—was every bit as inspired as Anquwan's approach had been.

"I thought it was about time the two of us shared a drink," he said, and smiled. In the half-light of her compartment, just her overhead on, it occurred to her that Jamie Lawton made Brad Pitt look as homely as one of Mo Jiggy's rottweilers.

"No, thanks," Dee said. "When I drink on airplanes, I become a hijack risk."

He reached into the minibar that was in each compartment and pulled out a wineglass for himself.

"From what you've heard," he said, "you probably figured me for a white wine drinker, right?"

Dee had a feeling that a call to that awful Dr. Laura, radio witch, was about to break out right here, over Buffalo.

"Well," she said, "half a glass probably wouldn't hurt."

Jamie Lawton, who really did have the kind of WASP nose

and looks she assumed were on the cover of plastic surgeon brochures, poured for both of them and said, "I'm actually not, you know. Gay."

Dee said, "When I hear somebody say that, I can't decide whether congratulations are in order, or regrets."

"I'm a little surprised you never asked," he said.

He was wearing a short-sleeved Lacoste polo shirt with a small tear near the cute little crocodile. The shabby preppy look, like the frayed collars she noticed sometimes on his buttoned-down dress shirts. His long, streaky blond hair was brushed straight back, going way past his collar. He had a light stubble of beard, the color of the wine. His eyes were nearly emerald green.

"I didn't think it was any of my business," Dee said, "one way or the other."

"I'm only mentioning it because most women, the ones who never get the thrill of hearing my teammates talk about me the way they do, throw themselves at me first chance they get."

Dee sipped her wine.

"I try to be strong," she said.

"Actually," Jamie Lawton continued, "even the ones who have heard the suggestion that I might . . ." He had a good voice, though not nearly as good as his smile. "They sometimes make a run, too."

"Thinking they can turn you around. So to speak."

He nodded. "Trophy deal. They think their powers are so tremendous, they *can* turn me. And I let them think they're doing just that." He gave her a mock toast. "They end up feeling like they somehow screwed the whole Halloween parade in the Village."

"Let me get this straight," Dee said. "About your straightness. You don't mind people thinking you're not."

"*Damn* straight," he said. "Absolutely. My fellow Knights especially. I'm sure you've noticed they generally treat me like some sort of leper."

Dee allowed as how it was about as easy to ignore as Anquwan's various hair statements.

"I *love* that," he said. "They leave me alone. But here's

the key." He was so pleased with himself. "They think it's their choice, not mine."

"There you go," Dee said.

"Let's have a real toast," Jamie said.

"To *your* feminine side," she said. "Even if it doesn't actually exist."

"Cheers," he said happily, and they clicked their glasses.

"How about we go somewhere when we land?" he said.

"It will be after four in the morning," Dee said.

"Oh, don't worry, I know some clubs. I know *lots* of clubs, as a matter of fact."

"Straight or gay?"

"Damned if I know sometimes."

"Thanks," Dee said. "But no thanks."

Jamie Lawton frowned the way they all did when that word—*no*—scurried between them like a rat.

"Is it because you and Eddie . . . ?"

Dee said, "It has nothing to do with Eddie. I'd just rather not."

"You're kidding."

"Not kidding," she said, smiling, trying to keep things light. "Just not interested."

"How about this? How about we have dinner some night?"

"I don't think that's a good idea, either."

He leaned forward. "I've gone about this all wrong. How about this? How about I call, like tomorrow, like I'm asking you out on a real date. We'll go to a show. Or a movie. I know you like music. I saw where Rosemary Clooney is doing a limited engagement at the Algonquin." He gave her the big smile now. "Look at that! Even though I'm not gay, I know about Rosemary Clooney."

Dee said, "Jamie, I appreciate your interest in me, I really do. I'm glad this gay-straight thing is working out for you. Really, I am. But the kind of social life I want right now is no social life at all."

He finished the last of his wine, stood up, his head nearly touching the ceiling of her compartment in The Calvin. "So," he said, "I guess the two of us going back to the trainer's room right now is out of the question?"

• • •

Listening to the guys talk now in the locker room, Dee looked at Jamie Lawton and smiled to herself. He'd really thought he could knock off a quickie with her on the team plane. And she knew exactly why:

He was a jock.

He'd never think of himself as a dumb jock, and in a lot of ways, he wasn't. But he was about women, in the same weird way some of the dumb-jock women she'd played with in Europe were about other women, when they'd decided to hit on her.

And no matter how they dressed it up, men or women, no matter what kind of approach they used, it always came down to them thinking that sex was some essential part of sports, some extension of the game, whatever kind of sex it was, boy-girl or girl-girl.

I like you.

We're here.

Why not.

After all, it don't mean nothin'.

We're all jocks, Dee thought, me included, sitting here with the boys joking about asses and assholes, about the booey and the bad. And somehow, out of all their backgrounds, all their egos and agendas, they had pulled themselves together to try to do this big thing: beat the Knicks' ass and beat the Heat's ass even worse, just like it said on Eddie's board, and make the playoffs. Out of all the dumbness that came with sports, the dumb *jockness* of it all, it was still the very best thing about it all, the way it could still come together this way.

The way Eddie Holtz—a lot of him and maybe a little bit of Miss Dee Gerard—had made it come together for the New York Knights with two games to play.

"I'm just gonna assume," Eddie was saying to them now, "that losing the way you guys used to lose must have officially worn your asses out."

Anquwan said, "Wish it was just our asses."

"Tell *me* about it," Thruston Howell said. "Was nights I hurt all the way down to Mr. Boo."

It made Dee giggle.

Eddie said, "I always thought you guys were better than your record under that little grease spot who coached the team before me. But I've got to level: It turns out you were even better than I thought."

"It's like our girl's man Mo Jiggy says in 'Balls in the Air,' " Deltha said.

"I must have missed that one on the greatest hits album," Dee said.

Dee knew Deltha fancied himself a future rapper. He rode around in the same black Suburban Mo did, had an ever-growing posse, was even talking about getting a dog.

Dee also suspected he had enough firearms in his possession to go toe-to-toe with a militia group.

He got up in front of them now, making some moves she could only describe as slouchy hip-hop, hands going everywhere at once, eyes closed, swaying from side to side as he gave them a little taste of "Balls in the Air":

> *Don't nobody 'member why you lost*
> *Uh-uh, uh-uh*
> *Just 'member that you fuckin' lost*
> *Uh-huh..*
> *So bitch-slap them 'fore they bitch-slap you*
> *Uh-huh.*
> *Bitch-slap them 'fore they bitch-slap you*
> *Uh-huh.*

Dee, the jock girl in the room, stood up and began applauding.

"Call me crazy," she said, "but by God, I still love a show tune."

Mo Jiggy said, "I knew I should have had Montell and Denzell bitch-slap him."

" 'Fore he bitch-slapped us," Dee said.

He looked at her, suspicious. "You know that song?"

She said, "I try to stay current."

He reached out and touched the newspaper as if poking something to see if it were really dead.

"How much of this shit is true?" he asked.

It was just the two of them in a back booth at the Athena diner on Seventy-ninth and Madison, around the corner from one of Mo's multiple residences, this one the apartment he'd bought from Reggie Jackson at Seventy-ninth and Fifth with the full park view.

The shit he was referring to was in the copy of the *Daily News* between them on the table.

Montell and Denzell were in the next booth closer to the door. Darnell and Shaheen were on the other side of Montell and Denzell. A new kid Dee hadn't met before today — Shawn — stood out on the sidewalk with Bill and Hillary. Mo said he had brought the boys with him because he didn't want him and Dee interrupted.

Dee thought: A SWAT team would think twice about interrupting us.

She was looking at the dogs, their noses pressed to the window, eyeballing Mo, when Mo said, "Earth to Dee. I *said,* how much of what the man said is true?"

She said, "Only all of it."

RANSOME NOTES
by Walt Ransome

You know that colorful daddy Dee Cody Gerard told us about when she first came to town?

Colorful Cool Daddy Cody?

The one from Boys High and Green Correctional and the Harlem Apollos?

The one who taught the girl everything she knows about basketball?

Well, after a couple of weeks investigating the life (and death) and times of Cool Daddy Cody — even making a trip to Gay Paree — I can tell you this: It's a good thing he didn't teach his daughter everything *he* knew.

It turns out he only moonlighted as some second-rate version of a Harlem Globetrotter.

The guy's full-time job was as a bum.

A grade-A certified creep.

He was at various times in his life a dope mule, a con artist, a thief. He was a career deadbeat if not a deadbeat father. In this country and abroad, he knew more big-time and small-time hoods than there are now on cable television.

He tried to hustle just about everybody with money he ever met, including his daughter. He stole every dollar and franc and English pound he could. From the research this reporter was able to do—it all started innocently enough, with some curiosity about how much about Cool Daddy Cody was fiction and how much was fact—it is amazing in retrospect that he had time to play any basketball at all.

"Let myself tell you what it was," said Earthwind Morton, who agreed to play a charity game in Athens that Cody had organized right before he died (a game for which Earthwind is still waiting to get paid, along with all the other players who participated). "If you was at a party tonight and somebody said, 'Hey, guess who all is comin' over? Cool Daddy and that Salaam Hussein,' everybody would say, 'Aw s——, Cool Daddy? That m——f——er?' Even that cute a—— daughter didn't want nothin' to do with him."

I think you get Earthwind's drift.

It was even suggested to me that when Cody died in that Greek ferry accident—the memory of which nearly got his daughter to give Barbara Walters the kind of tears she always wants from her guests—he had in his possession about $200,000 that didn't exactly belong to him.

Let me tell you more. . . .

And he did, the piece stretching across two pages of the *Daily News* sports section, with some old pictures that even Dee had never seen, including one of her and Cool Daddy when she was in high school, Dee in her Clinton uniform, the two of them standing on Seventh Avenue with the Garden marquee behind them.

There was one of her standing with the New York Apollos, this time with the Eiffel Tower providing the backdrop.

There was a blowup of the original wire-service story about the day the *Samina Express* struck that rocky outcrop off the resort island of Paros, where Cool Daddy had become a kind of court jester for some rich Greek guys; his name was just listed alphabetically with sixty-five other victims of the *Samina*, including the sixteen they never found.

There was the mug shot from when he had been arraigned back in 1964.

In the Athena, Dee said to Mo Jiggy, "I'm actually kind of surprised."

"What about?"

"That it took somebody this long to find out," she said.

Dee had discovered something about New York sportswriters in a pretty short time.

If it wasn't their story, they weren't interested.

They generally liked to chase somebody else about as much as lazy basketball players did.

So they didn't give her a hard time about Cool Daddy after practice that afternoon up in Mamaroneck, before she got into the town car Michael De la Cruz still sent for her every day the Knights were up there. She did one quick shot about Ransome's piece for all the television people, basically finding about ten different ways to say the same thing:

I never thought my father was perfect.

"When you're a kid," she said at one point, "you see what you want to see. Then later on you remember what you want to remember."

Then she gave them a variation of the line she liked to use about her ex-husband.

"Cecil Cody," she said, "was a good dad and a very, *very* bad boy."

Before she got into the car, a woman who introduced herself as Natalie Ferrare from *60 Minutes II* asked if it was cool if she could ask her one question alone. Dee said, Go ahead.

"You said you grabbed this shot at the NBA so you wouldn't have any regrets in basketball," Ferrare said. "What do you suppose your father's biggest regret was?"

"That's the funny part," Dee said. "He didn't have any. He always thought he was going good."

"He never got off the street, no matter where it was," she was telling Eddie later. "He used to tell me all the time. 'Little girl,' he'd say, 'your daddy was born to two places. One's a basketball court. The other's the wrong side of the goddamn tracks.' "

Dee and Eddie had actually managed to have a quiet dinner at the Union Square Café, a corner table in the upstairs room that Eddie said he rated now that he was coach of the Knights. Though, he said, they probably could have had the whole upstairs room to themselves if he'd made the reservation in the name of his new sweetie pie, Miss Dee Gerard.

I'm your sweetie? she'd asked over coffee.

Eddie said sure, he had the pictures to prove it.

They left the restaurant and took a cab uptown, and when they got to the Sherry she asked if he wanted to come upstairs for a nightcap. "What if somebody sees us walk in together?" he said. "Haven't you had enough bad press for one day?"

"You know what?" she said in the back of the cab. "I don't care anymore. My life is officially an open book. Remind me to tell Mo. That's the real book deal in all this. It's true what you told me back at the beginning. Everybody gets to know everything, it was a law they passed while I was away."

They went upstairs, and though Dee wasn't clocking anything, she figured they were in her big bed with its partial view of the park in less than five minutes and it would've been shorter than that if she hadn't fumbled around with her stupid diaphragm as if it were a live hand grenade.

Some of their clothes even made it into the bedroom afterward, though it looked as if they'd left a Hansel and Gretel trail of underwear and socks behind them, even the knee brace Eddie sometimes wore under his gray slacks.

Now she was telling him all the parts about Cool Daddy she'd left out the first time around, when she had given Eddie and Mo the sanitized version of her father's life, as if it were some kind of movie she had to clean up before it could be shown on television.

"It's like one of my shrinks said. He had the skill, just not the will. But he never saw that in himself. He just saw everything that happened to him as bad breaks. Him not making it at Marquette. Him not making the NBA. Him always being on the hustle or on the run right up until that stupid boat went down, it was *always* somebody else's fault. Always."

He was always in debt, she told Eddie. He was sitting up, his back propped against the headboard; she was leaning on an elbow, the sheet only half covering her, facing him. Even after her mother was gone, she said, in that period when Cool Daddy was actually acting like a real daddy, acting as if he cared about something more than her basketball, he could never get away from the street, all the street people he knew; all the ones exactly like him, just without the charm, and maybe without the capacity of bullshitting themselves about who and what they were the way Cool Daddy always could.

When she began as a teenager to realize just how her father was supporting her—supporting *them*—dealing dope at the nightclubs where he worked, taking overnight trips with a suitcase that looked fat enough for a whole summer vacation, even running numbers sometimes, she started to think of him as the eighth wonder of the world.

"Why's that?"

"Because he only did that one stretch of jail time."

There were always guys showing up looking for him, first at Franklin Plaza, later up in the Bronx. Some were picking up money, some were dropping off. She would find out much later, in France one night when he had gotten into his red wine, that the real reason he ended up out of the nightclub business for good was that the guys who had fronted the money for CD finally found out how much he skimmed after they made him manager.

"Even when we moved to Europe, what he said was going to be his big fresh start, he was still speaking the only language he ever really knew," Dee said. "Easy money."

The Apollos were a modest success for a few years, never going too long without gigs, always having a decent schedule, making a decent payday.

Of course, it wasn't enough for Cool Daddy.

So before long he was scamming again, with both hands, finding bad guys in France and Italy and Spain as easily as he always had in East Harlem. He made sure he and his daughter had a nice apartment in Paris while she went to the American School, located in a quiet neighborhood between the Invalides and the Eiffel Tower, right before the street opened up into Boulevard Saint-Germain. But he was never around much, even during those stretches when the Magicians were on hiatus.

Dee's position, she told Eddie Holtz, remained unchanged from when she first began to see Cool Daddy for what he really was.

"I didn't want to know what I didn't want to know," she said.

She opened the wrong drawer at the Paris apartment one day, looking for her birth certificate, and found all his fake passports, each one looking real, each one with the same young-looking picture of Cool Daddy. "He was always a dude," she said. "Always thinking he was better-looking than he really was, always thinking he was a better dresser in, like, these zippy Pierre Cardin suits." Each passport in the name of a different Negro League baseball player: Ed Semler, Joe Williams, Ted Radcliffe, Buck Leonard, Dick Seay. And James "Cool Papa" Bell, his favorite.

"You remember those names?" Eddie said.

"Despite what I told the press," Dee said, "I actually remember everything."

The real reason she got to play with the Apollos as much as she did, at least when the games were close enough for her to get to in a hurry by train, was that her father had disappeared suddenly on another one of his famous overnight trips.

"You know me, little girl," he'd say when he returned.

"Always out there beatin' the bushes, tryin' to drum up interest in our team."

"Like I believed him," she said.

Then he'd pull a fistful of money out of his pocket, saying somebody had come through with some money he was owed and how about you and me going shopping at one of those *rues* where all the nice clothes are?

Later on, with the Apollos history and Dee off playing pro ball, he'd disappear from her life for a year at a time, then suddenly show up where she was playing, looking for money. Always telling her that maybe just a thousand, American, would get him over. Or he'd call her collect from Italy or Greece or someplace, asking if she could wire him that amount.

And always he would tell her about some new friends he'd made, some exciting new business opportunity that was right around the corner, how he was finally gonna hit it big, get back up on his damn feet once and for all.

Or there would be some new version of the Apollos, only built around his little girl this time.

But for now, he just needed that thousand, American, real bad.

"Sometimes he'd just show up at my hotel, or outside the players' entrance at the arena," Dee said, "saying, 'Hey, baby, Daddy's home!' "

When she'd finally split from Jeremy and was running DC, he showed up there, after no contact in five or six months, saying that he was getting back into basketball, he had this big plan for Greece, a charity game maybe even she could play in — wouldn't that be fun, getting out there with the boys again? — there was just the matter of some money he owed some gentlemen in Spain that he had gotten his tired old ass on the wrong side of.

"Same old thing," he said. "Wrong side of the tracks again, this time in Valde-fuckin'-rama, Spain."

And that was it, right there and right then, underneath the blue lights of DC, right there at the front door. She'd had enough, she told him. Told him that she had cut herself loose from a husband and now she was doing the same with a father.

She gave him one more thousand, American, and told him she didn't want to see him again.

Told him she was moving on from all the men in her life.

Both of them.

"The ferry went down a couple of months later," she told Eddie at the Sherry.

⊕ twenty-four

"Was a saint compared to my old man," Dream Jackson said.

"Only saint mine was ever compared to was a Saint Bernard," Anquwan Posey said.

Anquwan and Dream had come down to her dressing room, along with Carl Anthony and Thruston B. Howell. It was, to the best of her recollection, the first time any of the Knights players had been in there.

"Least you had one," Thruston B. Howell said. "A father."

"What, your momma had one of those immaculate receptacle deals goin'?" Anquwan said.

Carl Anthony said, "My old man said he was goin' out for some red. That was 1982. My momma still got his damn supper on the table."

"That shit in the paper?" Anquwan said. "Now, that shit really *don't* mean nothin'."

Dream was looking around at her luxurious digs. "Tell you what," he said. "You take my apartment, I'll take this, straight up."

Carl Anthony was sitting on the couch, playing with the remote to the big screen like a zonked teenager, watching transfixed as one channel after another—soccer games, old sitcoms, news channels, cartoons, black- and-white movies, music videos—flashed before his eyes.

"We just come down to make sure you was cool," Carl said, eyes on the screen.

"I'm cool," Dee said.

"Anquwan's right for once," he said. "It don't mean nothin'."

"Yo," she said.

"There you go," Carl said.

Thruston B. Howell was in his purple warm-ups, making him look more like Barney the purple dinosaur than a Sea Lion. Dee and Eddie had walked into FAO Schwarz one afternoon from the Sherry and Eddie had explained that to a two-year-old, Barney was bigger than Mick Jagger used to be. One more thing she'd missed. This one a kid thing. Sea Lion flopped down next to Carl Anthony on the couch. "They line up all the bad fathers in the league?" he said. "Players included? Line'd stretch all the way to Philly. Which is where I believe mine was last seen."

"Still think mine was the mailman," Anquwan said. "My aunt Peg always maintained I favored his eyes and whatnot."

Dee looked at the clock, which said 7:15. Twenty minutes until the Knicks. She stood up. "I believe it's time for us to go kick some ass," she said.

"Asses," Anquwan corrected.

She shooed them all toward the door, but before Carl led them into the hallway, Dee said, "Hey?"

They all turned around.

"Thanks," she said.

The rest of the players were waiting for them near the opening to the court. She got into what had become her usual spot, last in the line, same as it had been for her in high school, then ran out into the loudest ovation she'd gotten yet at the Garden, even louder than the one the first night when Eddie'd first put her in. Joey had told her the place was disgusting with celebs, both ends of celebrity row and underneath both baskets. Dee was about as interested in that as she usually was. When she hit the court, she just gave a quick look to the place in the third row where she knew Sharmayne was supposed to be sitting with the rest of the girls' team from Clinton. She saw they were all there. When Sharmayne saw Dee looking at her, she jumped off and made this little dance move, finishing by pointing her two index fingers in the direction of No. 14 of the Knights.

The other Clinton girls, all dressed in their warm-ups, raised a banner that read:

Cool Daughter!

It was a Knights home game, which meant they had the home bench at the Eighth Avenue end. While the rest of her teammates were still warming up, or just stretching near half-court, the scoreboard countdown letting everybody know the game would start in less than four minutes, Dee went over to a folding chair at the end of the bench and sat down.

Eddie was at the other end, his usual seat near the press table, going over the notes on blue index cards he always wrote out for himself with Bill Flynn. When he saw Dee, he came down and sat next to her.

"Everything cool?" he said.

"Well, isn't that the question on everybody's lips?" she said. "Yeah, I'm cool."

"They gotta win, too," he said. "The Knicks, I mean. If they beat us, they lock up homecourt for as long as they go in the playoffs."

"Hey," Dee said, "I read the papers."

Eddie Holtz said, "That's what I'm always afraid of, kiddo."

"You know what I'm afraid of? The dog-and-pony show at halftime."

Eddie said, "It can't last that long, there's still gonna be half the game to play. Go with it. They'll probably give you a car."

"Did I ever mention to you, in a moment of searing honesty, that I don't know how to drive?"

"You're shitting."

"Nope."

"You don't know?"

She shook her head.

"I'll teach you this summer," he said. "After the playoffs."

She started to say something about where she really wanted to be this summer, but then the horn sounded. Then both teams went through the dopey rock-concert, light-show, video-game production that was the rule now for player introductions in the NBA.

When they were all on the court for the opening tip, Dong Li against her old friend DuWapp Piersall of the Knicks, Pooh Bear Moriarty got close to Dee and said, "Been meanin' to ask you: Who's your daddy?"

She knew she should walk away until the ref got between Dong and Kunta Kunta, but the bad Dee put an arm around Pooh Bear instead, like they were buddies who went way back, and said, "Just somebody else your momma gave it up for."

He pulled away, saying, "Say what?"

Dee said, "And another thing: Where'd you get that nickname? What, Kanga and Roo were already taken?"

"Bitch," he said.

"On wheels," she agreed.

The first time down the court, she went behind her back on Pooh Bear Moriarty, stopped at the free-throw line when Bad Levine came up on her, turned around as if she were going back outside to start the offense again, then threw a blind pass over her shoulder to a cutting Dong Li for an easy layup.

Yeah, she thought.

Bitch on wheels.

The Garden sounded like a downtown express.

Next time down for the Knights, Pooh Bear backed off her, and when he did, Dee stepped back and hit a three-point basket with the same kind of one-hand push move she used to see Cousy make in old basketball movies, right knee coming up in the same motion with hand and ball.

It went like that, against the best team in the league, for most of the first half. Poor Bear Moriarty finally got pissed that he was being shown up this way by a girl, and got hot himself. But the Knights wouldn't miss, either. They were up ten points at the end of the first quarter and thirteen at the half. Dong Li was in double figures, so was Anquwan, and so was Dream Jackson.

Dee had eight points and nine assists.

She had the numbers, had the crowd.

Not because she was the first woman in the NBA.

Not because they were happy to see her, so they could say they saw her at least once.

Not because Eddie and Michael De la Cruz—she saw De la Cruz during one time-out running up and down the steps near his seat like a crazed, hopped-up cheerleader—had picked her.

It was because of the way she was playing the game. Handling and passing and shooting when the shot was there, not just keeping up now, not just holding her own.

Beating them at their own game.

Dee was flying.

They had actually doubled the length of the halftime, to twenty minutes. Michael De la Cruz acted as his own master of ceremonies. Dee had to stay out there for the whole wretched thing; her teammates at least got to go and hide out in the locker room for a few minutes, promising they'd come back to catch the last few minutes.

"We'll be back for the good parts," Anquwan Posey said.

"What good parts?" Dee said.

"I got to go ice something," he said.

Dee said, "They shoot deserters in the Army."

"This little party," Michael De la Cruz was saying now, holding a wireless mike in his hands, turning this way and that, "is just our way of saying thank you, Dee."

There was a small burst of applause, like politicians got when they paused during a speech, no matter what they'd just said.

"Thank you for finally giving Knights fans a basketball season."

More applause.

"Thank you, as our little friends at Special Olympics like to say, for being brave in the attempt."

Kill me now, Dee thought.

"Thank you," De la Cruz said, "for giving us the most precious gift of all in sports . . . *hope*!"

Jesus, Jesus, Jesus.

The place, as if on cue, went crazy.

De la Cruz introduced Rosie O'Donnell then, who gave Dee a huge, framed blowup of the current cover of *Rosie* magazine, one that featured an action shot of Dee.

The mayor gave her the keys to the city, saying that the Yankees had left him a few to give out on special occasions like this.

The governor, who seemed to enjoy towering over the mayor the way he did, officially proclaimed Dee Gerard Night as Dee Gerard Day in New York State, while sheepishly admitting the day was almost over.

Sharmayne and the rest of the girls from DeWitt Clinton gave her a Clinton letter jacket, the old-school kind, with a wool front and leather sleeves.

Kathie Lee Gifford, who acted as if Dee knew who she was, came out and sang "New York, New York" in a voice that had what Dee liked to call shower-stall range.

The Rockettes did the big showstopping "Lullaby of Broadway" number from *42nd Street.*

Dee discreetly looked up at the scoreboard clock.

Three more stinking minutes.

Finally, Michael De la Cruz, wearing black jeans and black work boots and a black T-shirt to go with his Armani tuxedo jacket, told Dee to look past the Eighth Avenue basket because that's where she could take her first look—he'd turned into a game-show host now—at her brand new . . . BMW convertible!

Joey was behind the wheel, leaning out of the driver's-side window and giving her a jaunty wave.

Two minutes.

De la Cruz said, "Now I'd like the woman of the moment and the year and maybe the century to come up here and stand next to me."

The lights of the arena had been turned off. There was just the spotlight on De la Cruz, and the one following Dee as she went to center court, then just one spotlight on both of them.

De la Cruz put an arm around her.

"We have one more gift," he said.

Dee leaned into the mike and said, "Gee, boss, you've already done more than enough."

"Not quite," he said.

"More than enough, really," she said, faking a smile.

He wasn't listening.

Why should Dee Gerard Night be any different from the rest of them?

"I originally came up with the idea of Dee Gerard Night because I wanted to thank you for all the nights," he said, giving her shoulder a squeeze.

A drunk in the upper seats yelled, "Love you, Dee."

"We all do," Michael De la Cruz said. "And that's why I racked my brain trying to decide what you give the girl who suddenly has everything."

Dee noticed a spotlight dancing all over the Garden now.

"And then I got a phone call the other day that was almost like divine intervention," he said.

One more dramatic pause.

"I want you to say hello to someone," he said, in a voice that was barely above a whisper.

And from the Eighth Avenue end of the Garden, past where the BMW convertible had just been, strutting the way he always did, wearing a suit Dee was sure she remembered, a Pierre Cardin with a slight flare to the cuffs, big heels on his shoes, one hand on his stomach and one hand out as he did a little slide two-step, as if waltzing with himself, waving to the crowd as if they already knew who he was, came Cecil (Cool Daddy) Cody.

⊛ twenty-five

"Say hello to your father, Dee," Michael De la Cruz said, his voice back up now, deep and loud, a pulpit voice, as he stepped back with a wave of his arm to give them room.

Dee knew she was supposed to be overcome with shock or tears or maybe faint dead away—she was supposed to do *something*—but somehow all she could think was this:

He couldn't even stick with being dead.

She thought she heard "Daddy's Little Girl" being played over the p.a. system by a single unseen piano. Cool Daddy, saying something into her ear she couldn't hear, tried to hug her. But then he was hearing the same ovation she was, so he quickly pulled away, grabbed the microphone away from Michael De la Cruz almost in the same motion, and said, "Baby, daddy's *home*!"

Dee noticed they had suddenly been surrounded by Mini-cams.

What had the commissioner talked about after Michael De la Cruz fined Bobby Carlino? Bad reality TV? Now they were doing it, live with a dead guy at the Garden.

She grabbed the microphone away from her father.

"I'm not your baby," she said.

She walked toward the dressing-room area, walked away
from Cool Daddy and Michael De la Cruz into the darkness,
eating up the court in that long-legged walk that had bugged
the hell out of her actually dead mother, the spotlight trying to
keep up with her like a trailer on a fast break.

Behind her she could hear Cool Daddy saying, "Little girl,
don't spoil my big moment."

Over her shoulder, not slowing down at all, maybe im-
pressing him with her dazzling speed one last time, she said,
"I was actually under the impression that it was mine."

The houselights came up when she reached the runway.
Mo Jiggy, dressed in a white No. 6 New York Hawks football
jersey, was standing behind a temporary guardrail bracketed
by Montell and Denzell. Behind them Dee saw that Darnell,
using just his right hand, had lifted Harold Wasserman off the
ground by Harold's red power tie, which was not nearly the
full-bodied red that the little p.r. man's face was.

Harold Wasserman's feet were kicking wildly and he was
generally squirming like a tuna on a hook.

"You got any other bright ideas up your midget-ass
sleeve?" Mo was saying to him.

Wasserman was making a sound like a plunger trying to
unstop a toilet.

Dee tapped Mo on the shoulder. "My father?" she said.

"One just jumped out of the dead-boy cake?"

Dee said, "If he tries to get anywhere near my dressing
room, have one of the Earp brothers shoot him."

When she didn't answer the door right away, Eddie first
checked to see if it was locked, then opened it enough to poke
his head inside.

"Dee?" he said. "I know you're in here."

The only light in her dressing room came from a small
reading lamp on the small table at the far end of the couch. She
was lying there on her back, arms at her sides, eyes open, staring up at the ceiling.

"Knock, knock," he said.

She didn't answer.

Or move, for that matter.

Jesus Christ, he thought, they've done it up good this time, she's having one of her goddamn attacks right now.

"Hey," he said. "It's me."

She tilted her head slightly, fixed her eyes on him now.

"Listen," he said, "I know you must be freaked. I know I'd be freaked. But we've stalled them as long as we can out there, and now they're fixing to start the second half."

He remembered her in that bathroom stall the day of her first press conference, over on the other side, in the rotunda. Joey had told him what it was like for her in Cleveland that time, the day he came up with his tranquillity tea. And one night Dee herself had told him what it was like when it happened to her over in Europe.

Now—*shit!*—now this, after the shit they'd just pulled on her outside.

My life's an open book, she'd said to him just the other day.

That was the real book deal, she'd said.

"Dee," he said in a soft voice, afraid anything he did might startle her, make things worse, "just tell me how I can help you."

He walked in now, pulled a chair up to the couch.

"Talk to me," he said.

"Those fucking *fucks*!" she yelled suddenly, startling him enough that he nearly fell out of the chair.

Dee jumped off the couch and threw these wild punches in the air in front of her, spinning around as she did, even throwing in a few kick-boxing moves.

"Wait a second," Eddie said. "You're not . . . ?"

"Not what?" she snapped.

"I just thought . . ."

"What, that I was in here having another nervous breakdown? Well, you thought wrong." She walked over in front of him, chest heaving, staring down at him. "Did you have anything to do with this?"

"Hell, no."

"If you did . . . I'll get Mo to make you tell. There's some dog thing he says he does."

"Swear to God I didn't."

"Where's my not-so-late father, by the way? Already having his first press conference? Wait, is this one of those *Dateline* nights? Is he already on with Stone and Katie?"

"Jane."

"Whatever."

Eddie said, "I think Mo took him off somewhere with his ferret p.r. guy and Michael."

Even with the door closed, they could feel a cheer from inside the arena. Dee was back on the couch now, facing Eddie. She looked at him the way she did sometimes, asking a question by just raising an eyebrow, as if she expected him to read her mind.

"I told Flynn, if I wasn't right back, to tell them to go ahead and start," he said.

She was taking deep breaths now, as if doing one of her yoga things, still trying to calm herself down.

"Who's at point?" she said.

"Deltha."

"Deltha can't keep up with Pooh Bear on a skateboard."

Eddie said he'd noticed.

She clenched and unclenched those great hands of hers, those beautiful hands, the fastest Eddie had ever seen on a basketball court, then stood up.

"C'mon," she said. "We'll kill the Knicks first, then the rest of them, one by one."

"I can get behind that," Eddie Holtz said.

They won by twenty; it was just one of those nights. Dee ended up with twenty assists. With ninety seconds left, Pooh Bear Moriarty smart-mouthed her again, telling her not to pay tonight no mind, he'd see her in the playoffs, then asking if you called somebody a daughter of a bitch 'stead of a son of a bitch, he wasn't quite sure of the proper usage and whatnot when it came to somebody like her old man.

So when they were in the last minute, the crowd standing

for an ovation that seemed to be one long piece that wouldn't
end, she decided, What the hell?

Why should the boys have all the fun tonight?

It was a three-on-one fast break, only Bad Levine back,
and usually she would have just pulled up, pulled the ball
back out, run as much clock as she could. But she didn't stop
until she got to the foul line, just the way Cool Daddy Cody
had taught her in the gym at Hunter College, when he was
first teaching her the move.

There'd be a great shot of her in the *Daily News* the next
morning, showing her smiling like it was Christmas morning.

Before she leaned forward, just a little.

The ball was already behind her, balanced on her butt like
a cup on a saucer.

Now her hands came out.

Hey, where's the ball?

Her hands went behind her and came up with the ball,
which she was flipping now, over her head, to Jamie Lawton,
coming hard from her right.

She didn't know if Cool Daddy was still in the house or
not.

She didn't care.

This wasn't for him, or Eddie, or Michael De la Cruz.

This wasn't for any of them.

This was for her.

⊙ twenty-six

"Hell, I could *always* swim," Cool Daddy said. "Remember the girl lifeguard at Rockaway Beach that time, summer 'fore we left? Tryin' to be nice, tellin' your daddy she'd never seen a brother could swim like me?"

He was going to explain it to her, he said, even if it took all night. Even, he said, if she didn't want to hear. Shaheen had driven them back in Mo's Suburban, Mo in the front, Dee and Cool Daddy in the back, nobody in the car saying anything, the quiet bothering Mo enough that he played one of his biggest hits, "Closure," on the car's recording-studio sound system. They all listened to the *thump-thump-thump* of that all the way up Eighth, across Fifty-ninth, up Madison, and then back around to Fifth.

At the Garden, Dee had finally sent Mo into the interview room to grab Cool Daddy; Joey Shahoud had poked his head into Dee's dressing room and said that he could be off a little bit with his numbers, but that in the twenty minutes or so Cool Daddy had been in there with the media, he had told about six different versions of what had really happened to him after the *Samina Express* went down that night.

Dee and her father were watching one version now on New York 1, on the television set in the living room of her suite. Cool Daddy was staying across the street at The Plaza. When he'd called Michael De la Cruz from the town in Jamaica, Ocho Rios, where he was living now, De la Cruz had asked if he wanted to stay at the Sherry, because that's where Dee was. And Cool Daddy said, no, he'd always had a hankering to stay at The Plaza.

If it was all the same with Mr. De la Cruz, of course.

"You could say it was like one them *Cast Away* deals," he was saying on television, leaning into the microphones. "When I finally woke up, I was on one of those little islands they got over there near Paros."

"Which island?" someone asked.

"Never did find out, that's the thing," he said. "Just knew it had a beach and no people and was hot as a [bleeped for air] Harlem sidewalk in the summer. At that point, I musta had some of that water fever, 'cause I didn't know who I was or where the [bleeped for air] I was."

Dee watched his face on the television screen, fascinated, watched him make it all up as he went along.

Just like always.

He got serious now for his audience, shaking his head slowly from side to side, frowning.

"But it was the same with me as with Tommy Hanks in that movie," he said. "The will to live, she's a powerful thing."

He finally decided to swim for it, he told them. He'd been there for either a week, or two, surviving on what he described as "some of that nuts-and-berries [bleeped for air]." And it was when he was in the water, he can't even tell you how long he was in the water before that freighter picked him up, he knew there was even something more powerful than the will to live at work.

At the Sherry-Netherland, Dee said, "I will bet everything in my purse it was the hand of God."

". . . hand of God," her father said on television. "Lifting me up, carrying me over them waves. It was like I heard His voice sayin' to me, 'Cecil'—'cause I don't believe the Lord would traffic in no street names—'Cecil, you got yourself a

I think I told you about him once," he said. "He come lookin'
for what I owe, anyway, say he got business over there on
Paros, I should meet him there. At first, I was gonna pay him,
then figure out a way later to pay the ones I was borrowin' the
money from in Athens. Then I had one of my famous brain-
storms, little girl. I said to myself, 'Cool, maybe it's time to
just get out of Greece entirely with this two very large, American, and start a whole new life somewheres else. Which is
why I came up with the plan to go off the starboard side about
ten minutes after we leave Athens, knowing I can swim back,
no problem."

The memory of his own brilliance made him smile. He was
thinner than she remembered from the last time she'd seen
him, grayer, older-looking. But still handsome, his hair slick
and close to his head, reminding her a little bit of an aging
Billy Dee Williams. And somehow something else had not
changed as he'd gotten older: All the con, all the charm and
bullshit and pulp fiction, was still like some lightbulb inside
him. He was probably still catnip to the ladies.

No matter how small he acted, no matter how small he really was, Cool Daddy Cody had always looked in the mirror
and seen big staring back at him.

She idly wondered even now how much of this version
was true.

"The details of all this ain't important, little girl," he said,
as if reading her mind. "What's important is that I catch this
amazing break: the damn *Samina* does a *Titanic*!"

"Some break. More than sixty-six people die."

"Exactly!" he said. "And, praise the Lord, your daddy
ain't one of 'em!"

He nodded at the television set. "How 'bout we turn that
back on, watch me on the news a little more."

"You were always better live," she said.

Cool Daddy, white shirt hanging out of his pants, over his
own skinny butt, went over to the bar and poured himself
more red wine, drank a big slug as if it were soda pop,
smacked his lips. "Damn, I always did like that ro-zay," he
said. " 'Specially when it cost more than seven dollar a bottle."

"So the guys you stole from, and the guy who waited for you to pay him off, they all thought you went down with the ship."

"They did."

"And the guy you were sailing over to pay off, how come you owed him that much money?"

"Was a misunderstanding."

"Yeah," Dee said, "it was funny how misunderstandings like that always seemed to follow you around."

He tried to look hurt. "You used to have a more forgiving heart."

Dee said, "I used to be a nice girl, but I turned."

"Anyway," he said, "now that I was dead, I knew I had to stay dead."

"Especially now that you were two hundred thousand to the good."

"I got to admit, that there was a consideration."

Cool Daddy turned his head, as if he'd just noticed there was music playing. "That Ruthie Brown?"

" 'Mama,' " Dee said. "Comes right before 'He Treats Your Daughter Mean.' Honest."

"I wished there could've been another way," he said.

"You always did."

Cool Daddy said, "You was the one who said you didn't want me in your life no more."

They sat there now, listening to Ruth as she shifted into some rhythm and blues, Cool Daddy reminding her one more time that his "good friend Nipsey Russell" had emceed for Ruthie when she toured with Count Basie and Billy Eckstine in the middle fifties. Finally, Dee said, "So why now?"

"You don't know how I ended up down there in Jamaica. God*damn,* those people got to move on from that Bob Marley shit."

"No."

"Pretty good story there."

"Aren't they all?"

"I'm gonna tell you something, little girl. I'm a better man now'n I ever was."

Dee sipped some of her white wine, noticed that it was

2:30 in the morning. "You'd have to be," she said. "But you haven't answered my question: Why now?"

Cool Daddy Cody said, "Even if it meant blowing my cover, I had to see you with my own damn eyes. See you be what I never was."

That she believed.

In Jamaica, he went with the name of his favorite Negro League player of all, Cool Papa Bell, eventually buying a little reggae club down the road in Ocho Rios from the Jamaica Inn. He called the place Cool's. Eventually started to turn a nice little profit, he said.

"I'll be goin' back there tomorrow," he said. "It won't take long for them I stole from and them I owed to see me on that CNN International, or in the newspapers, or some such. I might do a little more press tomorrow, then be movin' on."

"You could pay them back," Dee said. "Though I'm sure that never occurred to you."

"I actually been puttin' somethin' aside with that in mind," Cool Daddy said. "A little nest egg. It just ain't hatched yet."

Dee sighed. "How much are you short?"

"Hundred thousand."

"American," Dee said.

He told her he had just picked up the phone a few days earlier, after debating whether to do it from the first day he found out she was in the league. He had gotten the Knights' main number from information and cold-called the executive office and asked the woman who answered the phone if he could talk to the boss. When she'd asked who it was, he said, "The father of the first damn woman to play in the NBA, that's who."

Michael De la Cruz came on about five seconds later, and before the two of them got off the phone that day, De la Cruz had come up with the idea for "Dee Gerard Night." He'd sent his plane to pick up Cool Daddy at the Kingston airport yesterday morning.

"It was all about him," Dee said. "And you."

"I didn't think you'd begrudge your daddy getting down

there on that Garden floor one more time. And that Michael sounded so happy-like, tellin' me on the phone, praise God, I was some big surprise he'd been prayin' on."

He stood up. "I'm goin' to bed now," he said. "But 'fore I do, how about giving me a real hug? That one on the court was about as warm as a doctor's exam."

Dee stood up herself, put her wineglass down on the coffee table, walked across the room and hugged her father, feeling the tears start to come now, out of nowhere, smelling the same cheap aftershave he'd always used. In her arms, he felt as if he'd shrunk somehow in the years he'd been gone.

When she pulled away, she said, "I'll have Mo cut you a check in the morning."

"You don't have to," he said.

"I know," she said.

She went to the front closet, took the polyester jacket off its hanger, came back and handed it to him. "After you have the money, I want you to do me a favor," she said.

"Anything, little girl, you know that."

Dee said, "Lose my phone number."

He flipped his jacket over his head, the way kids did, slid his arms into it, even shot his cuffs like a dude.

"I used to tell myself you were the best of me," he said. "That I was the one gave you what you got." He shook his head. "But with all due respect to myself," Cool Daddy said, "you so much better than me it make my heart hurt."

He took two steps toward the door, then stopped and turned back to Dee with a sly smile, as if he couldn't let the tender moment be, as if he had to get back into character, make his exit as Cool Daddy Cody.

"But that over-the-shoulder pass you throwed tonight?" He picked up the basketball Dee had left in the front hall, turned his back to her, still talking. "Throw it like this sometime, long as you got the man coverin' you on your side. Crowd will go wild." He looked over his shoulder at her, serious, the way he always got when he was showing her something in the gym.

"Trust me," Cool Daddy said.

Then he bounced the ball to her between his legs without looking and walked out the door.

She sat there another hour listening to Ruth, sometimes getting up and walking to the window and staring across at the Plaza, where Cool Daddy Cody had the best New York City digs of his whole improbable life, the smell of his aftershave still over here with her, along with the raspy sound of his voice. Wondering in the middle of the night exactly how much of it was true, the men chasing him and the one waiting for him, the two hundred thousand in the wet suit, finding out the next day about what happened to the *Samina Express,* that he had caught that break and was supposed to be dead.

Tried to imagine him, the jazz guy, the Apollo guy, as some cool reggae *mon* in Jamaica, another place Dee had never seen.

Pictured him doing his Garden strut.

She drank a little more of her wine.

Then she pictured the two of them on the court at Franklin Plaza on 106th, remembered the day when she was a sophomore at Clinton and got hot from the outside, him grinning at her and daring her to keep shooting, because the game was winners-out, just the way it had been with Eddie in Monte Carlo.

When it was over that day, he'd said, "Great game, little girl. You beat me fair and square. And now I ain't ever gonna play you a game of one-on-one again."

She'd wanted to beat him in the worst way. Show him. Then she had, and he was gone, upstairs, and she was still out there, by herself.

God, she'd played a lot of ball in her life.

Always trying to show somebody.

Herself, mostly, when she got right down to it.

She slept only a few hours, but then woke up refreshed when she started to hear the first car horns, traffic noises, rip right through the dawn. She got the ball Cool Daddy had left in the front hall and took the elevator down to the lobby, as if she were walking through the lobby of 225 East 106th, and

asked the young woman at the desk for the keys to the ballroom.

The woman, Kristin, said, "This early, Miss Gerard?"

"You know how it is in a man's world," she said. "You've
got to get the jump on them."

Kristin said, "Good luck tonight."

"You a Knights fan?"

"Not even a basketball fan," Kristin said. "Until now."

Dee didn't even wait for the elevator, the way she sometimes couldn't wait as a kid, took the stairs instead, two and
three at a time.

It was all going to be great now, she was sure.

She couldn't wait to tell Eddie.

⚾ twenty-seven

The game against the Heat was on a Wednesday night, the last night of the regular season. If the Knights won, they tied the Heat in the standings and won the season series; as far the playoffs were concerned, it was winner-take-all, the winner playing the Knicks in the first game of NBC's playoff triple-header on Sunday at 12:30. Even Eddie Holtz, who believed when no one else had believed, didn't think the Knights could upset the champs, get three games out of five, as good as they had looked against the Knicks the other night.

Just getting one game would be one of those moral victories sportswriters loved to talk about.

Shit, if they could get two, they could all feel as if they'd been carried out on their fucking shields.

Even in his heart, he was pretty sure that was it. Man's got to know his limitations, his old man used to say, saying it was a line from a movie, always saying he couldn't remember which goddamn one.

Eddie knew Dee would know. She was great with those old movies; she told him she had this amazing collection of them in her place in Monte Carlo. She acted embarrassed some-

times, quoting them as much as she did. But she quoted them
a lot. She was great with movies the way she was with old
singers. Good with a lot of things. Maybe women didn't even
think about limitations, maybe that was another way they
were smarter than men.

She told him after the morning shootaround that she
planned to get to the Garden early that night, acting excited,
telling him there was something she wanted to talk to him
about. He'd asked her what and she told him it was a secret.

Then Eddie'd asked how it had gone with Cool Daddy.
Dee gave him the outline of their conversation as they were
walking down the long runway toward Thirty-third.

"He hasn't changed much," she said. "You have to give it
to the guy. He's changed less than any person I've ever
known."

"He gonna stick around for the game?"

"He never stayed before once he had the money," she said.
"When you get a good move, stay with it. Isn't that what you
always tell me?"

Eddie said, "You think you'll see him again?"

"Remember the end of *The Sting*?" Dee said. "Newman
and Redford are walking out of the betting place after the
scam has gone down and the fake cops are escorting poor
Robert Shaw out of there. And Newman says something to
Redford like, 'Aren't you gonna stick around for your cut?'
And Redford says, 'Nah, I'd only blow it.' The money I gave
Cool Daddy today? He'll only blow it."

"I thought you said that money was supposed to be for the
guys he'd ripped off, the ones who thought he was dead?"

Dee leaned up before they came around to the street, gave
him a quick kiss. "You've got a lot to learn about men," she
said. "This man, especially."

They had come out into the sunlight then, where the television trucks were parked. Somehow there was the usual
crowd of teenaged girls waiting for Dee, even though it was
the middle of a weekday afternoon.

Eddie said, "Anybody else would've freaked last night
when old Lazarus came hip-hoppin' in there. How come you
didn't?"

She smiled at him. Her high-beams smile. It was like the first time he'd seen it in Monte Carlo, when she'd told him she'd been a girl her whole life, practically.

"I thought you knew by now," she said. "I'm cool." Then she disappeared into the crowd, all of them talking at once, laughing, all these basketball girls.

Eddie took a cab to his apartment on Fifty-sixth and First, napped for what felt like ten minutes, decided there was no shot he was going to be able to relax here, took a shower, went back downstairs, took a cab back to the Garden, went into the empty Knights locker room and began drawing plays on the greaseboard, as happy in here, alone, Coach Eddie of the Knights, as he'd always been in empty gyms.

Maybe happier.

It was funny how things worked out.

A girl turned out to be the kind of star he always thought he could be but never came close to being. Then the same girl turned out to be the reason he became a coach, and a little bit of a star coach, which is what he was maybe supposed to be all along.

So it wasn't just funny, it was fucking hilarious.

Five o'clock now. Still more than three hours to the game.

He had turned off his cell, but now the locker room phone rang, sounding like an alarm to him. He went over to answer it, even knowing it might be Michael De la Cruz, who always liked to touch base with him the afternoon of a game, at home or on the road, just to give him a pep talk that was always dumber than video games.

"Thought you'd be there early," Mo Jiggy said. "Doin' some of that X-and-O shit you coaches treat like the bad."

"Where'd you think the X in sex comes from?" Eddie said.

Mo said, "You got a few minutes? Want to show you somethin'."

"Where are you?"

"Right across the street. Boss's office."

Eddie thought he heard some kind of growl-type noise in the background.

"What was that?" he said.

"Was Hillary," Mo said. "Bitch generally get a little treat 'bout this time of day."

"You've got Hillary with you in Michael's office?"

"Bill, too. And Darnell."

Eddie said he'd be right over.

Michael De la Cruz, bug-eyed and pretty much scared shitless from what Eddie could see, was in the chair behind his desk. Looking, Eddie thought, like it was *the* chair. Bill, the slightly bigger of Mo's two rottweilers, was seated to his right, at one corner of the great big CEO desk, completely still. Hillary, who Mo had told Eddie before was the far more aggressive of the two dogs—"We had to send her back to that puppy college three times"—was at the other corner, to Michael's left, equally still.

Mo had explained that the reason the rest of the Knights' offices at Five Penn Plaza were empty was that he had instructed De la Cruz to give everybody the rest of the afternoon off before the big game.

"After that," Mo said, "I explained to Mr. De la Cruz that he gonna be fine, long as he don't move."

Darnell, man enough to wear a Dee Gerard No. 14 jersey with his black Knights cap and black jeans, sat on the other side of the desk, directly across from De la Cruz, as still as the dogs.

"Darnell's taken over as the dogs' primary trainer," Mo said to Eddie.

"Oh," Eddie said.

Michael De la Cruz, reminding Eddie somewhat of a ventriloquist's dummy the way only his lips were moving, said, "We seem to have a slight misunderstanding here."

"Oh," Eddie said again.

"Wasn't no misunderstanding," Mo said amiably. "I came over her to fill in some blanks, in light of last night's fes-tiv-i-ties. And now, because we open with each other, because we got that trust goin', we managed to fill in the rest of those blanks."

De la Cruz said, "Listen . . ."

Mo said, "Hush now." Then he snapped his fingers one time, which caused the dogs to move about six inches closer to De la Cruz's chair.

"Damn, 'Nell," Mo said to Darnell. "That is *good.*"

De la Cruz said, "You can't hold me hostage this way."

Mo said, "Michael, I ever tell you what Step One is when you negotiatin' with me in the rap-record business? And don't shake your head, on account of the dogs. Step One is shut the fuck up."

Eddie said, "Could somebody tell me what this is about?"

"Happy to," Mo Jiggy said. He was wearing a snow-white T-shirt with "FUBU" written on the front, and khaki painter's pants and low-cut white Nike leather sneakers, the swoosh outlined in little dots. His cell phone was clipped to his canvas belt. On his bald head was an Adams golf cap.

"After last night's game," Mo said, "I had a little talk with what's-his-name, Stuart Little the p.r. man. I asked him whose brilliant idea it was, springin' a dead daddy on my girl like that in front of the whole world. Thinkin' it was him, and that he just got Michael here to go along with him, bitch style."

"Where did this conversation occur?" Eddie said.

"The car, where you think?"

"Oh," Eddie said.

"Well," Mo said, "Stuart give it up in a heartbeat, saying no, no, no, it was Michael's idea, just like all the rest of the shit was, and he says it all started with the picture in the newspaper."

Eddie looked at Michael De la Cruz, his arms gripping the sides of his chair so tightly he could see the muscle definition like it was some drawing in an anatomy book.

"Is that true?"

"No nodding," Mo said.

"Yes," De la Cruz said.

Eddie couldn't decide whether it was Bill or Hillary making a low sound now that was a little bit like a chair being scraped on a hardwood floor.

"I didn't mean any harm," De la Cruz said. "I just wanted to keep a flame to the story. Give it some juice."

"Mixed metaphor," Mo said. "Hate that shit." Then he

turned to Eddie and said, "He told the little p.r. man he wanted it to be like a soap opera, a surprise every couple a days."

Darnell said "Shit!" suddenly in a loud voice.

Michael De la Cruz's eyes got even wider. "What . . . now?" he said in a tiny voice.

"Forgot to tape *One Life to Live*," Darnell said.

Eddie said to De la Cruz, "You hired a photographer to follow us?"

"I told the guy to stay loose, see if anything interesting developed. Then you kissed her on Fifth Avenue, for Chrissakes."

"Oh, I get it," Eddie said. "I wanted it."

"Tell him the rest of it, Motivation Guy."

"Okay, okay, okay," De la Cruz said. "I might've had Melissa do some research on the father. Before it turned out he was alive."

Mo said, "Information which you just happened to share with that shitweasel from the newspaper."

"Yes."

"Same shitweasel you leaked the very first story to, about Dee."

"Yes."

Mo sighed, and snapped his fingers again. The dogs inched a little closer, and what came out of De la Cruz this time actually sounded to Eddie like "eek."

"Aw, chill," Mo Jiggy said to De la Cruz. "I'm just playin' wit' you."

"I'm sorry, okay!" Michael De la Cruz said. He tried to force his buddy-boy smile. "My bad, okay?"

"My bad?" Mo said. "Jesus, you sure you got brown blood in you?"

"Eddie," Michael De la Cruz said, shifting imperceptibly in his chair. "Please make him stop with the dog thing."

"Eddie can't do that," Mo said. "Eddie gonna go coach his team now."

De la Cruz couldn't help himself. "My team," he said.

"No, dickwad," Mo corrected him. "*His* team. He gonna coach his team, and he not gonna tell anybody about what he saw over here 'cross the street. And that will actually be his way of protectin' you. 'Cause if 'Nell hear anything in that outer office between now and the end of the game, he gonna start snapping his fingers like one of them flamenco dancers and walk right out this office."

" 'Nell," Mo said now to Darnell, "you remember the new code?"

"*What* code?" De la Cruz said.

"Think I got it down," Darnell said.

"What *code*?" De la Cruz said, his voice even more of a whine.

"Code turns off the rotts," Mo said. "Like an alarm code."

"But what about the *game*?" De la Cruz said. "You're not going to let me go to the big game?"

"You and Darnell can watch it over here on the TV. Look on the bright side. Least you got a big screen and some of that surround-sound."

Eddie thought Michael De la Cruz might cry.

"But it's my big night," De la Cruz said to Mo.

At the same moment, both Eddie and Mo said, "Hers."

Then Mo said to De la Cruz, "By the way. That Melissa? Big girl, getting herself straightened when me and 'Nell showed up. I believe I'm gonna need her home phone."

As they walked across the wide expanse of Michael De la Cruz's office, Mo started singing "I've Got the World on a String" in a surprisingly rich baritone, his cadence as perfect as Sinatra's, smiling as he suddenly snapped his fingers to the beat. Behind them, Eddie heard a couple of growls, and rustling noises on the carpet, then Michael De la Cruz doing an excellent impression of a tea kettle coming to a boil.

"Relax," Mo said to Eddie, "I'm just playin'."

Three years before, the Miami Heat had nearly won the NBA title under Coach Stan Roiles, going all the way to Game Seven before losing to the San Antonio Spurs. And it was during that period, Dee knew, that Roiles had become the kind of hot-boy in coaching that Bobby Carlino had been in college, writing his own motivational books, giving his own big-ticket speeches. Eddie told Dee that for a while you couldn't see an

NBA coach interviewed on television without him suddenly
quoting some dead Chinese general—"The battle is won before the battle is fought" was Eddie's favorite—or talking
about how now he got to the office at 4:30 in the morning, the
way Roiles did, to start breaking down game film. Roiles was
also famous for his daily five-hour practices, though he did
get into some trouble with Commissioner Betts eventually
when it was discovered by a reporter from the *South Florida
Sun-Sentinel* that he sometimes made his players run their sui-
cide sprint drills naked as a form of punishment.

Dee remembered reading about that one on the Net.

"Shoulda seen," Heat All-Star guard Suge Day said at the
time, "guys' things floppin' around, whacking the guy next to
them when they got out their lanes, end of practice every day
looked like the Olympics of f—— garden hoses."

But now, according to Eddie and most of the Knight players, the guys on the Heat had finally realized something about
Stan Roiles:

He was a self-serving, player-hating asshole.

And this year's edition of the Heat had been playing out
the string, doing a free fall through the standings after Janu-
ary 1 until the team's owner—South Beach hotel tycoon
Binky Goldberg—had made his players a unique offer: If
they could somehow make the playoffs, he would fire Roiles
as soon as the season was over.

Binky Goldberg knew Roiles wouldn't quit, for the same
reason Michael De la Cruz knew Carlino hadn't quit all those
years, despite all the times he'd threatened to:

Too much money, in this case the money from Binky's
pink hotels, still on the table.

"So," Eddie Holtz was saying to the Knights now in the
locker room, five minutes before they were supposed to take
the court, "they'll probably play us tonight like they go to
Central Booking if they don't win."

"Aw," Anquwan said, "Winky probably fire his ass anyway."

Thruston B. Howell, stretching in front of his locker, said,
"Roiles another poodle who thinks people come out to watch

him run up and down the sideline like somebody set his tail on fire."

"Ooh, ooh, ooh, lookie here at me, I'm coachin'," Dream said, rubbing the new Chinese symbols he'd had tattooed on his right arm. Dream was under the impression that they were some war slogan, or so he had been told by the drunk down in Chinatown who'd done the job for him. But then an enterprising reporter from the *Post* had had them translated, and it turned out the meaning of the symbols, roughly, was Sick Bird Dirt Nap.

"Hey," Eddie said, "listen up for one second."

He had their attention, Dee thought, the way he had from the start.

"I've been thinking all day about what I wanted to say to you," he said, "mostly about what a goddamn trip this has been. But then I remembered something: I never heard a single locker room speech in my life, from any coach I ever had, made me want to play any better than I already did."

"There you go," Anquwan said.

Eddie smiled.

"Just go out there tonight and play like you did the first time you knew that playing ball was all you ever wanted to do," he said.

Dee stood up first.

"Gentlemen," she said, facing the group, "it's been a privilege flyin' with you."

"Wait," Dream Jackson said, "I know that one. *Apollo 13.*"

"There you go," Dee said in a deep, man voice.

She and Eddie were the last two out of the locker room. At the last second, Eddie pulled her back in, kissed her hard on the lips. It was their first moment alone since she'd gotten to the Garden, told him what she wanted to tell him, after she'd stopped giggling about where Michael De la Cruz was, and whom he was watching the game with.

"I wanted to tell you two things," he said. "First, I'm glad about your news. I really am."

"Not just my news."

"I know that."

"You could've told me what Michael said, by the way.

About you not coming back if I didn't. It would've made things a little easier."

"Then it wouldn't have been your call. And it had to be your call."

Dee said, "What was the second thing?"

"Thank you," Eddie Holtz said. "For everything, mostly."

Dee smiled at him, straightened his tie.

"God," she said, "don't go all girlie-man on me now, Coach." Then she ran up the hallway to join the guys, before they all ran into the explosion of noise, a bomb going off, that always meant you'd found the big game in sports.

The Knights fell behind fourteen points by the time the first half ended. Suge Day couldn't miss and neither could Predragon Kryzyzski, the Serb small forward, the two of them combining for forty points. If it hadn't been for Anquwan going a little crazy himself, scoring thirty points in the half, the game might already have been over for the Knights, their shot at the playoffs already gone.

They were actually down twenty points with a minute to go, but Dee picked up Suge Day in a half-court trap, stole the ball, outran everybody, and got an easy layup. Then Anquwan stole the Heat's inbound pass and made the jumper that got him to thirty points.

Finally, with three seconds left and Dee trying to get the ball to Carl Anthony, she stumbled as she came across the lane and started to go down. Knowing there was hardly any time left, she threw up this high hook shot without even looking at the basket, right before she landed at the feet of the Heat center, Onlyne Cooper.

When she felt even the Garden floor shaking like a platform for an elevated train, like she was still a kid waiting with Cool Daddy for the Number 7 at Shea Stadium, she knew the shot had gone in and the Heat lead was down to 68–54.

She had felt sluggish — not wanting to admit how tight she was — for most of the half, but she was into it now, into it all the way, riding the noise for her shot like a wave. She ran past

Mo Jiggy, making this big wide turn on her way to the locker room.

"So many effin' games," Mo said, quoting another of his famous songs.

"So little effin' time," Dee said back to him.

She gave him a high five and then gave one to Sharmayne, sitting next to Mo tonight on celebrity row.

In the locker room, all the Knights got something to drink, sat down in front of their lockers, bitched a little about the refs, yelled to Joey for more gum.

Eddie finally came in a couple of minutes later, smoking a cigarette.

He looked at them and said, "They had their shot."

"Tell *me* about it," Deltha said.

"They have no idea how much trouble they're in," Eddie said, and walked out.

"Yo," Carl Anthony said. "First man of few words in the history of coaches."

Dee said, "It's one of the things that makes him so cute."

The rest of them immediately made a sound that was like a bunch of barking dogs.

"What," she said, "it can only be sex, sex, sex in here with you guys?"

The Knights all laughed together then, went out to play the second half. Dee didn't know why she happened to look up when she got out there to warm up at the Seventh Avenue end, her eyes traveling all the way up to the cheap seats—if there was such a thing anymore at the Garden—up there and maybe back in time to when she'd first come here to watch John Stockton.

But way up there, in a runway next to a huge banner that read "Jamie's Juniors," she thought she saw Cool Daddy.

The Heat apparently didn't know how much trouble they were in, because they sure wouldn't quit.

Suge Day came out hot again, hit the first two shots of the second half, one of them a three-pointer. But Anquwan came right back with a three of his own, Dong Li got away from

Onlyne Cooper inside for three straight layups, and the Knights had cut the Heat lead to ten with eight minutes to go in the quarter.

And it was here that something happened, in the game, at the Garden.

Somebody showed up.

The young Dee Gerard.

The basketball girl only the ones who'd played against her in France and Spain, all the other stops over there, really remembered.

Twenty-two instead of thirty-two now.

Twenty-two and the fastest girl anybody'd ever seen on a basketball court.

The one no woman could get in front of.

And now, for this one night, no man.

It started with a fast break, one of those streak-of-light bounce passes from half-court to Dream Jackson.

Then came a rebound from Carl Anthony, an outlet pass, Dee catching the ball and, without looking up the court, just heaving the ball in the direction of the Knights' basket, because she knew Anquwan had snuck away from the pack early, cheated on the chance that Carl would get that rebound—*knew* Anquwan would be there.

The Heat lead was down to four by the end of the third quarter and the Garden was the way Eddie said some old sportswriter had described it once, when the Knicks were great in the early seventies, the Garden was the Monster of Madison Square Garden, that monster, Eddie said, quoting the guy, living in the throats of 19,000 people.

With eight minutes left in the game, Dee crossed over on Suge, beat him to the free-throw line, spun around when the Serb kid jumped out on her, then threw that bounce pass between her legs, the one Cool Daddy had shown her in the front hall of the suite at the Sherry, to a cutting Jamie Lawton for a layup.

The Knights had the lead for the first time, 94–93.

On her way back up the court, she looked up to that runway, to the "Jamie's Juniors" banner.

There was only an usher in his maroon jacket standing where she thought Cool Daddy had been.

The Knights were ahead six points, two minutes to go, when Eddie noticed that Joey Shahoud had come to sit next to him.

"Almost there," Joey said nervously.

Eddie put an arm around his shoulder. "We are there," he said. "It's in her hands now. She won't give it up, and she won't miss when they foul her."

"You know that, huh?"

Eddie said, "I know what I know."

"Well, god*damn*!" Joey said. "We did it. This year the playoffs. Next year, we win the whole fucking thing."

Suge Day had fouled Dee, who was crouched at the free-throw line, drying her hands on her socks the way she did, waiting for the ref to hand her the ball. Smiling at the scene — at her, really — Eddie said, "Isn't gonna be one."

"One what?"

"Next year."

"I thought that's what you did in sports," Joey said. "Wait till next year."

"Gonna be a long wait," Eddie said.

Dee made the first free throw, followed by another huge cheer.

"What're you saying here?" Joey said. "You're saying she's not coming back?"

"Says she's got a business to run. Says she's even better at that than running a basketball team."

Dee made the second free throw. Knights 106, Heat 98. Nobody in the stands was sitting. Eddie looked around, thinking: Sports can still do it, even turn a place like this into a high school gym.

"What about you?" Joey said.

"Joey," Eddie said, "have I ever told you that I thought the only pure form left of basketball was in Europe?"

Suge had missed a long one. Dee had the ball at midcourt. Ninety seconds left at the Garden, which was all about her now.

His mother was going to love Monte Carlo, Eddie thought. She'd finally get to see all that Princess Grace shit for herself.

With under a minute to go, the Knights ahead 110–102, the people in the crowd began to chant "Play-*offs*! Play-*offs*!" the way they had always chanted at the Garden for *dee*-fense, as far back as she could remember.

All the way back.

Suge Day hit one last three-pointer, cutting the Knights' lead to seven, but it was too late now.

Dee saw Mo Jiggy going up and down celebrity row doing his Chuck Berry chicken-walk, his golf cap turned around backwards on his head, stopping every few feet, putting a hand to his ear as if to say, I can't *hear* you.

The ball was in her hands as she crossed half-court.

Twenty seconds left.

Suge made a half-assed attempt to steal the ball. When he did, Dee spun away and went into this low dribble she had seen The Cooz use on some ESPN Classic show a few nights before, making the same full circle he'd made against the old Syracuse Nationals nearly fifty years ago, the ball so low to the floor it looked like part of the Knights' decal at center court.

She was still a Cousy guy.

Ten seconds.

Now they all chanted, *"Dee! Dee! Dee!"*

As if they were feeling the same beat she was now.

From over on the wing, Anquwan jumped up and down and yelled, "Hey, girl. We goin'!"

Thruston B. Howell, on the other side, put his head back and roared, "Boo-*eee*!" over the roar of the crowd.

Now Dee put the ball on her hip, looked up into the crowd once more, up to where she was sure Cool Daddy had been, up to where her dreams had begun.

Dee thought: Some of my dreams, anyway.

Not all.

AUTHOR OF BUMP & RUN

MIKE LUPICA

WILD

PITCH

PUTNAM

chance to start a whole new life here, one better than any life you ever known."

On the television, he put a hand to his face now, as if he had to compose himself. Dee knew it was all bullshit. But he did a long take before he looked out at them again and said, "The Lord had found me. Now I was sure I had to go off somewheres and find myself. Even if it meant letting my little girl, the only thing on this earth I'd ever truly loved, think I'd passed."

Dee pointed the remote at the set and turned it off.

She said, "Before we go any further with this, how much money are we talking about here?"

"I tried to tell you when we first got in the car, 'fore you clammed up. This ain't about money. Was just about getting swept away by circumstances the way I nearly did them waves."

"How much?" she said in a loud voice, putting some mustard on it.

" 'Bout two hundred thousand," he said in a small voice. "American."

"There was no island, was there?"

He shook his head.

"Did you even get on that boat? You had to, they had you on the manifest. Or was that part of the scam?"

He did get on at Piraeus, the port at Athens, just so they'd check him in. The boat was supposed to make six stops, the first one Paros, before it finally ended up at a tiny island called Lipsis, near the Turkish coast. The two hundred thousand from the charity basketball game he'd organized in the new Athens Olympic arena, the money he was supposed to deposit in the bank and didn't, was on the inside of the wet suit he was wearing inside the suit he was wearing, he said, right here in this room.

"My lucky suit, is the way I look at it now," he said.

Dee said, "At least luck never goes out of fashion, like lapels and flairs and so forth."

Then she said, "Obviously, you didn't have any intention of making it to Paros."

"Was a man there I owed somethin' to, Spanish-type guy,